SWING

Also by Rupert Holmes

Where the Truth Lies

SWING

A Mystery

Rupert Holmes

 Random House · New York

Library of Congress Cataloging-in-Publication Data

Holmes, Rupert.
Swing : a mystery / by Rupert Holmes.
p.   cm.
ISBN 1-4000-6158-X
1. Golden Gate International Exposition (1939–1940) : San
Francisco, Calif.)—Fiction.   2. San Francisco (Calif.)—Fiction.
3. Women composers—Fiction.   4. Jazz musicians—Fiction.
I. Title.

PS3558.O367S95 2005
813'.54—dc22

2004050765

Printed in the United States of America on acid-free paper
Random House website address: www.atrandom.com

987654321

First Edition

Book design by Mercedes Everett

For Wendy Isobel Holmes
(1976 – 1986)

To you, Treasure Island, farewell.

As the world has lived, your life was all too short. It seems but yesterday you lay beneath the sea.

The good and the bad have come to you and you have had gifts for all who would receive them.

But this is not Death for Treasure Island. The flowers may fade, the palaces may fall to earth, the music and laughter be stilled . . .

. . . but as God measures Time, it is but tomorrow that huge airplanes will glide down through the air which tonight is ruled by the Tower of the Sun . . . will roll across the ground where Pacific House now stands.

Let there be no sadness tonight . . . for remember, sorrow is of the past and joy is of the future. And so we salute Treasure Island . . . whose greater future starts—tonight!

Written by Glenn A. Wheaton for the closing ceremony—attended by an audience of over 85,000 and carried live on all three national radio networks—marking the end of The Golden Gate International Exposition, "The World's Fair of the West," September 29, 1940, Treasure Island, California.

OAKLAND
BAY BRIDGE
YERBA BUENA ISLAND
BATTLESH
BAY BRIDGE
C O
B A Y
BUILDING
EMBARCADERO
MARKET STREET
NCISCO
MISSION DOLORES

SWING

1

The Band Bus

We'd had a miserable drive down from Portland that day. The radio on the bus had been on the fritz since we'd left Spokane the week before, there are only so many hands of penny-ante gin rummy that seventeen men can endure without a card table or drinks, and while from time to time we might professionally be called upon to perform "Ninety-nine Bottles of Beer on the Wall," we sure as hell weren't about to sing it voluntarily. We were grown men. We all had stories to tell, great stories, but after a few years, we'd told and heard them all.

By the time we crossed from Oregon into California, I'd already read the first paragraph of *Seven Pillars of Wisdom* for several hours, my gaze wandering back and forth between the yellowed pages and the bleached green scenery outside. When you tour the country, you quickly learn that America is a pleasant view through a bus window that is then repeated eight thousand times before it yields to the dim prospect of a small brown city.

Frankie Pompano, tenor sax, first chair, made his way to my padded pew at the back of the bus. "Bored enough?" he asked. "'Cause I'm ready to cut my wrists with a reed trimmer."

He sat down on my left, just as he did on the bandstand each night, and flopped back so heavily that he caused the bus's rear door to swing open. It should have been latched and locked, but it wasn't. I watched his face fill with childish surprise as he began to fall smoothly out of the speeding bus, headfirst.

I instantly swooped after him and grabbed his collar with my left hand, which would have made for a fine rescue if my right hand had been holding on to something other than my *Seven Pillars of Wisdom*.

Now we were both halfway out of the bus, and Frankie was realizing that if we completed the fall, our heads would hit the roadway at a solid fifty miles an hour. He clutched frantically at my belt, pulling me farther out, tipping the seesaw the wrong way. They didn't teach science at the Juilliard School of Music, but I knew by the laws of physics and simple measurements that it was impossible for my right leg to stretch far enough to hook my foot under the base of the seat in front of me, or for the metatarsal bones in my foot to counterbalance the total weight of two men hanging out of the back of an eight-door Dodge bus. Fortunately for us, Isaac Newton had never factored adrenaline into any of his equations.

Suddenly I was being hoisted back into the bus by the confident arms of two trombonists, Danny Hodges and Harry Weidel, second and third chair respectively. They were well suited to the task, pulling me as if gliding their slides from seventh position to first. I held steadily onto Frankie, who looked up at me like a dangling mountaineer who was fearful I'd cut his tether. With one good yank, I had him inside again. I bolted the hatch and observed that most of the band hadn't even noticed our small drama, except for Tommy

Trego, our band boy and the one responsible for checking the bus's back door. His complexion was pale as milk glass as he averted his eyes from mine. I made a mental note that once we got to our hotel, I would have to tell him the story about how I once made the exact same mistake myself. I would have told Tommy the story then and there but I hadn't invented it yet.

"Jesus, you nearly killed yourself, Ray," said Frankie, brushing the road grit from his jacket. "I guess this makes you my hero."

I wasn't a hero, his or anyone's. To be honest, I didn't even care that much about Frankie. It's just that nearly killing yourself for a fellow saxophonist is easy when you've been considering doing the same thing for no one in particular.

Prior to September of 1940, I'd more than once soberly entertained committing the equivalent of what we musicians call a *dal segno al coda*, this being the written instruction in music that the player should abandon repeating what has gone before and leap forward to the end.

Luckily, the woman I love (who's just in the next room as I write these words and who—God help her—has agreed to review these pages when I finish my account of the innocent intrigue that became a personally harrowing mystery that revealed itself to be a deadly puzzle) has been able to help me make a most miraculous *da capo*, which for those of us who play jazz means "take it again from the top."

2

The Claremont

Less than an hour before we were scheduled to play, our band bus groveled its way up the wooded hillside near the border of Oakland and Berkeley, upon which is enthroned the genially aristocratic Hotel Claremont.

Usually when we had a hotel engagement, our band boy signed in for all of us, but a respectable dowager like the Claremont required each member of the band to register for himself. We hated this, as the trip had left us exhausted and we still faced a four-hour set on the bandstand that evening, entertaining a thin Monday-night crowd.

The hotel's faultlessly tailored lobby had undergone many changes since I'd first played there in my teens, but all I was interested in was a quick washup in my room before heading to the ballroom.

"Ray Sherwood?" inquired the desk clerk, looking at my entry in the hotel's registration ledger. He was a pleasant enough young man, although it was clear he had no close relatives who were dentists or cosmeticians.

"That's me," I answered, and he advanced me a key attached to a copper tag, which on one side read THE CLAREMONT, BERKELEY, CALIF., below which was my room number. On the other side were the words IF CARRIED AWAY, MAIL UNSEALED. POSTAGE GUARANTEED. I tucked the key into my billfold, under the flap where I always keep my room key until I inevitably find myself dropping it into a mailbox one city beyond the one I've just left.

The front desk clerk was searching some cubbyholes behind him. "Sherrrrrrrrrrrrrr-wood, hold on, I believe there's a—. Yes. A young lady left this for you late this afternoon."

He laid down an envelope bearing my name, which I opened. A letter, written in a precise, angular hand, began:

Dear Mr. Sherwood,

I would be honored if you would meet with me to discuss a business proposal that I believe may be of interest to you. Rather than bore you with the details here, I am hoping to bore you in person tomorrow morning at nine-thirty, when I will try my utmost to weaken your resolve over a cup of excellent coffee. Since I make terrible coffee, could you meet me at the Café Lafayette at the Golden Gate Exposition on Treasure Island?

These last six words were as clear as cuneiform to me, but I figured someone at the hotel would be able to direct me to this destination—that is, if I decided to meet her at the heathen hour of nine-thirty, a jazzman's equivalent of the crack of dawn.

"I'm performing in the Tower of the Sun at ten," her letter continued, still bewilderingly,

> so if you can't make it, it will not be a hardship for me. However, time *is* of the essence and it is important we meet as soon as possible. I am hoping my proposal will interest you, and if not, please know that three different underclassmen in the last month have told me that I am the cat's meow, pajamas, and whiskers, in alphabetical order. I am sure they are just being polite, but perhaps you might want to form your own opinion. Be advised that if I don't see you tomorrow at the Café (where I will know you by your photograph in *Metronome* magazine) I intend to track you down at the Claremont and lure you to your doom.

The letter was signed *Gail Prentice*. Beneath her signature was a phone number with a Berkeley exchange.

"You saw the girl who left this?" I asked the desk clerk.

"I did, sir, yes," he said.

I advanced him a dollar bill. "Tell me, if this girl had asked you to have breakfast with her, would you have said yes?" I smiled as if we were both men of the world.

"No, sir, I should say not," he answered, covering the bill with his right sleeve and sliding it off the marble counter into his waiting left hand. "I've been engaged for the last two years to a manicurist from Walnut Creek who works here at the Claremont. I'm sure she wouldn't like me keeping company with an Attractive Young Woman." He stressed the last three words and winked.

"How young?" I asked.

"Her twenties."

"How far into them?"

He shrugged. "She might be a little young for you."

I leaned forward. "How old do you think I am?"

He looked me over. I was disheveled from the long bus ride and could have used a shave. "Thirty-four?"

"Thirty-eight," I enlightened him gratefully as I slipped him another bill.

I hadn't had the pleasure of breakfasting with a woman in almost a year, and lately I'd been waking way too early (the dreams had come back). Keeping an intriguing appointment with an Attractive Young Woman sounded like a much better way of enduring tomorrow morning than sitting in my room playing cribbage for one. Gail (we were on a first-name basis now) had said she'd be honored to meet with me. How unchivalrous it would be if I were to ignore such a simple and charming request. I tucked the letter into my breast pocket, picked up my suitcase, and headed toward the stairs.

"What are you whistling about?" asked Raleigh Subbotin, who was crouched on the floor of the lobby and not at all happy about losing one of the wheels he'd strapped onto his bass fiddle case. I said I wasn't aware I'd been whistling.

3

The Terrace

On our second break that same evening, I went to the hotel's bank of coin telephones and tried calling the number Gail Prentice had given me. I was a little surprised when I got no answer. I suppose I'd pictured her breathlessly pacing by the phone.

I wandered myself as inconspicuously as possible to the bar in the Claremont's Terrace Lounge. Finding a narrow vacancy alongside a woman who was dressed in turquoise, which was this season's shade of evening blue, I brushed against her indifferent back and said to the bartender, "Rum and Coke. In the bottle."

He appraised me. "You with the band?"

"Tenor sax, second chair." I slipped a five-dollar bill alongside a small puddle of beer on the mahogany bar and we now understood each other.

"How much?" he asked.

It was like ordering gasoline. "Two dollars' worth," I said.

He raised a tufted eyebrow, opened a bottle of Coca-Cola, and wasted half its contents into the basin beneath him. He reached for the Bacardi (choosing the silver label from Puerto Rico, not the white label from Cuba—I was, after all, a musician) and carefully topped off the hobble-skirted Coke bottle. I took my bandstand stash with me out onto the Claremont's fieldstone terrace and was surprised to see that the island of Atlantis—an impossible Babylonian city whose iridescent walls gleamed in pastel shades of blue and pink, ornamented in gold and dull bronze—had chosen to arise in the middle of San Francisco Bay, halfway between Telegraph Hill and the wharves of Oakland, floating nonchalantly as if it had always been there.

As I puzzled over this inexplicable apparition, which hadn't existed when I'd last stood on this terrace over twenty years ago, I turned to see the ghostly glow of Jack Donovan's white dinner jacket floating toward me. A second later I was relieved to see that Jack was in it. As the leader of our band, Jack always wore a white dinner jacket with black pants. We in the band had elected to wear dark brown suits, primarily because they better hid stains. We tried to go as long as possible before having to visit the local French cleaner wherever we were playing. Some of us managed to tour the country with only four suits, two for the stage and two for the civilian world.

I placed my Coca-Cola bottle on a ledge behind me. I was sure Jack knew this was how we all sneaked booze onto the stage, but he seemed content to look the other way as long as we didn't force him to acknowledge the practice.

"Hello there, Ray," he said as if we hadn't just seen each other on the bandstand five minutes earlier. "Not a bad booking for us, wouldn't you say?"

Jack, who came from Vermont, had somewhere picked up the British habit of ending many of his sentences with a question. I'd always considered this to be a veiled way of daring someone to contradict you, but it was the only thing about him I didn't like.

I pointed toward the island of Atlantis, glimmering incandescently in the bay. "What is that, Jack? Do you know?"

"First time you've seen it, is it? That's the Golden Gate International Exposition. The West Coast's answer to the World's Fair in New York."

"That's interesting," I said. "I was thinking of meeting someone there for breakfast tomorrow." I stared at the island's tallest spire, which was greater in height than any structure on either side of the bay. "You know, I remember standing on this very spot when I was seventeen, and I could swear there was nothing out there. It's twenty times the size of Alcatraz. Where the hell did it come from?"

Jack lit a cigarette. "From the Army Corps of Engineers, I believe."

I shook my head. "No, I didn't mean the buildings, I meant the island itself."

He exhaled. "That's what I meant. That's what they built."

Before he could enlighten me further, I heard the unmistakable and much admired voice of Jack's wife, Vera, calling out to him. Jack Donovan and Vera Driscoll fronted our outfit. Jack played xylophone, which was a very useful instrument if you were underscoring a Mickey Mouse cartoon. The story on Jack Donovan's talent was that, as jazz musicians go, he had a wife who sang great.

Her looks were great, too, if what you liked was a genuine blonde with eyes the color of fresh cigarette ash, the sharp nose of someone who always gets her way, and the kind of permanently pouted lips that would cause intelligent, reliable men to ruin their lives. I mean, if that's what you liked, I guess Vera was okay. Her trademark hairstyle was a crimped pompadour angled to the right with the sides sweeping back into a chignon that made the nape of her neck as feminine as her forehead was challenging.

The fact that she was performing in the hotel allowed her to be one notch more intensely dressed than any other woman in the Terrace Lounge. But if she hadn't been performing, she probably would have dressed that way all the same.

She glanced right through me, as she had since we'd first met several years ago, and turned to her husband. "Jack, can I skip out on the last set?" she asked. "I need a little air." Vera then whispered something in her husband's ear. I could discern the words "monthly visit from my friend."

Jack nodded. "Certainly, why not?" It wasn't really a question, and she didn't answer it.

I have been afflicted since birth with the need to fill silences. I said, "You sang 'Believe You Me' especially well tonight, Vera."

"I had to," she replied, not taking her eyes off Jack. "It's an especially crummy arrangement."

The arrangement, of course, was mine. About three quarters of Jack's current book had been orchestrated by me.

"I suppose I've done better charts," I conceded.

"None that I've heard," she said.

For some unknown reason, Vera had been skewering me so much for the last few weeks that I'd debated getting a booster shot in case tetanus set in. Lockjaw could seriously impair my sax playing.

She brushed by me, pushing past my right hip as if I were hinged like a swinging door.

As she did, I heard a rustling noise, that of paper against fabric, something like the sound you might hear if you were a man and a woman had slipped a folded note into the outer pocket of your brown suit jacket while her husband was looking directly at you. That sort of sound.

"Sorry she was rude," offered Jack as soon as Vera left the terrace. "She says it's that difficult time of the month for her." He stared directly at my jacket pocket with his best impression of a smile. "Seems she wants to make it a difficult time for me as well."

I put my hands above my head as if volunteering to be frisked. "Jack, I swear to you, I don't know what gives."

He tossed his cigarette to the ground and stepped closer, but I wasn't as concerned about Jack hurting me as I was about Vera hurting him. I let him fish the note out of my pocket. He placed it, unread, upon the sand of a standing ashtray and lit it from a book of Claremont matches.

As we watched it burn, he said, "She just does these things to reassure herself that she's important. The more I tolerate, the more she knows she's the star of the band. And she is, so I tolerate it. It's no different from the actress who demands pink azaleas out of season because they're so hard to get. You've never responded to any of her overtures, Ray, and that makes you hard to get. You're just her latest pink azalea."

"Well, that's very nice of you to say, Jack," I replied, and followed him back into the hotel. The guests greeted him as we stepped through the lobby, and Jack gave each a cordial hello. He really was quite an affable guy.

As he stopped to sign an autograph, he confided to me *sotto voce,* "I'm not just the band's leader, Ray, I'm its manager. It behooves me to keep my star happy until such time as I can replace her with someone as good, or better." It was a strange way to talk about one's wife. "And should that day ever come," he added, opening the door to the ballroom for me and laughing lightly as he no doubt pictured such a day, "I'll just have to have Vera slaughtered, don't you think?"

4

The Ballroom

As far as the Claremont's patrons were concerned, the evening closed out pleasantly, even without Vera's presence. By the last chord of our signature theme, "A Temptress in Taupe," I had already disassembled my clarinet, and as I took apart my tenor sax, Jack stepped down from the bandstand to sign dinner menus and shake hands with the last of the dancers. Frankie Pompano asked if he could buy me a drink, but I had in my head the pleasant image of me in a Claremont bed between Claremont linens, with two fingers of rye in a water tumbler at my side, reading a medley of psalms from a Gideon Bible. I nonchalantly told Frankie (concealing as best I could some small amount of masculine pride) that I was meeting a young woman for breakfast the next morning and that I thought I'd call it a night.

I saw Larry Vance, trumpet, third chair, being handed his suitcase by Tommy Trego. When Larry wasn't touring, he made his home in East Oakland. He'd been counting the days until he could sleep in his own bed for two whole weeks. If you'd ever seen Larry, you'd know that his wife would start counting the days once he'd arrived.

Over the years, I'd learned that I could always rely on Larry to be there whenever he needed me. I asked him if I could borrow his car the next morning. I told him I could take a cab to his house around nine and that the loan of the car could square us for the hundred and six dollars he'd owed me for the last three years. The generosity of my offer was counterpointed by the certainty that I was never going to see that money anyway.

Larry said he wished he could help but had just that moment remembered he didn't really want to.

I asked him if his wife, Florence, liked funny stories. Sure, he replied, who doesn't, and I could see the dawn of suspicion rising within his squinty sky-blue eyes. I asked him if Florence had ever heard the one about the trumpet player who'd been arrested for playing "St. James Infirmary" in the nude on the front porch of the nicest bordello in Decatur. Larry told me he'd leave the car keys under a potted palm on his front porch and asked me not to race the engine.

It was a rare treat to be sleeping under the same roof as where we were playing, even if my room was in a part of the Hotel Claremont originally intended for those servants who didn't stay in the suite of their employers. Most venues merely offered us a rate at a businessman's hotel, usually named the Warfield or the Warwick, but a lesser chamber in a swank hotel is a lot better than the best one in a former flophouse.

I entered my room and flipped on the light switch. "You took long enough," Vera complained, looking up from the magazine she was reading upon my bed. She was fully dressed, except for her heels, and lying on top of the covers, but as far as propriety and my friendship with Jack went, she might just as well have been naked.

"How'd you get in here?" I asked, not taking another step.

"Bribed a maid who was turning down the beds. You were supposed to come up before the last set and leave the door unlocked for me. Can't you read?"

"I didn't look at your damn note," I told her. "Jack saw you slip it into my pocket, just the way you meant him to, I'm sure."

"Bet you five bucks he didn't read it." She gauged my reaction and murmured, "I should have made it twenty bucks."

"How could you treat the guy like that, Vera? What has Jack ever done to you?"

"Not what *you* could do, Ray, I'm willing to bet," she cooed, but Jack had been right; this had absolutely nothing to do with sex. She just needed someone to make a fuss over her. If I'd walked in holding the *San Francisco Chronicle's* rotogravure section with a picture of her on the front page, I probably would have aroused her just as much.

"C'mon, Vera," I said, picking up her silver ankle-strap heels from beside the bed. "You're clearing out of here before Jack catches on. He's always been square with me."

She crouched on the bed. "You want to run away? We could run away, take a clipper down to Panama—I've got my passport with me." She produced a green booklet from her bag and waved it at me. I wouldn't have been surprised if she was carrying traveler's checks as well.

Although I was angry with her, my vanity was primped by her obvious advance planning. "Gee, I'm flattered that for once *you're* making the arrangements for *me,* Vera."

"Don't be. I don't drive, so I have to keep my passport with me for identification," she explained, sticking a fork into the soufflé of my ego.

I snatched the passport from her hand.

"What are you doing?" she snapped. I weaved around the room and she followed me, trying to retrieve it.

"I just wanted to see if even somebody who looks like you takes a lousy passport picture," I explained with a laugh, but my real motive was simply to get her off my bed.

The photo in the passport had been taken a couple of years earlier, and I thought Vera actually looked a little nicer back then. She'd worn the same striking hairstyle, but there was a softer look to her face, as if she hadn't read any of her reviews yet and still wasn't certain if she'd make it.

I read her name aloud. "Edna Drisch Vernon?" I exclaimed with glee. "*Edna?!* Ohhh, Edna!"

"Give me that back!" she spat.

"Place of birth Hackettstown, Pennsylvania, nineteen-oh-*my!*"

Having accomplished my purpose, I let her grab the passport back from me. She stuffed it deep into her bag. "C'mon, Ray," she groused. "Jack always takes me back. He has to. I'll make him take you back, too."

I shook my head. "No, Vera, not in Panama, not in this room, not as long as Jack is alive and you're still his wife."

I opened the window closest to my bed, as I do most nights. I have to feel air moving across my face or I can't sleep. Although my room was one flight up from the lobby, the grounds of the Claremont rose alongside the hotel, so there was only about a five-foot drop from the window to the paved walkway below. I peered outside to make sure no one was there. "Come on, Vera, I'll let you down gently," I said.

She waved me off, put on her shoes, stepped over the sill, and smoothly lowered herself to the ground. My guess was she'd done this somewhere before. She took quick, assured steps along the walkway, which was glossy from being hosed down for the night. Without looking back at me, she made a one-fingered gesture in the air whose meaning in this particular context seemed paradoxical.

I went to the door, snapped off the overhead light, and returned to the window, drawing back the curtains as far as I could, in order to see what had so interested me earlier this evening: the floating city I'd whimsically named Atlantis, whose illuminated central tower reflected deep into the water, so that it looked as if the island had been speared through its heart by Neptune.

I looked at the telephone by my bed and checked my wristwatch. I couldn't call Gail Prentice at this time of night. If she was going to look for me at nine-thirty on the alluring island outside my window, as her letter had said she would with or without confirmation from me, she'd surely be in bed by now. It wouldn't hurt me to do the same, since I found myself with a rare reason to be up early the next morning. To be sure, my mysterious assignation would almost certainly prove to be mundane: a legal secretary who wanted saxophone lessons or advice on how to break into show business. The crafty Miss Prentice had been cunning enough to omit virtually all pertinent information, and I was allowing myself the fun of conjuring an intrigue from my ignorance.

I shed my clothes and slipped into the bed, which was still warm from Vera's body and smelled of her perfume. I was uncomfortable being so intimate with Jack's wife, even at such a safe distance. It made me further uneasy that the scent she wore was, in a word, enticing.

I got up and yanked the linens off the bed, at the foot of which was a neatly folded coverlet that I unfurled and bundled myself within, lying down on the otherwise bare mattress.

I worried that I'd have one of the dreams. These left me in terrible shape come the morning. I stared at the ceiling, dreading what I might see in my sleep.

I was lucky that night. I saw nothing, at least that I could remember.

But in the morning, less than an hour after keeping my appointment on the beckoning island, I would witness Atlantis's first human sacrifice—bloody, repugnant, and in broad daylight—within the Court of the Moon, beneath the Tower of the Sun.

5

A Broken
Engagement

Treasure Island, Golden Gate International Exposition, San Francisco   C-4

Larry Vance's new Nash sedan was a dream to drive, the lofty prow of its narrow hood jutting out like the barrel of a .45 automatic.

The first surprise of the day (there were to be many) was discovering that the exit ramp for the Golden Gate International Exposition was located in the middle of the bridge that spanned San Francisco Bay. The reason such an exit was not the invention of a homicidal architect was because the recently completed transverse really consisted of two bridges: the first stemming from San Francisco, the other from Oakland, both meeting in the middle of the bay on a small shale island called Yerba Buena.

The exit ramp chuted me through a veil of eucalyptus-scented mist that was already being sponged up by the morning sun and onto the slopes of the little isle that floated like a grass-covered buoy in the water. Through a break in the tall trees of its natural landscape, I got my first good look at the much larger island that human hands had built upon the waters alongside Yerba Buena while I'd been busy carpeting every square inch of the Midwest and Southeast with the Jack Donovan Orchestra.

What I saw (and I may have gasped when I did) was a sprawling walled city whose architecture seemed to be an amalgam of the Aztecan, Abyssinian, and Acropolisian. Beneath its ramparts were lavish gardens whose millions of blooms were organized in such disciplined fashion that they looked like the contents of a giant's paint box. I guided Larry's sedan onto a causeway that bridged the gulf between Yerba Buena and "Treasure Island" (this being its official name), paid fifty cents at a tollgate, and slow-cruised the Nash down a great boulevard lined with palm trees. Above what seemed to be the kingdom's gateway, I was astounded to see twin Mayan pyramids that served as stepped platforms for a pair of stone elephants trumpeting to a gleaming gilt phoenix atop the island's tallest tower. Through a second great portal in the crenellated walls, I saw a lofty yet graceful statue, a milk-white goddess standing taller than depictions of the Colossus of Rhodes or Athena at the Parthenon.

And then I came to the parking lot.

A half hour later found me seated in the Foreign Pavilion area of the Golden Gate Exposition, at the outdoor Café Lafayette, attached to the Palais de l'Élégance, dipping a warm brioche into a sweet, smoky bowl of café au lait while awaiting the arrival of a young woman I didn't know.

It seemed strange to be eating patisserie in this mock Montparnasse while Paris was largely deprived of the same treat. France had fallen to Hitler only three months earlier, and the sale of baked goods there had been banned four days a week. So I felt guilty enjoying my little breakfast on a sunny day flecked with soft breezes from the bay. But then again, for the last eleven years I'd generally felt guilty enjoying anything.

Just as, when driving, you will sometimes notice a distant oncoming automobile and get the idea that it is intent on meeting you head-on, I watched a young woman walk my way, more and more my way, until she was sitting uninvited at my table.

The desk clerk at the Claremont had underestimated her age as generously as he had mine. I placed her as late twenties. She was slightly taller than average, dressed in the same frock of green-and-black plaid that women seemed to have been wearing in every town Jack Donovan's band had played for the last two years. As if to counterbalance this ordinariness, she'd created an interesting arrangement of six fake emerald-and-pearl barrettes, three on either side of her head, holding her hair in a tight, complex construction, each plaited lock pinned to overlap the one above it. Her long neck and lack of chin caused her profile to resemble that of an ostrich, but when you looked at her straight on, she was more than attractive. If I were in prison and she'd been my girlfriend, I'd have dreamt about her easy enough. Her figure was trim, perhaps too much so. She wore white socks and penny loafers. It seemed a bit sad that she was trying to look younger than she could get away with.

Since it was she who'd asked me to be here, I thought it behooved her to start the conversation. I stirred my bowl of coffee and waited politely.

"Are you an American?" she asked in the guttural accent I associate with the south of France. I'd of course not "heard" her accent when I'd read her letter. I told her I was indeed a U.S. citizen, somewhat surprised that this would be her first question.

Her eyes went to my left hand and its unadorned fingers. "You're not married?" she asked—hopefully, it seemed to me.

"Divorced. For quite some time now."

"You have children?"

"A daughter," I said.

"Does she live with you?"

"No," I answered. "I wish she did. Now can we please discuss business?"

She put her hands flat upon the café table and leaned toward me. "You wish to screw me?" she asked.

The café's management was clearly showing commendable attention to detail in re-creating the Parisian atmosphere, from the big Pernod umbrella above me right down to the little streetwalker beside me. However, there was something so genuinely desperate, rather than seductive, in her manner that I felt only pity mixed with wariness. I told her I had very little money on me, which seemed the most courteous way to reject her offer.

She rose abruptly, her cheeks flushing as if I had slapped them. "What, you think I am a prostitute? No, I am a dancer, with Les Folies Bergère, there." She nodded her head toward the austere United States Federal Building, where, inexplicably, the Folies had apparently received permission to purvey their classy display of skin. "When I ask if you wish to screw me, it is to say that if you marry me, you then could screw me. *Le mariage,*" she stressed, though it was more of a plea than a stipulation, "but it would have to be today, now." She did a pirouette for me and urgently answered her own question: "I am attractive, yes?"

"*D'accord,*" I said. I'd taken a year of French at the Juilliard.

"And you like my outfit, my hair," she continued, giving me a second glimpse of the intricate arrangement. She flashed a camera-ready smile. "I have very good teeth—the Folies has them maintained here." The smile stopped. "And of course the beautiful figure that people pay money to see."

I told her I was immensely flattered by her offer, but no, at least not today.

She smoothed out her frock, reassembling her pride. "Well, don't be flattered of yourself. You are not the only man whom I have proposed this morning to."

It was the second time in less than twelve hours that my male pride had been shot down, and I permitted myself some small but justifiable annoyance. "Look, Miss Prentice, you leave a message at my hotel asking me to meet with you, I borrow a car and drive all the way here—"

She looked at me as if I were mad. "My name is Prasquier and I have never been leaving any message for you! I don't know you. You are just sitting here."

And with that, she walked quickly up the street and out of my life forever, one would imagine. One imagines lots of things.

6

Gail

"Well hello and everything," came the peppy voice of a young woman behind me. "I'm guessing you're Ray Sherwood."

I turned and allowed myself a moment to take her in, which she must have misunderstood as bewilderment on my part.

She winced. "Oh, gosh, sorry, you're *not* Ray Sherwood?"

I smiled at her, one of the easiest things I've ever done, and responded, "Well, if I weren't, I'd sure try to keep that information from you as long as possible. Yes, I'm Ray."

"Well, I'm Gail," she said, as if we were now all tied at 1.

She was dressed in what I'd read was the current rage among college girls on the opposite coast: men's clothing. Her camel-colored slacks were of soft flannel and her right-buttoning jacket was of forest-green wool, under which I could see a white oxford shirt and boy's suspenders. Oversized green-and-brown argyle socks bunched around her ankles above a pair of men's brown moccasins.

Still, there'd be no way you'd mistake her for a boy, even at a distance. She was pretty damn fetching, but she acted as if she didn't know that. Her wild brown hair, which had obviously been shampooed that very morning, clearly disagreed with her on the topic of where it should fall. Its mass formed a nice backdrop for her bright, expressive features.

She sat herself down at my table. "So thank you for meeting me here, Mr. Sherwood."

"Call me Ray," I said.

"Okay then, Ray. I'm really stunned. I mean, writing that note to you was a case of 'I shot an arrow into the air.' And here you are."

I nodded at her wardrobe. "That's some number."

She looked down at her clothes and laughed. "I don't always wear men's clothing, but I'm not exactly rolling in dough—you fellows don't realize how good you've got it. Women have to pay double or triple what men pay for an outfit, and how many times a week do you think we can wear it?" She toyed with her lapels. "I'm working my way through school, the Department of Music over at Berkeley, and this getup is one quarter the price of something from the Sather Gate Shop. And it makes quite an impression, I think."

That it did, I told her, and asked how she knew of me.

"Well, I have all of Jack Donovan's records, the three on Vocalion and the new one on Brunswick . . . 'Beef Lo Mein,' 'Soup du Jour,' 'The Music Speaks to Me' . . . I really love the arrangements. And then I read about you in Art Garnett's column in *Metronome* magazine and found out they were all your charts."

"It was a very short paragraph."

"But very complimentary. Seeing you here, though, I don't think the photo did you any justice."

I was much enjoying the drift of this conversation as the café's only waiter approached Gail with a look of ennui he'd most likely received on graduation day at the Sorbonne.

"Just a glass of water, but bring *me* the check," Gail seemed pleased to say, indicating my coffee and roll. The waiter's eyes conveyed the overwhelming futility of life, and he departed.

I asked her, "How did you know I'd be at the Claremont?"

"Last week, I saw a sign in the Claremont's lobby saying that Jack Donovan's orchestra would be appearing in the ballroom. I asked if they knew where your band would be staying and they said, 'On the premises.' So yesterday afternoon, I went back and left my note for you."

She didn't really look or act much like part of the hotel's crowd, which tended toward the society set. "What were you doing at the Claremont?"

She laughed again. "Drinking free booze." I raised my eyebrows and she advised, "It's a long story."

I shrugged. "It's a long day."

The waiter returned, set down a glass of water and the check for Gail, and departed with a twitch of despair.

She began, "Well, at the end of Prohibition, some killjoys at the university pushed through a local ordinance saying you couldn't operate a bar within one mile of the Berkeley campus. As if there wasn't plenty of hooch in all the dorms! Of course, this killed the Claremont, which is right along the border. But as it happens, I do a little cross-country running for Cal Berkeley. I can do a mile in under seven minutes."

"Pretty good."

"Well, thanks. So one day, for fun, I decide to run to the Claremont's gates and it takes me nine minutes. Even accounting for the uphill grade at the very end, I mean, nine minutes to run one mile? I have a friend who's studying engineering. I had him do a survey and it turns out the Claremont is more than a mile away from the very closest border of the campus. I went to the hotel's manager with this information, he got it confirmed, and so you're looking at the reason the Claremont can now serve liquor." The Reason did a little "voilà" with her arms. "As a thank-you, I get free drinks at the Terrace Lounge for the rest of my life. I'll probably drink myself to death and get shortchanged."

(The whole thing sounded very made up, but the bartender at the Terrace Lounge later confirmed to me that this was indeed the case, except for the part about her drinking herself to death.)

I asked about her business proposal.

Gail's index finger played around in her glass of water. "You're a jazz musician and a jazz arranger, but you have a classical background. Juilliard, right?" Technically, I'd attended the Institute of Musical Arts before it had merged with its rival, but it was the custom to refer to our alma mater as Juilliard. Gail continued: "Okay, well, I'm a composer, or studying to be. I'm pretty wild. I mean, modern. Schoenberg, Stravinsky, they're like Kay Kyser compared to the stuff I write. Anyway, the Pavilions of the Pacific part of the fair, that's right behind us—"

She pointed toward a gigantic lagoon, around which were structures evoking the architecture of the countries that harbor the Pacific Ocean.

"—they held this contest for a musical composition honoring the spirit of Treasure Island. I called mine *Swing* or, actually, *Swing Around the Sun,* with the subtitle *One Star, One Planet, One Orbit, One People.* Because, you know, we really are." Her eyes got shiny with conviction and she had to turn a nervous laugh into a cough to cover her embarrassment. "Hokey, I know, but I think it helped me with the judges. Anyway, guess what, Ray? I won, and it's going to be performed here on Treasure Island by the Pan-Pacific Orchestra, an Asian swing band, if you can imagine. Our music, their musicians. Kind of sweet."

"Sweet indeed."

"Yes, except I composed the piece for the piano and I don't know a *thing* about scoring it for five saxes, four trumpets, four trombones, and rhythm. So I'm asking if you would orchestrate it for me. My notes, your voicings."

It sounded like an awful lot of work to me. This must have been more apparent in my face than I imagined, for she rushed to reassure me, "Oh, I'm not asking you to ghost it, if that's the word. You'd get full credit for the arrangement. Like Ravel did, orchestrating *Pictures at an Exhibition* from Mussorgsky's piano piece. Or Ferde Grofé for Gershwin's *Rhapsody in Blue*. Eventually I'll learn to arrange my own work, just like Gershwin did, but not in the time that's left before the concert. And this, well, this could show a whole new side of you."

I smiled. If I wanted to show a whole new side of me, I'd be back in New York, not working in towns like Dayton and Eureka with the Jack Donovan Orchestra.

She pressed her case. "The prize money was a hundred dollars. I could pay you fifty."

I smiled further. Fifty dollars probably wouldn't cover the copying bill.

The earnest enthusiasm in her face was the most pleasant sight I'd seen in ages. In a further attempt to manipulate me against my better judgment, Gail got a breeze to conspire with her by having it tousle her hair. She really was just lovely.

"Gail . . . how about I hear the piece and see what the work would entail?"

"Yes, that's great. Absolutely. Let me see, it's—" She looked at her watch. "Oh damn, I'm going to be late. Come on." She tossed some coins onto the table and raced away. I followed her, since she wasn't leaving me much of an option.

It was nearly ten and the public was beginning to enter the Exposition in serious numbers. Gail moved so fast that I barely had time to take in what I was seeing as she hustled me into a side entrance of the Foods and Beverage Pavilion, past a mechanical Mr. Peanut, a map of the Del Monte empire, the Italian Swiss Colony wine garden, where a sign proclaimed that its "special sherry hour" ran from one to six, a Heinz 57 display of Kitchens from Many Nations, and free samples of Junket Rennet Custard.

As we swept by the displays, she uttered the unusual sentence, "Did I mention I play the carillon in the Tower of the Sun?"

"That's very nice."

"You know what a carillon is?" she asked.

I said that if I recalled correctly, it was a set of cathedral bells that could be played with great difficulty by manually throttling a kind of keyboard made from large wooden pegs.

She nodded. "Yes, this one's a beauty—forty-four bells. On loan from Grace Cathedral in San Francisco. The one I play at Berkeley only has twelve bells."

We passed some restrooms and a first-aid station, then stepped out a doorway that verged on a stunning plaza. Fluming arches of water spanned a long reflecting pool surrounded by a thicket of blue-and-white flowers. Mirrored from one end of the pool to the other, and demanding my immediate upward attention, was a rocketing octagonal spire at least four hundred feet tall.

"Made it!" laughed Gail. "With time to spare. I'm playing Bach at ten. Hey, Russ!" She waved to a robust fellow, perhaps in his late forties, who looked like a sportsman of the *Field & Stream* variety. He was standing with a stockier gentleman in a royal blue suit.

"Hi there, Gail," said the guy she'd called Russ, the far more tanned and casual of the two men. His features resembled a relief map of a rock quarry and his ready smile caused long furrows to be formed alongside his eyes and the corners of his mouth. "Do you know my friend here? Bob Culpepper. Bob's in charge of all police assigned to Treasure Island, so if you want to be impressed, go right ahead."

The man in the royal blue suit shook Gail's hand. "Russ tells me you're the cause of these bells I thought I'd been hearing in my head all summer."

Culpepper and Russ now turned to look at me with curiosity.

Gail began an introduction. "Russ, this is—"

There was a tremendous noise, as if an immense sledgehammer had been brought down upon a huge and succulent Hubbard squash.

Culpepper turned first and saw what the invisible sledgehammer had wrought.

It was wearing a frock of green-and-black plaid. The frock didn't fit very well, because her right arm was pointed in a direction no arm can point and her left ankle now lay beneath her left shoulder. The splattered confetti of her former torso was the color of dark blood and yellow bone, and many of those standing in the court bore some trace of it.

In profile, her face was just a porridge of blood. Most heart-breakingly, she was still wearing her little fake emerald-and-pearl barrettes, meticulously placed in her tightly arranged coif.

In one pocket of her frock would be found a woman's wallet, with a temporary working permit in conjunction with the Folies Bergère. She was from the south of France. Her Christian name was Marie. Her family name was Prasquier, as she had told me herself.

7

The Blunt Instrument

As the crowd gradually realized that the vile mess scattered across what I later learned was the Court of the Moon had moments earlier been a human being, many of us became occupied with retching. Bob Culpepper had clearly stomached worse than this in his time, but even he struggled with his gag reflex for a moment.

"Damn fucking damn," he swore to fortify himself, no one reprimanding him for his language. With the back of his hand, he wiped some saliva from the corner of his mouth and moved toward the woman's body.

The children in the crowd were the only ones not sickened, likely because they had no grasp of their own mortality and thus their correlation to this human refuse. Some of them had gathered around Mademoiselle Prasquier's faceless head with the same studious interest they might have given their first dead robin, covered with a tidal wave of ecstatic ants.

I had control of my stomach for the moment, but I knew I wouldn't if I didn't turn away. I did so and saw Gail splashing water onto her face at a drinking fountain. The man named Russ was trying to calm a wailing little girl whose father had fainted at her side. A nun was attempting to pray over Marie Prasquier and touched the torso as she gave a blessing. Pulling back her hand, she saw the blood upon it and her courage and stomach fled her. She crossed herself and raced for the sanctuary of the restrooms. No one in heaven and earth or the Court of the Moon would have faulted her.

A uniformed policeman was approaching at far too much of a saunter for Culpepper's liking. He waved the flatfoot over and snapped, "Horvath, I want you to run to the dispatcher and get as many men over here as we've got on the island. We could use some of the Pinkerton guards too, if they're willing to help."

Horvath ran away in Olympian fashion. Culpepper muttered to me, "I'd lock down the island but I have no idea what I'm looking for. If anything."

I nodded soberly. Apparently I was now his Watson.

Culpepper addressed the crowd in a voice that would have made a megaphone redundant. "Attention, folks! I am Lieutenant Robert Culpepper of the Oakland Police Department." He flourished a bright silver badge in a cheap black wallet and got it to reflect the sunlight nicely. "Everyone in this area is to move in an orderly fashion toward the Enchanted Garden, which is that way." He pointed with arrow-fingered fists toward a formal garden about a hundred yards away. "No one is allowed to leave the island until I say so."

I spotted Gail now leaning against an electric light stanchion. I said to Culpepper, "I'm going to see how my friend is doing, is that okay?"

Calling Gail my friend was an overstatement, but I detected a wish in me that it might not always be. The wish was a young man's feeling, a feeling I'd not felt in a long time.

As I moved toward Gail, Culpepper tugged me back by the crook of my right arm as if he were the straight man in a burlesque routine. "What kind of weapon," he said to me, apparently just because I was next to him, "could do that much damage to one person and absolutely nothing to anybody else?" His eyes swept the area in all directions. "It's like she was hit by a bazooka, but there's no scorch marks and no shrapnel, except for bits of *her* scattered in every direction. I didn't hear any kind of explosive . . ."

"Well, what I heard," I offered, thinking a musician's observation about sound might be of use, "was the kind of noise I heard when I was a kid, when we used to drop water balloons from the top of an apartment building."

He stared at me for a moment, then cursed and looked disgusted. "Oh, and I call myself a cop? Looking for a weapon and I'm standing on it?"

I glanced down at his feet, but there was nothing beneath his Florsheim brogues except concrete.

Culpepper pointed at the cement. "There's your blunt instrument. That's what hit her. At about sixty miles an hour." Seeing my puzzled expression, he pointed at the soaring obelisk. "She fell from the top of the Tower of the Sun. Or jumped." He bent his head back to view the tower's peak and muttered, "I'd have noticed if she'd screamed. Most of them scream. They change their mind and there's nothing they can do about it and then they have the wait, of course. Must be the longest three, four seconds anyone ever lived."

"Try three minutes," I heard myself snap. I instantly realized it was an odd response.

"What does *that* mean?" asked Culpepper.

"I only meant that it must have felt like three minutes," I lied and tried to change the subject. "But listen, Lieutenant, I do think it's pretty likely it was suicide, not an accident."

He looked at me with interest but said nothing, waiting patiently. As a professional, he knew that silence can be a very effective interrogating tool.

Unfortunately, as an arranger, I view silence as an eight-bar rest that must be filled at any cost. I added, "She had seemed pretty agitated, to the point of desperation, when she talked to me. That would have been less than half an hour ago."

Culpepper emitted a profound sigh and looked at me as if I were the ghost of an old friend whose ashes he was about to toss into the ocean. He said sympathetically, "Gosh, I bet you're already wishing you hadn't said that."

8

The Blunt Instrumentalist

The best thing I had going for me was my alibi. I'd been standing with the island's senior police official at the very moment Marie Prasquier had departed from Treasure Island's highest summit to keep her irreversible appointment with death. Of everyone on the planet, surely I, Gail, and the fellow named Russ (about whose relationship with Gail I was still ignorant) were the three people most likely to be excluded from the suspicions of Lieutenant Robert Culpepper.

He took my arm more firmly now and started to walk me away from the area. I looked back and saw Gail moving, as instructed, toward the Enchanted Garden.

"Gail!" I called out.

The noise of the departing parade of material witnesses made it hard to hear what she shouted back to me; I heard something about "another carillon concert at three, today" at "the tower" something, before her voice got lost in a muddle of sound.

Culpepper said, "Come on, my friend."

It was nice to have a friend.

"Meet me tonight at the Claremont!" I shouted to Gail, but she shrugged and indicated she couldn't hear me. A police officer instructed her to move along, and she turned away.

"I said, come on now, pal," urged Culpepper. I was clearly growing dearer to him every moment.

The offices of the Treasure Island division of the Oakland Police were located on the second floor of the Administration Building, which, unlike the rest of the island's architecture, was a substantial and sensible half-circle structure that would have earned a double-chinned nod of approval from a banker.

Culpepper showed me with civility into what he called the interview room, whose furnishings a Quaker would have deemed spare. Before he got any of my own vital statistics, the lieutenant asked me for a concise rendition of my encounter with Marie Prasquier, along with a description of her appearance. Having elicited this, he stepped away, asking me to wait for him. In a rather thoughtful gesture, he had a rookie policeman bring in a pitcher of ice water and some reading matter, consisting of a few *Collier's* magazines from last spring and a handful of pamphlets describing the allures and attractions of Treasure Island.

A short while later, I heard outside the building a steely voice over the Exposition's public-address system. Culpepper was wasting no time broadcasting a description of Marie Prasquier around the island, along with the request that anyone who might have seen or spoken with her should report to the authorities at the Administration Building. No mention was made of her death.

About an hour later, Culpepper was back. He opened the door and ushered three men into the room. One was a raffia-haired kid in his early twenties wearing a white uniform and peaked cap bearing the words THRELKELD'S SCONES. The second man was in his late sixties, garbed in a gray serge suit that was glossy from too many encounters with an iron (whereas his yellowing shirt had never met one). The third fellow was about fifty-five, overweight, and planted in a leather-cushioned wheelchair, his bandaged right foot clearly afflicted by the gout.

Culpepper asked us if we'd ever seen each other before and we all mumbled words to the negative. He showed the three men out of the little room, then ducked his head back in to grin at me.

"These were your rivals for the hand of Ma'm'selle Prasquier. It seems she proposed to them this morning as well. And last week to my friend Russ, I've just learned, and a college kid who works at the Chuck-a-Luck stand, and half the male skaters in the Ice Show. Stay put. I'll be needing a statement from you."

He shut the door, and I was left alone for a considerable amount of time.

I have a good sense of rhythm. I write fairly well for percussion. But there is a limit to how long I can entertain myself drumming my fingers on a hardwood table. So I turned my attention to the pamphlets on the desk and opened up one emblazoned PAGEANT OF THE PACIFIC!

It informed me that, some seven years earlier, the city fathers of the Bay Area had decided that a West Coast world's fair to rival the much hoopla'd World of Tomorrow in New York would be a boon to California commerce and culture—but where to put it?

One engineer, who had hitherto seemed quite sane, advanced the idea of building the world's largest man-made island within the shoals of Yerba Buena.

Much mirth greeted this notion until the engineer added that, once the fair was over, the island could then become San Francisco International Airport, ideally located within ten minutes of both its namesake city and Oakland. This could replace the outmoded San

Francisco Aerodrome (a fancy name for some unattractive farmland out in Alameda) without wreaking havoc upon any existing community. The Administration Building, where I was currently sitting, would become the airport's terminal and control tower. Two hangars built for the maintenance of the Pan American World Airways seaplanes currently harbored in the island's marina could serve land-based planes at the new floating airport as well.

A general contractor named R. W. Hewett, a guy who apparently knew what he was doing, enlisted the services of the United States Army Corps of Engineers, who said they could build an island in under nineteen months. And they did.

Culpepper came back into the room, all smiles. "Got the nicest book of mug shots you'll ever have to thumb through," he said, and slapped down an oversized souvenir program bearing the gold-engraved silhouette of a kneeling naked woman and the words *Folies Bergère.* "Flip through the pages and see if there's anyone in this book who looks familiar."

As police lineups go, it was eminently fair, since the program featured photographs of some twenty female cast members in absolutely equal states of undress. Searching for Marie among them was slightly challenging because I had only seen her with her clothes on. But I found her quickly enough. She was posed in three-quarter profile, which exaggerated her ostrichlike neck and chin, but with the way that angle presented the rest of her, no one would be focusing north of her shoulders. She was wearing a feathered toque and little else. The program indicated her specialty numbers were "Nightingale at Midnight" and "The Criminal's Ball of Pigalle." Poor thing, to have died as she did.

"That's her," I said, pointing.

"You're sure?"

"Absolutely."

Culpepper took the program back from me. "Yeah, you got her. And we know why she killed herself. She was Jewish."

I told him I wasn't aware that this was considered cause for suicide.

Culpepper sat himself into the unyielding wooden chair across from me. "Do some thinking." He reached to his outer breast pocket, produced a cigar, and toasted it, drawing a match's flame up the flue of the Panatella. "She's Jewish. She's French. What does that mean to you?"

"No ham-and-Swiss-cheese crepes?" I ventured, baffled as to what point he was making.

Culpepper blew a gray cloud of smoke my way. "Where've you been hiding yourself, Ray?" I was going to tell him the part about Dayton and Eureka, but he continued: "The fair closes in a little over a month. Where do you think that puts the cast of the Folies Bergère? Haven't you been reading the papers?"

"Oh," I said, embarrassed I'd been so dense.

After France had surrendered to Germany, the victors had allowed the eighty-three-year-old Marshal Pétain to govern Vichy France. This had turned out to be the equivalent of the cruel schoolmarm letting the class snitch preside over the students while she went to the ladies' room. Eager to demonstrate to Berlin that a goosestep would come naturally to a nation fed on paté de foie gras, Pétain had turned over to Germany all naturalized Jewish immigrants, even though they were French citizens, and passed laws against all native French Jews. Elected officials who were Jewish had to resign their positions. Jews could not serve in the armed forces, be teachers, or be involved in journalism or entertainment.

Hitler had promised France and the rest of Europe that his gift to them would be "a Jewless peace."

"I had a talk with the Folies company manager just now," said Culpepper. "When the fair ends, their plan is to sail to Lisbon, then Bizerta, then to Dieppe, at which point Marie Prasquier—she was born in Algeria—would have been separated from the others and delivered by freight train to a detainment center. Apparently if you're a Jew, you lose your job, your savings, your personal property. . . . It couldn't get much worse than that, could it?"

I'd read a story the week before about a ship that had been chartered by German Jews to get them out of their country. It was all done legally, with the permission of the German government, but no country would let them in, including the United States. They were finally booted from Cuba and sent back home. The ship's crew couldn't police every cabin. There were thirty-five suicides by the time the boat landed in Bremerhaven. Five other passengers leapt to their death in the harbor.

Culpepper said, "Apparently Miss Prasquier had been trying to snare an American for weeks, coming on to any tourist who wasn't wearing a ring on his left hand. Sorry if that hurts your feelings."

"I gave up my feelings for Lent," I reassured him and gestured toward Marie's nude photograph, which in addition to being lovely and mysterious would now be forever tragic as well. "You'd think somebody with her figure alone would have had no trouble—"

Culpepper cut me off. "The trouble for her was with the folks at Immigration. They've gotten wise to foreigners who fall in love at first sight. The way the law works now, an immigrant has to prove that their marriage to an American is the real thing. Apparently, Marie had found several likely prospects, met with the authorities to see if they'd grant her citizenship if the marriage took place, and flunked three times. The only thing that puzzles me is why she started up again today, knowing that Immigration was on to her. Shows she was cracking up."

Oh good, I thought, a federal board of review for the credibility of *amour,* as if love were a thing that made sense. When I'd married my lovely ex-wife, who didn't bob her hair or sport bee-stung lips, my male friends had thought her drab by flapper standards—until they themselves got hitched and discovered that they'd married a makeup kit. My wife had been beautiful enough to model in glamour shows with Sally Rand when she was seventeen and knew more about makeup than Clara Bow had forgotten, but she'd given that up for motherhood. I told my cronies that with my Nancy, I'd been greeted each morning by the same wonderful face to which I'd said good night.

Culpepper stood. "I'm going to ask you to make a formal statement, Mr. Sherwood, and I'd appreciate it if you'd emphasize how distraught and desperate Miss Prasquier was, telling you she felt like killing herself, that sort of thing."

I said, "Maybe it would be easier for you if I just put my signature at the bottom of a blank sheet of paper, and you can type what you want above it." He looked a bit startled. He hadn't been a bad guy, and I immediately felt as if I was being needlessly peevish.

Culpepper asked a woman outside the door to join us, then turned back to me. "All right, just go ahead and say what you think is the truth, in your own words. I was pushing you too hard to get what I wanted." He shook his head. "This fair, Treasure Island, it's a beautiful world but it hasn't been an instant success, though we haven't lost our shirts like those know-it-alls in New York." I noted him referring to the Exposition as *we*. The cop on the corner smitten with his neighborhood. "That's why any backspin you can put on Miss Prasquier's emotional state would help the fair an awful lot. We don't want the general public thinking people get killed here."

He pulled out the chair for the secretary, who sat down with no smile for me. (For all she knew, I was going to confess to murdering someone.) "Look, Lieutenant," I offered, "I'll be glad to make a statement saying she looked agitated and upset when I saw her. The fact is, she did." Culpepper smiled gratefully.

I would read in the next day's newspaper that the death of Marie Prasquier had been officially pronounced a suicide. The fact that Marie's motives for ending her own life were discovered by the authorities so very quickly after her death—enabling them to rule out the possibility of murder—greatly pleased the police, the press, the public, and, as you can well imagine, her killer.

9

The Other Tower

I walked out of the Administration Building and into a blindingly sunny midafternoon. My watch read 2:52. When I'd last seen Gail, she'd been calling out to me about playing another carillon concert in the tower at three.

I was very anxious to locate her. This had nothing to do with her engaging personality, her memorable looks, the dancing of her eyes. Nor was it because she'd already become the sound of bowling pins clattering above my head that had aroused me from my long-bearded sleep. No, of course not. It was because I really needed a laborious arranging job for very little money.

Since I was now outside the fair, I'd begun the long trudge back to the entrance gate when a motorized tram with striped awnings, emblazoned with the same braying elephants as those above the Exposition's portals, pulled up to the curbside. "Elephant Train to the Northwest Passage, Chinese Village, and parking," announced its driver.

Two minutes later I was entering the fair for the second time that day. I remembered that the Tower of the Sun could be reached via the gateway that was guarded by a giant statue of a woman. I walked quickly toward the serene deity.

I'd made a major geographical mistake when I'd called this island Atlantis, for the goddess of this kingdom was officially named Pacifica and symbolized the fair's theme of "Peace in the Pacific." She stood eighty feet tall, backdropped by an even higher metal prayer curtain that scattered an undulating shower of sound whenever the wind stirred. The style of her face was a mix of Grecian goddess and Nubian queen. Her wide eyes were blank, but I couldn't say whether this was because her eye sockets were void or merely closed.

For a moment, I fancied that Pacifica looked a little like Gail. I moved to one side and, from this different perspective, the statue reminded me a little of my ex-wife. I used to come in late from work. Nancy would have fallen asleep hours earlier. I'd stare at her for a minute, then look in on Linney. As I adjusted her goose-down comforter so that it rested reassuringly on Linney's shoulders, I would murmur soft words to her and go searching for Nancy's features in my daughter's face. Now I searched Pacifica's face and found Linney there as well.

Was this the sorcery of the sculptor? Would any man find any woman in Pacifica's face?

Her creator had placed her in a strange pose, arms bent straight up from her elbows, palms outward alongside her shoulders in a defenseless benediction. But it also looked as if she were trying to push away some flat stone that lay hard upon her, pressing against her, confining and smothering—

Unbearable.

I quickly turned away as the prayer curtain shivered horribly. I saw the view presented to Pacifica, and knew for certain that if she'd ever had eyes, they would now be closed forever, for the statue directly faced the Tower of the Sun. She would have seen Marie Prasquier fall.

A minute later, I was standing at the foot of the tower, near a large tarpaulin that covered a portion of the concrete where Marie had landed. There were probably still stains to be scrubbed away.

Stepping through one of the tower's open entranceways, I saw a sign that indicated the next carillon concert would be at three P.M. It was now a few minutes after that, but the chimes were silent.

Some twenty or thirty stories up, I could see the carillon's bells. A sinister web of cables and pulleys arced down from them to a curtained-off area on a balcony near the top of the tower. I guessed the keyboard that Gail played was up there.

There was almost no one inside the Tower of the Sun, since it had no gift shop, refreshment stand, displays, or dioramas. As it lacked an observation deck, there was really nothing for a tourist to do but look up and leave.

Still, I knew there had to be a way for the carillonist to get up to the keyboard. I saw a door marked NO ADMITTANCE and admitted myself.

I was in a closet-sized chamber built within the east wall of the tower. It seemed that the sole purpose of the enclosed space, whose ceiling was hundreds of feet above me, was to allow access to a narrow service elevator that could not have housed more than three people, and they would have had to like one another a lot. I called out Gail's name, got no reply, and called it again, upward and louder.

A uniformed guard wearing the insignia of the Pinkerton agency stepped from a door marked EMPLOYEES ONLY. I saw a small washroom behind him.

"Hi there," I said. "Sorry if I'm somewhere I shouldn't be. I'm looking for the girl who plays the bells at the top of the tower." I pointed up, as if this would help him understand. "Gail Prentice?"

"That's her name?" he asked, looking at his watch. He was older than me and slightly built, barely filling out his uniform. "I don't work here in the tower, I'm posted next door in the Hollywood Building. I just use this washroom whenever . . . well, whenever. But I think I know the girl you mean. There's a bell concert each night to close down the park, and she and I usually talk a bit before she plays. Saw her just last night. Maybe she heard about what happened and thought they'd closed the—" He looked about. "We had a jumper here today, you know."

I said I knew, and asked him if there might be a regular guard for the tower who could have seen Gail. This amused him. "There's no guard here. What's someone gonna steal, the chimes, the tower?" He looked at his watch again. "The music should have started by now. I mean, it's not like we wouldn't hear it." I thanked him, left the Tower of the Sun, and hurried over to the area called the Enchanted Garden, to which Gail and the rest of the crowd had earlier been exiled by Culpepper. Beyond a gateway with a mural depicting GOOD WILL BETWEEN EAST AND WEST, an octagonal fountain was splotting great long drops into the air, giving the illusion of water going both up and down at the same time. A pinwheel vendor told me that the sequestered crowd had been dismissed to the East Bay ferry landing over an hour earlier.

I didn't think I had a chance in hell, but I headed to the Key System's boat slip just in case she might still be there. I got to the terminal in time to see a big purple ferry already departing, but odds were Gail had left long before this.

There was a coin telephone booth around the corner from the terminal's ticket counter, and I dialed the number Gail had given me in her letter. The girl who answered sounded like she thought she had better things to do with her time than say, "Berkeley Club."

"Gail Prentice, please?"

"This is the front desk, there are no phones in the rooms, I can page her if it's urgent."

I considered, and decided it was. After holding the line for a few minutes, I was told Miss Prentice wasn't buzzing back. I left a message for Gail that I'd be at the hotel sometime after four. I knew that waiting for her to call my room at the Claremont was going to drive me crazy. There's no more irritating sound than a telephone that doesn't ring.

I started to walk back to the parking lot where I'd left Larry Vance's Nash. I could see the Claremont in the Berkeley hills quite easily from here. When I'd first played at the hotel, over twenty years ago, its façade had been a cross between dark English Tudor and Swiss chalet. Now it beamed across the bay like bleached bedsheets drying on a clothesline, its new owner having had it recently painted white so it would glint for the benefit of those on the eastern side of Treasure Island.

Something caused me to look a bit north of the hotel, demanding my attention like a child at a parade tugging on your sleeve. It was a spire, about the same height but of a different design than the Tower of the Sun, although either would have looked appropriate in a European piazza.

There was no one on the pier except a young fellow with a soda pushcart. I bought a bottle of Jic Jac orange pop and asked, "Do you know what that tower is over there?"

"Bell tower," he said. "I think they call it the Campanile. Part of Cal."

"Cal."

"Cal Berkeley. The university."

Idiot that I was. Gail had told me she also performed on the carillon at her college. *The one I play at Berkeley only has twelve bells,* she'd said. Was that the tower where I was supposed to meet her for her three o'clock concert?

The Berkeley tower winked at me. That is to say, some beacon or reflection from a telescope or mirror at the top of the tower flashed on and off. It was as if it were letting me in on a joke. And although this might sound fanciful, I'd soon learn that it was Gail who was doing the winking.

10

The Campanile

When I'd first worked at the Claremont, drinking my way through its inventory of booze as if it were all going to disappear (which it was, thanks to the impending advent of Prohibition) and wooing my way through much of the Bay Area's female population as if they were soon to be outlawed as well, a number of young college women I'd dated had suggested we dine on Telegraph Avenue, where the foreign restaurants were always intriguing and an outrageous bargain. I remembered that at the termination of Telegraph, there was a circle where the trolleys turned back to Oakland and, in front of that circle, a big gateway that marked the beginning of the

Berkeley campus. I parked Larry's car just around the corner from Sather Gate (its name was embossed in its wrought-iron arch) where a vociferous crowd was waving placards bearing the words STUDENTS FOR PEACE, F.D.R. WANTS W.A.R., NO CONSCRIPTION WITHOUT REPRESENTATION. There was a small platform upon which a nicely dressed fellow with a shock of red hair was leaping from one lily pad of grievance to another. The government was steering us into a war that was none of our affair. The Selective Service Act was unconstitutional and no right-minded man should cooperate with this attempt to create Roosevelt's Horde. The current ban on delivery of scrap iron to any nation but Britain was yet another intentional blow against the hard-pressed Japanese, and made a lie of any claim to neutrality on the president's part.

I worked my way around the rally and through a side doorway within the gate. On the other side was a much cheerier cluster of students, handing out circulars to all who passed by.

"What's cooking?" I asked an agreeable fellow, taking the flyer he offered me.

"We're reminding everyone that to be seated in the men's rooting section of Saturday's game, you must wear only white shirts or sweaters. It's being strictly enforced this season. No white, no seating, no matter what your ticket says. This comes down from Ed Brewer himself."

I raised my eyebrows. "*Ed* said this? You heard him?" I asked gravely, wondering who Ed was.

"I did, and he was dead serious, mister, you can take it from me. We've had people showing up in yellow and light beige, but no more. We'll supply the reversible caps for making the Big C, and the cards for the card tricks, but if a man doesn't own at least one clean white shirt, what's he doing at Berkeley, I ask you?"

I asked him in return for the quickest route to the Campanile, the top of which I could see over several imposing buildings. He pointed me along a path to my right and I continued my uphill walk, envying in a not resentful way those who got to attend this university. On those rare occasions when I'd stepped onto a campus, usually to play a sock hop or prom, I'd always felt estranged from the students, even though for a number of years I was very close to them in age. I'd watch the girls moving about in groups of four and five, who strictly observed the rule that saddle shoes must be worn only while giggling. I particularly envied the guys who had so much sweet time ahead of them before they'd have to buckle down or knuckle under. I felt like I'd lived on a different planet, and I suppose I had. I'd been playing professionally, taken a wife, become a father, and departed Juilliard to support a family well before my peers had their diplomas. I didn't feel this made me one iota better than any of the campus crowd. Just apart from them.

I felt that difference now as I picked my way through the boys in sleeveless sweaters and cuffed trousers, many of them without ties, the girls in jumpers or skirts with little vests or their beau's over-sized U.C. jacket. All of them seemed to be heading in the opposite direction.

The afternoon had turned cool but bright, as if September were trying to provide us with a keepsake of the summer now behind us. I rounded a steep corner and saw the tower. It was stemmed by a square cupola with Roman arches, below which a clock on all four faces gave it purpose.

I entered a short esplanade filled with the strangest trees, a mustering of bent, crazed growths in a plaza that was almost perfectly filled by the tower's shadow. There were several rows of these angry, deformed gnomes, their resentful branches groping and twisting at the air. I felt as if I were standing in an orange grove gone mad. Their leaves were turning brown and crumbly. An elderly Japanese gardener was clipping at the swollen knuckles of their branches as if to remove their fingers.

Church bells began to toll, but not the standard "Westminster" chiming that we associate with Big Ben. They were playing . . . yes,

"St. Louis Blues" by W. C. Handy. It was no challenge to Louis Armstrong, but it was still pretty astonishing to hear. The sun glinted off one of the larger bells in the Roman arches as it began to swing. I realized that this was the "wink" that had summoned me from Treasure Island.

I tried to imagine the kind of musician who would have the pluck to play the blues on carillon chimes. "Gail," I murmured to myself with a smile.

Inside the tower, a lone guard doubled as ticket vendor. He requested twenty-five cents, "not for the view, for the elevator." He also served as the elevator's operator. We didn't talk on the way up because the bells grew ever more deafening as we ascended. Reaching the elevator's only stop, he pointed me to stairs leading to the observation platform. I took the steps two at a time until I realized there were five flights' worth of them. Short of breath, I arrived at the observation platform and saw an open door leading to a small mahogany-paneled cabin. The sun slashed bright bands across its walls.

Inside the small room, a woman with her back to me was assaulting a bizarre keyboard. The closest thing I could liken it to were the rows of billy clubs found in Spanish galleons, their handles protruding.

Between the din of the bells above us and the grunting and heavy breathing of her exertions, the young woman didn't hear my footsteps. Her wild thick hair (certainly now I knew it was Gail) flew about as she gasped little phrases of the song: "Oh, that St. Louis woman . . . with her diamond rings . . . she pulls my man around . . . by her apron strings!"

I could see she was wearing dark, thick gloves that made her look like a falconer, and she slapped the carillon's leather-padded handles a beat ahead of the tune because of the inherent delay in the cable-and-pulley system at which she was thrashing away.

She brought the song to a finish, slamming a last peg on her left, which caused the deepest bell to sound, and raised a gloved fist. "Try and make vinegar out of them grapes," she said aloud, pleased with her performance.

"Gail?"

She spun around. "Ray! Boy, I thought maybe the police sent you up the river." She was wearing denim overalls, the legs rolled up above her ankles, and a flannel work shirt unbuttoned devil-may-care at the neck. Her brow was dappled with droplets of sweat, making her face sweetly glossy in the sunlight. "Hey, can I gut-bucket them spots?"

"A clambake," I verified.

"Not too lollypop?" she asked, a might concerned.

"It was solid dillinger."

She took off her gloves. "Okay, well I guess that's quite enough of *that* kind of talk, don't you think?"

"Thank merciful heaven," I sighed, much relieved.

Producing a red bandanna from her front overalls pocket, she began to mop her brow with it. She asked, "Do jazz musicians really talk like that?"

"Sure they do. Don't you go to the movies?"

She collected her various music folios and wrapped a book strap around them. "I didn't know if you could hear me when I was calling out to you. I'm sorry I didn't wait around, but I had to clean myself up after that accident. I had some blood and . . . stuff on me—you know what I mean, right?"

I told her I understood. Culpepper and I had lucked out and been spared getting splattered by the remains of Marie Prasquier.

"The police held the crowd for about an hour, taking names and checking identification, and then they got a ferry just for us. It went to San Francisco, then back across to Oakland and the landing here in Berkeley. By the time I got back to my room, all I wanted was me sitting in a tub of scalding hot water with an open box of 20 Mule Team Borax soap on my lap, and then I had to play this concert here.

I figured if worst came to worst I'd get back in touch with you at your hotel." She smiled at me. "The great thing about Jack Donovan playing at the Claremont is that I knew exactly where I could find you at eight tonight."

She led me out of the carillonist's cabin and the tower itself and we ambled downhill, crossing a little footbridge over a gossiping stream. Gail stopped in her tracks and began rubbing her right hand. "I think I may have jammed my wrist on one of the carillon bars," she said. "Would you mind carrying my books for a few minutes while I flex my hands?"

I said I wouldn't mind one bit and took her book strap from her, manfully holding the bundle of volumes against my right side.

It seemed that every third male student whose path we crossed knew Gail by name. She jauntily acknowledged greetings from the opposite sex more efficiently than a politician working the crowd at a Labor Day parade. I caught more than one fellow looking back over his own shoulder, mostly at Gail, although one sporting young man flashed me a low "okay" sign, while several others simply shot daggers my way.

Gail said, "I'm going to get out of these clothes now, is that okay?" I looked around at the crowded street and she laughed. "No, I mean, we're here, where I live."

We were standing in front of what looked like a small, Occidentally run museum for Oriental art. A neatly painted sign read BERKELEY WOMEN'S INDEPENDENT COLLEGIATE CLUB.

"Nice digs, don't you think?" Gail said.

"Your dormitory?" I asked.

"Well, it's not really a dorm—or a sorority for that matter. The club is owned by a group of female Berkeley graduates, and they rent some of the rooms to students. Mine's tiny, but it has a little terrace." She twitched restlessly. "I *have* to get out of this clothing, and then I thought we could plan out our work schedule. Assuming you're still all aboard."

I recalled having said only that I would listen to her composition. This, however, was before I'd carried her books.

"Oh, I'm all aboard," I reassured her.

Her face lit up. "Great. Now listen, I can't even bring you up to the reception desk without many plucked eyebrows being raised. Will you wait here for me?"

She indicated the square of sidewalk upon which I was standing.

"Sure."

"Promise you won't budge an inch?"

"Swear."

"Give me fifteen minutes," she said, and made a spin up to my right cheek, planted a quick peck to prove that she'd reached that elevation, and scurried away. I would still be feeling the small brand of her kiss on my face when I went to sleep that night.

11

The Other Girl

As Gail had asked, I stood waiting outside her building for some fifteen minutes. I felt a bit lame. It was one of those situations in life that cause people to take up smoking. I reflexively reached into my pocket for a stick of gum and discovered that my pack of Beeman's peppermint was empty.

I noticed a Rexall drugstore alongside Gail's domicile. They were having one of their penny sales, which meant that for just one additional cent, you could buy two Rexall products for the price of one. In honor of the sale, Rexall had festively doubled all their prices.

I had promised Gail not to leave my spot, but surely I could scoot into the store, make my purchase, and be back out here again in record time.

I stepped inside and was instantly overwhelmed by that American incense that lurks within every corner drugstore: the toasty aroma of powdered malt in open urns and the sweet fragrance of frosty smoke hovering above chromium tubs of ice cream, the griddle's ever-present scent of grilled everything, the sinister bouquet of oil in deep-fat fryers that quietly await their next victim, the pungent odor of fresh magazines and comic books, and always the underlying reek of gelatin from medicine capsules and that sour-martini smell of a doctor's waiting room. I'd been out of touch with the world of real people, and so I was mildly disoriented by these powerful olfactory memories from my childhood. It took me a second to regain my bearings, and as I did, I discovered that, apparently, Gail had an identical twin. Because I saw her matching sister at the back of the drugstore, with the exact same mass of hair as Gail but in different clothing (a rust-colored shirtwaist frock that buttoned down the front), sitting in a phone booth, talking to someone while her right hand rocked the booth's folding glass door back and forth in what could only be described as a nervous or agitated fashion. After a while, she closed the door completely and turned her back on the rest of the store.

I ducked behind a revolving rack of magazines, stealing a peek every now and then.

After about five minutes, I watched Gail hang up the pay phone, but she continued to sit in the booth for another few minutes, even though her conversation was obviously over. Then she opened the door and went to the pharmacist's counter to have a few words with a druggist whose hair was as white as his uniform. She shaded her eyes as if the sun were shining into them. The druggist fetched her a squarish tin with a black-and-tan label, offered a few words of counsel, and rang up her purchase. She gave him a dollar and he made a great silliness of counting out her change. Men.

I had no idea how Gail had gotten into the store without me seeing her, but if it was all quite innocent, she would certainly walk right out the front door over to where she expected me to be waiting on the sidewalk.

It was not all quite innocent.

She slipped out the back of the store, where clearly there was also a nearby rear entrance to the Berkeley Women's Independent Collegiate Club.

Once she left, I moved quickly to the pharmacist's station. I picked out a pack of Beeman's gum and casually commented, "Funny thing. I heard what the young lady was ordering and that's exactly what my wife told me to pick up, too."

He nodded and went to his shelves. "We get a lot of call for it this time of year. Between allergies and infestation." This last phrase was an odd one. He put a black-and-tan tin into a paper bag for me. "Make sure it doesn't come in contact with your skin. Diluted it's fine. Unless you drink it, of course. That wouldn't be a good idea."

I looked into the bag. "Boric acid," I said. "Sounds dangerous."

"It is, to pests, but it's safe for humans as long as you don't do something foolish like eat it straight out of the container. Keep it away from baby, if you have one."

I said I would, if I did. He counseled, "Your wife's eyes are irritated, I assume?"

"Allergies," I said.

He nodded. "Mix half a teaspoon with two cups warm water. Bathe each eye for about a minute. If she doesn't have an eye bath, an eggcup or shot glass will do just fine."

"Do most people buy it for allergies, like that girl who was just in here?"

He smiled sadly. "Well, she either wanted to poison the man who broke her heart or to soothe her eyes from the tears he caused her to cry."

I looked at him, not understanding.

He said, with some pride, "A pharmacist is trained to be observant. That girl had clearly just been crying."

12

Berkeley Square

Outside the Rexall, I stuck a stick of gum in my mouth and tossed the bag containing the tin of boric acid into a trash can.

About ten minutes later, Gail came trippingly out of her place of residence. Remarkably, she had changed into the identical outfit her twin sister had been wearing in the drugstore.

"Sorry if I took too long," she said, somewhat out of breath. "There was a personal matter I had to attend to."

"A phone call?" I asked.

It was an innocent enough question, as was the look she gave me. "No, we don't have phones in our rooms. There's one at the desk, but we're supposed to use that sparingly, as it's the only line for everybody. You all torn up with me for keeping you waiting?"

I told her I was still of a piece. Her eyes looked okay, as much as I could see of them. Of course, I couldn't exactly stare into them, although I very much would have enjoyed doing so. Either the boric acid had been effective as prescribed or the pharmacist had exaggerated her distress.

You're making too much of this, I told myself. There were any number of reasonable explanations why she might need to place a telephone call surreptitiously. Maybe she wanted to cancel a date she'd already made but didn't want me to know how willing she was to do this. Maybe her boyfriend had then yelled at her and caused her to cry. I wondered how old a boyfriend of Gail's might be.

I asked casually, "By the way, who's that fellow I met named Russ?"

A much younger man than I approached, dressed in casual clothes that clearly cost as much as most people's Sunday best. "Hi, Gail," he said. "You look like you jumped into something comfortable and missed." He laughed the hardest of the three of us.

Gail did the honors. "Ray, this is Toby Ackland. He's a major in economics. Toby, this is Ray Sherwood. He's a major talent."

Toby's eyes flashed green with either envy or old money. "A talent at what?" he inquired.

"Ray does arrangements."

Relieved, Toby turned to me. "You're a florist?"

"Well, I've done 'Second Hand Rose,' " I conceded.

His brow furrowed. "Used flowers? Doesn't sound very appealing."

"Neither does economics," I responded.

We were well on our way to a bad start when Gail intervened. "Ray plays tenor sax with Jack Donovan's band."

"Oh. You're that man who writes out music," he said, making me sound like a calligrapher. He nodded toward Gail's residence and told her, "I was about to leave word at your boardinghouse that I can give you that lift to the Claremont you wanted."

Gail piped, "Oh, sorry, Tobe, turns out I won't be needing the lift after all." She nodded in my direction. "The mountain came to the corner of Mohammed and Vine. But thanks so much, really." She gave him a little salute that was her invitation for him to leave, which Ackland reluctantly accepted. He gave me a departing glance that was the retinal equivalent of manslaughter.

"Your boyfriend?" I asked, trying to camouflage any show of concern.

She laughed and said, "Toby is a very sweet guy," uttering the words that no man wants to hear spoken about himself. Good. "The front desk gave me the message you left, by the way. And I got another from the program coordinator at Treasure Island, wanting to know why there was no three o'clock carillon concert today."

I had wondered why Gail had scheduled herself to perform on both sides of the bay at the same hour, and said as much to her.

An annoyed look came over Gail's face as she said that it definitely had *not* been her turn to perform on Treasure Island that afternoon. "I alternate with another girl, her name is Adeline Head, she lives in San Francisco. She played the evening concert last night, I would have played this morning if that woman hadn't fallen from the tower, and it was Adeline's turn again this afternoon." Gail scowled. "This is the third time Ada has done this. I have to call her and find out why."

"There's probably a telephone booth in the Rexall," I said lightly, indicating the drugstore.

She shook her head. "It's been out of order for a couple of weeks now. There's a soda fountain called the Campus over in Berkeley Square that has a coin telephone. We can go there."

I could now discount any notion that Gail really did have a twin sister. Obviously, she was afraid that if we went into the Rexall, the pharmacist might comment on her speedy return. But it was easy to overlook her little fib on a sunny afternoon as we strolled to an ice-cream parlor together.

"So, Ray," she said, and God help me, she took my arm, slipping her right hand around my left arm and oh, we were snug now as she walked me away from the drugstore, her head against my left shoulder, "we have the obvious problem that you're working evenings at the Claremont. So what do we do about getting together?"

"I'd rather not start before eleven, to be honest," I answered. "Sounds lazy but I'm used to musician's hours, jazz musician's. I finish work after midnight, so I often don't turn in until at least three or four in the morning."

Gail nodded. "Me too. And I'm not even a jazz musician."

"Well, are the afternoons out?" I asked.

"No, I'm pretty free and clear, although I was counting on Ada to sub for me in a pinch and now I don't think I can rely on her." She frowned. "I'm sure she's trying to show her disdain for me and the Exposition simply because my composition beat out hers. She's an aspiring composer, like me, only very, um . . ." Gail searched carefully for the right word. "Traditional." I could tell she meant this to be a synonym for "boring."

I made what I misguidedly thought was a joke. "Did she call her composition *Suite Adeline*?"

She shook her head, vigorously. "No, listen, if you meet her—and I'm sure you will—do not so much as whistle the tune of 'Sweet Adeline,' and don't call her Addy, either. She's Adeline or Ada or you face her wrath, which is a fearsome thing." A small shudder caused Gail's hair to ripple.

The street now seemed to be populated only by couples, and we were all casting long shadows across the square. I realized I'd soon have to start thinking about getting back to the Claremont.

We'd arrived at the Campus, in whose vestibule was a phone booth. She fumbled through her bag. "Do you have any change? I seem to be fresh out."

I found a lone nickel in my pocket, which she dropped into the coin slot. It made a most satisfying *ting*. I was continuing to be impressed with Gail's way with bells.

She dialed Information and asked, "Hello, operator? Could I please have the number of a Miss Adeline Head?" As Gail waited, she produced an eyebrow pencil from her bag. "You don't? Oh, wait, you're looking in Alameda County, she's in San Francisco. Do you handle that too? She's on Larkin Street—oh, and her first name might be listed as Ada or just the letter *A* . . ." She turned to me. "You have anything to write on, Ray?"

I gave her the paper wrapper from a stick of the gum I'd bought. Gail licked the pencil's tip, tossed me a mischievous glance that instantly embarrassed her (and that I wasn't going to forget for a long time), and scribbled a number on the inside of the wrapper. She thanked the operator, who hit whatever it is operators hit on their end of a connection that makes a coin telephone regurgitate a nickel. Gail retrieved the coin and, flipping the handset's cradle, dropped the nickel into the slot once again and dialed the phone number.

"Hi Ada, it's Gail," she began, her expression immediately darkening. "Look, a friend of mine was at Treasure Island today and he said you didn't show up. Did you think—?" Her shoulders dipped a little in acknowledgment. "Okay, but then why didn't—?" Gail went silent and listened thoughtfully with widening eyes. "Really."

I wasn't sure what the correct male etiquette was at this point, so I stepped a discreet distance away and ran through the entire chart of "Soup du Jour" in my head.

Three minutes later, Gail came over to me. "Well, that's nice," she said drily. "Ada's eloping with a fellow from Nob Hill whose parents don't approve of her."

"What do Ada's parents think of *him*?"

She winced. "Nothing, I'm afraid. Ada lost both her parents in high school. She was brought up by an aunt in Alabama who liked everybody, especially vacuum cleaner salesmen, it's rumored. Ada is running out on her apartment with a month's rent due, and guess who's been elected to break the bad news to the landlady one hour from now, after Adeline has flown the coop?"

"You."

"Me." She grimaced. "Well, I'll see if I can get this fellow I know in Emeryville to spell me on the carillon. I'm not going to give up all of my afternoons, not when that's the only time I can work with you."

She asked me with a hopeful look if I'd like to lend her some moral support when she broke the bad news to Ada's landlady, and I said I'd be glad to drive her there—but then remembered I had to allow myself time to pick up Larry Vance at his home on my way to the Claremont. I told her this, saddened that we'd have to call it quits for the day and elated that she looked equally glum about it.

I did walk her down to the landing at the Berkeley pier. She started to ask a few questions about me, but I'd developed lots of effective ways to duck that dread topic over the years and was able to smoothly steer the conversation back to *Swing*, explaining that my job, in part, would be something like that of the person who colors the Sunday funnies. "The cartoonist draws the comic strip in black and white, but an ink artist adds the tints. I'd try to do that for your piece, adding brass and reed colors to your existing notes. The trick is to get to know you well enough that I can shade the orchestration the way you might have done it yourself, if you had both the time and the expertise."

Gail cast me a jaundiced eye and a barely hidden smile. "And if we were to, say, socialize, would that better help you to capture the pigmentation of my personality?"

I flushed with embarrassment and rushed to assure her, "No, I hadn't meant it like that," not knowing if I had.

"Oh," she said, looking downcast. "Well, can we socialize anyway?"

"Absolutely," I replied before she had even completed the question.

Unfortunately, there was a double-decker ferry at the landing all ready to take her away from me. We agreed to meet the next day at the house where her mother lived, because Gail felt it would be more pleasant working on the piano there than in one of U.C. Berkeley's windowless practice rooms. I jotted down her mother's address and Gail gave me directions via a combination of bus and trolley. We said good-bye and I watched her skip up the metal gangway.

I'd look very foolish, I thought, if I just stood there watching the boat pull away, so I started back to where I'd parked Larry's car.

An earsplitting whistle stopped me dead. I turned and saw Gail already on the ferry's upper tier, leaning over its aft rail. "Hey, what gives?" she yelled. "You weren't going to see me off?" She shook her head in dismay. "I don't know what we're going to do with you, Ray!"

A little boy asked his mother why the lady was yelling at me.

I called out to Gail, "Sorry! I didn't want to look stupid!"

"Perish the thought, Mr. Sherwood!" she called back with a grin. A loud horn sounded as the ferry slid away from the dock. Over its second blast, she bellowed, "Promise you'll write me every day?"

I nodded in the affirmative. Gail said something to a man next to her, and he handed her his white display handkerchief. She held one end of it and waved it at me, as if she were sailing to Kathmandu.

As the ferry picked up speed, she returned the handkerchief to the man, who gave her a wary glance before stepping away. She stood with both her hands planted on the rail, regarding me with a comfortable smile. I watched until I could no longer discern the features in her face. It said a lot about my life that this had been the best afternoon I'd had in over a decade. It also said a lot about Gail.

13

Swing Time

The swing craze got its start in Oakland, at a dance hall run by a U.C. Berkeley professor of agriculture named William Sweet. The dance hall was originally called McFadden's, but everyone knew it as Sweet's Ballroom. And the reason swing took hold here was because the sun sets three hours later in Oakland than it does in New York.

When I'd first started playing professionally, still in my teens, Paul Whiteman had billed himself as the King of Jazz. But of course his music wasn't real jazz, not the reborn blast of Dixieland that had blown into New York from Chicago. Whiteman's sound was rinky-tink dance music, with a few real jazz soloists like Bix Beiderbecke and Joe Venuti riddling the blandness like chopped walnuts in a cream-cheese sandwich.

But now Benny Goodman was being hailed as the King of Swing, and his swing *was* real jazz. Just a couple of years before, Benny had been one of the house bands for the *Let's Dance* program, which was broadcast live from New York across the country all Saturday night. Benny was told to keep the music pretty tame, since the show was aimed at a national audience. But as the hour grew late, he'd play some of the wilder numbers from his book, arrangements that were too hot to pump into respectable East Coast living rooms in the mid-evening hours.

That fall, Benny toured the country for the first time. Everyone in the East and Midwest knew him as this polite dance band and the crowds stayed away—until he hit California. What no one, including Benny, had figured out was that the hot music he'd played very late at night in the East had hit the young California crowd mid–Saturday night, and they'd been eating it up all this time.

After five miserable months, Benny and his men wheeled into Oakland and saw a line outside of Sweet's Ballroom that went around the block. That night, the fans either jitterbugged and Lindy-Hopped themselves into a frenzy on the packed eight thousand square feet of Bill Sweet's dance floor or simply surrounded the elevated stage, six, seven deep, just basking in the heat. And while Negro bands like Chick Webb's and Fletcher Henderson's had been playing this kind of music for years, this was really the start of swing as a national art form.

The names given our kind of musical aggregation were *dance band, swing band, big band,* and we were big all right, big enough to justify calling ourselves orchestras, though the only strings permitted were strung on the bass and the rhythm guitar, or closeted inside the piano. Violins were not invited. Everyone knows a violin can't swing, except the French, who also hold the accordion in high regard.

It was a tight, fat sound. Five saxes: two altos, two tenors, one baritone, all doubling on clarinet. Four trumpets, each carrying a toy box of mutes: the throaty Harmon, steely straight, comic wah-wah, rubber cup of a plumber's plunger, and derby hat.

Four trombones with all the same gizmos.

Add to that a four-piece rhythm section. Our guitarist, Chop Halliday, played a Guild acoustic to which he'd attached an electronic pickup. I didn't much like the resulting sound, and I was pleased a week earlier when there'd been a power failure at the Nortonia Hotel in Portland. Until electricity was restored, Chop's right arm was forced to work for a living like the rest of us.

Our billing was "Jack Donovan and His Orchestra of Note," which somebody over at the MCA booking agency had thought was cute when they'd coined it. We may not have been as popular as the half dozen or so biggest name bands in the country, but we weren't bush league either, and the bookings were steady. Most important for all of us in the swing bands, the music we wanted to play was, miraculously, the music the public wanted to hear. It was one great time for a jazz musician to be alive. Unless, of course, you were me.

Musically, I couldn't have been in better company. Dave Wooster, baritone sax, fifth chair, was just okay, but the three reed players on my left were as good as any I'd ever worked with. Frankie Pompano, Jerry Garden, and lead alto Billy French. It was jazz writer John Hammond who'd first started calling our sax section the "French Foreign Legion." He'd caught us at the White Willow Ballroom in Ann Arbor, Michigan. Looking up from his planter's punch, he realized that four fifths of the sax section were not where they should be, meaning that based on our talent we should have been ensconced in New York or Los Angeles, or at least touring with a major ensemble like Goodman's or Woody Herman's. John Hammond decided that there must be some hidden explanation for this phenomenon, and began to ask around. The answers he got proved to him the adage that when anything is too good to be true, there is always, but *always*, a reason.

Frankie Pompano. He'd had a huge run-in with the law some years ago regarding an overdue library book that was in the glove compartment of a car he'd stolen. As thieves go, he'd been as measured and meticulous as his artfully trim solos. When he was first struggling in the business, he'd accepted a few gigs in cities that could be reached only by automobile. He'd had no money. So he would steal the car of someone with whom he was slightly acquainted and, upon his arrival, play the gig and receive his pay in cash, at which time he would put the car in a parking lot and send a special-delivery letter to the vehicle's owner, informing them of the location of their automobile and enclosing one-way bus fare to the city where it was parked.

He'd done this on four occasions, and three of his victims had pressed charges. These warrants for his arrest weren't important enough to justify his extradition, but Frankie knew that if he so much as got stopped for speeding or spitting on the sidewalk in New York, New Jersey, or Pennsylvania, he'd be facing prison. So he signed on with Jack Donovan, with the understanding that he'd be excused from any bookings in states where he might get booked.

Jerry Garden, alto sax, second chair, faced a similar dilemma. He refused to pay his wife alimony. This was not as unreasonable as it might sound, since his wife had run off with Jerry's stepfather. Jerry took issue with the idea of paying alms to someone who had broken his nuts and his mother's heart in one fell swoop. What made it worse was that Jerry wouldn't have had to pay alimony if his ex-stepfather had married his ex-wife, but in his home state at that time, the law said you couldn't marry the co-respondent who had caused your divorce.

There were papers out on Jerry, and Jerry knew that his wife would have no problem tracking down the Glenn Miller or Jimmy Dorsey bands (both of whom had made Jerry offers to play on the East Coast). But to locate Jack Donovan's orchestra while it toured the Great Plains, send a process server out there to hunt Jerry down, and extradite him before the band had moved on to another state would have been a major undertaking and expense for his ex-wife. Jerry considered it a matter of principle not to pay her, and he stood on his principles by sitting second chair in our band.

Billy French's story was the darkest of the three.

Late one foggy night, Billy was driving home from a job at Jack Christie's club on Fifty-second Street in Manhattan. There was a kid working in the kitchen there who, like Billy, lived in Queens and, exhausted after working two shifts, decided to save himself the effort of pedaling home on his bike. So he did what kids have been known to do. He took some twine and tied the steering post of his bike to the rear bumper of Billy's car, leaving himself about eight feet of slack, and waited in the dark for Billy to drive home along the empty city streets.

So Billy is cruising home at twenty miles per hour when he notices this kid on a bike behind him, matching him in speed. Billy accelerates. Naturally, the kid and the bike stay right with him, and now of course the kid can't jump off the bike. He hardly dares to take his hands from the handlebars, but he risks it for a few seconds, trying to wave Billy to stop. Maybe Billy had drunk a few more than usual, or taken a hit on the weed, but in his rearview mirror, it appears as if the boy is taunting him. Billy hits forty miles an hour as he ramps up onto the Fifty-ninth Street Bridge. He looks behind him, the kid's still there like the Headless Horseman to Billy's Ichabod Crane. The car's doing sixty-five now, and Billy sees the kid has his eyes closed, face grimacing. It's very late, there's no other car on the bridge, so Billy tries to rid himself of this demon by performing a one-hundred-and-eighty-degree turn. This maneuver works fine for Billy, but it catapults the kid into the air, whipping him into a pylon, probably killing him that same instant if luck was with him. The boy's body holds almost magnetically for a moment against the pylon, then slides quickly down into the East River, which lies much too far below.

Billy could have just driven away. There were no witnesses. But he was a decent guy and understood that the kid's family would want to know why and how their son had died, so he went and got the police.

He also got a good attorney, who was able to make the point that his client had no idea the boy's bike was tied to the car's bumper, that in accelerating and turning about on the bridge, Billy had only been trying to evade someone he thought was in some way "after him."

So Billy ended up paying a speeding ticket in exchange for killing a kid. He paid in the basement of the city courthouse, and then told his family he was leaving town and would never be coming back.

That was Billy's story.

My story I kept to myself. But I had one.

Nothing bad had ever happened to Dave Wooster, baritone sax, as far as I knew, other than him being just an average saxophonist.

But for Billy, Jerry, Frankie, and myself, our past lives were why Jack Donovan possessed arguably the best sax section in the country. The French Foreign Legion, John Hammond had named us, after the army where men went to forget. I knew that for me, forgetting was impossible. The best I could manage, for a moment or two in the course of the day, was simply not to remember.

14

The Bandstand

It was a staid crowd that night in the Claremont's ballroom. The male patrons had generally opted for white dinner jackets. The women were favoring taffeta or crepe, most of them in black, turquoise, or silver.

A few minutes into our last set, I was muscling my way through an extended solo in our version of "Christopher Columbus" when I saw Frankie Pompano elbowing Jerry Garden. He directed Jerry's attention to the side of the bandstand, where I, too, saw a young woman leaning gracefully against a pillar, a champagne goblet in her hand. She was listening intently to what I was playing and gave me a small, encouraging smile. She looked smart and sleek in a black crepe sheath, over which she wore a sleeveless gold-and-pink bolero jacket. Her hands were cloaked in opera gloves. Her hair was pulled back in a French twist. She could have been a debutante heiress, toasting the whims of fate after losing the family fortune at Monte Carlo. A moment later, I realized she was Gail, and she was there to hear only me.

As the set progressed, it was clear she'd arrived unescorted. I liked this an awful lot. She arced appreciative glances my way as if I were a game of ring toss, and I savored both the hungry looks my musical compatriots launched in her direction and the resentful looks they hurled in mine.

Usually in the last set, Jack would have me sing a number I'd penned called "Beef Lo Mein." It was standard for a band to have a couple of sidemen vocalize once or twice in the course of the night, adding some variety to the evening at no additional expense to the bandleader. Since I was being paid salary and a half as the band's arranger, it behooved me to do this without complaint.

Not much was expected from an instrumentalist's vocals except that he have some swagger. Jack introduced me as "that man about town from the sax section." "Beef Lo Mein" was a crowd-pleaser that everyone smiled at but me, because although its title was silly and its tempo bouncy, I knew in writing it that it was actually a very sad song.

Over the crowd's applause as I finished, Gail gave me a long, loud whistle.

She vanished just before the set was over, to my momentary dismay. But after packing up my instruments, I found her where I'd hoped she would be waiting for me, in the Terrace Lounge, seated before a second champagne cocktail.

Despite the fact that she already had a drink, Warren Taplin, trumpet, second chair, was trying to purchase her a new one. As I arrived, I heard her say, "Sorry, you can't buy me a drink on three counts. First, I'm still drinking this one. Second, I get my drinks free. And, three, I'm reserved for Ray Sherwood."

Serenaded by this music to my ears, I sat down next to her and brushed Taplin to the other side of the room with a stare.

"Hi," said Gail. "After you left me, I thought, you know, just because we spent the afternoon together doesn't mean I shouldn't get to see you play at night. You sound great."

"Thanks."

"There's a lot of heft in your tone that you can't pick up from a record." She stretched. "Hope you like my outfit, and if you don't, would you lie and say you do, because it's the only formal number I own." She removed first the sleeveless bolero and then her gloves as artfully as Sherry Britton. I could hear the creaking of chairs as most of the lounge's male patrons strained to get a better view of her. At least, I assume it was their chairs that were creaking.

I ordered a Scotch mist from the bartender and asked, "Is that Arpège you're wearing?"

"Yes, how'd you know?"

"Because it's French for *arpeggio*," I said. "Figured it was the one perfume a musician ought to be informed about." I didn't tell her that I also knew this because Nancy had worn the scent (her only extravagance, a single bottle that she'd stretched out over the course of a decade) and because Linney had loved the picture of a mother and daughter on the bottle.

Vera walked into the bar and made a point of greeting everyone from the band except me. At last she walked over and said, "Hi, Ray. Buy you a Shirley Temple or have you already bought one?" Gail dealt with this in the most interesting way. She just continued to have a conversation with me as if Vera simply didn't exist. Vera stood around for a moment, not knowing how to respond, and finally left the lounge.

My drink arrived. I picked up Gail's as well and walked us over to a table for two by a window overlooking the bay. A small lamp with an amber shade bathed us in a pool of warm light while, alongside us, the island where we'd met glistened cool blue and icy pink. Every man in the lounge wished he were me, which was amusing, since most of the time I wished I were anyone but.

But Gail was making me remember when I had wished for other things.

15

Prelude and Fugue

G. G. I. EXPOSITION

TOWER OF THE SUN

I got the impression that Gail might have been illegitimate. She clearly had no inclination to discuss her father, if she knew who he was, and politely told me as much the moment I raised the topic. But on the subject of her uncle Joe, she came to life.

She'd grown up in the Avondale part of Cincinnati. Her mother had moved there from San Francisco to be near Gail's uncle Joe, who'd come from Europe to teach composition at the music department of the nearby university. "The most wonderful man, Ray. Whatever love for music I have, he gave me. He taught me piano. Patient? If I didn't want to practice and wanted to go to the movies instead, he'd say, 'Today we'll practice by going to the movies.' He'd point out to me how film composers manipulated my emotions, especially in scary pictures.

" 'Where's the music coming from?' I'd ask him.

" 'Don't worry,' he'd say.

" 'But the music is scaring me,' I'd tell him.

" 'No, no, dear one. It's just people playing little notes on paper. Dots on paper.' "

It wasn't until her uncle knew she'd be leaving Cincinnati to attend Berkeley that he decided to return to Europe to compose for some film studios there. The money being offered was excellent, and he'd left her a small trust fund that helped cover her room and board. She was rightfully proud that she had won a working scholarship at Berkeley, the work consisting of playing the carillon (which she adored) and accompanying voice majors at recitals (which she frequently loathed).

I gleaned that her mother doted on her a bit more than Gail liked. "She's far too overprotective, moved out here just to be near me. It makes her crazy that I have a room of my own on campus. She thinks it's a waste of hard-earned money, but I'd go loopy living under the same roof with her seven days a week. As it is, I feel obliged to spend my weekends in Chancery Lane, where she lives with Russ Hewett, just to keep her happy."

"And who is Russ?" I asked her for the second time that day.

"Russ is . . . well, to be honest"—she lowered her voice—"it's kind of sweet, I guess. He's supposed to be a casual friend of my mother's. They share a house along Fruitvale Creek. A really lovely place. The story is that she does housekeeping and cooking, he's a bachelor and one of those fellows who's great about building things on an elaborate scale but can't take care of himself. I think everybody knows that she's his girlfriend, although for propriety's sake they never, *ever* behave romantically in public. I mean, you'd think my mother would at least admit it to me, but I suppose it's—. She's just this very self-contained woman."

I asked her what Russ did for a living.

"He's sort of, I don't know his official title, a general contractor. For the state, and sometimes the W.P.A. He seems to make sense out of complicated construction projects. Anyway, he helped build Treasure Island, if you can build such a thing, and I guess you can."

I remembered reading about an R. W. Hewett in some of the pamphlets Culpepper had given me to read while I waited in his office earlier today. I asked Gail if "her" Hewett was the fellow who had brought in the Army Corps of Engineers for the building of the island.

"That's our boy," she nodded. "The island is his baby. He'll be overseeing its conversion to an airport when the fair closes in October. Not what you'd call a profound guy, but he earns an honest living, does the right thing with the public's money." She looked a little alarmed. "Oh, but listen, when you meet her, please remember that you don't know anything about her and Russ. It's their shady little secret." She fidgeted in her seat. "What about you, what are you hiding?"

So as not to seem evasive even as I was being so, I told her all kinds of useless details about myself. That I grew up in New York, worked there almost entirely until about ten years ago. That I was divorced. Why not let her know I'm single? "And then I decided I'd work the Midwest, towns I'd never been to."

"You wanted to see new places, make new friends," she put forward.

"No, I wanted to be anonymous. When you're always in places where you have no past history and never will, you're close to invisible. It's like having a Saturday afternoon to yourself in a strange town and you walk into a football game between the Dayton Somethings and the Eureka So-and-Sos. The winning side jumps for joy; the losers are crushed. And lucky you, you don't feel anything."

She looked like she was trying to understand why I'd think this was a good idea, and ventured, "I get stage fright sometimes. I suppose it would help me if I thought I was playing for people I'd never see again." She gave me a very direct look that I knew had something good in it for me. "Of course, *some* people I'd definitely want to see again. Do you come to California very often?"

I tried to give her an intelligent answer even as my mind was turning to creamed farina. "As a matter of fact, Gail, before this booking, I hadn't been back to California since I first started playing in the business. I wasn't even eighteen at the time."

"Where were you playing?" she asked.

"About five feet from where you're sitting."

My first professional job had been at the Claremont, performing in the house orchestra. I was seventeen, though at the time I confessed with faked chagrin to being only twenty-four, which sounded old as the hills to me.

My classical training, combined with my total enslavement to Dixie (the music, not the province), made me a strong utility player, which compensated for my being, as Ernie Shumaker used to call me, an absolute babe in the woodwinds.

I told Gail that I remembered the Claremont best (and my conscience remembered it worst) for being where I spent the last big drumroll leading up to the cymbal crash of Prohibition, which marked for most Americans the day when the locating and partaking of booze became our national pastime.

"Was the Claremont very different then?" she asked.

"The god-awful part, Gail, is that I remember very little of my stay out here in Oakland, except the music itself, and being astounded by what I could pour into my body and still function." I confessed to her—or she drew out of me—that the most thrilling revelation for me had been how effortlessly a teenage musician could attain sexual congress with a realm of women even more intoxicated and impressed with him than he was. With what staggering (literally) ease were achieved those conquests of mine.

Gail nodded with profound understanding.

"You were a trollop," she said.

I pleaded my losing case. "I was seventeen, there were six months left before the United States went dry forever, I was playing jazz for a living—imagine being paid to do something you'd gratefully pay to do—and girls who wouldn't have given me the time of day a year earlier were now admiring me on the stage of one of the swankest hotels on the West Coast. What would you have done in my position?"

Gail smiled. "But plenty, I suppose."

"Unforgivable," I reprimanded myself. "And the most shameful part of it is I don't even remember the faces or names. Admittedly, all the girls that hung around with us aspired to the same identical look: cinched-down bosom, carmine lips the shape of Louise Brooks's, penciled eyebrows drawn on a blank canvas, rolled stockings that got lost in the parking lot behind the hotel—" I stopped myself. "Not much of a portrait to paint for you, I'm afraid. You shouldn't have gotten me started."

She shrugged gracefully. "I appreciate your honesty if not your behavior, and as you say, you were very young."

I walked Gail to the hotel's taxi stand and rode back with her to her lodgings. I took the same taxi directly back to the hotel. She wasn't the kind of girl I'd ever have made a play for on a first date (if what we'd had was a date). I wouldn't have wanted her to be. I didn't even try to kiss her good night. I think the cabdriver may have been surprised by that. In light of all I'd told her, maybe Gail was too.

16

The Recurring Dream

That night, I had the dream again.

It was the worst dream in the world.

It's as lovely as a spring day gets in not-so-upstate New York. I am walking through the front door of our small house. My wife, Nancy, is in the kitchen. I hear her doing things with metal pans.

I've come from playing at the Bobbin Inn, an unusual job for me since it isn't in the city but fairly close to home, and for some odd reason my work has ended in the late afternoon.

I walk into the kitchen and I see that Nancy is basting a small roast. The room is filled with the strong, reassuring smells of beef and slightly burnt new potatoes roasted in drippings, and the steam from a pot of big, mealy peas with sprigs of mint. *"Nancy?"*

She's holding the roast on a tray. "I can't give you a hug, honey, my hands are full," she says.

"So I notice." I take advantage of her momentary handicap and scoot my arms through the handles made by her arms and firmly cup both of her breasts. She laughs and I gently kiss the nape of her neck.

"Stop that," she scolds, "it tickles and I'll drop our dinner."

"I thought you like when I do that."

She turns to face me. "Later, I'll like that." She looks out the window at the perfect day. "It's so unusual to have you home at dinnertime." She sets down the roast and turns around. "Okay, now I can give you a hug."

She always has the right buoyancy in my arms. She's the best kisser I've ever known. Or maybe it's simply that I love her more than anyone else I've ever kissed.

"Where's Linney?"

"She's upstairs, napping."

"She's tired?"

"Not one bit. But I've made a new rule that if she insists on having storytime with you whenever you come traipsing in from work at two in the morning, she has to take a nap each afternoon. Otherwise she's going to lose too much sleep."

My daughter and I have an agreement, her stipulation. No matter how late I get in from a playing job, I am to wake her and tell her a story. Today is different, though. My work is done, so I can tell her a story while the sun is shining. A treat for me.

I go up the stairs and make a right, past the lone bathroom in the house, which has a tub but no shower, and open the dark mahogany door of Linney's room.

Her name is really Linnea, but I soon made it Linney.

She's asleep, wearing that expression Nancy calls "careless rapture." She's in her blue-and-yellow-checked dimity frock. (I didn't always know these terms, but Nancy makes most of Linney's clothing and I've picked them up from her.)

Linney's arms are splayed out in total abandon. Her mouth is open and beads of healthy sweat dapple her forehead. She smells like cookies.

I sit at her bedside and allow myself a minute or two to absorb some of the youthful goodness that floats around her, as if she is already so full of loveliness that her body can't contain it all, and so it hovers over her in the air like the scent above a bed of blue and yellow pansies.

"Hi, Daddowee," she smacks from a dry mouth, not yet opening her eyes.

"Would you like some water?" I ask.

She nods yes. I put my arm beneath her shoulders and gently lift her up, and then I guide the glass of cool water I find in my right hand up to her lips. I let her control how much she drinks. *"Enough?"* I ask. She nods and I let her slip back onto her pillow.

"Story," she asks, probably thinking it's two A.M.

I nod. *"Once upon a time there were two bears named Iggy and Ziggy, and they lived in a hollow forest in the middle of a beautiful tree—"*

"No, no, you got it wrong!" she laughs. This is a mandatory part of our ritual. I have to display my ineptitude three times as the prelude to the actual story.

"Sorry. I meant, once upon a time there were five bears named Igworth and Zigworth—"

"No, no, no." She shakes, weak with laughter.

"Right, I'm sorry. Dumb Dad."

"Dumb Dad."

"I of course meant twice upon a time, there were three bears—" This error is a new innovation of mine, it takes her a moment, but then she gets it and howls with delight.

Nancy calls from downstairs. "Linney, some of your friends want to know if you're coming out to play?"

All business now, she sits up. "Story later, dumb Dad?"

"*Of course. Put on your Poll Parrots, not your Sunday shoes.*"

She dutifully slips into her scuffed-up brown leather gum soles, pleased with the double knots she ties. "Where's my clicker?"

She wants the yellow clicker with the parrot on it she was given when we bought the shoes. I go to what is the equivalent of her toy box, which looks like a tall, floor-level safe that is set into the wall. It's a home fur vault, a kind of sealed closet where furs can be stored for the summer. Nancy owns no furs, and with the modest income of her office work and my playing, she probably never will, so we converted the vault into shelves for the storage of Linney's books and toys, removing its mechanism so it can never be locked.

I pull the handle and open it. Her clicker is next to her books: *The Poor Little Match Girl, Little Nemo in Slumberland, A Visit to Davy Jones' Locker.*

I do my usual Mack Sennett routine for Linney, where I pretend to catch my finger in the door as I close it, and then, as I register pain and suck on my "injured" fingers, I pretend to crush the other hand as well. This proceeds to the mock-squashing of both sets of my toes, my kneecap, both hands, any combination that will cause Linney to create that most lovely of the universe's inaudible noises, a child laughing so helplessly that he or she cannot produce a sound.

It is a foolish game to play if you're a man who needs full use of his fingers in order to earn a living, but it makes her happy. She asks me what would happen if my fingers really got stuck; I say I'd open the door. She asks what if the door got locked. I explain it can't be-cause we had the lock taken out. She asks why. I say because things that lock on the outside but not on the inside are dangerous, like bank safes and the trunks of cars.

She runs down the stairs to play outside with her friends, and we tell her to be back in an hour. Nancy looks up at me, in the same way she did just before the first time we ever made love, when it was Nancy who said that today we should.

An hour later, Nancy and I have spruced ourselves up and laid out dinner. Linney comes in the door. She likes roast potatoes if we mash them for her and the burnt end of the roast beef if it's cut into squares. These things are all prepared for her and I ask her to sit at the table. She keeps wandering away while my back is turned. She also likes peas with a lot of butter and salt so they taste more like corn, and I set these down for her. In a tradition that we observe because Linney likes it, we join hands at the table, bow our heads, and say grace. Linney usually recites it, but today the honor has fallen to me . . .

There is a transition period. It won't fully hit me until two or three minutes after I wake. Then I will cry out, always, which is why I never sleep in the same room with anyone, because it would terrify them, though not as much as it terrifies me.

"No, no, please," I implore anyone who will listen, but no one does, because I'm a man alone in a hotel room with nobody near me, this being how I've arranged my life—in part to spare others, in part because it's simpler this way.

It was the worst dream in the world. Because it allowed me to wake.

17

Chancery Lane

Gail's mother and Russ Hewett lived at the end of a cul-de-sac that overlooked Fruitvale Creek, one of several clandestine assets of a very agreeable part of Oakland known as the Dimond District (named for one Joseph Dimond), the area being to all purposes an amiable, welcoming town that happened to be pressed right up alongside a major city. The other houses on Chancery Lane were sand-colored stucco, similar in design and neatly spaced to make them seem like two files of sentries standing guard for the one very different house where the street stopped. Hewett's home was of dark wood, built low and modern in style without making a big fuss about it. It was fronted by a high fence of light gray planks. Parked in the driveway was an olive-green Studebaker sedan. A grassy hill to the right of the house slipped down to friendly trees that were trying to keep the creek a secret, but the stream was betrayed by its benevolent gurgle and the sparkling sunlight that leapt from its busy surface like flames from a log fire, only the fire was a cold, clear blue.

It looked like it would be a particularly pleasant place to work, and that was just as well because there weren't many alternatives. I didn't have a piano in my room at the Claremont, of course. I could have tried using the one in the ballroom, but there were a lot of social functions there in the afternoon. Gail said the Berkeley practice rooms were the size of telephone booths and not conducive to spending long hours with the broad sheets of pale green music paper on which I would be writing my orchestration of her *Swing Around the Sun*.

But Russ Hewett and Gail's mother shared a house that went virtually unoccupied during the day. (Gail's mother augmented her housekeeping obligations with temporary office work in medical practices around the area.) Hewett owned a console piano, purchased simply because one bought such things for a house, and on it Gail could play me her award-winning composition, and I could use it to pen my orchestration of same without distraction.

I'd offered to pick up Gail by taxi so that we could arrive at her mother's home together, but she'd insisted this made no sense, as Berkeley and Chancery Lane were in equal and opposite directions from the Claremont. Thus I found myself ringing the doorbell of a man named Russ Hewett, alone.

He answered the door. I remembered his robust appearance from the few seconds we'd had before Marie Prasquier had landed—no, *landed* was not the right word—nearby us. I had a little more time to appraise him as he in turn surveyed me. He seemed about fifteen years my senior. He had sun-bleached hair on his arms atop the kind of uncultivated tan a person acquires while working outdoors. His eyes were a friendly gray, with a permanent squint as if he were always looking into the sun. His features formed a smile readily enough.

"So, you're Gail's jazz musician? I think I half-met you when that girl killed herself."

"Yes, sir." Stupid response. I was thirty-eight years old. "Yessiree," I appended, trying to make it sound as if that's what I had meant all along. I introduced myself.

He nodded toward the parlor. "Well, come in then." He called out, "Martha! Company's here."

I walked into the cool, dark parlor. It was manly and comfortable-looking. There were a lot of built-in bookshelves and a room divider with a glass display case. A simple dining room verged on an enclosed porch whose windows oversaw a near jungle of foliage. Russ waved me toward a sofa and explained that Gail had called a short while earlier to say she'd missed her bus and might be a half hour late. She'd have to take a trolley into Oakland and change for an eastbound bus from there. This left me with the horrendous task of sitting alone with the man of the house as if being scrutinized prior to a first date with his daughter.

"Get you something to drink?" asked Russ. "We have mixers, with and without, bottled beer, and, uh, we have some soda pop, I think." He raised his voice. "Martha, do we have any pop?"

A female voice shouted back, "No, but I fixed some orangeade."

Russ made a face and called out, "Well, I'm having a beer!" He turned to me. "Joining me?"

I shook my head. "No thanks, Russ, I'm sort of here to work."

He laughed deeply. "I'd love to tell my Caterpillar men that you call listening to piano music 'work.' " He called out, "He'll have your orangeade, Martha! I'm having myself a beer!" He didn't get up. "So, Sherwood, you have an interesting occupation. How'd you fall into your line of business?"

"Well, my parents weren't particularly musical but they wanted me to have—"

I stopped as Mrs. Prentice walked in from the kitchen. She carried a tray with tumblers, a glass pitcher, and an odd cone-topped can. She said, "Pardon me for not shaking your hand but I have to set this down."

She was about Gail's height, maybe an inch taller, and at one time she'd surely been just as attractive. Now she seemed faded, like a framed photograph of a smiling woman that had been left in a shop window for too many summers. And yet she wasn't that old at all, certainly still in her forties. She wore a simple blue-and-white cotton tattersall dress.

I stood, to show that I'd been raised properly, and Russ grudgingly did the same. She took her first real look at me and seemed almost startled, presumably by my age. She looked at Russ, then turned back to me and apologized: "Oh, I'm sorry, I didn't mean to force the orangeade on you. I'm expecting one of my daughter's friends, and I didn't know Russ had a guest. Can I make you a real drink?"

Russ said, "No, Martha, this is the fellow who's working with Gail."

Martha frowned. "Are you with the university?"

"Lamentably not." Her frown did not improve.

Russ took the oddly shaped container from the tray and held it up for my appreciation. "You seen this yet? Canned beer. Sounds just awful, doesn't it?" He reached into his pocket, pulled out a multifunction knife, and tugged off the cap on the can's cone top. "Martha buys me beer in these things because it stays colder, but it tastes of metal." He took a tumbler from the tray and poured himself a glass. "Waste of good tin."

The three of us sat and Russ urged me to continue the saga of how I got into what he called "the music game." As I talked, I noticed Gail's mother staring at me with more interest than my story warranted, and her expression ranged from distrust to disapproval. I made a few comments that passed for jokes and Hewett laughed appropriately, but Martha Prentice was not finding anything humorous about me. Each time I aimed words in her direction, she looked away, her eyes darting about the room as if I were about to pocket something, an ashtray, a piece of wax fruit.

I wondered how Gail had depicted our budding relationship to her mother. Perhaps in her enthusiasm, she had forgotten to mention that I was probably closer to Martha Prentice's age than her own.

In search of an ally, I turned to Russ and complimented him on the creation of Treasure Island.

He took a small sip of his beer. "Well, you're more than kind, but a general contractor is not so much a creator as he is a combination foreman, interpreter, referee, and chaplain. Lot of emphasis on the last part. I did more hand-holding than a gigolo in a home for spinsters." He looked at Martha with a good-natured laugh, and perhaps his timing could have been more gallant. "I got the army engineers to talk with the civilians, the civilians to the politicians, the politicians to the gangsters—although the politicians were on pretty good speaking terms with the gangsters to begin with. But yes, it was some job, and it doesn't seem to want to end: building an island where there was nothing, raising a city on top of it, then come this October dismantling that same damn city and building an airport in its place. Can you imagine those planes taking off and landing by the hundreds each day from a location that was once considered nothing more than a menace to navigation? That's going to be something." He took another sip of his beer. "Really something."

The front door wasn't locked and Gail walked in, a bit unkempt and breathless. She looked at me with pity. "Poor Ray, have you been getting the third degree? I'm so sorry I'm late."

"Not at all," I said.

"Isn't he great?" she asked the room.

Martha Prentice replied, "Have some orangeade, Gail. You must be thirsty."

We made small talk for a while, Gail stealing the occasional glance at her mother, gauging her reaction to what I was saying.

Russ certainly tried to be cordial, and he cast a few curious looks at Martha's demeanor, which was running the gamut from sullen to very sullen.

Finally Gail clapped her hands together and grimaced. "Okay, can't stall any longer, I have to play my composition for Ray, so . . . you'll excuse us?"

Russ stood quickly. "As it happens. Yes, I was thinking of taking a little stroll as far as Dimond Park and back. Join me, Martha?" He moved toward the front door.

"I'm not going anywhere," said Gail's mother flatly. It may have been the first words she'd spoken in over ten minutes.

Russ inquired softly, "You feeling okay, Martha?"

She took a kerchief from her dress pocket. "I've been so busy filling in at Dr. Corwin's that I've completely fallen behind on the cleaning." She turned to Gail. "You two do what you have to at the piano and I'll try not to be a bother."

"Hope you'll join us for dinner, Sherwood," said the departing Russ. Martha glared at his back.

Gail walked me up three steps to a slightly elevated extension of the house and indicated a doorway on her left. "My garret away from my garret," she said. "Where I sleep when I stay here on the weekends." I entered a room painted a blanched yellow, the same color as the promised piano, a console model, the kind you knew from kindergarten. Adjacent to the keyboard was a drafting table with blank manuscript paper and a coffee can filled with twenty or thirty lethally sharpened pencils. A small bed looked the right size for Gail. I could picture her napping there. Several orange crates were lined up against the opposite wall.

"You better sit down," Gail said. "It's not that short a piece, and I intend to play it through twice for you. I want you to like it, and with music, familiarity breeds content."

There was no chair in the room, other than the piano stool. "You want me to sit on the floor?" I asked.

"No, just sit on my bed, Ray, but take off your shoes first."

I did so and sat myself at the foot of the bed, leaning forward attentively.

She protested, "No, you're too close, it's making me nervous. Stretch out."

I dutifully wadded a few thin pillows behind the small of my back and lay there like a pasha on a divan, propped up on my right elbow.

She turned to face me, mock formal, posing with her right hand upon the cabinet of the piano. "It gives me now great pleasure, mingled with terror, to perform for your express enjoyment the original composition *Swing Around the Sun,* Opus Thirty-seven in D Major, composed by G. Prentice, circa 1940."

I wondered if she'd really kept track of how many works she'd composed to arrive at Opus 37 and when she had started counting.

She dropped her tongue-in-cheek grand manner and added, "Hey, listen, Ray, all I ask is that if you really don't like it and think it's not for you, that you'll lie to me, tell me it's great, and do the arrangement anyway. Is that too much too ask?"

"Sounds eminently fair to me," I replied. Who was I fooling? An albacore tuna in a net had more freedom of choice than I had at this point.

She walked over to the side of the bed. "Could we shake on it, Ray?" she asked. "It'll be a lot less harrowing for me to play this for you if you tell me in advance that you'll do it, no matter what you think. I mean, it *did* win the competition, so *somebody* thought it was good, right?"

"I'll do the best I can for you."

She reached out her hand. "So when you give me your critique, you'll be gentle?"

I reached up from the bed and assured her, "I'll be gentle with you, I promise," as the door opened and Gail's mother walked in.

I don't know if Martha Prentice heard this last utterance of mine.

But given the presented tableau of a jazz musician in his late thirties lying upon a college coed's bed within an hour of first being admitted into her mother's home, his arm apparently tugging the coed down onto the bed with him, I thought it was more than tolerant that Gail's mother merely said, "If you don't mind, I'll leave Gail's bedroom door open, since I love hearing her play the piano." She gave me a smile that would have turned a Gorgon to stone. "I'll just be in the next room, listening with great interest."

18

Swing Around the Sun

Gail went to one of the orange crates against the far wall and took from the top of it a thick sheaf of music manuscript paper. The pages were hinged together and folded accordion style. She opened the first five pages and spread them out like a banner across the piano, contemplated them for a moment, then launched into *Swing Around the Sun*.

Having only heard her play the cumbersome carillon, I hadn't been able to appraise her skill as a performer. I could tell immediately that she was an accomplished pianist, but then, I'd expected her to be.

What I'd not expected was as startlingly original a harmonic style as I'd heard in over a decade.

Describing music with words is somewhat the equivalent of making a painting of a novel. Here are some words one would *not* use in conjunction with Gail's composition: *pedestrian, bourgeois, mushy,* dated, innocuous, clichéd, schmaltzy. Another word you wouldn't apply to it is catchy. This was not easy music. It made demands on the listener. Some untrained ears might hear it and think that something was wrong. Not that it was overly discordant; it just had its own unique tonality. Her stance on harmony was akin to Grandma Moses's position on perspective. I was impressed that the Pan-Pacific judges, whoever they might be, had picked the inventive audacity of Gail's composition over more traditional submissions.

Of course, I had wanted Gail's work to be good, or at least competent. She'd told me on our walk to the ferry that she wanted me to orchestrate it, not rewrite it. Since I'd agreed to respect the integrity of her composition, I was desperately hoping it actually had some. Thankfully, the piece was clean, harrowing yet sprightly. It just refused to stay put.

As she concluded her preordained encore, I despaired a little for myself and the task ahead of me, since the harmonic underpinnings of the work seemed remarkably evasive. She must have seen the concern on my face as she turned away from the piano to receive my reaction.

"Well, what do you say?" she asked, and as I fumbled for the words, Gail blurted out in horror, "You don't like it. Oh, you can't not like it! It only means the world to me—"

I cut her off. "Gail, it's wonderful. I don't know that I'm fully qualified to appraise it, but—I mean, I was expecting it to be something uniquely your own, but it's . . ." My voice trailed off. "Gail, it's not for everyone's tastes. But it's flat-out terrific."

She hugged me and shrieked with delight. "I knew you'd hear it the way I hear it! I've been worried that it was only the judges and myself who could understand, that everybody else would say it was just a lot of racket—"

"Why, has anyone else heard it and disapproved?"

She rolled her eyes. "Oh, Toby, Ada—"

"Well, Toby Ackland strikes me as a jerk," I said, "and you told me Adeline lost the competition to you. What would you expect her to say?"

"She pretended she wanted to learn from my style of writing, and I felt guilty about beating her, so I tried to be a good sport." Gail frowned. "She made a big fuss about giving me the first draft of her piece for the competition—*Self-Portrait*, she called it—so I sort of had to let her play *Swing*. I should *never* have done that. And of course my mother and Russ, they don't understand it at all, so when someone like you, someone I truly admire, says it's wonderful—" She hugged me again with another cry of pleasure.

Her mother was in the doorway. "Gail, are you all right?" she asked, looking accusingly at me.

Gail let go of me. "He likes it, Mom. I mean, I knew he would, but until he said he did—" She whirled on me. "You're not lying, are you? Oh what the hell, it doesn't matter, you can't take it back now."

"Of course he likes it," said Martha, who walked away but didn't close the door behind her.

I asked Gail if I could look over the score. Her musical hand was much more precise than mine. That was a plus right there; I wouldn't be spending my time trying to decipher what she'd composed.

"It doesn't really voice naturally for big band instrumentation," I began. "It's not like there's a lead melody with chord changes behind it."

"I'm sorry about that, Ray," she said, her voice pitched to indicate that she would leave me no way to back out. "But you may very well be the only one who can make it work for the instrumentation they're giving me."

"Right here I've got a chord that has five low notes in it that can only be played by a baritone sax or a trombone in pedal stops or a bass. I don't know how I'll do that."

She looked at me as if I were crazy. "You weren't going to completely scrap the piano, were you? There's nothing here that doesn't lie on the piano."

I felt foolish. "Oh, how stupid of me! I was so busy thinking about how to take a work written for the piano and voice it for wind instruments that I forgot I still have the piano to work with. And drums, I assume, yes?"

"Yes, I'm told the Pan-Pacific Orchestra has the same instrumentation as Jack Donovan's band, minus the guitar, xylophone, and vocalist, of course."

I asked her what she wanted me to do about the drums, since obviously there was nothing resembling a drum part in the piano piece, although *Swing* didn't lack for rhythm.

"I leave that to you," she said, somewhat surprisingly, seeing as she'd told me she expected total fidelity to every other aspect of the work. "I can't get the hang of a drum kit. I hear the end result of a drummer playing all those different things at the same time, but I don't see how it's put together. So do what you will with it, Ray."

We went over the score bar by bar, and she was very receptive to almost all my ideas. I told her that although the job would be more difficult than I'd originally imagined, if we worked together, me orchestrating and Gail proofing my work, we should be able to complete the orchestral score in a couple of days, leaving more than enough time for a music copyist to then notate the individual parts for the performance.

Martha Prentice came in and said that she was serving supper and had set a place for me. She said it was lucky that they always had an early dinner, as it would allow me to get back to the Claremont in time for my eight o'clock start. The looks she gave me seemed a little more tolerant now. Perhaps this was because, in eavesdropping, she could hear that Gail and I were genuinely collaborating on this project and had been talking about nothing but notes and rests and instrumentation for several hours.

Dinner must have always been at the same appointed time in the

Hewett-Prentice ménage, for at the very moment that Gail, Martha, and I took our seats, Russ walked in the door and sat in the chair at the head of the table. "Pass the bread and butter if you please, Sherwood" were the first words he spoke.

"It gets a little warm in the dining room this time of year, because of the angle of the sun through the windows," said Gail's mother. "You fellows take off your jackets if you like."

Russ grunted gratefully and draped his jacket over the back of his chair. I wasn't too warm but felt I should do the same.

Clearly, Hewett liked to set a substantial table, and Martha did him proud. We started with steak scallone, which was a kind of seafood meat loaf made from a purée of shrimp and abalone that Martha then cut into slices and pan-fried. A boiled brisket of beef in a sweet-sour vinegar sauce was brought out alongside a gravy boat of fresh grated horseradish, along with bowls of buttered parsnips, creamed cauliflower, boiled potatoes, and spring peas. A dimpled bottle of Roma Dry Sauterne was set out on the table, but no one was moved to disturb the dust on it.

"They were setting up for some sort of festival in the park next week. Looks like a pretty big to-do." He frowned as he stabbed his fork at a browned slice of the sautéed scallone. "Don't like the feel of it one bit."

"What kind of festival?" asked Gail.

"Whole thing is supposed to be, you know, German heritage, German culture. To compensate for the bad name they say they're getting from Hitler and from the president, who they say is prejudiced against German Americans. Only in their speeches, they're calling F.D.R. 'President Frank D. Rosenburg' and calling his economic plan 'the Jew Deal.' That's not right. Look, I'm voting for Willkie this year, but still, he's our president." His displeasure didn't harm his appetite, as he filched the last two remaining slices of the scallone from the serving plate. "Could be terrible publicity for the Oakland area, and for the fair."

Martha asked in a dry tone, "Is that why it's wrong, Russ? Because it would be terrible for the fair?"

Russ made quick work of the food before him. "Just plain terrible. And right up the street from us. They're expecting thousands."

Gail was studiously cutting her food into neat pieces without actually eating anything. "There's nothing illegal about what they're doing," she said.

"But we're on England's side," said her mother.

"We're not supposed to be," said Gail. "We're supposed to be neutral. It's the only hope we have of not getting dragged into this terrible mess in Europe."

Russ asked me where I stood on world politics and I shrugged, trying to steer clear of any family disputes. "I'm not neutral. I'm irrelevant. First credo for a musician: if a fight breaks out at a dance, stay up on the stage, don't get involved or even watch. I work in a band, and the band plays on."

"Didn't Shakespeare say that the hottest parts of hell are reserved for those who remain neutral?" Russ said, misquoting Dante. "Say, Martha, you think you could carve me some of that brisket?"

"It's probably easier if I just bring it around to you." The beef was on a small carving board with a gleaming knife and fork alongside it. Martha held the twin-barbed fork and carving knife against the left side of the board and brought it around the table. "Since you're our guest, Mr. Sherwood, why don't you carve first? I'll just squeeze in here on your right, if you don't mind."

I did mind. For as she moved alongside me, I felt a searing hot pain in my right arm. I cried out and she looked aghast.

"Oh my God, I'm so sorry!" she blurted. I turned my head to my right and saw that the left tong of the carving fork had gone into the back of my arm. As she pulled it out of me, I felt a slight tearing sensation.

"Ray!" Gail came over to me and barked at her mother, "You *stabbed* him?"

"It's nothing serious," I assured everyone before I really knew if it was. I felt a warm wetness against my shirt.

"I was holding the fork against the carving board at an angle, and as I moved to put the brisket down, it must have gone into his arm," Martha rushed to explain. I looked over my right shoulder as an uneven circle of blood grew larger on my shirt. She held a napkin against the hole in my arm. "Russ, apply pressure and it'll stop the bleeding."

Russ stepped over. "It's just flesh there, Sherwood, nothing to worry about, I'm sure."

"I just washed the fork before we sat down," said Martha, "and it's touched nothing. I'm sure there's no chance of an infection."

"I'll get Mercurochrome and bandages," said Gail. "Are you all right, Ray?"

I flexed my right fingers. There was no problem with them, just some soreness in my right triceps. I told them I didn't think it would affect my playing.

"I'll get you a fresh shirt, Mr. Sherwood," said Martha. "Again, I'm so terribly sorry for my clumsiness."

She looked straight at me, clear-eyed, with just the hint of a smile on her face before she walked out of the room at her own good speed.

I suppose it was better to learn early on that insanity ran in Gail's family. For there wasn't the slightest doubt in my mind that Martha Prentice had just stabbed me intentionally, with premeditation and malice aforethought.

19

The Recurring Dream

Russ wouldn't consider letting me take a trolley or taxi home. He drove me back to the Claremont, Gail riding silently in the back.

I should have been the one at the wheel, with Gail at my side as we breezily made a joke out of her mother's attack on me. Instead, I sat in Hewett's Studebaker like an overgrown collegiate being escorted back to my dorm by my date's father.

When we arrived at the hotel, I got out of the car and opened the rear door so that Gail could move to the front seat. Russ was taking her back to her place alongside the Berkeley campus. She told me she was "booked" all the next day, playing a morning concert at the Campanile, then traveling to Emeryville to coach Adeline Head's replacement. We agreed to start work in earnest on Friday. With Russ sitting there, his car's motor idling, any thought I might have had about giving Gail a good-night kiss was laughed right out of the town where my good judgment was rumored to live.

At the end of the band's stint that evening, I went to my hotel room, where I took a washcloth and soaked it with the contents of a half-pint bottle of emergency rye I keep in my suitcase. I howled as I held it against my flesh wound and lay down on the bed, waiting for the throb to grow dull and eventually subside.

The New York Chemical Bank was crowded with shoppers like me who had thought that fifty dollars would more than amply pay for the Christmas presents on their list. Yet Nancy, Linney, and I found ourselves standing on a line at the bank, because we had not included in our calculations that while Nancy took Linney to Santaland at R. H. Macy's, I would go and purchase most of the dolls that had been manufactured since the previous Christmas.

I was greeted by the bank's junior manager, a man named Felton who was a jazz aficionado and who knew me by name.

He asked what brought us to the bank. I told him we were withdrawing some money, which he seemed to take personally.

Nancy said, "Mr. Felton, each week, I deposit one dollar in our Christmas Club here, and you stamp a page in our booklet. And each year, at the end of fifty weeks, we turn in our books and you very kindly give us fifty dollars."

Felton nodded amicable agreement.

Nancy continued, "So, may I ask . . . why are we doing this?"

Felton said, "Why, for the convenience."

I whirl on Nancy. *"Where's Linney?"*

Nancy said, "I thought you were watching her." I run around the bank and see that my little girl has somehow managed to cross into the office area unnoticed and is now stepping into the open bank vault, unseen by its guard.

"Linney, come back!" I call out. She could have plucked a few thousand dollars from the vault and no one would have paid any attention. I lecture her on the danger of going into bank vaults. At night they get shut and they don't open until morning, and all the air runs out. Air is important. I need air to play my instrument.

"How long can you hold a note, Daddowee?" she asks.

I tell her I once tried to blow a note for two minutes but almost passed out. *"If you don't get air after three minutes, you get dizzy, what they call unconscious, and after that, you'd get very sick. So be very careful when you're near things like bank vaults."*

She promises she will be, and she and Nancy and I leave Mr. Felton and the bank, and I don't find it odd that directly outside the bank is our living room with a decorated Christmas tree. Linney is unwrapping presents. The phone rings and my arm is sore from where it was stabbed.

20

The Vanishing Woman

This time around, it wasn't as emotionally painful to wake from my recurring lovely dream, because in this instance the lovely part hadn't lasted very long. The phone had seen to that. By the time I answered its third ring, you would have been hard-pressed to detect anything wrong with me at all.

"Hello?"

"Ray." She didn't have to say the next part. I only needed one syllable to know the voice. "It's—um—well, it's Nancy, how are you."

Her voice had not changed. I would have hoped the years might have altered its familiar warmth. I wished she hadn't called.

"Where are you, Nance? The connection is very clear."

"Actually, I live on this coast now, Ray. I wrote to you and told you that last year."

"I never got the letter. The hotels I stay at don't always forward mail." And of course sometimes I never leave a forwarding address. "Where are you living?"

"San Francisco. I saw that Jack's band was playing at the Claremont and thought I'd see if you were there."

The good thing about touring with a band is that when you leave a town, the people that you met there can't really hold it against you that you've left *them* behind as well. That's one of the very reasons some people tour with a band. The bad news is what Gail had already pointed out: when your band comes into a town, everyone knows where they can find you come eight P.M. And if you *stay* in the same hotel where you're playing, well, you might as well pitch a tent in the lobby.

Not that it was awful to hear Nancy's voice. It was something much worse than awful.

"Where in San Francisco, Nance?"

"Oh, I've just got a simple room near Willow and Polk."

There was the obligatory question. "How's the kid?"

"Fine, and doing well at school, but hardly a kid, Ray."

"Sorry," I said.

"Listen, I have to interview someone for a job not too far from you, at a luncheonette, of all places. Would you be able to meet me for a bite, say in about an hour?" She hesitated. "I actually have a little proposal I want you to consider." It was over two decades since I'd said almost the same words to her, and I wondered if the sad irony did not escape her.

With Gail off to Emeryville for the day, I didn't have a ready excuse for why I couldn't see her.

The entrance to the strangely named Centaur Luncheonette was successfully hiding from potential customers behind the elevator bank of the Brogan office building, located at Broadway and Eighth Street. Nancy was in the last of the shop's five booths, as she'd said she would be.

She looked a little older. Well, it had been how many years since

I'd last seen her—nine, ten? She was nicely dressed in a brown suit of a thin wool, probably part of her wardrobe from the East Coast that had been able to make the segue to California.

She saw me and offered a slow, sympathetic smile. She looked down at the tabletop and back up again. A reflex of hers.

I sat down across from her. "Hello, Nance. Have you been waiting long?"

She folded and unfolded a serviette like a shopgirl in Gimbel's scarf department. "I just got here myself. You look good, Ray. Not very different at all." She confided to the tabletop, "It's different for women."

I assured her, "Nance, when you were seventeen, you were thrilled you could pass for twenty-one. Be thrilled that at thirty-seven you can pass for twenty-six."

"In the dusk with the light behind me," she said, looking down. When she looked back up, she caught me searching for the wedding band someone else had bought her.

I asked, "Where's your ring? The Second Mr. Nancy is having it polished?"

She waved away how life works with a flutter of her hand. "Oh, it was simply what happens when two people worry too much about each other. Cliff was always painfully sensitive to the fact that when he was unhappy, I would become equally unhappy. So in a desperate attempt to cheer me up once and for all, he made himself extremely happy with a woman in Perth Amboy."

She broke off a little piece of a laugh for me as if it were a corner of peanut brittle and put her head in her hands, shaking it back and forth with a cheery woefulness. "Oh, it was such a bad mistake! Anyway, about then, Sally called me . . . Sally Rand. Wanted to know if I'd like to work for her again."

"As what?" I demanded.

She pshawed me. "Oh for heaven's sake, Ray, not as a stripper, if that's what you're thinking! I handle the office work for Sally, like I used to after I had Linney, only a lot more so. She called me, begged me to come out here and do the typing, booking, haggling, pleading. Most of the time I'm hamstered away in a cubbyhole at the Music Box Theatre, but this summer I've mostly been at Sally's showplace on Treasure Island—have you been out there, by the way?"

The luncheonette's sole and overburdened waitress entered from the kitchen with a stack of plates for other customers. She was the kind of blonde only a chemist could love, with a uniform whose lumpiness was probably not entirely the uniform's fault. I signaled to the waitress as I told Nancy that I had indeed been to the fair. I didn't share with her that in my one visit, I'd been proposed to *and* seen my would-be bride's body tragically shattered to a bloody pulp. Nancy worried about my mental state too much as it was.

The harried waitress had no time to greet us but wordlessly pulled out a pad and pencil and scribbled frantically as Nancy ordered the day's special, along with coffee and rhubarb pie. I ordered the same. As the waitress slapped our check down on the table, I asked her if she could bring me milk for my coffee instead of cream. She looked at me as if it were the strangest request she'd ever heard, cracked her gum, pivoted quickly, and rushed back to the kitchen.

"Whatever made you pick *this* place to hold a job interview?" I asked Nancy.

She smiled. "I'm booking a new road show for Sally. *Burst My Bubble* it's called. Sally's putting her name on it, but she'll only join the show in major cities. It's a real hinterland tour, thankless schedule and salaries to match. I'm having a lot of trouble booking talent for it. Anyway, I got a call from this girl with the cutest Georgia drawl who said she was a friend of Ann Pederson, a very reliable dancer who at the moment is ridiculously pregnant somewhere in Mexico. This girl from Georgia says she has great credentials and wants to do the tour in the worst way but can't meet me in San Francisco because she works as a switchboard operator in the Brogan Building, that's this building. She implored me to meet her here. I told her what I'd be wearing and that I'd either be alone or with a good-looking man in his thirties."

She had always tossed off thoughtful little compliments this way, saying that they cost her nothing. I put my hand affectionately over hers and said, "And you, being the person you've always been, came all the way across the bay just to meet with a hoofer who's desperate for work."

Nancy conferred briefly with the tabletop again. "Well, not exactly. I suspected you'd be at the Claremont and I thought this would also be a chance to talk to you about—. Well, that's why the trip to this luncheonette is in no way a waste if she doesn't show up." She looked at the Bulova watch I had given her for her twenty-first birthday. "Miss Georgia Peach is already ten minutes late, so the heck with her." Nancy was kindhearted to a fault, but she was also pragmatic enough to know that someone who was late for a first interview, especially when Nancy was doing the girl such a big favor, would certainly show up late for the job itself. In Sally Rand's world, that was not allowed.

"What is it that you wanted to talk to me about?" I asked, not unwarily.

She leaned forward. "Ray, I'd like you to consider being Sally's orchestra leader at the Music Box. Fourteen pieces. She's doing very well here on the West Coast, and when the fair at Treasure Island is over, she's doing a new show in a big way. It's going to be racially mixed, too. The Nicholas Brothers are going to be in it, and I know how much you've always loved them. It's going to be a good show. I think it'll have a long run."

She leaned back and judged the initial reaction on my face. Disliking what she saw, she added in the reproachful tone that still inspired fear within me, "You'd be in one place, Ray. Imagine! Living in the same town for more than two weeks of your godforsaken life."

I looked around for our waitress, hoping that the delivery of our meal might buy me a few extra beats to figure out my response, but she was nowhere to be seen. "It doesn't sound like I'd get to play very much, Nancy," I said. "That means a lot to me, you know. I get to lose myself when I'm playing."

She was annoyed with me now. "You've lost too much of yourself already, Ray. Who does it serve? Who does it help?"

"Me, Nancy. It's how I get by."

She sat back in the booth. "Well, the other offer was to do the same job for Sally's road tour, but I don't think I'd be doing you any favors there. Tough schedule, crummy accommodations. The only appeal for you is that it would get you even farther off the beaten track. But the Music Box job . . . please, Ray, come along with me back to Treasure Island and at least meet with Sally. You've never sat and had a real conversation with her. She's a swell person."

So as not to be rude when Nancy obviously was trying her best to help me, I agreed to go with her and discuss the offer with Sally Rand. We decided, since both our waitress and our food had clearly been spirited away by gnomes, to get something quick to eat at the fair.

Nancy signaled to a very distraught man with a big head of shiny black hair who was stationed at the luncheonette's cash register. He rushed over to us. "Yes, yes?"

"Are you the manager?" Nancy asked.

"I am, sadly, the owner." He spoke in what I thought might be an Aegean accent, a thick one, whatever it was.

"I'm sorry, but we're going to have to leave. The service here is very poor," said Nancy, who rarely complained about anything.

"Not poor, miss. Vanished." He displayed inexplicable anger toward us. "What did you say to my waitress?"

I intervened. "Hold on a second. We had about as brief an exchange with your waitress as anyone could have. We ordered today's special and I asked for plain milk with my coffee. She never said a word to us."

The owner glared at me. "You were the last table she waited on.

After that, she went straight into the kitchen and out the back door, so my cook tells me. Out the back door into the street, you understand? In her uniform that I supplied! So I lose the uniform, I lose my waitress, now I am the waitress for the rest of the day."

I wanted to say that if *he* was going to be the waitress for the rest of the day, it was probably just as well that he'd lost the girl's uniform. But I thought better of making the joke.

His eyes raged first at me and then at Nancy. "What did you say to her that would make her leave?" he implored. "Tell me! Why did she leave?"

I started to feel sorry for the guy and looked over the check that the vanished waitress had left us, figuring I'd pay half of it, just to be kind. I discovered, to my immense curiosity, that our waitress had known even as she took our order that she was never going to bring us our food, because at the bottom she had written "5," which I took to be our booth number, and by it an "NC," for "No Charge."

I put two dollars down on the table and showed the check to Nancy, pointing out what I'd found odd about it.

"I agree," she said. "If she wasn't going to charge us, why on earth would she leave us the check?"

With that we departed the Centaur Luncheonette, which I vowed never to visit again. But as Nancy well knew, my vows were more than capable of being broken.

21

The Gayway

Every high-minded exposition over the last fifty years (Nancy explained to me) has opened with great fanfare and received waves of public acclaim for its glorification of the noblest achievements and loftiest aspirations of humanity, its celebration of our greatest ideals and endeavors presented in edifying displays housed in grand galleries and pristine palaces.

And when that fails to draw a crowd, they bring in the girlie shows.

The amusement area of the fair, located next to the parking lot and behind Pacifica's back, was officially deemed the Gayway. Ah, now we were in our element! Farewell Atlantis, hello Atlantic City. The smell of burnt cotton candy, the happy staccato of shooting galleries with the celebratory clang each time a bullet finds its mark, the sweet fumes of frying dough and frying tube steaks and frying onions, and the stirring polyphony of converging music: "East Side, West Side" on the carousel's calliope concurrent with the penny arcade's player piano spooling out a chorus of "Twelfth Street Rag," while "Tuxedo Junction" emanating from a public address speaker on my left intersects with "The Boulevard of Broken Dreams" on the countertop radio at Bascomb's Butter-Bathed Corn-on-the-Cob.

Across the way from Ripley's Odditorium and the Hindu Temple of Magic, flanked by the Mystery of Life exhibition (where responsible parents could learn how babies were made) and a tropical drink stand (where Nancy and I pacified our appetites with frankfurts and grapeade) stood the proud effrontery of Sally Rand's Nude Ranch.

There was no promise in the billing outside that admission would buy you a glimpse of Miss Rand or her famous fans or bubble. But twice a week, Sally did visit the rodeo-themed girlie show that bore her name, signing autographs and consoling those exiting gentleman who'd mistakenly believed that the word *nude* actually meant nude.

With a smile of apology for the lurid spiel of the Nude Ranch's carnival barker, Nancy led me past a kiosk where a brunette who might herself have been one of the cowgirls was selling tickets. "Hi, Miss Carmack," she said to Nancy, "how are you today?" I savored that Nancy was no longer Mrs. Parminter, her second married name. Small victories.

Nancy led me through a door behind the ticket booth marked PRIVATE. The dark, hot corridor beyond it had the pleasing amusement-park smell of timber that has sat all summer in the sun. One bare overhead lightbulb offered just enough assistance to guide us past a doorman who was sitting guard by the wings of the stage.

We were careful not to wake him from his vigil. We passed a makeshift changing area where dressing tables and wardrobe racks were walled in by sheets hanging from a suspended clothesline. A sheet of paper held in place by a clothespin said: DRESSING ROOM— NO VISITORS.

"Are you sure it's all right for me to be here?" I asked Nancy. "I mean, isn't it private?"

She laughed richly at my concern. "Don't be foolish—they wear more offstage than they do when they're on."

We came to a door marked MANAGEMENT. "Just wait here a minute while I see if Sally's busy," said Nancy. She knocked on the door, then entered, leaving me alone for the moment.

A woman emerged from the changing area and asked if I had a light. I searched my pockets, knowing I probably didn't. She was dressed from the waist up in nothing more than a long western kerchief hanging loose around her neck, which covered some but never all of her bosom. She also wore a fringed apron made from fake buckskin, like the abbreviated front of a very short cowgirl skirt. A small holster containing a toy gun was stitched on the apron's waist just below her navel. She may have had on some sort of G-string, but if so, it was completely obscured by her graciously ample derriere. End of wardrobe.

I apologetically informed her I was matchless. She chose not to challenge my assertion and was about to say something interesting when the door to Sally's office opened. Nancy waved me in, rolling her eyes at the tableau of me standing there with a half-naked woman at my side. "Boy, I can't leave you alone for thirty seconds. Get in here."

The office had enough room for a small rolltop desk and a card table. There was an old-fashioned vertical phone sitting on the desk. A map of the United States bore little paper flags of different colors that denoted either Sally's upcoming tour or her secret plan to conquer the United States where its citizens would least expect it.

There was an unreasonably beautiful blonde sitting at the card table writing a letter. She put down her fountain pen and graced me with a smile.

"Hello again, Ray, it's a pleasure to see you," she said and stood to greet me. All of five foot one, she looked as graceful and lithesome in a flowered rayon shift as she did onstage in a thin layer of mother-of-pearl body paint. Her hand, as she shook mine, was cool and small. It was rumored her shoe size was four and a half.

We talked about the days in which our lives had overlapped, when I'd first met Nancy and she and Sally had alternated between being artist's models in the afternoon and "living statues" in the late-night glamour shows of the period. Years later, Sally had cleverly concocted her fan dance and then her bubble routine, which had kept her exposed to the public for well over a decade, even as she concealed a reputation in the industry for being a financially savvy entrepreneur.

She moved the conversation fairly swiftly to business but was very human about it. "Nancy and I talk," she said, "as one does with a trusted friend, and we think we'd like you to try your hand at being my musical director. I know from the discs you've cut with Jack Donovan that you're a fine arranger, and everybody knows you play a remarkable tenor sax." She waved her hand at the map with its paper flags. "And there's no one who knows the road better than I, so I know what your life is like. I've got a top-notch show moving into the Music Box and, knock wood, we'll be good there for a couple of years. San Francisco is a beautiful city. You could pick your own house band, I figure fourteen pieces with you playing tenor and leading it. I'll let you do a specialty number each night, and you play for dancing, too, so you can work in a couple of jazz numbers there. It may not be a swing band, but it's also not traveling on a stale-smelling bus for fourteen hours trying to get to the Hotel Mandrake in Lansing, Michigan, where the crowd will ask if you can play 'Lady of Spain.' "

Nancy added, "You could also be doing more recording if you were here. It's not New York or L.A., but there is session work and KPO has just built a new studio . . ." She looked at Sally, who finished the pitch.

"It's nice here, Ray. You could even make some new friends, instead of being limited to the guys in the Donovan band and the bartender at whatever hotel you're stuck at each week. So how about it?"

I knew she was offering me this primarily because it was something Nancy wanted, out of concern for me. That's why I couldn't even begin to consider it. Sally Rand had not sat up in the middle of the night and said, "Ray Sherwood! He's just the man for the job." It was extremely kind of Nancy (and Sally), but it sounded an awful lot like charity.

"Sally, it's a very generous offer. My problem is that I've just agreed to orchestrate an extremely modern, adventurous composition that's going to be performed here on Treasure Island, and for this I've been paid top dollar." (Well, it was as top as Gail's dollars could afford.) "I really can't undertake any other assignments until my creative obligations are met."

Sally gave Nancy a look that asked, *Did I do the best I could?*

The girl from the ticket booth appeared in the doorway. "Miss Rand, the badminton match just ended and we usually get a lot of file-outs at this point, so if you want to . . . ?"

Sally nodded. "Ray, wonderful to see you after all these years. Please do come to any of my shows, as my guest." She followed the box-office girl out of the room.

"This was very kind of you," I said to Nancy when we were alone.

Nancy shrugged, sat down at the desk, and started thumbing through some telegrams. "The offer was real. You have too much talent to be working the way you're working."

"Jack Donovan runs a good outfit."

"That life's only okay for kids on the way up, or for guys your age who can't do any better. Excuse me." She picked up the phone and asked the Treasure Island operator for an Exbrook exchange.

She had a little frame from Woolworth's on the top of the desk. There was a picture of a teenage boy in it, a little full in the face and full of himself, in my opinion. I asked her, annoyed, "Is that Parminter's kid?"

"Busy?" said Nancy into the phone. "Thank you, Operator, I'll try again later." She hung up and turned to me. "I told you before, he's not a kid, Ray. He's in college now. I may never see him again but he *was* my stepson for a short while. There's nothing wrong with me having his photo on my desk."

"But where's a picture of Linney?" I demanded. "You have Clifford Parminter Junior but not Linney? What kind of a mother are you?"

Nancy moved her hand toward a drawer in the rolltop desk, hesitated, then opened the drawer and took out a small rosewood frame. "I'm a good mother, Ray. And I wasn't the worst wife, either." She handed the frame to me. "I put it away when I knew you'd be coming in. That's why I had you wait outside."

The picture was slightly more recent than the one I kept in my wallet.

She asked, "Okay?"

I handed it back to her. "Yes. I'm sorry." She gave me one slow nod. "And thanks for trying to help me."

She started to put the frame on top of the desk, but thought better of it and kept it in her hands, facedown. "Thanks for coming out here," she replied. "I'm sorry if it was a waste of your time. Maybe I'll see you again before you leave town. Here's my telephone number." She scribbled something on the back of a business card and handed it to me. "If you lose it, I'm in the telephone book, under Carmack." I put the card in my wallet and gave her a clumsy hug good-bye.

Just around the corner from Sally Rand's was an area called the Scotch Village, and God knows I liked Scotch as well as the next man. In this case, the next man was on the bar stool to my left in the Village's Tam O'Shanter Inn. Usually I didn't drink before eight, but the way my meeting had ended, I needed one.

I probably didn't need the two further that I had. I wasn't ossified, but I wasn't sober either. In the twenties, we used to call this state "soaked with a bar rag." I walked out of the Scotch Village with my nerves still on edge, but the bathos in the booze was making me feel sorry for myself as well. A bad sign.

To reach the ferry back to Oakland, I had to walk through the enclosed sideshow part of the Gayway. I disliked freak shows intensely, particularly where they were real. Luckily, most of the attractions here were either circus art, such as sword swallowers or human pincushions, or patently fake, like the Headless Man, or this one here—

"Sealed in a glass coffin without food, water, or oxygen for over two months, owing to her amazing ability to suspend her heartbeat and intake of oxygen. Step inside and see this lovely young thing buried alive, and yet she survives!"

A barker in a boater hat waved with a narrow cane. A crowd was forming around him, including a number of children without parents. I was always horrified at how many adults, arriving at noon at an amusement park or fair, could actually hand their eight-year-old child a quarter or two, say "Now meet me back here at five o'clock," and assume that the world would not go awry in the ensuing five hours, that nothing would fall, collapse, jump its tracks, go wild, or catch fire. My own parents did that with me, and they were caring and well-intentioned.

The barker accelerated the tempo of his pitch. "See this beautiful young woman, who through powers learned in ancient Tibet only requires the amount of air contained in a balloon this size—" He blew up a small pink balloon that had the words BURIED ALIVE printed on it. "Here you are, kid, you can keep that—she only requires *that much air* to remain alive for over a month. This is not magic, ladies and gents, these are skills that anyone can acquire, even you kids, if you dedicate yourself as this young woman has—"

"Don't tell them that," I said to the man. If he heard an aggressive ring to my voice, he heard right.

"What's the problem, pal?"

I was at his side. The platform gave him a four-foot advantage over me, but I didn't care. I had the three shots of Scotch on my side. "I said, Don't tell them that stuff, they're kids, they'll believe you."

He spoke in a low voice. "Listen, it's a harmless little novelty, everybody knows—"

"It's not harmless!"

"All part of the show, folks!" he announced, then hissed back at me, "Go find somebody else to bother, jughead, it's been a slow day in a dead season and I'm trying to earn a living here. Now move along." He raised his voice, "Skills that anyone can acquire—"

"I'm serious," I said. "Stop it or else."

He gave my shoulder a firm shove with the tip of his cane. "Buzz off."

Men standing on platforms shouldn't shove me with a cane, especially near the part of my arm where I was stabbed the night before, and especially if I've had a few drinks. I watched myself grab the end of the cane, pull it from his hand, hook its handle around his ankle, and yank him down off the platform.

The children screamed as he fell clumsily to the ground, but he got right back to his feet in an instant and came at me hard. I managed to poke him back with the cane as an excited crowd gathered, but he wasn't going to walk away without paying me back.

"Don't you dare tell them that!" I snarled in a voice I didn't recognize. "Don't you ever tell them a person can go without air for ten days or ten hours or ten minutes!" It sounded like a hell of an asinine thing to have a fistfight about, but as he grabbed the cane from me and tossed it aside, we apparently were going to. He was a better fighter than I was, but to my advantage, I wasn't minding anything he did to me as long as I could do something—a blow—something—another blow to my stomach. We grappled, neither able to throw a punch. I yelled out to the frightened children, whose parents were wisely moving them away from me, "Kids, listen, he was lying! You can't live without air. After three minutes, you get dizzy, what they call unconscious, and after that, you'd get very sick—" He kicked my knees out from underneath me and clamped his hand over my mouth, and it felt like the bastard was deliberately trying to stop me from saving the kids, he wouldn't let me warn them. He was on top of me now and with his other hand he pinched my nose, and I couldn't breathe. Winded from the fight, I needed air, but then I thought, This was what it was like, let it happen, let me learn what *she* felt. The noise of the crowd moved them farther and farther away along the shoreline of the big black pool that was forming around me . . . I started counting the seconds, to see if I would reach two hundred . . .

22

The Sleep

"One, two, three . . ."

Linney looked around, thrilled. No game other than hide-and-go-seek made her heart pound so. The counting, those precious, breathless seconds in which to find somewhere safe! Often, at the last moment, having no recourse, she would simply duck behind a tree or the corner of the building, but that was rarely any good. The seeker needed only to shift his vantage point slightly to spot her skirt, shoulder, or rump. It was humiliating to be called out so early in the game, "I see Linney, one-two-three, behind the telephone pole." Sometimes the accusation was vaguely worded and she would wait, in case it was a bluff. "I see Linney, one-two-three, over by the building": anyone could say that. Of course, if she piped up, "Which building? You can't just say 'by the building'!" she'd give up her location. There ought to have been demerit points for people who tricked her that way, but that was life.

The ecstatic terror as the seeker would approach her hiding place! They would be within a few steps, breathing heavily. She would try not to move.

Then the unbearable silence.

Had she been seen? She could try bolting from her spot and out-racing the seeker, gasping a "Home-free-home!" as she tagged "It" (whatever "It" might be—a fireplug, the door to the O'Lunneys' cellar, the telephone pole with the green stripe).

Or she might feel confidence in her hiding place. It took such willpower to do nothing when the seeker was only a few feet away. The urge to abandon the effort, the dread of the big face suddenly thrust into hers, bellowing, "I SEE YOU!" But at last the hunter would move along. She was safe.

Then, after a long silence, the mocking drawl of the seeker. *"I see Linney, one-two-three"*—as if you had fooled them for even a second!—*"hiding behind the stoop of the Butrams' house."* How foolish she would feel.

Or perhaps there would be no call. They had *not* seen her at all. Not at all!

That would be the greatest thrill. All the kids have been called out and you are the last and no one—*no one*—can find you. The place they never thought of looking, the coal bin next to the Cicchettis', the unlocked cab of the Nankins' van. Was there ever such a gorgeous sound as "Linney, you can come out now, you win!" not just called out of hiding by the seeker but by everyone? "Come on, Linney, it's not a trick, we're all in, the game's over!" And finally, you rise from your perfect hiding place and the others marvel, "There? She was there? I would never have thought to look *there*!"

"Thirteen, fourteen, fifteen . . ."

She'd had enough of the embarrassing stoops and humiliating lampposts and being caught first, having to stand by Home for the duration of the game.

"Seventeen, eighteen, nineteen . . ."

There! At the back of the O'Lunneys'. That had never been there before. It could probably just fit her. They'd *never* find her! She raced to it, and just as the cry of "Twenty-five! Ready or not, here I come!" rang out, she nestled into the old icebox that lay abandoned on its back and closed the door above her with a satisfying *clunk*.

It was 6:27 P.M.

I was walking in the front door. "Nance?" I called.

She was in the kitchen, going over some figures in a ledger she'd brought home from work. "I'm here," she said.

"Me too," I said. "That's it for my day."

"You don't have to go out again?" she asked.

I was happier than a kid who's just heard that school is closed on account of snow. "Nance, it turned out to be one of those garden-party socials. They started folding up the chairs at half past five."

I opened the icebox and started looking for the pitcher of ice water we kept there.

"I didn't expect you home for dinner," Nancy said.

"That's okay. Where's Linney?"

"Out playing," she said.

I hummed a chorus of a tune I'd been working on.

"What's that?" Nancy asked.

"Nothing. A Bix Beiderbecke number I'm doing a little chart on." I set down the pitcher. "Linney's playing around here?"

"At the Butrams'."

"Who are the Butrams?"

"They moved in next door to the O'Lunneys."

I poured myself a glass of water and drank it empty without taking a breath. I slapped the glass down on the table. "Think I'll go over there and tell her to come home. It's not often we get to have supper together."

Nancy smiled. "Hate to tell you but she's already had her supper. We usually eat by five-thirty around here, or didn't you know that?"

"Gee, what time is it now?"

She looked at the wall clock. "Six-thirty exactly."

"Isn't that late for Linney to be out?" I asked, grabbing two eggs from the icebox and closing it with a satisfying *clunk*.

Nancy reassured me, "It's July, the sun won't set for hours, she's having fun. I think she can stay out till seven. I mean, she's with all the other kids."

"Okay. I guess I can wait a couple of minutes. I don't mean to be selfish. It's just that I can't get enough of being around her."

I heard a boy's voice calling out, *"Home-free-all!"*

"What are you making?" Nancy asked.

"I'm making myself breakfast."

She closed the ledger and laughed. "You never eat breakfast."

I took out a pot from under the sink and started filling it with tap water. "That's why I'm having it now. You want some?"

She shook her head. "I ate with Linney. I made you up a plate. Didn't you see it in the icebox?"

"I'll have it for breakfast," I said with a laugh. "Right now, I'm going to have me two soft-boiled eggs with toast and marmalade. And coffee."

She said, "You want me to make the coffee?"

"I sure don't want to have mine. Where's the egg timer?"

She got up, pulled open a drawer and handed me the miniature hourglass. "Flip it when you put the eggs in."

I was insulted. "You think I don't grasp the premise?"

She smiled at me. "Twice now you've flipped it over when you turned on the gas below the water. And then you've wondered why your eggs were underdone."

I put the pot of water on the flame.

"Hey," I said. Her head turned quickly as she recognized a specific tone in my voice.

"Ray . . ." she said.

We kissed and tussled with each other for a few moments. She broke away from my embrace and, catching her breath, said, "Your water is boiling."

I dropped the two eggs neatly into the pot and flipped the timer. Nancy was by the door. "Where are you going?" I asked.

"I'll fetch Linney after all. It's so rare the three of us have the evening together. We can get in a game of Uncle Wiggily before she goes to bed."

"That'll be great."

Nancy went out the door. I stared at the egg timer and thought about a chart I'd been wanting to write of "My Blue Heaven." I hummed a bit to myself. I'd voice it for two trumpets, trombone, and tenor sax.

"*Lin-ney! You can come out now!*" called a voice outside. It was a kid, not Nancy. I heard the cry again. The sand or salt or whatever it was in the egg timer was halfway gone.

"*Lin-neyyyyy!*" Nancy's voice took up the call. Well, if there was one thing that always summoned Linney, it was the sound of her mother's voice. They had an understanding with each other. Sometimes they communicated in ways I couldn't comprehend. It was an almost mystical—

"*Linney!*" snapped her mother. I guess she'd done something wrong. That was not a request. That was Nancy's voice of authority.

I decided I'd go outside and give Linney a hug and hoist her onto my shoulders. So what if the eggs were hard-boiled.

I went out the door and angled down to where the kids were. They were calling, "Linney, you can come out now, you win!"

I saw my wife searching hastily about our neighbors' yards, wearing an expression of mounting anxiety that frightened me, for she was always the calm one in a crisis. She kept calling out our daughter's name. I joined in, and with each plea for which there was no response, I felt an ominous panic rising within me.

Nancy came down the far side of the O'Lunneys' and I moved quickly toward her. We both saw the icebox at the same moment.

Our eyes met and we knew. We raced to the icebox. I was closer and I screamed, "Look away!" as I pulled open its door . . .

23

The Wake

. . . and air rushed into my lungs.

I heard a loud scuffling sound and saw Lieutenant Bob Culpepper standing over me, while his friend Russ Hewett was doing an effective job of holding on to the barker, stopping him from trying to smother me again.

The lieutenant shook his head and took out a handkerchief from his breast pocket.

"You're a mess, Sherwood," he said, and held the handkerchief against a cut on my forehead. "I don't think anyone's going to be proposing to you today."

24

The Cover-up

"I'm currently holding you as a material witness to your own stupidity," Culpepper told me in what was quickly becoming my permanent digs on Treasure Island, the interview room at police headquarters in the Administration Building. "Stu Webster, that's the fellow you had the fight with, he's not going to press charges against you. You can thank my friend Russ Hewett for that. He has a lot of sway on the island. But Maria Elisea may file a complaint. Here, hold this against that big bruise." He tossed me an orange Popsicle Twin bar, still in its wrapper.

"Thanks. Who's Maria Elisea?" I said.

"The blond receptionist at the desk downstairs. Russ Hewett and I were bringing her back an order of Chicken in the Rough from the Estonian Village when we saw the commotion. I save your skin, Russ finds your wallet where it fell from your pocket, Stu starts to say it's his, I have a second exchange with Stu about that, I take you here while Russ tries to convince Stu not to press charges against you, and in all the confusion . . . we lost Maria's Chicken in the Rough. Here's your wallet, by the way—Russ just came by with it. I understand you had dinner with him last night. Small world."

I pocketed the wallet. "Thank him for me, will you?"

"You can thank him yourself. He's giving you a ride back to your hotel. Meanwhile, madame, your makeup artiste has arrived."

I'd called Nancy at the Nude Ranch and asked her to come over with a full theatrical makeup kit. I wasn't going to be able to take the bandstand at the Claremont with my face in its current condition. My only hope, unless Culpepper's Popsicle had supernatural properties, was for someone who knew her way around stage makeup to ply her craft on my face. The only one who was immediately available on the island, had access to such makeup, and whose help I knew I could bank upon was Nancy.

"She's here already?"

Culpepper nodded toward the hall. "I've been with her out there for ten minutes. Wanted to get some background on you."

He stared at me for a second, and I realized why he was being so helpful to a man who'd started a brawl at his beloved fair.

"Sorry about your daughter, Ray," he said.

I nodded. "Thanks."

"Can I ask how old she was?"

"She was eight, Bob."

He sat down across from me, crossed his hands, and slouched over the table. "Listen to me, okay? Myself, one guy, I've had to deal with four such deaths in the time I've been on the force. All four kids had loving, devoted parents. Starting around 1929, people started tossing out their old iceboxes and the death rate for kids started climbing. There ought to be a law says you have to remove the goddamn door before you can throw it in a dump or leave it sitting out in your backyard, but there isn't."

His look invited me to speak, and so I did. "Hers was a broken-down icebox in the backyard of the O'Lunneys. A man was going to come cart it away for them the next morning. The O'Lunneys wouldn't have harmed a fly. They loved my daughter. O'Lunney had a stroke a few months later, and I swear it was because of that."

"Game of hide-and-seek?"

I nodded. "Yeah."

He mumbled to himself, "Yeah. Hide-and-seek. You have no idea . . . what am I saying? Of course you do." He fumbled in his pocket and produced a sealed pack of cigarettes. "Smoke?"

"I don't smoke," I said.

He put the pack away. "Yeah, it just helps to have them to offer, in my work. I'm cigars myself." He looked at me. "Ray, you can tell a kid not to do this, not to do that, there are a million ways kids can hurt themselves, and if you made a list of ninety-nine don'ts, you'd still forget to say 'And don't put your tongue on the railroad track in freezing weather' or 'Don't put the Philco by the sink when your brother's taking a bath there' or 'Don't hide in the trunk of the DeSoto when it's a hundred degrees out and everyone's gone home.' The things I run into, Ray. And half the time I'm the one who has to break the news to the parents, and usually they're the most conscientious people. It's a miracle any kid gets through life, but most of them do. Other parents ignore their kids, leave them alone while they step into a store to do some shopping, let them play out in the street, and somehow nothing bad happens. Why you? It was just the odds getting played out."

I took the Popsicle still in its wrapper away from my face. "You have any kids, Bob?" I asked.

"Nah, not me. I'd need a wife for that," he said.

"Well, then I don't know if you can understand. You're walking down the street and if your child gets hit by a meteorite, it's your fault. You should have done something about it. You shouldn't have walked on that street, or on that side of it, or on her left instead of on her right. You're her parent. You're not allowed to let her die."

He owned a memorable scowl. "So what then? You tour from one dead town to another—"

"Towns that Linney and I never went to. Towns where she was never likely to go. So there are no memories there, real or imagined. Linney isn't there, wouldn't have ever been there, she's missing nothing there. . . . I don't see her friends growing up, don't see the high school she would have gone to, don't meet the boys she might have kissed. And that's the prescription, Bob. If you have a better plan for me, just let me know."

"It's no way to live," he said.

"It's the only way I can, Bob. And I don't know that I'm right to even be doing that."

He got up. "I'll send your wife in. After that, you're free to go. You ever start another fight on my island, I guarantee you'll stay in one place for a while, and it won't be the Hotel Claremont." He indicated the Popsicle in my hand. "Make sure you leave me the wrapper when you're done with that, okay? I'm saving up for a Schwinn racer."

He left the room and a minute later Nancy was allowed in. "Nice," she said, appraising my face.

She opened her makeup kit. I'd last seen that case in the days when her motionless pose as Lady Godiva had been the best frozen treat at the Fourteenth Street Theatre. She'd been seventeen at the time, although she'd claimed she was eighteen. I forgave her the lie, since I'd told her I was twenty-five. At nineteen and eighteen respectively, we'd been among the youngest parents in the maternity ward of Columbia Hospital, although back then it wasn't that unusual for people to get married and have kids straight out of high school.

I didn't mean to be an ingrate, but I said, "Did you have to tell the lieutenant about Linney?"

She set out a few tubes of makeup. "He was going to arrest you. His understanding was that you had started the fight. He told me what the sideshow exhibit was and I felt that if I explained to him, he might not bring you up on charges."

"I don't like sympathy," I muttered.

"No fooling," she said. "Lift your head a bit."

Nancy did a fine camouflage job with my bruises and reassured me that I'd probably be two hundred percent better tomorrow. We walked out of the room together. Russ Hewett was chatting with Culpepper and a uniformed officer by the water cooler. Their conversation stopped dead as I appeared.

Russ tossed away his drinking cup. "Sherwood. Well, not too bad. Your wife is a miracle worker."

I agreed with him. "You're right. Nancy has always made me look good."

25

Railroad Tracks

I said good-bye to Nancy, thanked Culpepper, and headed with Russ to his Studebaker, which had its own reserved space in the crescent of the Administration Building. In three minutes, we had scooted onto the Bay Bridge back toward Oakland.

"Traffic's getting lighter every day leaving the fair," noted Russ. "It's a darn good thing we're making an airport out of the island. Otherwise this whole exposition would have been a financial disaster. Can you imagine those idiots in New York? When their fair closes, they won't have a thing to show for it, not one tick."

"They're keeping the Trylon and Perisphere, aren't they?" I asked.

He shook his head. "Nope, it's all coming down. You understand that, as a contractor, the idea of building something that's only supposed to last two years is—well, I guess it would be like you forming a band that could only be heard once."

"If only that had been true of Guy Lombardo," I muttered.

We reached a tollgate, and he indicated a sticker on his car that allowed him to drive through without paying. He told me he needed to swing by his home to get some schematics for a meeting he had with the planning commission not very far from the Claremont and asked if I minded stopping there before he dropped me off. I told him I was grateful for the lift and to take as long as he needed.

"I was wondering," I began. This was awkward, and I tried to sound casual. "I don't suppose Gail might be at your house just now?"

"No, generally she only comes by on the weekends, to please her mother. She likes having her own place on campus. I can't say as I blame her."

I indicated the swellings on my face. "Well, obviously, Gail is going to see these bruises when we get together tomorrow. I was wondering if it would be all right with you if I gave her a different explanation as to how I got them."

His eyes creased whenever he smiled. "You mean, lie."

"Not really lie as much as omit. I'd rather not have her aware of my daughter's death. It can color working relationships. I don't want people making allowances for me just because something horrible happened to a little girl. It's Linney who lost her life, not me."

He considered this and said, "Well, since she's not my daughter, I suppose it's okay." After a moment, he gruffly mumbled, "Sorry—of course I was referring to Gail, not your child . . . must have sounded heartless."

I assured him I had understood what he meant.

You could tell that the modernization of the neighborhood around his home was not a high priority for the city fathers, because it still relied on the old two-light semaphore signals on the corner. A bell rang as a stop sign went up with an accompanying red light.

After a few seconds of silence, Russ said with some discomfort, "But if I were you, I would mention to Gail that you're married, seeing as the two of you will be working together and I note you don't wear a wedding ring. I *would* feel the responsibility to say something to her about *that*. If you didn't."

"Nancy and I were divorced a year after my daughter died."

"Oh," he said. "Oh, well, I suppose that's all right then."

He eased the Studebaker into his driveway and silenced the engine. "I won't be more than a minute." He paused. "Do you need to make use of the facilities?"

I told him I was fine. He left me and let himself into his house.

My face was burning. I stepped out of the car and slouched back against the trunk, hoping the cool afternoon breeze fresh off the bay would soothe my skin. The street being a cul-de-sac lined on both sides by a tight row of houses, the breeze came at me as if I were standing in a wind tunnel.

A woman at the end of the block had turned in to Chancery Lane and was now walking toward me with an even gait. She was all in white, including her shoes and stockings. It was disquieting, because the last person who'd approached me from a distance in such a steady, assured manner was Marie Prasquier, who'd sat with me, propositioned me, and died. Now it seemed I had an appointment with the White Angel of Death.

I was not much relieved when I realized it was Martha Prentice. She *had* stabbed me, after all. Gail's mother was outfitted in a white uniform that evoked the offices of a doctor. She came to a halt about four feet from me, but her demeanor made it feel more like the distance of a ten-foot pole.

"Good afternoon, Mr. Sherwood," she said in the same tone used by my fourth-grade teacher when she'd caught me cheating on a geography test. "If you're waiting for Gail, I'm not expecting her."

I looked to see if her hands contained any sharp objects. "No, I'm waiting for your . . . for Russ. He's inside. He's giving me a ride to the Claremont."

She looked at my face, which was side-lit by the sun. "Do you always wear makeup, Mr. Sherwood, or is this a special occasion?"

I offered what I thought was as good an explanation as she deserved. "I had a little fracas with a librarian who wanted to rearrange my face in alphabetical order. I'm a hard-line Dewey decimal man." This didn't play, so I tried being honest. "Truth is, I was over on Treasure Island and I didn't like what one of the barkers was telling some of the kids. I took issue with him and . . ." I gestured to my face.

She allowed herself a clinical look at my various contusions and obtrusions. "This shouldn't be too bad by tomorrow. Try and keep some ice against it while you sleep."

I've always been annoyed when receptionists in doctors' offices act as if they have medical degrees. "Is that your expert opinion?" I said, nodding toward her mock nurse's uniform.

Her back stiffened. "The fact that I show up at a medical practice dressed appropriately has always indicated my professionalism. I work any day I want for the top doctors and dentists in the area. I'm always on request. The waiting list is mine, not theirs."

"I'm sorry, Mrs. Prentice," I said. "I didn't mean to be rude."

"Of course you did," she said. I heard Hewett's front door open. Her eyes looked beyond me and monitored Russ. "Listen to me now," she said in a low tone. "It was convenient our meeting this way, because otherwise I was going to have to call you at your hotel. I want to see you tomorrow. I'll meet you in the Claremont lobby at one o'clock."

She didn't ask if it would be convenient for me. "All right," I agreed, because I couldn't think what else to say.

"One more thing," she added hurriedly. "I don't want you working with my daughter again until after I've met with you."

I heard Russ's footsteps approaching. "But we're starting on the arrangement tomorrow morning."

"I can't meet with you any sooner, it would be pointless. Tomorrow at one is the earliest it can be. You're not to do anything with her until then. Hello, Russ," she said, instantly shifting tone.

Russ had several rolled-up charts under his arm. "Martha, I have to go over these diagrams with the idiots at the commission and they'll have the usual lame questions, so make something to eat I can warm up when I get home, would you? Shouldn't be later than seven or eight. Ready, Sherwood?"

There's a symbol in music indicating a dead stop that the player must observe until he's directed to continue. In swing parlance, we refer to this symbol as "railroad tracks," because it's notated by two parallel slashes in the music.

Martha Prentice had just given me my second slash.

Russ got back into his car and Martha gave me a last, pointed look that pricked at me like a vaccination. "I'll be seeing you, Mr. Sherwood," she said.

As we pulled out of the driveway, her stare pulled at me as if it were drawing blood.

26

Railroad Crossing

My appearance caused some minor comment on the bandstand that night. Jack did not have me sing "Beef Lo Mein" or "Too Bad for You." Frankie Pompano could see the makeup I was wearing from where he was sitting and asked if I wanted to go out with him tomorrow for a henna. Vera stated for the benefit of the trombone section that she'd known I had a swelled head for years.

I didn't know what the hell to do about Martha Prentice's admonition. Gail and I had agreed to begin work the next day at eleven, at her mother's home. How was I supposed to cancel it, and what reason would I give?

On my breaks, I tried calling Gail at the Berkeley Club from the coin telephones near the men's lounge, but the first time she was out and the second time the club's switchboard was closed for the night. I realized I'd just have to try her in the morning. I requested a wake-up call from the Claremont operator for nine.

The next morning my phone rang at the appointed hour. The soreness from my fistfight came on slowly, like music from a radio as the tubes warm up.

"Hello," I uttered with some effort.

"Good morning, Mr. Sherwood, this is your nine A.M. wake-up call."

"Thank you, Operator," I grunted.

"Rise and shine," she advised.

"Yes, thanks."

"Up and at 'em, sweetie," she further counseled. "Don't want to keep the world waiting. Big day, lots to do."

"Operator?"

"And just between you and me, that girl you're meeting? I think she likes you."

I was awake now. "Gail."

"Morning, Ray. See, I've been here in the lobby since 8:30 but they wouldn't ring your room for me because you had a wake-up call for nine. So at 8:59, I told them to let me be your wake-up call. I thought maybe we could go out for breakfast before we get cooped up for the day. Oh, you're not in bed with some shameless hussy, are you?"

"No, but listen, I haven't shaved—"

"Gee, okay, then you better get yourself in gear. Oh, and Ray? Dress your sharpest, 'cause several lounge lizards down here have already mistaken me for a woman named 'Hey Good-looking.'"

Ten minutes later I came down the stairs. She had been accurate in her description of herself, but when she beheld my somewhat lumpy countenance, she chirped, "Wow, is it too late to cancel our budding relationship? I mean, I could be back in Berkeley in less than half an hour if I catch the right trolley, and we could pretend we never met and go our own ways. Gosh, Ray." I grimaced as she ran her cool hand over the bump on my forehead and the small swelling on my upper left jaw. "What the Sam Hill happened?"

I told her the story about my dispute with a sideshow barker, omitting any reference to Linney, and she seemed to accept it. But I still hadn't figured out how to explain that I'd been temporarily banned from seeing her.

What exactly was it that her mother had warned me against? Her emphasis had been on when we started the *work*, hadn't it? My memory was conveniently blurry about this. If so, maybe she simply didn't want us alone in the house together, at least not until she knew more about me. Perhaps she was making arrangements to *not* be working on those days when Gail and I *were,* so that she could serve as our de facto duenna.

But if Gail and I were simply out, in public . . . what possible objection could she have? The hell with Martha's railroad tracks across my garden path.

We stepped outside. The forecast had been for rain in the afternoon, but the morning was as lovely as Oakland could be. I assumed Gail was largely responsible for this.

I turned to Gail and said, "Listen, when we made our plans, I forgot that I have to meet with a booking agent here at the hotel at one. Between getting banged up yesterday and having to be back here in a couple of hours, we're not going to get as much accomplished as I'd like. While it's still sunny, why don't we just sort of lark around, go to a zoo or a park or something?"

"Why, what a great way to kick off our project," she murmured. "Like beginning a piano recital with a forty-eight-bar rest. Or attacking the enemy with a truce." She studied my face, seriously and searchingly, and continued, "Look, I know I act kind of flip, and we both know some of it is to try to charm you into doing this immense job for me, and if along the way I'm finding myself more than a little charmed by you, that much the better. . . . But look at me now, Ray. This composition of mine, its performance at the fair—this means more to me than heaven and earth and all the rice in China. You're not going to let me down, are you? You don't know how important *Swing* is to me or how much I'm counting on you to make it happen. I'm not as tough as I look, you know."

Yeah, she looked so tough. I mussed with her hair because her hair was perfectly suited for such activity. "I won't let you down. I have a pretty good sense of how much time our work will take. Believe me, I've had my ration of stupidity for the year." I indicated the bump on my head. "I'll be smart from here on out."

Lake Merritt

LAKE MERRITT AND LAKESIDE PARK, OAKLAND

In addition to knowing how to build an island, it seemed Oakland had equal success in building a lake. They did this by damming an inlet of the San Francisco Bay and surrounding its banks with apartments and government buildings, so that it now sat like a huge, flat amethyst gripped in a formal triangular setting.

Our "motor launch" wasn't quite what I'd envisioned when I'd seen a sign near the Lake Merritt boathouse listing hourly rental rates. It was just an electric-powered dinghy with two seats side by side. But look who was at my side.

There was a grassy border on the narrow southwest bank of the lake. I noticed a double flash of light coming from it and aimed our way. It took me a moment to realize it was sunlight reflecting off someone's binoculars. Enjoy the view of Gail, lucky bystander, I thought. I sure was doing the same.

I'd been pretty excited that the boats were billed as "radio equipped." I'd pictured ship-to-shore communication, but as I searched for the microphone, Gail pointed to the dashboard, where there was a simple Philco car-radio tuner. Thirty seconds later, "Sunrise Serenade," with Glenn Miller's reed section playing in cheerfully octaved thirds, drifted up from below our knees out of a speaker planted somewhere under the dash.

While I'd been standing on line for the boat rental, Gail had gone to a sandwich shop so that we could have a shipboard brunch before I returned to the hotel. Now she produced from a brown paper bag two expertly folded wax-paper packages and two pop bottles. She was able to figure out a way to open the bottles using a fixture on the side of the boat that may or may not have been designed for that purpose. We split our sandwiches fifty-fifty, Neufchâtel with olives and a deviled ham, both of which inexplicably and for the first time in my life tasted wonderful to me. The radio station played a string of great recordings until suddenly Vera Driscoll's voice came over the speaker crooning "Believe You Me." I was uncomfortable listening to Vera while I was with Gail, and particularly restless with the sound of my noodling on the clarinet during the song's intro.

I snapped off the radio, and Gail protested, "Why'd you do that? I love that arrangement of yours." Here on the glazed lake under a smooth blue sky, the song suddenly evoked smoky ballrooms, shrill laughter from intoxicated couples, and lonely hotel rooms. It was like stepping inside on a flawless afternoon so as to catch a breath of stale air. I mumbled something about liking the moment we were living right now better than a playback of my recorded past, and it surprised me to realize I meant it.

I noticed the same dual flashes of light aimed in our direction as before. They were much brighter now, because we were on the southwest side of the lake, closer to whoever was watching us.

It was such a strange sensation, being in a huge body of water, miles wide, yet in the center of a city, walled in at all compass points. I felt confined yet also exposed.

I was becoming extremely interested that the person with the binoculars continued to be extremely interested in us. The reflection from his paired lenses danced around our little motorboat with the persistence of two bumblebees who refused to be waved away.

Whoever was so intrigued was certainly not a trained detective, for no professional would do such a clumsy job of allowing me to note his curiosity. Unless, of course, he wanted me to know we were being watched.

I said nothing to Gail about this, because there was every possibility that our onlooker was not a he at all but her mother, shadowing me to make sure I hadn't violated her edict.

I was surprised how quickly the sky went dark at the thought of Martha Prentice. Several brown clouds had intervened between the sun and the lake.

We'd been doing a mixture of drifting and cruising. I guided the motorboat at an oblique angle, moving south of our watcher on the west bank, seeming to leave him—or her—behind us. But as I did so, I also slowly edged closer to the shore. I then turned the boat around and headed back north and east, directing our prow and my gaze away from our observer, moving at our slowest powered speed.

I said, "Gail, if it's okay with you, I'd like to make a very sharp turn as fast as I can get this boat to go."

She regarded me with amused interest. "Any particular reason why?"

"I'm a motorboat enthusiast," I said. "Just curious how this maneuvers compared to the Broome 218," I said, inverting the street address of my first apartment in Manhattan.

She laughed and said, "You want to take a joyride, you found yourself the right girl, Ray. As a matter of fact"—she reached under the dash and flipped a little switch—"you've sort of been cruising in second the whole time."

I flushed. "You might have told me."

"Oh, I kind of hoped you were setting me up. I was waiting for you to tell me that the boat's run out of voltage and we're stranded here together until help comes in the morning." With studied mock innocence she batted her eyes, and as far as my heart was concerned, she'd hit one right out of the park. Her mother's admonition was getting harder to adhere to every minute.

I cautioned her to hang on to something. She grabbed the side of the boat with her right hand and gripped a handle on the dashboard with her left. I eased the boat halfway through its turn, as if we might be heading back to the south, letting the boat seem to swing on its own just a little to the west, and then I floored the accelerator, spinning the wheel to my right as I torpedoed our craft directly at the watcher on the shore.

All right, it's not like we were going to set any speed records. But we were the fastest thing on Lake Merritt at the moment and I'd achieved my goal, which was to catch our observer off guard. I'd kept in mind that anything you see coming at you through binoculars seems to be closer and gaining on you faster than it really is, and our watcher was startled.

Gail screamed with delight, and whether it was our oncoming vessel or Gail's cry that was more startling, our observer lowered the binoculars, froze for a moment, then turned and headed up the slope to Lakeside Drive.

I swerved the boat hard to the left, as a number of people having their lunch on the slope had started to retreat from us as well. Easing back on the accelerator, I quickly had us cruising toward the middle of the lake again.

"Yeah!" said Gail. "Let's have another one of those!"

I'd seen our watcher for only two or three seconds. It was a woman in a plain brown shift, with longish, stringy blond hair, the color of which looked pretty fake to me. She'd done a decent job of keeping her hand in front of her as she turned and ran, so I had only a general impression of her face.

Of the very limited list of women in the Oakland area who knew me and might have wished to spy on me, I had only a few blond candidates. I very much doubted it was Sally Rand. It's hard to judge the height of someone running away from you uphill, since they're a bit bent over and appear small against the slope, but I certainly thought this woman was taller than Sally's five foot one.

Culpepper had made reference to a blond receptionist at the Administration Building whose lunch of Chicken in the Rough I'd spoiled, but I didn't think she'd take a day off from work to avenge herself.

Of course, it could very easily have been Martha Prentice in a blond wig. The drab, shapeless shift seemed very much her style.

And it might have been Vera. She'd already pursued me to my Claremont bedroom uninvited, so I knew she didn't lack for a sense of intrigue. However, Vera's hair had always struck me as natural looking. Then again, a real blonde who disguised herself with a fake blond wig would be displaying a level of subtlety that I would greatly admire.

But of all the women I'd encountered since coming to the Bay Area, the departing watcher reminded me most of one person I'd first encountered only yesterday and of whom, as today, I'd had only the most momentary glimpse before she ran away.

She looked like the waitress at the Centaur Luncheonette. The woman who had taken a lunch order from Nancy and me and then vanished from the premises without explanation.

28

Martha

HOTEL CLAREMONT
The Beauty Spot of California
BERKELEY, CALIFORNIA

Gail had said she could find her own way from Lake Merritt to her mother's home and asked me to join her there as soon as my business appointment (as we were calling it) was concluded. I hoped that whatever it was that Gail's mother had to say to me, it wouldn't take so long that we couldn't get going on *Swing* that same day. We needed to start our work, and I needed to be back in Gail's exhilarating company.

I walked out of the quickly darkening afternoon and into the Claremont lobby, where I saw that Gail's mother was waiting for me.

She had dressed up for the occasion, and looked . . . pathetic. Her outfit hadn't been fashionable since before the stock market crash. It must have come from the attic or an old trunk, and I could detect the scent of camphor as I approached. The dress's low belted waist drew a stare from several passing women. An equally outdated hat, what they used to call a cloche, sheathed her head like a brimmed skullcap, with a tiny silk flower stitched to its side.

I hadn't fully considered quite how pitiable a life she led as the unacknowledged common-law wife of Russ Hewett. He would probably leave her a pittance if she outlived him. She'd shown such pride in her self-supplied white uniform—her "respectable" side. If we ever got past our rough beginning, and if things evolved warmly between Gail and myself, I vowed to show some kindness to this rather sad woman.

She turned to face me and pushed away her hat's short veil. She'd made herself up far too much, again in a manner reminiscent of the days of Coolidge. Her mouth was painted small but garishly. If one of my fellow band members saw me with this tarted-up version of my maiden aunt, I'd hear about it for days.

"Come on. Outside," she said with no warmth in her tone. Already I was feeling less sorry for her.

By now a battalion of pewter clouds had strategically assembled in the west, directly above Treasure Island, and looked as if they were merely waiting for the right moment to charge the Claremont and spend themselves above us.

Since she ignored the taxis at the cabstand, I assumed that Martha was heading toward a car, although I didn't recall her owning one. Instead, she led me along the path that took us to the rear of the hotel, where a narrow patio faced the gardens that sloped steeply uphill. Aware of the imminent rain, white-jacketed waiters were hurriedly gathering up the linen and silverware from the patio's tables.

We reached the rear parking lot of the hotel, a leveled-off area at the top of its own drive. An attendant in a small shed put down a copy of *Look* magazine. "Your car, sir?" he asked, buttoning up his jacket.

Martha said, "We're just taking a stroll," and handed the boy a dollar bill.

"Stroll away," he said with a broad smile, and went back to his magazine.

Martha led me toward the very back of the lot and turned slowly in the gravel to face me. She took off her hat. Her hair was bobbed in tight curls that verged on the grotesque.

"Well?" she asked, offering me a challenging glare.

I didn't know what she expected me to say. "You've changed the way you do your hair." When she said nothing more, I added, "It's very nice."

Her face registered disbelief and consternation. It was an expression I'd seen on several women's faces when I hadn't understood that I'd done something incredibly wrong.

She gestured to her face and then her dress. "I do all this, make myself look ridiculous, and you still don't recognize me?"

I was bewildered. She *knew* she looked dreadful? "Well, you're, you're Martha Prentice, of course," I said.

She looked around the parking lot as if she desperately needed another woman to come and bear witness to my unspeakable stupidity. "No, I mean, from before. *Here.*"

"Here at the Claremont?" I fumbled. "You mean you saw me on the bandstand before I came to your home, or . . . I'm not sure what you—"

"We were lovers, you crumb," she said quietly, but making no attempt to hide her bitterness. Her painted lips formed a straight line. "Maybe the word *lovers* is a little too kind. We did it together." She nodded toward a parked car. "Where that maroon sedan is parked. In the rumble seat of my girlfriend's new Ford." She looked back at me. "It was only the one night. But you might have remembered."

"I haven't been at the Claremont in over twenty years, Mrs. Prentice."

"That was when it was." She laughed without humor. "And I think under the circumstances, you can call me Martha." She smoothed out the dress with her hands. "I still fit into this pretty well, don't I? A little tight in the waist, but even that . . ." She seemed so very hurt.

"I'm terribly sorry," I said, meaning it. "I don't remember. I did a lot of ambitious drinking at that time. Prohibition was just around the corner."

"Yes, you drank a lot. It almost ruined your performance, but you came through in the end. Would that you hadn't."

I forced myself to a question for which I didn't want an answer. "Were you a virgin, Martha?"

"Did you 'ruin' me?" Another short, nasty laugh. "No, I had at least five years on you. I suppose I was a virgin sometime in my life, but I certainly wasn't by then. And you certainly weren't, you little bastard. You went down the line of my friends like a pail of water in a bucket brigade."

"Martha, are you sure you don't have me confused with somebody else?"

"No, Raymond Michael Sherwood, out to the West Coast for the first time in your life, hottest young saxophone player in town. The joke about you back then was that a long line of women were waiting for your services, but at least the line moved fast. You drank like there was no tomorrow, and talked about how you couldn't wait to go back to New York to enter some fancy music school." She stared at me, stunned by my lack of recall. "You *still* don't remember me? You showed me one of your most cherished possessions, or did you do that with every girl? I had the idea you didn't."

I ventured cautiously, "What was it?"

"A broken clarinet reed. Autographed by someone named Sid something or other. I'd never heard of him, but you seemed pretty impressed about who he was. I hadn't ever seen a clarinet reed up close. The maker was something like Van Dyck. Their name was in blue ink. The signature was in a darker shade of blue from a fountain pen. Sid something."

"Sidney Bechet," I said soberly.

I removed my wallet from my hip pocket, opened it, and withdrew a small pharmacy envelope that was hidden away between the billfold and my driver's license. From the envelope, I extracted a number three Van Doren reed, its tip broken like the jagged outline of a mountain range. On the back of the reed was written, in fountain pen, *Sidney Bechet,* and below that *1917.* "I was fifteen when he gave it to me back in New York. Talked my way into the Savannah Club in Harlem to hear him play."

I openly studied her face, seeing her in a new light even as the sky grew ominously dark. Take twenty years from her, fill her with giggle water until she's juiced, let an honest smile cross her features, and yes, she might have been one of my conquests back then.

"I understand that you might dislike me," I said.

"Oh, you're much too kind to yourself," she said, taking a Pall Mall from the clutch bag she carried.

I was sure I hadn't forced her to do anything; I at least knew *that* about myself, no matter how much I'd had to drink. We had both been young and wild. There really was a limit to how many pounds of flesh she should be entitled to extract from me.

"Is this why you stuck that carving fork into me at dinner the other night?" I said coolly. "To get back at me?"

She laughed the first honest laugh I'd heard from her lips. "No, you dimwit. I did it to get your blood. And I got plenty, on your shirt, on the napkin I held against you, off the fork when I cleaned it."

An undefined sense of dread was coming over me, as if a smiling malevolent valet was placing onto my shoulders a thin robe that had been stored in a freezer.

"Why did you want my blood?" I asked, remembering where Martha Prentice often worked.

"To learn your blood type."

The clouds were now directly above us. A slow drizzle began, which we ignored.

"Dr. Corwin works closely with a lab that identifies blood types," she explained. "And a Mr. Tucker there was glad to help me out. If he had asked me, I had a very good explanation prepared for why I needed to know the blood sample's type. But he didn't ask me. That's the kind of trust I generate from the people I work with."

She walked over to where we had apparently consummated our passing acquaintance almost twenty-two years ago.

"I just got the results from him late this morning. That's why we couldn't meet until now. If your blood type had been AB, I would have met you today, apologized for having treated you in such a cool fashion, told you I was a bit concerned about my daughter being attracted to a man old enough (albeit just barely) to be her father, and never have mentioned what happened on this location when you were still in your teens."

I turned up my collar against the rain.

She said, "My blood type is as common as you probably thought I was back then. Type O. Gail's type is the same as mine. Do you know *your* blood type?"

I said I wasn't sure.

"Well, you might want to know, Ray, should you ever need a transfusion, because someone has, say, stabbed you or shot you or hit you with their car"—she enjoyed reciting these possibilities—"that your blood type is O as well. O plus O always equals O."

"That doesn't identify me as Gail's father. He could be any one of millions of men."

"Not millions!" she snapped, adding sarcastically, "I wasn't *that* easy." I thought she might spit at me, but she continued sadly, "I'm ashamed to say that her father could have been any one of three men that I was familiar with during the time in question."

"Well, have you found out *their* blood types?"

Her eyes rolled ironically. "The other two haven't been kind enough to drop by as a dinner guest of my daughter's. I have no idea where on earth either one is. You were the catch of the bunch, the closest thing to a celebrity I ever knew. I recognized you the instant I saw you in the house." I remembered her sullen stares when we'd met. "I hope you appreciate that I didn't have to tell you all of this. I could have pretended that the only possibility was you."

The rain was suddenly assaulting us. From his shack at the bottom of the lot, the attendant yelled to us over the pounding of the downpour, "Get in the truck!" He indicated a livid green Ford pickup that was sitting alongside our fateful parking space. "It's okay, it belongs to the hotel!"

We scrambled onto the running boards and into the truck, gasping as the water poured from our clothes onto the bench seat and the rain did a Gene Krupa solo on the roof above us.

"When was Gail born?" I asked when I had my breath back.

"Her twenty-first birthday was two weeks ago. You can count backward from nine, can't you?"

"But she says she's been drinking at the bar here—"

"Please. No one questions a girl like Gail about her age."

I could hardly think straight. I asked her in a near-whisper, "What do you want me to do?"

"I don't *want* anything. I'm going to *tell* you what you're going to do, and you'll do it."

She took a handkerchief out of her bag and started to wipe away the thick lipstick on her face. "First, understand that I had my fill of men in your profession long ago. But Gail seems to believe you're the one person who can help her complete this work she's written, and it means everything to her. Even if there were someone else who could do the same for her, there's no time left to find them. So you're going to help this girl who's grown up so splendidly without a father."

I snapped, "You don't have to *order* me to do that. I'm doing this strictly because I believe in her music. It's wonderful to see someone who's young and passionate about—"

"Young and passionate and desirable," said the woman who was Gail's mother. I felt the blood rushing to my face, and not from anger. "Which brings us to what you *aren't* going to do. I know my daughter, and it's likely she has at least the beginnings of a crush on you. I'm not saying it's profound or that it couldn't blow away in an instant. But you understand the position you're in here. You may very well be her father. As long as the two of you are working together, you can do absolutely nothing that would encourage or reciprocate any romantic feelings she may have for you."

I would have cursed her, but she was Gail's mother. "Do you think I'm depraved?"

"I have no idea. Finally: until the day comes when medical science has progressed to a point where it can tell me for certain *if* you are Gail's father, you are never to say a word about this to her. Never. I've worked in the offices of psychiatric physicians, and I know from typing their notes that for a young woman to discover that a man about whom she's had fantasies might be her father . . . this could be shattering to a girl who, at the moment, has a very optimistic and sunny view of the world and her place in it.

"And just in case you wonder where my own self-interest rests: I've worked very hard to paint a picture of a fine father who was killed in an accident overseas just after Gail was conceived. Russ Hewett, whom I love very deeply, also believes this to be true. I've lived a very respectable life since I learned I was pregnant, and I wouldn't want Gail or Russ to ever learn what kind of a young woman I was when you knew me."

She grabbed my left wrist, dug her nails hard into my arm above my wristwatch, and held them there. "So you're going to say and do nothing beyond helping her with this performance of her composition, and then you're going to leave our lives, at least until someone invents a blood test that can determine for certain if you are her father. But if you turn Gail's life into a shambles by telling her what you *might* be to her, even though we may never know for certain if you really are . . . or if you in any way let her down with this project . . . and especially if you make the slightest overture to my daughter, I promise I will take that carving fork I used on you two days ago and drive it into your heart, over and over again. Look at me. Do you have any doubt I would do it?"

"No," I said.

She let go of my arm. With her nails she had once again caused me to bleed, but this time it was not to acquire medical information. Martha added, "And there wouldn't be a jury anywhere in California that would find me guilty of murder."

29

Coming in from the Rain

Water streamed down in thick ropes from the gutters of Russ Hewett's level rooftop and twined to the ground, where it formed sloppy puddles. I rang the doorbell and could hear Gail stepping quickly to the door, almost in a run, making no attempt to feign nonchalance. She was sweatered now in a light Irish cable-knit top above her pleated skirt. Her hair spilled down upon her forehead. She looked very happy to see me, as if I'd made it home through dangerous weather.

"Hello, kid," I said.

#

It could not have been more difficult that Gail was expecting to work with me directly after I'd met with her mother. God, I needed at least a day, days, maybe the rest of my life to understand what I was feeling. Instead, I'd had little more than an hour to collect my senses before I met with the girl who'd been charming me since the moment we'd met, whom I'd been falling—no, I couldn't put it that way—for whom I was feeling such tenderness and . . . and loving affection, that was what it was. Loving affection.

An hour earlier, I'd stood outside the Hotel Claremont helping into a taxicab a woman who loathed me and was the mother of a child who might be ours, handing the driver her fare and tip, watching the cab pull away. After a while the doorman came over to me, holding a large umbrella. He asked, with a surprising measure of concern, if perhaps I'd like to step out of the rain.

I walked into the Terrace Lounge and, dazed, took a small table in the corner by a window. Just beyond it, the slate terrace was tiled with water, the rain dancing on it like a casting call of invisible chorus girls in tap shoes.

"Something to drink?" asked the waiter.

I'd never wanted a shot so bad in my life, but it was the last thing I needed. "Coffee," I said. "Wait. Can you do beef bouillon?"

"Beef consommé."

"Yes, in a coffee cup, extra strong."

"I'll have the chef boil it down. And I'll get you an extra napkin to dry your hair."

You'd have thought just once the fates would have given me a bye. Nearly a dozen years I'd spent allowing myself nothing closer to love than near-nameless encounters with women who knew I'd be leaving in a day or two. I'd shut down my feelings in the hope that being numb to pleasure might also make me a little more numb to the pain. Nancy I couldn't even talk to for the first few years. I didn't blame her, she didn't blame me; we each blamed ourselves. We'd been necking, just necking, but a couple of doors down the street Linney had been breathing her last minutes of air, maybe calling our names, her small hands pushing at the—

I hit my fist against my leg under the table, not to inflict pain (it didn't cause enough pain to call it punishment) but just to break my train of thought.

I find someone who starts to make my life feel livable again. Therefore, of course, a way is devised so that I cannot have her, not because she doesn't care for me, not because she loves somebody else, but because of something for which there is no remedy. Can't happen. No way around it. She could throw herself at my feet and I would still have to turn my back on her.

"Nice going," I bitterly addressed the fates aloud, and the waiter, arriving with my cup of beef broth, misunderstood and told me it had been no problem. "Brought you a nice hot dry towel, too, from the kitchen." I received both benisons gratefully.

I took a sip of the consommé. It was as strong and hot as I needed it to be. It didn't improve my spirits, but it gave me a small physical lift.

Reflexively I said aloud, as I always did when some little thing in life went my way, "Thanks, Linney." It was a habit that had been honestly born and was nowhere near as pious or precious as it might seem. When I found a steel mouthpiece I thought I'd lost, when my fuel tank was reading empty and a gas station materialized on a desolate mountain road, when I was fifteen minutes late for the last train out of Elkhart and I got to the station and discovered the train had been delayed a half hour, I found myself automatically saying, "Thanks, Linney." I refused to give credit to anything so deformed as my supposed luck. So it had to be Linney.

I had another sip and began to think about what in the last hour I had just lost, and what I had gained.

By the time I rose from the table and went to my room to change out of the wet clothes I'd foolishly been sitting in, I thought maybe I understood things better.

"Thanks, Linney," I murmured.

30

A Labor of Love

So here I was, in a house at the end of a street that went no farther than where I stood, saying hello to my Gail.

"I made us some coffee, if you'd like it," she said, heading to the kitchen.

I told her I was fine.

She spun neatly back to me. "Oh, that's right, I told you about my coffee. Or was it written on the wall in the men's locker room? Men have no sense of discretion."

"Gail, I think we should get right to work. I only have until seven."

"This night job of yours is really undercutting my efforts to royally exploit you," she said, breezing her way to the bedroom that had the console piano. Over her shoulder she added, "Frankly, you may have to make a decision here. On the one hand, I'm offering you fifty dollars for a tremendous amount of work so that your name may be associated with an unknown college student's composition to be performed once at an exposition that in a matter of weeks will be dismantled for all time. On the other hand, Jack Donovan is offering you a good salary, travel expenses and accommodations, and the chance to play top-notch swing with a highly respected aggregation of sidemen in luxurious settings. Something may have to go. The only question is how we break the bad news to Jack."

We entered the bedroom. She had set up a card table and straight-backed chair for herself next to the orange crates and, probably for lack of anything else to do, had sharpened several dozen more pencils.

Her piano score was unfolded across the length of the bed. I sat beside it and began, all business: "Okay, now obviously we have very little time and my orchestration needs to go to a music copyist in a couple of days. I'll be there for you right through to the concert, but after that, you know I'll be leaving town, right?"

She picked up an already sharp pencil and started to sharpen it. "Where does the band go next, Ray?"

"Three weeks in Seattle, then back to the Midwest—that's our strength. We have a whole bunch of one- and two-night stands for several months."

"If you're free at Christmas—"

"Bands don't take a Christmas break, Gail. There's no musician on the face of the earth who can't get work around Christmas and New Year's if he owns his instrument."

Gail ceased her sharpening and stared at me, looking mildly hurt. "No, Ray, I meant where will you be playing when I have *my* Christmas break?"

It would be easy enough for her to find out by looking in *Variety* or *Metronome*. "Jack always plays the Heathman Hotel in Portland, Oregon."

She rolled her eyes. "What the hell am I going to do with myself in Portland?"

The conversation had to move elsewhere. At the moment, I had no idea what if anything I could ever do about Gail, or if I would even get to see her again once our work was completed. I knew I delighted being in her company, and felt as if I'd received the miraculous chance to be graced by a glimmer of what Linney might have been in my life. But what I wanted or needed meant nothing. I had to steer Gail away from caring about me as anything other than an ally. One good way to do that would be to make sure both of us were working studiously, soberly, and industriously on *Swing*. "Gail, we can talk about all this some other time. Right now we have a ton of work ahead of us, and that's what we have to focus on."

She said I was the boss, and I told her that, yes, I would have to be while I was creating the orchestration. Rolling out an eight-bar sheaf of blank orchestral manuscript on the drafting table, I said, "Look, you'll save me ten minutes an hour if you label all the lines for me. The first staff is for bar numbers, each number in a circle. Staves two through five are the four trumpets; leave staff six blank; then four trombones; staff eleven blank; five reeds. That takes care of all your horns. Staff seventeen blank; eighteen through twenty-two are rhythm. . . you get the idea, right?"

She smiled. "Got it."

"Now for the clefs and keys. You've chosen to write this chart in the key of D, even though it's so atonal I suppose it could be in no key at all. Why D?"

She sat on the chair by the card table and scrunched her shoulders together. "Looks nice on the page. Two sharps. Sounded right. *Swing Around the Sun* in D Major."

I winced. "Putting the tenor sax and trumpet in four sharps, and the alto and baritone sax in five? In your future writing, keep in mind that jazz musicians just love composers who write in flat keys."

"Sorry."

"Just a tip. Well, no matter what the key, we're going to write a transposed score, not a concert score."

"Where all the instruments are notated in their own keys, right? The same as their individual parts?"

I nodded. "Yeah, it saves the copyist time and saves us money. It also forces you to think of where the notes lie not on the piano, but on the instruments themselves."

"Then that's what we should do," said Gail, and she began the thankless job of preparing each big sheet of score paper for my contribution as orchestrator, which was ludicrous, as she was the composer. It was something like hiring young Mozart to tune the harpsichord for the premiere of his first sonata.

For me, the assignment was like nothing I'd done before. Clusters of notes that may sound fine on a piano can seem muddy, grating, even comic if directly assigned to a group of wind instruments. Yet Gail had made it a point of personal pride that not one note of her piano composition was to be changed, and I respected that. So it was up to me to find the combinations of instruments that would sound best playing the piano voicings she'd obliged me to commit to. Certain melodic passages had leaps in them that no one wind instrument could ever make, and so, right from the start, certain choices were simply not available to me. Much as I might want a trumpet to take an entire phrase, at some point I would have to give his part over to a trombone or baritone sax, only to switch it again to alto sax or clarinet. But this only served to dramatize the departure from the norm that Gail's *Swing* represented.

We worked quietly. She was finished with her task in less than two hours. She stepped behind me and watched as I filled in notes and rests and dynamic markings like a lightning sketch artist at a sidewalk café.

"Wow, Ray, look how fast you work." She peered at the landscape of pencil lines. "Isn't there a chance you'll get some of my notes wrong?"

"That's why you're going to be proofreading very carefully. As I finish each page of score, you're going to be responsible for checking my orchestration with your piano composition to see that I got it right." I set down my pencil. "I'm sure you envisioned me doing this like a medieval monk inscribing illuminations of a holy text. But I think you'll find very few mistakes." I rolled my shoulders, which were stiff from writing, and went back to my inscribing.

Standing behind me, she put her hands on my shoulders and began to knead them.

It was the smallest, most harmless and innocent thing to do, undoubtedly prompted by a momentary rush of gratitude for the effort I was making on behalf of her work.

Only it wouldn't be enough that my intentions were noble if I allowed hers to be anything but the same. I couldn't let her unknowingly do, say, or feel anything that would cause her revulsion or self-recrimination were she ever to learn what our relationship might be.

"Uh, thanks, Gail," I said, squirming out of her grasp, "but doing that actually interferes with my concentration. It makes it harder to write. Please, um, don't do that."

"Oh. Oh, okay," she said, a bit taken aback, and returned to her chair.

I continued to write, more briskly than ever. She shifted in her seat.

"So is there anything you want me to do now?" she asked at last.

I didn't even look back over my shoulder. "When I finish this page, you can start proofing. I promise you, from that moment on, you'll never be ahead of me."

She came over and collected my discarded dull pencils and made a show of sharpening them at her station.

"Do you want to get together at the Claremont tonight? For a beer or something?" she asked.

God. "Here's the thing, Gail. I'm working two jobs now, so I really need my sleep. From here on out, I think we should start no later than ten in the morning. So I'm going to try to go from the bandstand directly to bed. You understand? I need to be well rested for my work on your composition."

She nodded glumly. "I understand," she said, and went back to her pencil sharpening, humming to herself. It was throwing off my pitch, and I asked her to stop.

"Is something the matter, Ray?" she said at last. "Did I do something wrong today at the lake?"

"You're a wonderful girl, Gail. And I'm so proud of . . . I'm proud to be working on this piece with you."

She seemed relieved. "And I with you," she murmured in a voice huskier than I liked.

In another minute I handed her a sheet of score paper, every inch of which was covered with my musical hieroglyphics. "Here you go," I said. "Page one. Proof it like crazy, Gail, because you're the last line of defense."

She took it from me gratefully. "You think we're okay? That we'll get it done? We don't have much time, you know."

I put down my pencil for a moment and watched her as she scrutinized the page. "That's very true," I agreed. "But we do have what we have. I'm grateful for that."

Concern floated upon her features. "You think it will be enough time for you?"

"Oh gee, Gail." I waved vaguely at the drafting table. "Of course I'd like to have more time than I've been given. But you should see what I've gotten used to. On the road, working alone. . . . This is, working with you, this is more than . . ."

I couldn't finish the sentence honestly without betraying my feelings, so I let her finish it for me. "Enough time to do the chart," she said, looking much reassured.

When Linney had died, I used to think (when I could think at all) about what might have happened to Nancy and me if we'd already had a second child. If that would have kept us together. But after Linney's death, the idea of having another child seemed out of the question.

To some, I suppose that might sound strange.

Nancy and I found ourselves unable to look at each other, or spend time with each other, without thinking of who was not there. She and I would sit to have dinner at our table and there would be this empty chair to my right, her left, where Linney had always sat. It would be so glaringly vacant that we found we couldn't eat together. It became easier for me to work late, or dine with strangers, or alone, or in places Linney had never been. It became easier to talk with people who didn't know I'd had a child. I could, for a little while, be part of the normal world, where one complained about salaries, or the price of steak, or the unreliability of the Penn Central. For a little while . . . until I would compulsively mention something about Linney and make the stranger in my company woefully uncomfortable, and that would be the last I saw of them, for which we both were grateful.

But for Nancy and me to have tried to conceive a new child, perhaps hoping it would be a girl, maybe even hoping she would look and sound a little, or a lot, or exactly like Linney . . . it would have felt as if we were trying to replace our lost child. And that would have felt like we were the worst people on the face of the earth. Lose a child, make a new one, forget the old one, this one's even better!

We could never have done that.

But if, when Linney died, we'd already had another child, one we would still have had to take care of, who would have been frightened about death and who would have needed to be reassured that the world was still secure and as safe as we could make it, perhaps that might have kept Nancy and me together. We could have done this for our other child. Linney would have wanted that, I was sure.

Now it seemed I'd had that second child all along. And I didn't have to feel that I was betraying Linney, to whom I'd devoted most of my waking thoughts and all my troubled dreams. Gail had been conceived *before* I'd met Nancy, before I'd ever dreamt of having a daughter. If I'd neglected anyone all these years, it was Gail, the big sister Linney had never known. Who could say how much the two of them might have grown up alike, how much of the woman that Linney might have *become* would have been the way Gail *was*, this very minute, sitting near me in this small room, studiously reviewing the page of music I had orchestrated for her.

At about half past six, Martha Prentice appeared in the doorway of the bedroom. We had heard no sound of the front door opening, of her calling out to see if anyone was home, of her step upon the stairs to where we were working. It would be unnatural for someone to venture that far into her own home without making a sound. Yes, she was wearing the rubber-soled shoes of her part-time profession, but that would not have totally accounted for her silent entrance. Stealth would.

"Hello," she crackled out of nowhere. Gail jumped the veritable mile, and I landed only a few yards short of her.

"Mom," said Gail after regaining her breath and heartbeat. "You scared me."

"How are things coming along?" she asked, not looking at anything but me.

"Oh, fine, I suppose," said Gail. "Since we started, Ray speaks softly, if at all, and carries a big stick-in-the-mud. All work and no play is our Ray."

A look of satisfaction crossed Martha's face. "That's good, Mr. Sherwood. I'm glad to hear you're taking Gail and her work so seriously. It would be a terrible thing if her big debut were anything but perfect."

"I understand, Mrs. Prentice," I said to Gail's mother.

"It would just kill me if anything went wrong. You too, I'm sure."

31

No Picnic

That evening and the few days that followed were hallucinatory for me. I was actually grateful for the hours I spent on the bandstand. The bandstand I knew. It was my fixed place in the universe and had been for many years. From town to town, ballroom to American Legion hall, my fixed position in the universe was always with Frankie Pompano two feet to my left and Dave Wooster two feet to my right. Sometimes where the piano was located might shift from one side to the other, but within the sax section and in correlation to the trumpets and trombones, I knew my place.

After our last set, Jack stepped over to me as I packed up my instruments and said good-naturedly, "Hello, Ray. Your solo work tonight was the worst I've ever heard from you, wouldn't you say?"

"Was I hitting a lot of bad notes?" I asked. "I wasn't listening."

"Not bad, no. Just not very many."

Vera had plenty to say to anyone who'd hear her out on the subject of cradle robbing. She talked her loudest about it when I was within shouting distance.

My dreams? Alternately wonderful and nightmarish. Linney turning into Gail, Gail turning into Martha, Martha turning into Nancy. In one much-too-vivid vision, Pacifica came to life and, humming the discordant notes of Gail's composition, tore away from her pedestal and walked with eyes closed down the Court of the Seven Seas until she stood alongside the Tower of the Sun. Then, horrendously, her eyes opened . . . but the sockets were empty and black. She reached through the similarly empty and dark arches atop the Tower and plucked a screaming woman from amid the carillon bells, then hurled her to the ground below, into the Court of the Moon. But whether the woman was Marie Prasquier or one of the other women who now held dominion over my life, I couldn't say.

My hours with Gail were maddening. I wanted to let her know how proud her father was of the woman she'd become, how admiring he was of her engaging personality and daring creativity. She continued to be wounded by the way I quarantined any of her attempts at playful sparring. I knew I was hurting her feelings, but that was the goal: to impair and impinge any emotions she might have that might border on romantic, until she regarded me the way she regarded the Uncle Joe of whom she'd spoken so fondly, the one who'd helped her through life and shepherded her into music.

The work itself was progressing well. I'd never had an assistant, not to mention someone who knew the piece I was arranging better than I did. Having another person to take care of the secondary tasks dramatically accelerated our pace.

On Saturday the weather cleared, and with Martha Prentice home for the weekend and policing the hall outside Gail's bedroom for any frivolous laughter or conversation, we got a lot accomplished. But I was miserably aware that once we were done, I would not be seeing Gail again for a long time, perhaps forever. I loved simply being in the same room with her, hearing the sound of her erasing a mistake and sweeping away the dottles of rubber with a swipe of her forehand. It seemed nearly criminal that if I were to have only this short time with her, we couldn't enjoy it more, that I had to be this dour stone-faced statue in the corner.

When I left for that evening's stint at the Claremont, a sadness overtook me. I'd see her again the next morning, but this collaboration would last only a few days longer. I reminded myself that losing someone because she was far away or shut out of my life would be a far different sadness than losing someone to death. I'd at least have the solace of knowing Gail was out there somewhere, living a life, having adventures. Perhaps I might become Gail's unknown benefactor, leaving presents at her doorstep on her birthday, attending her concerts—

I was revisiting these thoughts on Sunday afternoon when Gail interrupted my maudlin scenario by slapping down her pencil lengthwise on the table. "Enough!" she declared. "We're way ahead of schedule. I hereby declare this regatta open. Come on, Simon Legree, I'm hungry."

"Just let me finish up these four bars, Gail."

I'd never actually been lifted by my collar onto my feet prior to this moment. Gail hiked us down the hall and into the kitchen, where Martha was drying dishes as an excuse for monitoring my every move.

"Ray and I are going out for a while," said Gail.

I shot Martha a look that I hoped more than conveyed "Let me assure you I have nothing to do with this."

She said, "I'll fix you two some lunch. Go sit out on the deck."

"Nope," said Gail flatly. "I've been cooped up in a room for days making more scratches than a crooked horse race. We'll see you back here in a little while."

I'm not sure what Martha would have done next if Russ hadn't come through the front door.

"Oh, hello, Sherwood, Gail. Um, Martha, do you have a beer?" Martha moved to the fridge as Russ sat down at the dining table. "Just saw them filing into Dimond Park. That Heritage Picnic I told you about? Drawing a surprisingly big crowd. Ran into Carl Brauner, the lumber-supply fellow, and he asked us to come around."

Martha brought him a tumbler and a bottle-capped can of beer. He nodded thanks but didn't open it.

I asked with genuine curiosity, "So is it like a Bund rally?" I had heard about these. The Ku Klux Klan with nattier uniforms.

Russ shook his head. "No, I don't think they allow Bund rallies anymore, since their members swear allegiance to a foreign government. This is a celebration of German culture. Carl Brauner thinks that the press is working overtime to give Germany a bad name."

I nodded. "Yes, that annexation of Poland got blown way out of proportion."

Russ grumbled, "Of course, I know, but he means that German Americans are getting lumped in with the Nazis." He frowned. "When I asked him who's behind this festival, he was pretty vague. Nobody I know from Oakland or San Francisco. Sounds like a lot of East Coast people, probably some America Firsters." He turned to Martha. "Anyway, he wants us to stop by and show our faces. Do you mind? He's a good man, and he came through with a ton of the lumber we used on the island with absolutely no profit for himself. I owe him the favor." Russ looked over at me. "Carl's a big jazz fiend. I'm sure he'd be thrilled to meet you."

"Once he met me he'd know better," I said.

Russ laughed. "Well, it looks to be a nice picnic. You're welcome to join us."

"We're going on one of our own," said Gail.

"That's nice," said Russ.

Martha's face tightened and I said impulsively, "Actually, it would be fun to join you, Russ, if you don't mind. The four of us?"

Martha said, "Yes, wonderful idea—let's do that right now."

Russ couldn't have been happier and said this was just the ticket. Gail gave me a look, but it didn't matter. I knew I was doing the right thing for her.

She glowered. "You've become as much fun as shooting monkeys in a barrel, Ray."

I told Gail she was confusing her metaphors, and she replied that she meant exactly what she'd said.

It was a splendid afternoon, the turnout beyond everyone's expectations, the crowd festive, the bunting colorful. The German band was as good as that sort of thing can be, while the wursts and sauerkraut and warm potato salad were absurdly delicious. The Linden beer was cool, the Kabinett wine was only mildly sweet, and both flowed at ten cents a glass. It was as delightful a day as you could have while hearing that your life would soon be controlled by Nazis.

The Heritage Picnic started out amiably enough. Russ introduced us to Carl Brauner. It was easy to see why Russ liked him, because the two were so similar in size, shape, and demeanor. Brauner was a red-faced fellow in his mid-fifties who was speaking enthusiastically to a group of dour, dark-suited men. I was a bit alarmed to see another one of them, a little fellow named Gunther, outfitted in a silver shirt, a black tie, and breech pants, the uniform of the Bund, which had been suspected of sabotage and espionage. But it was certainly not yet illegal in our country to dress inappropriately, or they would have locked up Cab Calloway years ago.

Brauner himself seemed delighted that the picnic was going so well and said that he was looking forward to the speeches that were going to be made from a grandstand he'd had built for the occasion. He also seemed very excited to meet a jazz musician from a band he admired. He asked if, were he to come to the Claremont for our last performance on Saturday night, I would autograph the recordings he had of my arrangements. I said I'd be glad to do so during any of the band's breaks. Brauner said he'd see me then. All in all, he struck me as a decent fellow saddled with the difficult task of convincing the public that there was an understandable reason why Germany was currently behaving the way it was.

The Prentice women and Russ Hewett and myself were quite the happy family. Martha had put on a floral print dress and looked almost pleasant. Russ was, as usual, the hail fellow well met, and at least some of his bonhomie seemed genuine enough. Gail looked politely glum, like a bobby-soxer who's been forced to attend her father's company picnic. But a bauernwurst on a roll swabbed with sweet mustard and a glass of cool wine on a sunny afternoon can make the most sullen prodigy crack a smile.

Russ took Gail by the arm and led her a few steps away to introduce her to someone from the War Memorial Opera House whom Russ had met when Treasure Island's outdoor concert shell was being built.

A roving photographer had been taking pictures and handing people his business card. He went over to Russ, Gail, and the others and arranged them in a little tableau.

"Ray." I turned to see Martha looking at me with sympathetic eyes. "Would you like a picture of you and Gail together?" she asked. "For you to have, on the road?"

Something in her expression told me there was a woman behind that face who hadn't had it easy in life, who knew how much all this was tearing me apart and what such a photograph would mean to me. "Yes, Martha. I really would. Thank you."

She called the photographer over and had a few words with him. He fetched Gail and Russ and positioned them on either side of me. "Put your arm around her!" he encouraged. I looked to Martha for her approval. She closed her eyes and nodded enough to let me know it was all right. I did as the photographer had instructed, Gail mugged for the camera, and the moment was captured. The cameraman called to Martha, "Now let's get your friends in the shot!" He was obviously looking for multiple sales.

Carl Brauner came over and put his arm around my shoulder, happy to be snapped with a "celebrity." I kept Gail in the shot with me, happy to be with her. Brauner waved some of his friends over, and the photographer kept snapping away. I was standing in a park on a lovely day with Gail at my side. I could smile for the camera till Kodak ran fresh out of film.

The German band had been playing near the beer barrels but now moved to chairs on the grandstand. As the crowd (there must have been over a thousand people on hand) gathered in front of it, Russ looked concerned. He pointed out to me that the fellow in the Bund-inspired outfit was part of the delegation assembling around the podium.

The first bad sign was that the band played "The Horst Wessel Song" and that the master of ceremonies, a fellow named Fred Kuhn, who apparently helmed the Friends of the New Germany, encouraged the crowd to sing along.

"That's a big mistake," muttered Russ. "That's the marching song of the storm troopers."

The first speaker, Carl Brauner, talked about the great unfairness being done to German Americans, how the president clearly was an Anglophile and viewed German people on both sides of the Atlantic with disfavor.

A unique aural phenomenon began to take place. As the speakers on the rostrum stated their case in ever more specific and poisonous terms, a portion of the crowd fell gradually more silent while the remainder became increasingly enthused. Thus the volume of the crowd remained level, even as its depth and character changed.

The next fellow said he was from New York, where a year earlier they'd been able to fill Madison Square Garden with over twenty thousand Nazi supporters. "I will tell you a little something about

New York City, my friends: they have an Easter parade there, where the people walk by Saint Patrick's Cathedral in fancy clothes and Easter bonnets. And who wrote the song 'Easter Parade'? Of course. A Jew named Irving *Balin*," he said, "who changed his name to—all together now—"

"*Berlin!*" chimed some of the crowd lustily.

"But he will never get to be a part of our—"

"*Berlin!*"

"And someday the name of New York will be New—"

"*Berlin!*" yelled a considerably smaller group.

Russ turned to me. "It's not like I believe for one second there could ever be a German occupation of the United States. But I'll tell you what isn't so far-fetched. Say Hitler takes out England, as I'm afraid looks likely. Meanwhile, completely separate from this, Japan wins out over China, then the Philippines and Guam, and they shut down our trade with Asia. Now we can't import or export, and that breaks our economy. The people blame Roosevelt, you get a new Congress elected that thinks a new order in Europe and across Asia doesn't have to be bad news for this country. One day you look up and you're living in a different America."

"I know that boy over there," Gail said, pointing to a fellow with curly brown hair. "Nathan Federman. And he's with Mort Kaplan. They're president and vice president of the student ACLU. And see over there, by the beer barrels? The Wald brothers, they're from Berkeley as well. That's odd. Why would they be here?"

The picnic sponsors next scummed up the fellow in the Bund uniform, whose name was Gunther Günstling and who, I later learned from the *Oakland Tribune*, had been charged with helping four Nazi saboteurs enter the United States via a German U-boat that surfaced off the coast of Long Island.

On a technicality, Gunther had been allowed to go free. He was now boasting about an explosion that had taken place just this last July Fourth in the British Pavilion of the New York World's Fair.

Gunther implied to the crowd that, while he himself had not planted any such bomb, he knew full well who had.

"Bastard," said Russ. "Tries anything on Treasure Island, I'd personally draw and quarter the son of a bitch."

Gunther was speaking about when he was questioned on the witness stand in New York. "I was asked by the district attorney, 'How do you salute at your Bund meetings?' And I said, 'Like this!' "

He gave the *sieg heil* salute.

"Then he asked me, 'Is that how an American salutes?' And I answered, 'It will be!' "

He faced the crowd and saluted. *"Sieg heil!"*

And some in the crowd, the sort who had filled a rally at Madison Square Garden the year before, responded in kind.

I looked around, wondering where the police were, but then again, I wasn't sure if anyone was breaking the law. At this point, the Wald brothers unzipped their Berkeley jackets and hurled tomatoes at the speaker. Apparently about eight other friends of theirs were similarly lardered, and instantly Gunther was splotched and oozing with pulp.

Nathan Federman of the student ACLU grabbed at the sleeve of the heavier Wald. "Let him speak, he has every right!"

Federman's ally Mort Kaplan chimed in, accusing the brothers of acting like the Gestapo.

Immediately the Wald brothers pivoted and began pelting the ACLU boys with the remainder of their tomatoes. "Call *us* the Gestapo, Kaplan?" yelled the slimmer Wald.

Suddenly the Jewish group and the ACLU group (which apparently was also predominantly Jewish) were beating up on each other.

Meanwhile, Russ had turned a shade of purple that would have won him a prize at a flower show. He bellowed up at Gunther, who was still at the podium, "Go back to where you came from!"

Martha looked with contempt at the near-Nazis on the grandstand. "Little puffed-up weasels. They're only a threat if we take them seriously."

Gail was running toward her Berkeley friends to try to intercede. I caught up with her and pulled her away. "No, Gail, it's not our quarrel."

And in truth, it was hard to know whose quarrel it was. You had some highly principled Jewish boys duking it out with some other highly principled Jewish boys over the right of ersatz Nazis to speak hatefully about Jews. You had varying shades of fascists on the grandstand watching the boys fight. Most of the crowd, repelled by the speeches, had started to drift out of the park, though a few pro-Nazis were still locked in their *sieg heil* salute. Some police officers made the rounds of the refreshment stands, telling the vendors the picnic was over. I was pretty sure I saw Bob Culpepper trying to separate some of the college boys, and I began to wonder if the lieutenant was solely assigned to scenes of violence to which I was a witness or participant. It was all very confusing.

But despite its nasty ending, the event had, in fact, been very effective for the person who had viewed the picnic as an unintended means to an ill-intended end, and whose simple mission had been achieved smoothly and without mishap.

And in my masterful ignorance, I'd done nothing to stop it. In point of fact, I'd helped out a bunch.

32

Opus 38

Jack Donovan's orchestra didn't play Sunday nights, which meant I could put in a full evening on *Swing*. I worked alongside Gail in the comfortable knowledge that Russ and Martha, our chaperones, were just down the hall, listening to Jack Benny.

It was pleasant to be accepted as one of the family. Martha whipped up a light supper while Gail and I made it our goal to reach the last bar of her composition by that end of that night.

Russ was very upset with what had happened in Dimond Park and spent most of the evening drafting a letter to the editor of the *Oakland Tribune*. He then retired to his bed, but Martha stayed up, probably to make sure I didn't retire to Gail's. It gave me the creeps that she might think me capable of such a thing. I guess her perception of jazz musicians' morals was shaped by the licentious behavior of certain members of my profession back in the days just before Prohibition.

Gail was totally occupied with proofing her composition, poring over the score in what was as hard a musical task as I could imagine. Gail's piece did not follow any traditional rules of harmony, and a miswritten note would not be something you could "hear" by spotting a missing accidental. I'd been peeling away the glued joining paper from each fold of the original piano score so that I could give her back each page of her composition as I finished orchestrating it, to compare what I'd just scored to what she'd first written. She caught a few errors, but overall it seemed I'd done a very accurate job.

I finished the last bar of music, took a straight edge, and drew a double bar down the right-hand side of the page with what I imagine would be the same feeling of satisfaction that an author gets typing "The End." In the bottom right-hand corner I wrote, "Composed by Gail Prentice," and in smaller letters below that, "Orchestrated by Ray Sherwood, Oakland, California, 1940."

As people often do when finished with an arduous task, I started to look for approval in a seemingly humble way, even while pointing out how much I deserved it.

"So would you say I did an okay job?" I asked, knowing I'd done an amazing job.

"Mm, yes," said Gail, not looking up from her work.

"See, here . . ." I pointed to a section she was working on. "I've tried to underline some of your leitmotifs with identical instrumentation each time they occur," I said.

"My leitmotifs?" She looked up from the score with a smile. "Isn't that word reserved for Wagner?"

I shook my head. "No, lots of composers have recurring musical phrases that run through a piece. Here's one of yours, this little phrase. I'd call that a leitmotif, wouldn't you?"

"I didn't think of it as anything that highfalutin," she said modestly.

"And here. You don't use this A very often, but when you do, you always seem to go down a fifth to the D below it."

She sang the two notes. "*Ding-dong.* Dominant to the tonic, very reassuring. My uncle Joe used to sing it to get me to sleep."

I unpeeled the joiner between the last page of her original piano score and its protective back cover. "Well, here you go—the last page of what you wrote, to proof against my last page."

She rubbed her eyes. "I know you're finished, but I shouldn't be doing this when I'm beginning to see double." As Gail noticed what I was doing, she said, "Oh, you don't have to undo that sheet. It's just there as a cover, to protect the last penciled page from smudging. And for the dedication."

The back cover read, *Dedicated to a World of International Understanding.* I suppressed a smile and Gail winced. "Yeah, I know, I was hoping you wouldn't see my apple-polishing for the judges. But I guess it worked."

I handed her the last piano score page, along with my final orchestrated page. "No harm done. The copyist will only be working with my orchestration, so you can keep your original piano score with you here. What's this?"

The reverse side of the piano score's back cover was actually further music. It looked like the very beginning of a tenor sax part Gail had started to write for a different piece, called "A Bach Ache" (cute), and beneath the title was the billing "Opus 38." She'd obviously abandoned it soon after beginning. The part was almost nothing, less than twenty notes. Above the G clef, Gail had written a memo to herself: "Clef?"

Gail saw my interest. "Oh, that's nothing, I'm loath to say. A waste of manuscript paper, so I made use of it as a back cover. You have no idea how frustrated I was that I couldn't do my own orchestration of *Swing.* This was before you mercifully rolled into town. It was a blow to my vanity that there are still things I don't know how to do as a composer. So I tried arranging my own jazz version of a Bach air." She took the page from me. "You like the title? You do get the joke, right?"

I told her I got it.

"I figured I ought to be able to handle a simple sax part like this. And I could, Ray." She laughed. "All the way up through bar thirteen. That's when I learned that, hallelujah, Jack Donovan was moving into the Claremont for two weeks. The one arranger I thought could handle the chart was going to be fifteen minutes away from me. Some miracle, was it not?"

I agreed that it had all been quite miraculous.

A radio had been turned on somewhere in the house, closer to where we were working. It was loud, and we could hear it clearly from where we sat: a live broadcast from the California Coliseum, Treasure Island's largest indoor theater. The American Society of Composers and Publishers was putting on the greatest pop concert of all time, one great American tune after another performed by the men and women who had written (and set) our standards.

George M. Cohan was just finishing a rendition of "Yankee Doodle Dandy." To top that, Irving Berlin began belting out "God Bless America" and the crowd at the coliseum sang along. The radio's volume increased. I stepped out into the hallway and realized the music was coming from Russ's bedroom, the door of which was closed. It must have been deafening in there.

Then I heard a sound I'd heard many a time over the years through the thin walls and ceilings of hotel rooms in which I and my band buddies were staying. That slow, steady chugging of bedsprings, the relentless creak of the floorboards, the odd banging of the headboard against the wall, punctuated by the occasional coarse grunt or shivery moan.

The bedroom's occupants must have thought the radio was drowning them out, but it wasn't. Russ and Martha were going to town on a buckboard. It sounded like Russ was enjoying himself, but Martha Prentice was either able to keep her voice down or simply along for the ride. I suddenly realized that I'd been in Russ's position, literally, some twenty-plus years ago, and that notion made me more than a little squeamish. I looked back toward the doorway where Gail was standing and felt embarrassed, for myself and for her. We returned to her bedroom, where we were expected to conduct ourselves with decency, and studiously reviewed our work.

33

The Copyist

The next morning, I found Jack Donovan sunning himself on the Claremont's patio and asked him if he knew where one went in Oakland to get fast, reliable music copying done for a reasonable price.

"Well, this isn't New York or Los Angeles, is it?" he replied. "There used to be a decent service in Oakland that I used when I was broadcasting from the St. Francis, before you joined us. RC Copying, I think they were called." The name rang a bell; an old chart we had of "Shanghai Lil" bore the company's monogram.

I'd taken a combination of the last trolley and a late local bus back to the Claremont the night before. Gail had still been proofing my arrangement when I'd left. She must have risen with the dawn, because the score was waiting for me at the front desk at eleven, along with a note saying she had rehearsals for a big student recital she'd been neglecting and would call me tomorrow or Wednesday. The thought of not seeing her for that long, when I was only going

to be in town another week, was oppressive. But I had my responsi-
bilities to the score to attend to.

RC Copying was run by a man named Gilbert Rice. I'd later learn
that his company had originally been called Rice Copying and that
all the music that came out of his office bore the emblem RC. People
had started calling the company RC Copying, so Gilbert had eventually given up and put that on his letterhead as well.

RC's office was located near the wharves, at Alice and Fourth,
wedged in between Oakland's working harbor and its Chinatown, in
a drab building where every other door boasted the name of a shipping firm.

A bell attached to the door gave a small ring as I entered.

The room itself had been laid out and decorated in a way that
would make its inhabitants envious of Bob Cratchit. Twelve wooden
tables were each topped by large green blotters that now more
closely resembled the world's most ambitious Rorschach test. Blank
music manuscript and onionskin paper stood in stacks on the left
side of each table. Overhead fluorescent lights bleached away any
shadows that twelve goosenecked lamps might not eliminate.

There were seven men of various ages and one woman in her
mid-forties, all at work on different projects.

A long counter intervened between this work area and the entrance to the office. Behind it, a man with a thin salt-and-pepper
mustache was jabbing at an Underwood typewriter. He consulted
some notes in a ledger to his left. "Yes, sir," he said to me, not looking up from his work.

"I have a score I'd like extracted into parts for a rehearsal this
Saturday. Can you give me an estimate?"

"An estimate takes time. Are you in the union?"

"Yes, I am."

"See your card, please?"

I got out my wallet and handed him my A.F. of M. Local 802
card. He handed it back and resumed typing. I thought he was just

finishing up something, but after a full minute I had the feeling if I didn't speak up, we'd never converse again. "So?" I asked.

He rolled the paper out of the typewriter. "We try not to do out-of-town jobs."

"But this is to be performed here, on Treasure Island."

"But you're from out of town. We'd need payment in advance, in full."

"Fine, how much?"

He shrugged. "There's really no way to tell until the work is done."

At that moment, a very tall, elderly man walked in—early seventies perhaps, but far from frail. You don't see a lot of very tall old men. His white beard and hair were stunning against his slightly sunburned face. He had a small satchel in his hand. I realized that I knew him.

"Professor Haffner?" I asked, and he nodded. "Sir, I was a student of yours at the Institute of Musical Arts in New York some twenty years ago."

He peered at me.

"You were a student of mine?" he asked somewhat disbelievingly, though I don't know why.

"Well, just first-year theory. But what an honor it was, Professor."

Haffner looked at the mustached fellow behind the counter. "Attention, Gilbert. Across your threshold comes an honest man." He turned back to me. "What year did you have the pleasure of studying with me, young man?"

I told him, and he reeled off a list of names I hadn't thought of for quite some time. They were all classmates of mine; he had the right year. I was slightly stung that he didn't mention my name. Aw, damn. I hadn't made an impression on him.

I introduced myself and told him I now played for the Jack Donovan Orchestra. "That's a swing band," I explained. "And I arrange for the band as well. Some of my orchestrations have been recorded."

He patted my right shoulder in a fatherly way. "We all have to put bread on the table," he consoled me.

Haffner was the sort of composer you hired for the opening of a museum or a city centennial. The piece would admirably fill the bill, be loud and majestic, conclude to very respectful applause, and never be heard again. His work was as sound and astute as his teachings on musical theory. Unfortunately, sound and astute is rarely what drives an audience into a frenzy.

He turned to Gilbert. "How are you today, my little sunbeam?"

"Fine, Professor," replied Gilbert.

I asked Haffner, "So is RC doing some copying for you, Professor? A new work?"

He gave me an angled nod. "I am working with RC, yes." He whispered to me, even though everyone around us knew the secret, "In truth, I am working *for* them. As a copyist."

I must have displayed more pity than I meant to, because he rushed to assure me, "No, it will only be for a short while longer. I will get a commission soon, I am very sure. A few years after you were my student, I went back to Germany. We were hoping to rebuild not just the country but its music as well. But it became clear to me last summer that I had to get out. I have family in Walnut Creek, so I have been here a month or so."

Stupidly, my hand moved toward my wallet. "I'd be very grateful if you would allow me to advance you a small loan—"

He glared, deeply offended. "If I would accept charity, do you think I would be working here? You think my family has no money to give me? Now: What do you have for me here?"

Could I *really* have him copy my work? "I don't know, Professor, I feel—"

"Come! Better you than a stranger." He turned to the man behind the counter. "If I don't do this one, what do you have for me?"

Gilbert looked at a stack of much-handled score paper. "Re-arrangement of a stage chart so it can be played by any instrumentation from solo piano to pit orchestra."

Haffner shuddered and looked at me. "That is my version of heavy labor. Let's look at yours, please."

Gilbert shoved Gail's score over toward Haffner. "He's from out of town," he warned. "We'll want payment before you start, so you'll have to estimate in advance."

I said, "It's a very original and unusual composition, composed by a wonderfully promising young woman, a student here at Berkeley. I'm just the orchestrator. It's going to be performed at Treasure Island in a few days by an Asian ensemble, but I assume they know all the Italian terminology for dynamics."

He took a rudimentary glance at the first page, making a series of light popping sounds with his lips as he appraised the chart.

I added, "Swing band instrumentation, but not a swing arrangement by any means. As you can see, I've written all the instruments in their own keys, so there's no transposition for you to do."

Haffner flipped the pages. "Ah, what a fabulous investment you are making to have me copy this!" he murmured. "Years from now the composition may be worth nothing, but the copying, Ah, they will say, this was in the hand of a master." He flipped back to the first page. I knew he was capable of looking down a bar line and hearing what was written, but in the case of *Swing,* even his gifted mind would be tested.

He gave a small scowl. "Hm. A strange composition."

I nodded my agreement. "A very new composer."

"Hm." He made a few more of those little popping noises and looked up at me. "Why don't you have yourself some lunch? When you come back, I will tell you what I think and if I can do it."

I looked at the satchel he carried with him and pictured the sandwich it contained. "No, Professor, please, at least have lunch with me, as my guest, no matter what you decide about the copying.

It would be a wonderful honor after all these years. I'll meet you in an hour, wherever you like. You can give me your appraisal then."

"Very well. You can meet me at two o'clock at the First and Last Chance Saloon, and I will accept your hospitality. They serve a very good German beer there. As opposed to Berlin these days."

34

The First and Last Chance

I had snagged a table for us in the First and Last Chance Saloon, which was an accomplishment, as there were only four tables to go around. The entire bar was permanently tipsy, skewed at a downhill angle courtesy of the Great Earthquake of 1906.

Haffner entered, bringing Gail's score with him. Standing over me, he asked, "You said this piece you have so excellently orchestrated was composed by a young woman?"

I was really pleased that he liked my orchestration. It meant so much to me. "Thank you, Professor. Yes, a young student, a wonderful girl, just twenty-one."

"She is attractive?"

"I think most people would say that readily."

He nodded and plopped himself into the chair at our tiny table. He pulled out a briar pipe whose bowl was shaped like a barrel and which had a hinged metal top like a beer stein. "You mind?"

he asked, striking a loose match against the old cast-iron wall beside us.

"Not at all," I replied. He worked the pipe. Scents of cherry and autumn bonfires wandered my way.

He smiled somewhat weakly at me. "I will do the job. I estimate it will be seventy dollars. It might be less, it will not be more. Fair enough?"

"Of course," I said. I'd kick in the extra twenty dollars out of my own pocket. "But, Professor, what about the piece itself?"

He finally allowed, "I am very glad the young woman is attractive."

"She's a remarkable talent," I added.

He patted my right hand with his left. "You, my boy, are most certainly in love." He gave the slightest nod toward the musical score on his right. "And this composition is noise."

I was disappointed in his response, but I quickly realized I'd expected too much from the elderly man, who'd thought everything written after Bruckner was either bilge or redundant, with the notable exception of his own work. Still, to call the piece noise . . .

I countered, "They also said that about *The Rite of Spring*."

He frowned. "I'm still not sure they were wrong, but at least when Stravinsky wrote it, he had already demonstrated he could write excellent Rimsky-Korsakov. You have to know the rules before you break them. That is the difference between revolution and anarchy. This young woman, what else has she written, has it all been in this *style*? Understand, I call it 'style' to be polite. I am, after all, your guest." He laughed and took a small sip of the dark beer that had been set before him.

I couldn't give an intelligent response to what he said, because, in point of fact, beyond *Swing*, the only other composition of Gail's that I had any knowledge of was her abandoned attempt at orchestration, "A Bach Ache."

"I understand, Professor, but I think most composers who attempt to do something new in music are, in the beginning, invariably accused of writing, as you say, 'noise.' I used to get this from my classical friends regarding jazz. They called it the sound of barnyard animals in heat!"

"*Und?*" he asked. He leaned back, wreathed in smoke like Father Christmas. "This"—he flicked his hand disdainfully at Gail's score, and I really didn't like him doing that—"this is a mediocre composer hiding in the uncharted *Sumpfland*, the swamps, of the avant-garde."

I told him I would have to respectfully disagree with his opinion. His response was a temperate sigh.

"You may be right. There is really nowhere left for artists like myself. I went back to Germany hoping I'd be in the company of the composers and musicians I knew and admired, but so many were dead, or imprisoned, or their work declared decadent. Those that were not able to emigrate . . . Thank God I got out in time. It was not easy, and I am not even a Jew." He took a puff from his pipe and set it down; it was designed so it could sit on its barrel. "You know your government is doing everything it can to delay visas for those trying to leave Germany for here. The argument is that among the refugees will be spies, saboteurs, and *die Lagerschwellen,* what you call 'sleepers.' "

It was hard for me to imagine. It seemed to be happening on that other earth, the one *Life* magazine reported about on a weekly basis. And yet I thought about the pro-German picnic that had tried its very best to turn pro-Nazi.

After lunch, we walked back to the copying office in leisurely fashion, because I knew that Haffner could not manage otherwise.

At the offices of RC Copying, Gilbert greeted me with a cordial "So I'm going to need seventy bucks cash from you now, based on Haffner's estimate."

"Yes, lunch was delicious, thanks," I replied and gave him four twenties. He stepped into a small side office to get change as Haffner thanked me again for the meal and went to his desk.

As I waited, I had nothing better to do than look at a stack of individual music parts sitting on the counter. Atop the stack, one of Gilbert Rice's billing forms bore a scrawl that read *Adeline Head. Will call Friday afternoon.*

The name was unusual enough that I knew I'd heard it before. It took me a moment to recall that she was the carillon player who'd alternated with Gail and eloped with a fellow from Nob Hill whose parents didn't approve of the marriage. The honeymoon was apparently a short one if she was going to be in this office in a couple of days. Or perhaps this was something she'd composed for the wedding. I remembered that Ada Head had entered the Pan-Pacific competition and been jealous of Gail's victory, wanting to hear what was deemed better than her own work. Was this the rival piece?

I slid the billing form aside and saw that the music bore the title *Apaches of the Night.* Didn't sound like an appropriate title for a wedding march, nor an inspiring anthem for world unity. It might have been written for something like the Cavalcade of the Golden West show near Treasure Island's Gayway. I wondered why Ada would have used a copyist in Oakland when she lived in San Francisco, but then I remembered that she had abandoned her abode there.

I made a mental note to mention this to Gail when I next saw her. I fancied she'd pay me a visit by the bandstand that evening, this being our first "night off" from the task of orchestrating *Swing.*

That evening, no Gail.

The next day went by for me in jittery aimlessness, and every time I looked up from my music that evening, I saw her not standing there.

She'd told me in her note that she had a big student recital to prepare for and that she was woefully behind, owing to the time we'd spent on *Swing,* so there was a logical explanation, of course. But still it seemed odd that she hadn't called. I feared the obvious: that with my arrangement of *Swing* completed, I was no longer important to her.

I was also growing increasingly restless with the fact that I would likely never know if Gail was my daughter or not. I would have to be stoic about this, possibly forever.

I can manage stoic for about three days.

If science couldn't assist me, how else might I better judge if Gail was my child? I found myself wishing I had some hereditary trait, like an attached earlobe or a webbed hand, the kind of "clew" in a Gothic novel indicating that the peasant girl is really the lost Princess of Gastonia. I wondered if a police expert, looking at photos of our faces, would be able to detect any common features.

Then I had what I thought was a very bright idea. And even if it wasn't, the idea would give me an excuse to drop by the Berkeley Women's Independent Collegiate Club the next afternoon.

♯

The switchboard operator buzzed Gail on the intercom to let her know she had a guest. She greeted me in the lobby six minutes later. She was wearing a long black dress, and her hair was pinned back. She had many sheaves of classical music under her arm. "Hey there, Ray, I'm just leaving. What's the story?"

It was not quite the greeting I had imagined, but she was cordial enough. I told her that although the orchestra parts wouldn't be ready until Friday, I wondered if she'd like to have lunch with me tomorrow. I said I thought it would be nice to just get together without having to think about the chart.

I said I also wanted her to meet a friend of mine who lived in the area.

I didn't seem to have her full attention. "Lunch. Um, sure, I suppose. I have a carillon concert on Treasure Island at three tomorrow. The new fellow who was covering for me last week expects me to return the favor. That's one of the reasons I'm spread so thin right now. Where would you like to meet?"

This suited my own purposes perfectly. I suggested the place where she and I had first met, the Café Lafayette, around one-thirty. She said fine and that she had to run, that tonight was the dress rehearsal of the fall recital. I offered to walk her there, but she said no, that she *literally* had to run, and that it would look silly for the two of us to be sprinting in tandem to the concert hall. She added apologetically that the rehearsal was a closed one. I said I understood and looked forward to seeing her on Treasure Island the next day.

I received no peck on the cheek this day.

I needed some dinner before the evening set, and I had to make a phone call as well, so I decided to walk to the Campus, the soda fountain where Gail had made her phone call to Adeline Head.

Damn. I'd meant to mention to Gail that the copying company for *Swing* was also handling a piece of music for Ada.

At the Campus, I ordered a chili size and a lime phosphate, then went to the phone booth, put in a nickel, and dialed Nancy's number from the card she'd given me. An operator asked me for five more cents; I'd forgotten Nancy was across the bay. I fed the slot another nickel. She answered on the third ring, and I asked her if she'd like to have lunch with me tomorrow on Treasure Island.

I told her I had a friend I very much wanted her to meet.

35

After Hours

That night, despite knowing she had an evening rehearsal, I once again looked for Gail in the Terrace Lounge after our last set. I wondered if, five years from now, playing at an Elks convention in Mishawaka, Indiana, I'd still be expecting to find Gail by the bandstand.

The one good thing I saw, from my point of view, was that Vera seemed to be setting her sights on Dave Wooster now. Jack Donovan's point of view regarding this was poor, since he was seated with his back to the bar, where Vera and Dave were flirting and trading quips with the Claremont bartender. I invited myself to Jack's table, as I felt it must have been awkward for him to be sitting there alone while his wife was loudly telling the one about the Texan who entered the roping contest at the rodeo.

"Well, hello there, Ray," he said. He nodded over to the bar. "We could manage to play without Dave Wooster, couldn't we?"

All seated at the bar exploded into laughter as Vera punch-lined, "Lariat? Who said I used a lariat?" As a regaled Dave rocked back, he allowed the arm he had around Vera's shoulder to slide down her side, to where it could rest momentarily against her der-riere.

"Of course we can do without him, Jack, he's probably our worst player." I added with concern, "But maybe this is not the time or place to deal with it."

Jack smiled blandly. "Poor Ray, always so concerned for me. You misunderstand. Dave wants to visit his ailing father in San Diego this weekend. It's Dave's last chance before we head to Seattle. He'd miss Friday and Saturday. Do I need to hire a sub?"

I told Jack that in our book, the baritone sax and the fourth trombone were the most expendable. I asked if there would be any critics reviewing us. Jack said that both the *Tribune* and the *Chroni-cle* were saving their serious ink for the bands at Sweet's Ballroom and, of course, the major venues in San Francisco. I told Jack to save himself the money, that I'd cover on the tenor any solo lines Dave played. I'd written very few for him.

"Thanks," he said, relieved. "It's getting so expensive to tour. Every nickel and dime makes a difference. An orchestra used to be three trumpets, one trombone, four reeds, and rhythm."

"Don't forget the xylophone," I said.

"Ah yes, can't do without a xylophone, can we?" He looked around the room. "Your young lady from the other night, I haven't seen her again, have I?"

I explained that she'd been busy rehearsing as an accompanist at a Berkeley recital.

Jack looked concerned. "Oh, she's a musician herself, is she?" He turned to summon a waiter.

"Yes, an excellent classical pianist as well as a composer." Some-thing about Jack's comments regarding "nickels and dimes" was troubling me, but I had no idea why.

"Gail's quite a performer."

"A performer. Ah. Well. Best of luck to you," he said, turning away from the sight of Dave stroking his hand along the nape of Vera's neck. "Best of luck to you indeed."

36

Trio Non con Brio

The café was much busier at lunch than when I'd breakfasted there. After moping and mooning about the Claremont grounds for the last few days (the liveliest alternative being canasta in the Bamboo Room with Jack and some of the hotel guests), I found it pleasant to be part of a keyed-up crowd. The Café Lafayette was a bit pricey for the family set, and the chatter around us was smart and merry.

I'd arranged to meet Nancy fifteen minutes before Gail arrived, giving me more than enough time to tell Nancy about my *Swing* commission and the female student who'd employed me.

Nancy punctuated my account with the occasional judicious "of course" and "certainly" and "naturally" and wore a serious expression on her face with a certain set to the corner of her mouth that let me know she was trying not to smile at my earnest explanation.

I of course omitted any reference to the possibility that Gail might be my daughter.

"So you've been working very long hours with this girl," she said. "At her home?"

I explained the setup of the Hewett household.

"Well, it's nice that you've gotten yourself out of the hotel for a change," she said. "It must feel strange for you to spend the day in a place with a backyard."

I told Nancy we hadn't had much time to be outside, except for the sunny unpleasantries of the Heritage Picnic.

"So you've stayed mainly in her house," she said, still gently needling me. She was not going to let me off the hook easily, and I couldn't explain to her that any kind of love between myself and Gail beyond that of father and daughter was out of the question.

The same jaded waiter as last time, despairing over the unrelenting consistency of the sun's daily rising and setting, asked if we too, like so many others in the café, were going to want something to eat. Nancy was working on the books at the Nude Ranch today and only had an hour. I was suggesting she order without waiting for Gail to arrive when I thought I heard the waiter say, "Nancy?"

But it wasn't the waiter. It was Bob Culpepper, with Russ Hewett at his side. "Yes, it is Nancy. And Sherwood, hello." Our waiter seized this golden opportunity to leave us.

Russ Hewett looked from me to my female companion. "It's nice to see you again, Miss . . . ?"

Nancy offered him "Carmack" and Russ reminded her that they'd met briefly at police headquarters on Treasure Island. Nancy said she recalled.

I hoped the men wouldn't want to join us. It was Nancy's undistracted appraisal of Gail that I wanted.

Russ looked about approvingly. "Nice weather we're having here," he said, as if he might speak to his foreman about ordering some more.

"And the fair's doing well today," said Culpepper, pleased. "Business seems to be picking up."

Russ asked, "How are things going at the Claremont, by the way?"

"Why don't you and Martha and Gail come over and see for yourself?" I replied. "I can't guarantee it, but they might lift the cover charge, as you're friends of mine."

I was showing off here. The Claremont would never do such a thing for a mere musician, but they might for Jack, and since I'd saved him the cost of a sideman for the rest of the stint, he'd likely be glad to intercede.

"Well, I think we'd like that," said Russ.

"Like what?" asked Gail, arriving breathlessly.

"Hi, Gail," said Russ. "Mr. Sherwood's invited you and Martha and me to the Claremont. How would tomorrow do for you?"

Gail took a seat at the café table. "Yes, good. Haven't seen Ray in action for way too many days." I caught Culpepper giving Russ a little look.

I introduced Gail to Nancy, explaining that she was my ex-wife. Gail's eyes widened. "Gee," she said. "So we've both put in a lot of hours in the bedroom with Ray, huh?"

All of us but Gail decided it would be a good time to do whatever throat clearing we might have been putting off until now.

I said to Culpepper, "By the way, regarding the Claremont, the same invite goes to you, Lieutenant."

Culpepper looked a little embarrassed. "Well, actually, Nancy and I have a date tomorrow."

I was quite surprised—no, stunned—by this. "Oh, sure, by all means," I said idiotically.

The two men excused themselves, with Russ assuring me he'd bring Gail and Martha to the Claremont at eight-thirty tomorrow.

I turned to Nancy as they departed, showing my surprise. "You've been seeing Culpepper?"

She looked at the table for a second. "Just friendly. The first time I met him was when I was covering up your bruises. We're both around the fair, obviously, and he dropped in to say hello to me at Sally's a couple of days later. We had dinner on Tuesday."

The waiter decided to give us a second chance and took our lunch order. Gail, Nancy, and I chatted, and Gail was every bit the vibrant girl I'd been captivated by since she'd introduced herself to me only a few tables from where we now sat. The two women gleefully shared observations about my flaws, my nervous tics, expressions I used that they wished I'd retire, how I always say this when I mean that, my odd way of pronouncing certain words, and how I am unable to success-fully mix brown and gray in my wardrobe. These kinds of conversa-tions are what I believe most men must endure when two women whom the man has hitherto known individually finally meet and con-fer. The women are invariably relieved, even elated, to know that they haven't been alone in suffering that which they've so heroically toler-ated. You could call it ganging up, but it is still mysteriously pleasur-able for any man to hear two smart, attractive women speak only about himself, even if in a relentlessly patronizing way.

Eventually the two moved on to topics other than my failings. Gail was particularly interested in Nancy's show-business past, a topic my ex-wife didn't always warm to, but Gail was able to draw her out. Now that I was off the roasting spit, I chimed in with my own recollections and provided the setups for some anecdotes that I knew Nancy told well. Gail's face was alive with curiosity, her laughter generous, and she quickly nodded agreement whenever Nancy ventured an opinion.

It occurred to me that this immensely pleasant lunch was the kind Nancy and I might have had with Linney, had she lived. It would have been wonderful to see her grown up, fascinated with life, and making an indelible impression on those she met. This was as close as I was ever likely to come to that, and I cherished the hour.

Gail had to leave, regretting that she did, but she and Nancy exchanged numbers and vowed to meet again when I had left town. Nancy was particularly interested in seeing the Berkeley campus and the Greek amphitheater there, and Gail said she'd be delighted to give her the grand tour.

"She's quite wonderful, don't you think?" I asked Nancy, once Gail had left.

Nancy ventured carefully, "She seems to me to be a very smart, very attractive young woman. I'm sure she knows how the things she says and does affect other people, and she makes a charming impression, which I'm sure is deserved." She hesitated. "I do think that maybe she puts on the girlishness a bit much."

I was shocked to hear Nancy do anything but gush about Gail. I said as much, and she hastened to reassure me: "No, Ray, of course, I'm sure she's a very lovely person. I just don't think she's unaware of how engaging she is. At least not as much as she would have you think."

Ignoring what I assumed could only be a tinge of jealousy on Nancy's part, I moved us to the real purpose of the lunch.

"Nancy, I was wondering . . ." How on earth could I even begin to broach this? "I was wondering if she reminded you of anyone."

I sat back and let the spotlight of the sun set me apart from the crowd.

Nancy pondered for a moment, and the realization hit her. "Oh. Oh, you think? Yes, I suppose . . . in a way. I mean, I was several years younger than her when you and I met, but I suppose I did have her kind of energy. Is that what you mean?"

I was annoyed, but I should have hidden it better. "No, not really, Nance. No, I thought she might have reminded you a little of, well, *me*."

Nancy gave me a mildly quizzical gaze. "Hm. Uh—no. No, I don't see that."

"Oh," I said, sulkily.

The waiter brought me a check. It being a French restaurant, I wondered if the tip was included, but he'd made sure to notate the abbreviation for *Service Non Compris*. I overtipped to see if I could get a smile. He sneered at my attempt to buy his friendship. "Too much," he said and returned a quarter and two dimes.

I put the receipt in my wallet and turned back to see Nancy drawing invisible lines with her finger on the café table. "It wasn't really very nice, you know, showing off your new girlfriend to me this way," she said.

She'd been so friendly to Gail during lunch that it had not occurred to me for an instant that she'd been insulted or hurt.

"Oh, Nance—" I began.

"A bit mean-spirited, Ray. I wouldn't have expected it of you. I guess you *have* been on the road too long. And don't you think she's just a bit . . . I mean, how old is she?"

I told her.

"Well, Ray, I mean, Ray, the last thing I would ever want to do is stop you from feeling happy, but, Ray, she's—. Ray, do I have to say it?"

"Say what, Nancy?"

"Oh please. That you're old enough—" She stopped and looked at me.

Into me.

"Oh, Ray," she said quietly. "What are you doing?"

"I know what I'm doing, Nancy," I said, although I really didn't. Boy, I sure didn't. "It isn't as simple as you think."

"Ray—"

"There are things you don't know."

"Ray. Listen to me, my dearest boy." She reached across the table and held my face in her hands. "You can't get her back, honey."

She looked in my eyes for a moment, then took her hands away from my cheeks and sat back in her seat.

"Ray, do you want to come home with me tonight?" She saw a startled look on my face. "No, don't flatter yourself," she scolded, the third time I'd been told this of late. "I mean, come to my home. When was the last time you ate a meal that you didn't order?"

In point of fact, I'd had a home-cooked meal just a few days earlier that had been very enjoyable, except for when the woman who'd prepared it had stabbed me.

I told Nancy thanks, but that the food was pretty good at the Claremont.

She reached for her pocketbook and took out a compact. "You really don't want any help, do you?" I said nothing, and as she fixed her makeup, she asked, "Do you still sing 'Beef Lo Mein' on the bandstand each night?"

"My most popular number," I assured her. The vintage tune was a variant on the old "for want of a nail" proverb, relating in ever-compounding terms how one event can radically alter the course of one's life. In this instance, a lack of Beef Lo Mein at a Chinese restaurant causes the narrator's marriage proposal to be rejected. And thus "*there went the son who would run the bank, and marry into money with some honey born with swank; there went the new governor of the state of Maine, and his ascent to president, for lack of Beef Lo Mein.*"

Nancy closed the compact with a precise *snap.* "You know you only perform it to punish yourself," she said. "The audience is laughing up a storm while you're singing 'in disbelief, some call it grief, I call it Beef Lo Mein.' And you're dying inside with a pretend grin on your face, thinking about *your* child who never got to grow up. It's a way to keep your own grief fresh each night, isn't it?"

"No, Jack asked me to do the song because he thinks it helps the set, and I want to help Jack," I said. "I'd feel the same way whether I sang it or not."

"Ray, you're in some strange place right now, I can tell. Maybe I can help you with it. You're still my friend and the first man I really loved."

How could I tell her that there was so much more to this than she could possibly begin to realize? The tragic part was that my good news, about Linney having a half-sister, wasn't going to be *her* good news. Only mine. It would give nothing to Nancy. It might even wound her further, if such a thing was possible. I could never share this with her. I'd hoped our lunch might in some way confirm my soaring hopes, but it had only made me feel more distant than ever from Nancy and from the life we had shared.

37

Surprise Symphony

I went to Lake Merritt the next afternoon, on my own (I know, a little pathetic, but it was a beautiful day and I *had* to get out of the Claremont). I called RC Copying from a coin phone and Gilbert Rice confirmed with his endearing "Yeah" and his heartwarming *click* that the music parts for *Swing* were ready to be picked up.

I'd not realized how close the lake was to the waterfront. In less than ten minutes, I was watching Professor Haffner put the last touches on the drummer's part. These were the most difficult pages for him to copy, since as a classical composer he was not used to writing for a drum kit, what we called "traps."

"Almost done. Sit, I have some questions." He indicated an empty chair next to his desk. You could have framed his handiwork and enjoyed it, whether you read music or not.

"Beautiful, Maestro," I said, using the term without the slightest trace of levity.

"I concur wholeheartedly," he said, autographing the lower right-hand corner of the drum part as if it were a lithograph. I told him that the composer would be very thrilled to see her work so admirably rendered, and he muttered that this was one orchestration that would be better enjoyed by the deaf than by the blind. I wasn't as amused as he was by this.

He went over several places in my orchestration where he hadn't been able to tell what the hurried scrawl of my pencil had intended. A flat sign that might have been a quarter rest. Some unflagged sixteenths that unintentionally made a bar of four beats into a bar of seven. "And here," he said, pointing at the score. "This note in bar twenty-three, did you and your lady friend mean this to be a B or an H?"

"Very funny, Professor." I scowled. "I do think you've insulted the composer enough for one afternoon." As even those only passably familiar with music knows, the lettering for musical notes starts at A and stops at G, but whenever one of my arrangements gets a little adventurous, Larry Vance says, "Wow, this chart is in the key of H!"

I gathered up the instrument parts and turned back to see Jurgen Haffner looking very perplexed, still waiting for an answer to his question. He said softly, "*Nein, nein,* I was not making the insult. I just can't tell if this note is supposed to be a B or an H. In the previous bars you alternated flat sign, natural sign; this time here you have no sign at all. Is this H what you want?"

I didn't understand and told him so. "Professor, that's a B-natural."

Haffner muttered, "*Jemand hat mein Gehirn gestohlen!* I am growing too old, they must put me away soon! You didn't know that in German music we have an extra note?"

"An extra note?" I couldn't imagine what he meant. Beethoven was played with the same notes in Hamburg, Germany, as in Hamburg, Alabama. "You mean, a quarter tone, or a blue note . . . ?"

He chuckled. "No, nothing that *ungewöhnlich,* that unusual. The note that you Americans call a B-flat, we call just a B. And the note you call B-natural, we call H. Our Führer has convinced himself this stands for Hitler, but of course it goes much further back. You never heard of Bach's Mass in *H Moll,* that is, H Minor?"

I told him I knew it as the Mass in B Minor, but his mention of Bach reminded me of a question I had meant to ask him. "I have a question for you, Professor. The young woman who wrote *Swing* tried writing an arrangement of a Bach air and I'd thought, as a parting gift when I leave Oakland, I'd give her an arrangement of it for her to study, as a kind of tutorial. No one knows their Bach repertoire better than you. Do you recognize this melody?"

I have what most people consider an excellent musical memory. I took a sheet of blank music manuscript and wrote lightly in pencil, so that I wasn't wasting the page, the theme Gail had been arranging for her "A Bach Ache."

He studied the notes. "Not to look at it. An interesting theme, but it's not Johann Sebastian. This leap here of a major seventh is not his style. I would remember such a thing. Are you sure she meant Johann Sebastian Bach? Not, say, the son, Carl Philipp Emanuel? The grandson, Wilhelm Friedrich Ernst?"

I had no idea and said I'd have to ask her. The bell on the entrance door gave a little ring as a customer entered behind me.

I went through the parts one last time to make sure they were all there. He'd gotten each part onto four hinged pages, except for the piano-conductor part, which was naturally longer. It did not contain the full chart by any means, but it would be helpful to whoever was leading the band, whether at a podium or from the piano.

I slid the parts into a large manila envelope Haffner gave me that bore the name RC COPYING.

Haffner picked up my thirty-eight-page orchestral chart, from which he had extracted each individual part. "Is this the only copy of your orchestration?" he asked. I told him it was. He made that little popping sound of his with a grave look on his face. "I don't like that you have only the one copy. It is a fine arrangement. Even the best musical mind would not be able to re-create this orchestration if it was lost—the voicing is too unusual. We should have a Photostatic copy made. I have preserved my last two works this way. It is an expense but also a reassurance."

He turned to Gil. He was settling up some business with a blonde, who was looking at a chart from his side of the counter and had her back to me.

Haffner asked, "Gilbert, my friend, how much would we have to charge my former student here to make a Photostatic copy of his arrangement? Reduced in size, of course?"

Gil, who was reluctant to tear himself away from the blonde, turned to face us. "No way to really know," he said.

Haffner pouted. "This would be for my friend," he said, indicating me.

Gil said, "Forty dollars?"

Haffner silently mouthed the words "My friend."

Gil said, "Twenty bucks will cover it," and turned back to the blonde. He seemed much more interested in the way her green serge dress draped over her rear than in the transaction with me.

Haffner winked at me and urged, "You should have it done. This may be that rare case where the orchestrator is more talented than the composer, and we certainly know the copyist is better than the composer and orchestrator combined. Take the parts themselves and I shall have delivered a Photostatic copy of the orchestration to your hotel tomorrow morning. You said you were at the Claremont, yes?"

I shook his hand and thanked him for his thoughtfulness and his fine work. He said he hoped we might have a beer together before I left town. I said that sounded great.

I walked past the counter and saw that Gil was explaining to the blonde his billing for the piece called *Apaches of the Night*. He was doing all the talking; she was doing all the paying, like myself, in cash. Apparently she hadn't had to pay in advance. Next time I brought in an arrangement to Gilbert Rice, I'd dye my hair blond.

I suddenly stopped at the door as I remembered that the person with the arrangement called *Apaches of the Night* was Adeline Head.

I slyly turned and said, "Gail Prentice sends her regards, Adeline," offering my friendliest smile. She looked up and gave a little gasp. I uttered a small gasp myself.

It would seem that Adeline Head, carillonist, composer, and runaway bride, was also the runaway waitress from the Centaur Luncheonette. She grabbed her music, pushed her way past me, and likewise became the runaway customer of RC Copying of Oakland.

38

Dance of the Sugar Plum Ferry

I'm generally not in the habit of chasing after women who don't want to be in my company. But this was thrice now she'd fled from me, and I couldn't imagine why I would be the cause of her fear. Yet that seemed to be the emotion that had swept across her features as she'd spun away from me.

The music parts in my hand were too valuable to take on some merry chase. I slapped them down on the counter. "Will you watch these for me?" I asked Gilbert. He would have quoted me an hourly rate if I'd waited another moment.

I dashed out the door and saw Ada entering the building's birdcage elevator. Its door closed, but luckily it descended at a leisurely pace.

I raced down the zigzagging stairs that cut through the building's five galleried floors and was pleased that I reached the lobby well ahead of the elevator. I was somewhat less pleased to see the elevator stop on the second floor and watch Ada run to a door at the far end of that gallery. I ran back up the first flight of stairs and raced to the door through which she'd slipped, which bore the word RESTROOMS.

Beyond that was a short corridor with two doors, LADIES on the right and MEN on the left. There was no other exit. I decided I could wait here in the hall for just as long as she could wait in the bathroom.

Then I realized I couldn't. I would eventually have to go back to the Claremont or leave Jack Donovan in the lurch. After all, the only real problems I had with Adeline Head were that she was popping into my life with startling regularity (considering I had never formally met her), that she'd abandoned my booth at the Centaur Luncheonette, and that she'd been spying on Gail and me during our morning on Lake Merritt. All I wanted was to ask her why she'd been monitoring us through binoculars and why she'd gone to the trouble of writing Nancy and me a check that said there was no charge.

I knocked on the ladies' room door. There being no reply—was I really expecting a "Come in?"—I did the unthinkable and opened the door slowly, stepping into the room with my back turned. The room made an inverted L, and I stood in the crook of that right angle, staring at a paper-towel dispenser as I called out, "Excuse me. I just wanted to have a short word with you."

There was a long pause. Finally she answered, "What about?" It was hard to tell much from her voice except that it seemed educated and youthful.

I offered, "It seems like our paths keep crossing, and I was wondering how much I can reasonably attribute this to coincidence."

Again she seemed to consider her reply. "Well," she said at last, "right now it seems like we can attribute our paths crossing to you."

"How do you mean?" I asked.

"Oh, I don't know," she answered in a sarcastic tone. "The fact that it says 'Ladies' on the door."

"You were watching me," I protested. "Last week. At Lake Merritt."

There was a pause. "I *live* along Lake Merritt. I walk through the park there every day. I watch lots of people—I find people interesting, including the odd man now and then, and you certainly are the odd man. Look, if you want to discuss this in a sane fashion, walk out of here, past the elevator, and you'll see the second door on your right is marked 'Litras Imports, Inc.' Step inside and tell them you're there to have a word with Miss Patnode. They'll tell you I'll be back in a few minutes. I'd very much appreciate it if you'd not say where we met."

I suddenly thought it possible I'd made a slight mistake. I stepped out of the ladies' room and bumped into a stout fellow in a three-piece suit of dark green tweed who was exiting the men's room. He looked as if I'd made his day.

"All right then!" he said as much to himself as to me. "All right then, something's definitely up when you have a lady in the men's room and a man in the ladies' room. Thought maybe it was me who had it wrong, but no."

I ran back out to the gallery's railing and saw Adeline Head running out of the lobby below me and into the street.

By the time I'd hit Fourth Street, it was clear I had lost her. There was, however, one possible checkpoint at which I might catch her again. I knew that Ada used to live in San Francisco. If for any reason she was going back there now, she'd certainly take the ferry from the Embarcadero. I hailed a taxi and told the driver I wanted the Key System's landing off Clay.

As I got out of the cab, and as my luck both good and bad would have it, I saw Ada stepping onto one of the smaller damson-colored ferries, the *Castro*, a second before its metal gangway was removed. A horn sounded and the ferry began to move away from the two piers that flanked it on either side. There wasn't that great a distance from the port side of the boat to the landing, perhaps four feet but widening . . . I foolhardily took the leap and found myself on board.

"There's a fine for doing what you just did, buddy," said the ferry conductor.

"I'm sorry, I'm from out of town. It won't happen again."

"Don't let it," he said and walked away. I looked to my left and right. No sign of Adeline. I laced my way through the crowd that was queuing up at the refreshment counter and reached the other side of the open deck. Still no trace of her.

I moved quickly to the stern of the ferry, stepping around some coils of rope and avoiding a puddle of oil. I looked back to the pier and groaned as I spotted Adeline standing like a crane, raising one foot to put her shoe on, her long-necked profile completing the ornithological image. Dammit. Somehow, just as I'd leapt onto the ferry from the port side, she must have taken off her heels and leapt from the starboard side onto the enclosing pier. I felt a perverse sense of importance that she would have gone to such measures just to avoid me.

As the ferry towed me farther away from her, I saw her spin around to make certain I hadn't managed to return to the pier myself. Seeing nothing, she completed her pirouette and walked quickly to one of several identical DeSoto Sky Tops on the taxi rank. Unless I wanted to swim to shore, I had lost her.

There were cocktail lounges on most of the Key System's ferries. I sat myself near a window and ordered an Indian tonic water with lime. I had to travel to San Francisco and back. This gave me plenty of time to think.

When I went to pay for my tonic water, the receipt from my lunch with Nancy and Gail at the French café fluttered from my billfold. I looked at where the waiter had indicated at the bottom of the check that service was not included, and it made me think again about the check that Adeline Head had handed Nancy and me at the Centaur Luncheonette.

When I finally disembarked back in Oakland, I walked not to RC

Copying but to the Centaur, where the manager had found someone to fill the vanished waitress's job but not his empty seats.

He sat in the same booth we'd occupied. He had a prop sandwich in front of him and was reading the newspaper, trying to look like a customer. The new waitress was sitting in another booth, doing her nails.

He saw me enter and became excited, but I counseled him to stay seated. "I have a few questions to ask you," I said and slid five dollars across the table as I sat in the booth.

He took the money but said in his thick accent, "Only if you have some coffee and a slice of pie while we talk. If someone comes in, you must look like you're enjoying it. Arlene, the rhubarb pie, cheese, and coffee."

By the time I was done eating and drinking and asking, I'd learned why no one wanted to dine there, and that the vanished waitress had started working for him the same morning Nancy and I had encountered her. She'd shown up with no references, just a driver's license identifying her as Adeline Head of San Francisco, eyes brown, five foot six. She'd told him she had moved out of her apartment owing to a romance that had gone bad, and while she looked for suitable employment, she'd work for him dirt cheap, off the books, mainly for tips if meals came with the job. She'd walked out after taking our order and had never come back.

I asked him what her voice was like. He said, in an accent that oozed of retsina, that he'd only been in this country a few months and that everyone's accent sounded foreign to his ears, including mine.

I asked him if we were currently sitting in booth five of the luncheonette's five booths. He said no, that we were in booth one. Things were beginning to click.

I walked back to RC Copying. Professor Haffner had already left for the day, but Gilbert Rice was still there. I thanked him for staying.

He laughed in a quick staccato. "I didn't stay for you. I'm here most nights till eight or nine at the least. Everybody wants everything by the morning. If it weren't for overtime charges, I'd lose money on the whole operation. By the way, thanks a bunch for scaring off a customer."

"I thought I saw her paying you," I said.

"Yeah, but I bet she never comes back. What did you do to her?"

I ignored his question and asked, "How'd she sound?"

Gilbert looked at me. "What do you mean?"

"When she spoke to you. What was her voice like?"

He must have thought I was crazy, or in love with her.

"I think she had, you know, some kind of speech impediment. She said as little as she could."

"By the way, that copying job you would have given the professor if he hadn't taken mine, rearranging a stage-show chart so it would work for smaller combos . . . was that the chart Adeline brought in?"

"Yeah, it was a specialty dance number. *Comanche* something."

"*Apache*," I corrected him and left with the *Swing* parts under my arm. The orchestral score itself and a Photostatic copy of same were to be delivered to my hotel the next day.

I rode the birdcage elevator down to the ground floor and hailed a cab to take me back to the Claremont, where the band would be playing in less than half an hour.

I sat back in the taxi and thought about what had brought Nancy and me to the unlikely meeting place of the Centaur Luncheonette. We'd been there because a dancer who worked in the building wanted to meet with Nancy. Except that she hadn't shown up. It was a strange coincidence: a no-show dancer and a vanishing waitress in the same lunch hour.

Strange unless they were the same person. People in show business often fall back on jobs as waiters and waitresses in between bookings.

What if the dancer had fled the luncheonette before she'd even seen Nancy, fled because of something she saw.

Me.

Just as she had fled from me today and at Lake Merritt. Was she frightened to see me? Or frightened I'd see her?

What had prompted these thoughts was the check from the French café that I'd looked at on the ferry. The café's bored waiter had indicated that a tip was not included by writing the standard abbreviation for *Service Non Compris*. SNC.

I'd originally thought our waitress at the Centaur had jotted down "5NC" for table five, "No Charge." But her 5 could easily have been an S. And I now knew that we had been seated at table one.

On her first day at a low-paying job where her tips would be important, a waitress might have reflexively written SNC at the bottom of the check.

If she were French.

We had never heard the waitress speak. The heavily accented owner of the luncheonette wouldn't have been able to discern where the waitress was from, and Gilbert Rice thought she had a speech impediment that caused her to speak very little.

She'd been picking up dance music from RC Copying, rearranged so it might be played by any size instrumentation, the kind of arrangement someone would take with them on the road.

I'd originally thought Adeline was a patron of RC Copying because she was a composer. But what if she were there because she was a dancer. Among whose specialty numbers was a Parisian Apache dance.

I thought of the neat pirouette Adeline had made after she'd leapt to the ferry landing, and the vaguely familiar birdlike profile made not only by her one-legged stance but by the curving neck that became her chin.

Take away her bleached blond hair (or wig) and the rumpled (or padded) wardrobe, and suddenly we no longer have Adeline Head, aspiring composer and carillonist, leaving town to get married to a boy from Nob Hill.

Instead we have an unemployed French dancer with an ostrich-like visage who is eager to tour in the sticks for low money and is afraid that I may recognize her.

Were it not for the fact that she had died ten days ago, she might well have been Marie Prasquier, whose bloodied body had landed at my feet in the Court of the Moon after having fallen from the Tower of the Sun.

39

An Intoxicating Evening

I had just enough time to make it to my room, change into my stage suit, and hit the bandstand for the first tune of the set, "The Music Speaks to Me," which, of course, I was also expected to sing. I would have loved to beg off for the night and sort through all that was seething in my brain, but Dave Wooster had left for San Diego that morning to see his father, and I was hard-pressed simply to fill in all the empty spots that occurred in his absence.

I'd made a reservation for Hewett, party of three, for eight-thirty. Jack had been kind enough to get their cover and music charge lifted, so they were basically getting the evening for whatever they drank, and in Russ's case, that turned out to be a stiff price.

They arrived at five after nine, which I considered to be the height of bad manners. But it's a rule of thumb that the people you get in for free are the ones who cause a scene, or insult the management, or arrive late, or leave in the middle.

Worse, their party of three turned out to be a party of four, with Toby Ackland serving as Gail's date. He was decked out in a white sports coat, and Gail looked quietly stunning in pale blue chiffon. Russ was wearing a three-piece suit with the vest unbuttoned. Martha wore a plain black dress and flat heels, neither of which did anything for her. A silver mesh clutch bag was her one concession to fashion; my guess was that it had been a gift from Gail.

The maître d' was gracious enough to extend the "no cover" to the unexpected (and unwanted, from my point of view) fourth guest, and sat the Hewett party fairly close to the stage. Ackland talked through every number we played. I could hear his bray from the bandstand, even over the trumpets.

What I wanted to do more than anything was sock him in the nose, walk Gail out onto the terrace, and ask her if she had any idea why someone who looked like the deceased Marie Prasquier was now picking up music in the name of Gail's rival Ada Head.

On our first break, I stepped over to their table. Russ, mopping his face with an oversized handkerchief, was polite enough to stand. Ackland didn't even look my way, although he knew I was there, but continued talking to Martha Prentice about a trip he'd taken to Guatemala.

Russ smelled strongly of gin and seemed to sway ever so slightly as he said, "Sorry if we were a little late, Sherwood. Had to pick up the two kids, then stop by my office on the island and pick up a few things I need for the morning. Toby, this is Ray Sherwood." He had a little trouble getting to the *w* in my name.

Toby looked at Russ without looking at me. "Yes, we've already met," he said and resumed his conversation with Martha, who at least nodded politely in my direction.

I turned to Gail, who had a neat little Manhattan sitting in front of her. "Evening, Gail."

Gail said, "Very nice of you to have us as your guests, Ray. I hope you don't mind that I brought along Toby. I figured there's no way on earth that *you* can dance tonight."

Russ was served a second pitcher of some cocktail, and he spilled its pinkish fluid in the vicinity of his martini glass. "Damn good music, Sherwood. And Miss Driscoll is a damn handsome woman. Love to put a saddle on her sometime and take her around the corral." Yes, he'd been drinking. "I'm having pink gins tonight, would you like one?" The drink was exactly what it said it was, straight cold gin with just enough Angostura bitters to add a blush of shame.

I told him not while I was playing, which of course had never been a strict policy of mine, but he didn't have to know that.

Vera came over to us, giving me my best chance to show off. She'd opted that evening for a cellophane-cloth frock that look like liquid gold. Its puffy short sleeves heightened the shock of her décolletage. Vera shook hands all around and took my guests' names and compliments in stride.

"What a lovely little dress that is," Vera said to Gail. "Didn't I see you and Ray having drinks after the show last week?"

Martha looked at me with her usual hatred, and I said solely for her benefit the otherwise meaningless "Yes, that was before I'd met Martha here and got to know more about everyone."

Russ planted his feet a little wider apart, as apparently his part of the room was experiencing a slight yaw. "It would be my pleasure to buy you some champagne, Miss Driscoll."

Vera said, "Well, that's very kind of you. You could have it delivered to the Olympic Hotel in Seattle, where we're next playing, only make sure they mark the crate 'Fragile.' Ray, a word with you?"

I excused myself and followed Vera, who eventually halted by the ballroom's exit. Reviewing the contents of her pocketbook, she said in the most casual voice, "Ray, I'm going away for a few days. I wanted you to be the one to let Jack know I'll rejoin him in Seattle, that I'm fine, but that I need a break."

Suddenly Dave Wooster's story about his ailing father sounded a lot less Samaritan, or even credible.

"Vera, you're going to San Diego, aren't you? Don't do this to Jack. It's going to be so obvious. Dave left today, you leave tomorrow—"

"Tonight, actually. Right now. I'm catching the last train out of Emeryville."

"But it's the band's last weekend here. You're a draw, Vera, you can't skip out."

"Just have Jack tell the crowd what I tell him every night before we go to sleep—that I'm indisposed."

I sighed. "And why am I the one who has to tell him this?"

"Because you feel bad for Jack, so you'll make up a good story. He might even buy it coming from you."

"Give Dave my regards," I said.

She shrugged. "Could have been you, Ray. You should see what I'm not wearing under this dress." She started to leave but added in a low voice, "And you think I make nice sounds when I *sing*."

She left the ballroom and I walked back to Russ Hewett's table. "So, Ray, tell me," Gail asked, "did the *Swing* parts get done?"

It dawned on me that while I had a hundred questions for Gail, I was too confused at the moment to know which ones I should be asking. "Um, the parts are a thing of beauty. Or things of beauty. I'm sure you'd prefer me to bring them to the rehearsal tomorrow rather than burden you with them now, right?"

Gail said she'd be grateful if I'd do that, as Russ, who'd been rocking back a bit too far on the rear legs of his chair, toppled backward.

"Steady there, Russ," I said, righting him with the help of two waiters.

"Whoops-a-daisy," Russ commented. He sat there mopping his face.

"He's stinking," Toby observed. Such a help.

"Why are you doing this, Russ?" snapped Martha.

Russ gave a big smiling shrug with outstretched hands and

turned to see several patrons staring at him. "Hello," he said. "Any-one get the license plate of the bus that just hit me?"

Gail went over to him. "Russ, stop it."

He put his arms around her. "Oh, Gaily, Gaily, I love you daily. You never give your uncle Russ a hug and a kiss, do ya?" He began to fall backward in his chair again and reached out toward Gail to stop his fall. His hand grabbed the left shoulder of her evening gown and, in doing so, exposed her left breast for two seconds. The women at the next table gasped and reflexively put their hands up to their bosoms. For the second time in the last minute, I helped Russ to his feet.

Gail's cheeks flushed. "Okay, come on, Toby, we're going." She turned to me. "See you at the rehearsal, Ray?"

I suggested we rendezvous around two-thirty at Pacific House and walk to the three o'clock rehearsal together. She agreed and de-parted with Ackland, who made no offer to assist with a tip or the cost of the drinks.

"He's completely soused," said Martha, looking at Russ with the loathing she usually reserved for me. "We'd better walk him around outside."

I heard Jack tap his baton on a music stand, our three-minute call. "I'm sorry, Martha, my break is over."

Russ was laughing quietly now at some personal joke. He mopped his brow again and put his handkerchief in his pants pocket.

Martha asked, "Do you have time to get him to the men's room?"

I looked at my watch. "I can get him there, but he'll have to find his own way back. Russ, come on, we're going for a walk."

He wasn't too bad on his feet as long as I was there to serve as his training wheels. We turned past the impressive tropical fish tank near the elevator bank and stepped into the men's room. There was an attendant seated by the sinks, guarding a long row of aftershaves, colognes, hair tonics, talcs, and mouthwashes. The Pinaud and the

Wildroot Cream Oil were running a little low, but everything else seemed available in ample sufficiency. I loved that there was a bottle of Drene shampoo available. Was someone really going to shampoo his hair before returning to the ballroom? The attendant stood up from his leather upholstered captain's chair and helped me help Russ into it.

"Evening," I said to the attendant.

"Yes sir, it sure is that," he answered, sensing an opportunity in the making.

"My friend here partook of some pink gins that disagreed with his sobriety," I said, laying down a five-dollar bill. "Maybe a prairie oyster with a lot of Worcestershire, and a tall tomato juice?"

"You leave him with me," said the attendant. "I get a case like this three, four nights a week. We'll give him hot towels and a cold compress, get him smelling nice, too, and have him back to you in under an hour."

I laid down three more singles. "A little coffee wouldn't hurt, either."

"Right as rain he'll be, you leave that to old Duke."

I sincerely hoped that *he* was, in fact, "old Duke." Otherwise, I had a dreadful image of Russ being hurled about the washroom by an oversized Doberman pinscher until he was scared sober.

I returned to the bandstand, took my seat with an apologetic nod to Jack Donovan, and remembered that I still had to invent a credible reason why Vera had told *me* (but not her own husband) that she was leaving for a destination and purpose I'd yet to invent, while simultaneously transposing Dave Wooster's baritone sax part on the fly thirteen whole tones below where it was notated.

A cinch.

The washroom attendant was better than his word. In well under the promised hour, a sober-looking, pale-faced Russ had returned, murmuring some grim apologies to Martha, who looked away from him unforgivingly.

On our next-to-last break, Jack stopped by my music stand and asked, "No idea where our Vera has gotten herself, have you? I saw her chatting you up earlier."

I explained that she'd asked me to convey to him that she'd gotten a message at the front desk from a friend or relative (I said I couldn't remember which) who was going to be somewhere in southern California for only this weekend before flying to somewhere in Australia to retire. Vera found that if she left that very instant, she could just make the last train out of Emeryville, that she didn't even have time to pack, that she would rejoin us in Seattle, that Jack shouldn't worry about her, and that she'd be fine. She'd suggested he explain to tomorrow night's crowd that she'd come down with laryngitis.

He listened to my explanation, nodding assent to each vague turn of this ham-fisted story I'd had to create with enough slack built into it to cover Vera's damnable tail.

"Yes," he murmured. "Yes, I mean, yes, that's actually quite odd that she suggested the laryngitis. I was, actually, going to say that anyway. Even if she hadn't left for, where'd she say? Southern California?" He gave my arm a reassuring squeeze. "Thanks for conveying the message as thoughtfully as ever, Ray." He asked me if I'd lead the last set for a few minutes while he went to place a phone call. I said I would. As he started to leave the bandstand, he added, "Oh, by the by: I think you should start scouting up a new baritone sax. I think we deserve better than Dave Wooster."

I told him I agreed.

I headed to where a contrite Russ was seated, doing hard time alongside Martha. Although he now seemed as abstemious as Henry Ford at a Mormon temple in Oklahoma on a Sunday, he actually had a shot of neat brown liquid sitting in front of him. I could smell the toastiness of a bourbon.

"Apologize for the scene I caused a while ago, Sherwood," he said gruffly.

Swing · 223

I waved his words away. "I think you need to apologize to Gail and Martha, not me. I'm afraid I've been just as tight as you were a couple of times in my life." I hadn't consciously meant this to be a message to Martha, but her expression showed me she'd taken it that way. For a fleeting moment, she looked almost human, until she corrected herself. I pointed to the bourbon. "But don't start all over again."

"Hair of the dog that bit me," he said. "This stuff I can handle."

"You should never touch gin," Martha said. "The juniper berries make you crazy. I still don't think you're anywhere near fit to drive."

"Nonsense." He tossed down the last of the whiskey and stood. "Stuff and nonsense. Well, at least the music was excellent. And tell your Miss Driscoll that champagne will be waiting for her in Seattle." He gestured to the bandstand. "Is she going to sing again this evening?"

I shook my head. "She came down with laryngitis. Caught it from a friend in San Diego."

Russ gave Martha a quarter, and she went to get her wrap from the cloakroom. He threw some money down on the table. "So there's a rehearsal tomorrow of Gail's composition?"

"Yes, at three."

"Look forward to hearing it. You'll be there?"

I said I would.

He confided, "I appreciate all the help you've been giving her. Made a fool of myself tonight, but she's become almost a daughter to me, if that doesn't sound too foolish."

"Not at all," I said.

He gave a low grunt. "Hate that little twerp Toby Ackland."

"Me too," I agreed, to his mild surprise.

I led the first twenty minutes of the last set. It wasn't a big deal, not as if I stood there waving a baton. It just entailed giving a count-off. After each intro, I sat with the rest of the band and only got up for the cutoff.

Jack returned to the stage looking reinvigorated. His hair could have used a comb. My guess was he'd gone outside to take in some clean air and exhale some Vera.

After the last number, Tommy Trego took my instrument cases and wished me a good night. I wandered over to the Terrace Lounge to see if for any reason Gail had returned, but no. I wondered if she was still out with Ackland.

I walked through the lobby and saw a bellman and a uniformed custodian gravely inspecting the tropical fish tank near the elevator bank. I wondered what held their attention. I stepped over and saw that all the fish in the tank were dead, forming a colorful ceiling of delicate cadavers above a model of a deep-sea diver, an underwater castle, a bubbling clam shell nestled against a sponge, and some coral.

I walked up the steps to my room, withdrew my mailable key from my wallet, and opened the door. The lights were on in the room, although I was next to certain I'd turned them off before leaving.

It was an absolute shambles. Someone had broken in and searched the room, and they hadn't given a damn if I knew it. They'd overturned a chair as if I might have hidden something beneath its seat. The writing desk's drawer was inverted on the floor. The covers had been pulled from the bed and the mattress raised and moved off the bedsprings.

I heard a rustling noise behind me, turned, and saw that the curtain I'd been leaving closed until I went to sleep had been drawn back and was being buffeted about by a breeze that was taking advantage of my much too widely opened window. My uninvited caller, who was no friend to hotel furniture, could easily have used that portal to leave. If he had left. . . .

I looked cautiously in the closet and then the bathroom, but there was no sign of anyone. Interestingly, the bathroom did not seem to have been searched at all; everything was as I remembered having left it. This made me suspect that whatever it was the intruder had been searching for, they had found it, or they would have made an equal shambles of the bathroom as well. I wondered what—

Oh God, the *Swing* parts! I raced to the dresser's second drawer, where I'd put the music when I'd hurriedly changed for the evening, and pulled it open. No, they all seemed to be there, sitting neatly on the clean butcher paper that lined the bottom of each drawer of the dresser.

In fact, nothing seemed to be missing from the room.

I considered calling the front desk to complain, but I didn't know what they could do about it. The Claremont probably had a chambermaid on duty between midnight and six, but I wasn't about to ask the poor thing to make up my disaster of a room simply so that I could turn in for the night. So I righted the chair and the night table, fixed the shade on the reading lamp, and otherwise restored the room to normalcy.

I went through all the instrumental parts. Each was intact, and nothing had been changed. Thank God for that. If I had thought Martha's wrath was a dreadful thing to witness, imagine Gail's fury if I'd lost the parts for her masterpiece the night before its rehearsal.

I couldn't imagine anything worse. Until the next morning.

40

The Next Morning

There was a knock on my door. I travel with a dark gray charmeuse robe that packs well. I went to the bathroom to get it off a hook on the wall, knotted its sash around my waist, and opened the door to my room.

It was Bob Culpepper. "Morning, Lieutenant," I said.

"Russ Hewett and Martha Prentice are dead."

I said that ridiculous thing. "They can't be, I just saw them last night." He'd probably heard this many times.

"I understand. They're dead, all the same." It was such an easy thing to say, and his saying it made it so. "I remembered you'd invited them to come see you here last night. Can I have a word with you?"

I showed him into the room.

My first thought was only of myself. I thought, *If Martha's dead, my chances of ever knowing the truth about Gail are frailer than ever.* Worse, unless Martha had left some message for Gail—you know, "To Be Opened Only in the Event of My Death"—how would I ever be able to tell her or anyone else about the possibility that I'm her father? I wondered if Martha had let anyone else on earth know about this. Perhaps her brother, Gail's beloved uncle Joe? But he was, where, in Germany? I found it hard to believe that Martha would have shared our secret with Russ, but even if she had, Culpepper was saying he was gone now, too.

My second thought was that I had, in the last dozen days, witnessed the death of Marie Prasquier, been stabbed in the arm by Martha Prentice, had a woman who called herself Adeline Head flee at the sight of me on three occasions, discovered the possible reincarnation of the aforementioned Marie, and now learned of the deaths of Martha and Russ. All of these people I'd only encountered because of Gail. There was much I could tell Culpepper, including the fact that my hotel room had been ransacked the night before, but I didn't dare speak a word until I knew if the girl who might be my daughter was in some way connected to, or even at the center of, this atonal medley of events.

I sat on the bed and he pulled over a chair. "What happened?" I asked.

"Car accident. On Grizzly Peak." He grimaced. "*Off* Grizzly Peak, actually. There's a piece of road where I've been trying to get a guardrail installed for six years now. Coming downhill about halfway between Tilden Park and Fish Ranch Road, there's been a half dozen cars gone over the edge in the last five years alone. Now add another. His Studebaker went off the cliff, and there was nothing to stop the fall until four hundred feet later. Imagine that fall, Ray." He was a tough guy, and trying to be professional, but I could see he was upset.

I asked him if he wanted me to order up some coffee. He looked like he'd been awake awhile.

"No thanks, I've had too much already. Got the call around three this morning. They found the plates belonged to Hewett, and the officer in charge knew he was an acquaintance of mine. Not a great friend, we knew each other from working on the island, but, you know, we'd had dinner more than once. I was over to his house, met his lady friend."

"When did this happen?"

He moved his neck about within his suit collar. "That's what I've been trying to figure out, not that it does any good for Russ or Martha. The area is completely desolate up there. It would make for a great lovers' lane but there's not a lot of places to park without risking your life. An hour can pass without a car going by. The only reason anyone knew there'd been an accident was because the car caught fire after it crashed and the flames could be seen above Claremont Avenue. The fire was reported around one-thirty, so it stands to reason it happened some time between one-fifteen and then. By the time we got there, both of them were pretty much burned to a crisp—" He went pale for a moment and coughed into a handkerchief he produced from his pants pocket. "Excuse me, I'm used to this stuff, but it's different when you know the person."

Sitting there, I suddenly panicked as I envisioned Gail and Toby Ackland borrowing Russ's Studebaker in order to park and pet amid the wilds of Grizzly Peak. This was not impossible. I hadn't actually seen how the four of them had arrived or departed last night. Perhaps Gail, leaving in a huff, took Russ's car, figuring that in his drunken state, it would be safer for him and Martha to take a taxi home.

"Are you *sure* it was Martha?" I said, trying not to show my anxiety.

Culpepper reassured me. "The coroner's had a busy morning. We found a little black book in Martha's metal clutch bag with all her telephone numbers, including her doctor and dentist, and the same for Russ. We got her dental records at nine A.M., his by a quarter after, and by ten we had a positive I.D. on her. Russ we're still working on—apparently there was some damage to his jaw on impact—"

"But as far as Martha goes, there's no way it could have been anyone else?"

"You can speak to the coroner himself if you like; it was a perfect match." He permitted himself the smallest smile of understanding. "Listen, if you're worried about what I think you're worried about, let me reassure you that I talked to Gail this morning."

"In person?"

"Yes, I went to her dormitory, if you want to call it that, on Bancroft Way. She had already heard from the coroner's office, which was a helluva way for her to be told. I don't think Russ meant that much to her, but the girl at the front desk said she'd gotten hysterical when she heard the news. You know: 'What'll I do now,' that sort of thing, just like you'd expect from a kid. But she'd pulled it together by the time I got there. Real emotionless, state of shock probably. She just wanted to know what she had to do. I guess she's all alone in the world now."

I needed to call her then and there, but Culpepper wanted to hear about the previous night. I gave him a thumbnail sketch of the evening, including everyone's time of departure, and felt obliged to mention Russ's three pitchers of pink gins. I omitted his pawing of Gail because I didn't think it was in any way relevant. "I did my best to sober him up, and he seemed lucid enough when he left, although he did have a bourbon."

Culpepper wriggled his shoulders in disgust. "Gin, then bourbon. Not my idea of a chaser."

"It didn't occur to me they'd be going anywhere other than home, which is almost a straight line from here. What in God's name were they doing in the hills at that hour?"

Culpepper said finding the answer to that was one of the foremost reasons the City of Oakland paid him a salary. He said he was going back to inspect the accident site in the overhead spotlight of noon, and asked if I'd like to join him.

I asked if I could call Gail first and he said that would be fine. I had the Claremont's operator try her at the Berkeley Club, but the desk clerk there said she was out. I tried her at Russ Hewett's number and got no answer.

I hadn't liked Martha Prentice one bit, except for one giddy night almost twenty-two years ago. But I owed it to her, to Gail, and to myself to visit where her unlovely life had concluded.

Culpepper drove a Cord cabriolet, God love him, and I would have savored the drive were it not for the circumstances. It was, to me, a gangster's car, dangerously handsome and serious business. It had a coffin-nose hood with a wraparound louvered radiator and two pontoon fenders in which retractable headlights hid until needed. Brand-new, it could not have gone for less than two thousand dollars. Replying to my eyebrows, he said, probably not for the first time, "Bought it secondhand from somebody who owed me a favor. I'm a bachelor, don't go out on many dates, have a one-bedroom flat in the old part of town, plan to keep it for twenty years. It's my one indulgence." That might have been the story, or it might not. He was a well-placed officer on a big-city police force. This, in my experience, was often a more profitable franchise than Nedick's or Schrafft's.

Coming out of the Claremont, we motored up the green canyon hillside, leaving Berkeley at our backs. I couldn't imagine why Russ and Martha had headed this way at that hour.

I asked Culpepper, "So what does one find on Grizzly Peak?"

"Grizzly Peak," he answered, downshifting to low. "So . . . you didn't go back very far with Russ Hewett?"

"I met both you and Russ at the same moment, Lieutenant, remember?"

"Oh yeah. What a lousy moment that was, huh?"

"For Marie Prasquier, yes, it was terrible." I then asked, in what I thought was an eminently casual way, "Did she have any family in the area? You know, brothers or sisters?"

Culpepper let me marinate for a moment, then looked at me out of the corner of his eye. "Funny question. Why do you ask?"

"I have no idea. Just making conversation, I guess."

The Cord's engine exulted as the grade grew more extreme. "Someone at the Folies did say she had a sister who'd been in the business, but they thought she was still in France and in the same pickle that Marie Prasquier was so terrified of."

The scenery was becoming scrubby as we made a hairpin turn onto Grizzly Peak Boulevard, rising higher and farther north.

"So you had no connections to Russ or Martha or Gail before the day I met you, huh?"

I wondered what he could possibly have learned. "Why do you ask, Bob?"

"Well, it just seems odd that you got yourself sort of adopted by this family that isn't quite a family, considering you're a musician just passing through town. Spending your days at their house, in Gail's bedroom . . ." I asked him how he knew that, and he told me that Russ had mentioned to him, a little uneasily, how I was there every day and he'd hoped I wasn't up to something.

"I don't know what 'up to something' means," I said, annoyed. "I worked very hard arranging Gail's composition, and anyone who has some awareness of my craft would tell you it was quite a challenge. It's amazing I got it done in the time allotted. I've run around getting the best copyist for her composition, I'll be assisting the first rehearsal of the piece this afternoon—probably without Gail under these terrible circumstances—and for my services I'm receiving all of fifty dollars, even though I've already spent close to a hundred for the copying and related expenses."

Culpepper smiled at me. "Why?"

"What?"

The road angled sharply. We were now on a cliff, and the most spectacular view suddenly revealed itself on our left. But Culpepper knew he could see this view anytime and kept the questions coming. "I mean, it's very nice of you to lose money on the deal, but how come, Ray? I look at Gail and have to ask myself, Is it because you're sweet on her? Fooling around with her?"

"Certainly not!" I said indignantly.

He laughed pleasantly, and I realized he was far more dangerous than I'd thought. "Why the outraged 'certainly not'? What would be wrong with the two of you having a necking session? You're single, so's she, she's plenty attractive—so why is that idea such an insult? I'm trying to figure you out, Ray, and it's not the easiest thing to do."

We passed a black-and-white squad car that was parked alongside the edge of the cliff. Culpepper made a tight U-turn, and for a moment I thought we'd be going off the cliff ourselves. But he knew the cabriolet down to the last dime it could turn on, and we pulled up perfectly parked behind the police car.

When we got out I, being on the passenger side, found myself warily regarding the edge of the clumpy cliff only a few feet from where I set down my feet.

A policeman, introduced to me as Officer Ciancimino, conferred privately for a few moments with Culpepper.

I detected a criminal lurking on the premises. It was the City of Oakland. How could they not have installed a guardrail or, minimally, a row of reflectors along the cliff's edge, which patiently waited only a few hundred feet beyond a sharp, blind downhill turn.

Staring straight out to the southwest, you could easily scan past the bay to where the Pacific's horizon became a thick line of navy blue ink drawn with a wide-nibbed pen.

Staring straight down, however, you could see a plateau bearing the remains of more than twenty cars, mangled and misshapen in a Sargasso Sea of Lost Sedans. Each looked as if it had been ripped apart and torched by a dragon's claws and breath.

I could just make out the blackened green body of Hewett's Studebaker in the graveyard below. It was charred worst on its right front side, but the impact and ensuing fire had been more than enough to speed both the car's passengers to their final point of termination. I don't pray, but I did now, for the cold, unforgiving Martha Prentice. My thoughts, for whoever could read them, were that, father or not, I'd try to watch out for her child as best I could.

I looked back and saw Culpepper take a glassine envelope about six inches square from the police officer. Culpepper pocketed it and sent the squad car on its way.

We were alone, high above the world.

Culpepper sidled up to me. "You're wondering how come all this wreckage hasn't been cleared yet. There's a dispute about whose responsibility the heap is. Only been going on for about twenty years, should be resolved by the turn of the century. The property we're standing on is Oakland. But where the cars land belongs to U.C. Berkeley. Cal says it's Oakland's problem; Oakland says it's Cal's."

He began to point out to me landmarks for which I needed no pointing. Literally beneath my feet was the Hotel Claremont, where Gail had first left her note for me, her mother had left her mark on me, and Russ had bid good-bye to me. A seeming stone's throw to my right, the U.C. campus, its Campanile, and Berkeley Square, where Gail had phoned Adeline Head. Straight ahead, Treasure Island, where Marie Prasquier had died, only to apparently rise like the phoenix atop the tower from which she'd fallen, and where, in a few hours, Gail's *Swing* would be rehearsed for the first time. If I looked hard enough on my left, I could see the neighborhood where Gail and I had together created that very same composition.

"You're an idiot, Sherwood," said Culpepper softly.

I entertained the possibility that he was going to push me off the cliff. I turned and saw him shaking his head disapprovingly at me. "Nancy was no one to leave just because your life got painful."

I'd forgotten for a moment that he'd dated Nancy. I was glad they were getting along. Most of the time, he seemed to me to be a good man.

"Has life really been that much better for you alone?" he asked.

"You don't understand. Did you ever have a partner on the force?"

"Officer Dan Sprayberry. We were squad car eighteen," he said without a moment's hesitation.

It was so hard to explain. "Well, say that one night you and Dan see a man at the back of an alleyway, and you think he has a gun, and you both hear a shot, and the two of you fire back. He drops. And now you run to his side and you see he's a twelve-year-old kid with a toy gun and the shot you heard was a truck that backfired. The kid says, 'Why'd you kill me?' His face turns blue and he's dead.

"Now you and Dan, you're the only ones who saw what you did. You bundle up the kid and you take him to a reservoir and you toss him in. No one finds out, there's no repercussions, and you go about your lives. Except that the two of you both have this knowledge. Sometimes it goes away for a while, but it always comes back. You like each other, trust each other . . . but wouldn't you eventually want a partner who doesn't know that this thing happened . . . so that you could pretend for a little while each day that you and your conscience were just fine?"

Culpepper said, "Yes, but, Ray, the thing is: you didn't kill anyone."

The wind made our jackets flap for a moment. We were like two perched birds figuring out where to roost this evening.

Culpepper continued to stare straight ahead. "Now, Ray, I'm going to show you something that you didn't see. Understand? You're not going to talk to anyone about it, and if you do, I'll say you took it out of my glove compartment while I was talking to Officer Ciancimino. He just gave it to me now. They found it in Hewett's cigar case, one of those metal-sleeve jobs that'll hold five Panatellas. They didn't think to open the case until a while ago."

He reached into his vest pocket and took out the glassine envelope that he'd been given by Officer Ciancimino. It contained a folded sheet of blue paper.

"I've talked with your ex-wife and additionally God gave me this pair of eyes. I can see there's something you feel about Gail Prentice other than admiration for her musical talents, and before you say *how dare you,* understand I'm not saying your feelings are necessarily romantic or sexual. I'm also aware that Gail is close to the age your daughter would be if she were alive today. It happens that I like you, Ray, or maybe I like your wife and since she likes you, I want to like you, too."

He reached into his inside pocket and produced a set of white cotton gloves, as if he were about to do an impression of W. C. Fields.

"Put these on," he said.

Apparently, I was the one who was going to do the impression.

He said, "Now even though I'm supposed to be the detective here, I don't know quite what to make of what I'm going to show you, or how it might help or hurt you. I was very surprised by it, to say the least. But I know you're leaving town soon, and I thought you might want to factor this into any feelings or thoughts you have about what happens next in your life."

He handed me the envelope. "It hasn't been checked for fingerprints. Read it for yourself and you'll understand why, receiving such a letter, Russ would have wanted to both keep it, and keep it private."

He handed it to me. It seemed to be the last page of a letter written on standard stationery. There was a large violet ink stain in the top left-hand corner of the page that I thought for a second was blood but on closer inspection clearly wasn't.

I knew from the handwriting who had written the letter long before I read its signature.

... and then we can put this dreadful time behind us. Sometimes the desk clerk here at the Berkeley Club will buzz me on the intercom and tell me I have a phone call. I fly to the phone, and before I reach it, I've convinced myself it's you, that you've managed to get away if only for one blessed morning or night and I need only rush to the Hotel Oakland or the Fairmont across the bay and you will be there in the lobby, waiting to lift me up into your arms. I am younger than you but does that mean I am stronger? I have no idea. This is such an immense charade I am living, for your sake, for mine, because it is what I must do today to make sure we have a tomorrow that will be like our yesterdays. Soon we will be together and all will be as it was. Do reassure me this is true, if only in another note. I am doing terrible and ridiculous things in the name of our future. I lie in my bed here and in Chancery Lane praying that love can travel through walls and reach you, and that you can feel my embrace. I live for when I can be honest again and we can be together again. We must both be strong and do what we must do to make this happen.

You don't work long, focused hours over someone's musical composition, reading their indications of *fortissimo* and *pianissimo*, each requested *sforzando* and suggested *delicato* without learning their writing hand. And so I had absolutely no need to look to the signature to see who had written this fervent letter to Russ Hewett. I looked all the same, if only to see how she worded the closing.

Love now, ever and always,
Gail

41

The Castle

*S*wing was to be performed in the Pavilion of Japan, a thing of exquisite grace and beauty, patterned after an Asian feudal castle and containing, within that fortress, a baronial Samurai house.

I knew from the reading I'd done while first waiting in the "study hall" of Bob Culpepper's interview room that a Japanese liner had been the first ship of serious tonnage to make its harbor at Treasure Island. Russ Hewett's construction team had stopped their work as, fascinated and enlightened, they watched their Asian equivalents, garbed in blue-and-white kimonos and sandals, creating the entire pavilion without the use of a single nail, lashing together the beams with rope until each join could be dovetailed into the next. The final construction seemed to float above, rather than upon, the lagoon that surrounded it, the largest on the island, and when one sat in its inner garden for rice cakes and a cup of green tea, it placed the rest of the world an ocean apart.

I was waiting for Gail in the nearby Pacific House, as we'd previously agreed. I wasn't sure if she would appear, or how I would feel when I saw her. But I knew she might need my help on many fronts.

Two hours earlier, Culpepper and I had driven back in silence to the Claremont.

I'd gone to the front desk of the Claremont and asked if a package had arrived from RC Copying. The clerk had handed me an oversized manila envelope that contained my full orchestral score and the Photostatic copy that Haffner had made for me.

I'd gone to my room and tossed the copy of the score (photographically reduced in size and a negative image with white notes on a black background) onto my bed. Then, remembering what had been done to my room the night before, I opened my top dresser drawer, lifted the sheet of white paper that lined its bottom, and placed the score underneath it.

I'd called Gail again at both the Berkeley Club and Hewett's home and gotten no response.

I have seen people perform for the public on the same day someone close to them has died. I had no way of knowing if Gail would show up for the rehearsal. Professionally and personally, I owed her my presence. But the "personally" part was all balled up now.

So she'd had a romance with Russ Hewett and, from the tone of the letter, a consummated one. (And *I'd* been worried about being too old for her!) She'd said in her note that she was living a lie, but what was it? That Russ and Gail barely knew or liked each other? Did her mother suspect the relationship? I wondered if Gail's flirtatious behavior with me had been part of the deception, or just the way she was. Then I allowed myself the hope that this was an old note she'd written to Russ, that he'd kept it as a wistful souvenir of the briefest crush an impressionable young girl had once had for a day or two at most. Now it was over. Yes, that was possible, very possible indeed. It would also explain Russ's drunken behavior and momentary pawing of Gail. After all, the only thing that dated the letter was that she'd been living at the Berkeley Club when she'd written it. She might have moved in there years ago.

Waiting for her now in Pacific House, I stared at a leaded-glass mural depicting the trade routes of the South Seas and watched the decorative clock alongside it reach two forty-five. If I was going to have to explain Gail's absence to the Pan-Pacific Orchestra, it would be best for me to arrive at the rehearsal a little early.

I entered the impressive, high-timbered portal of the Japanese castle and passed an exhibition on the manufacturing of silk. A young Japanese woman in a kimono bowed to me and said in a delightfully high voice, "*Yoroshiku onegai shimasu. Irasshaimase.* Welcome to Japan." She handed me a little card with Japanese phrases on it and pointed to the translations of what she had just said.

"You do speak English?" I asked.

"Oh yeah, the staff is all Japanese American. To be honest, my Japanese has gotten kind of rusty. I can tell you all about the Pavilion though."

I told her why I was there. "Oh sure," she said. "The band is setting up in the rock garden. I think someone there is supposed to be greeting you. Phil . . ." She turned to a sober-faced, darker-hued youth, his hair pulled back in a tight bun appropriate to his samurai garb and long, sheathed sword. "Phil, can you cover for me while I take this gentleman to the official with the swing band?" She gave him her handful of phrase cards.

A low, broad platform about a foot high had been placed upon the white gravel of the rock garden, and the Pan-Pacific Orchestra was seated upon it, playing that universal, unwritten overture of a band warming up.

The Kimono girl escorted me over to a serious-looking gentleman in a nicely tailored charcoal suit with black pinstripes. He was studying the activities of the orchestra with great intensity. She said to him, "I think this is one of the people you've been waiting for, Mr. . . ." clearly not remembering his name she smiled and left us there.

"Hello," I said. "My name is Ray Sherwood, and I've brought the musical parts for the piece that won your competition."

He gave an efficient bow, reached into his pocket, and produced a card that identified him as Mr. Fumio Dakuzaku, special envoy from imperial Japan to the office of the Japanese general consul in San Francisco. He said in a crisp but courteous voice, "I had the honor of serving on the committee that selected the winning composition. May I ask if you are with the woman who composed it?"

I explained in a lowered tone about the tragedy that had occurred and said that I didn't know if she would be able to attend. He made some low, sympathetic sounds and observed how tragic it was that her mother would not be able to witness her daughter's public success. I agreed and assured him that I had overseen the arranging of the score from start to finish and that I would stay close at hand in case there were any questions, difficulties, or changes that had to be made.

He nodded gratefully and told me that, to help reduce expenses on the long trip with the orchestra from Tokyo, he was also serving as the band's librarian. (Actually, he used the word *curator,* but I got the idea.) He asked for the music, which I gave to him, and invited me to meet the ensemble that would be playing *Swing.*

42

The Verdict of the Court

He escorted me across the sea of white pebbles to the musician's platform. The band members, all seemingly Japanese and all male, wore white shirts, pants, socks, and bucks. Their ties were bright red. Whether they were intentionally emulating their flag of the rising sun, I couldn't say. I saw them go quiet as Dakuzaku led me toward the piano, which I assumed had been rented for the occasion. It was a creamy white, and its top was propped open.

Fumio stiffly introduced me to Mr. Katzumi Kitahara, leader of the Pan-Pacific Orchestra, who was also the band's pianist. He was a young man with a great mop of black hair and golden skin.

"Mr. Sherwood! It's an unexpected honor to meet you," he said with earnest enthusiasm. "How did you become involved with this composition?"

His apparent awe took me by surprise. I wasn't exactly Harry James or Woody Herman. I gave him a vague explanation about being in town and wanting to help rising young talent. I also explained why Miss Prentice was not present at the moment and told Katzumi to call me Ray.

"Thank you, then I will," he replied. "And you should call me Kat. It's done by everyone I know."

He stepped in front of the orchestra, and their conversation ceased instantly. (Jack Donovan was lucky if his band stopped talking while we were playing.) He made an announcement in Japanese, and I noticed that when my name was mentioned a murmur went around the orchestra. I was then introduced formally, and the band members applauded.

"May I be allowed to introduce you individually to the musicians?" Kat asked. I said it would be my pleasure. He took me to the lead alto player, who is in a way the swing band equivalent of an orchestra's concertmaster. He is also, in my opinion, the person who defines the "color" of the reed section.

"Mr. Ray Sherwood, may I present Mr. Shuki Kinoshita, our first alto saxophone?"

"Beega-fahn," said Shuki intently as we shook hands.

I looked at Katzumi, who explained, "He's saying he's a big fan of your work."

"Oh, thank you very much," I said to Shuki and shook his hand again. I turned to Kat. "I don't understand. Jack Donovan isn't that well known even here in the U.S.A. How do you know me?"

"Oh, from your arrangements for the Robbins-Feist-Miller corporation," he said respectfully.

I had to laugh. Over the years, I had written a great number of what are called stock arrangements. These were charts of current hit songs, existing standards, and special-purpose numbers that anyone could walk into a music store and buy for their own ensemble, whether it was an amateur organization or a professional band that didn't feel the need to make their own artistic statement regarding "Auld Lang Syne," "Happy Birthday," "The Anniversary Waltz," or

"The Girlfriend of the Whirling Dervish." Jack Donovan even had a few of my stock arrangements in his book, not out of respect for this side job of mine, but because if he was requested to play something approximating Benny Goodman's "Let's Dance," Glenn Miller's "Moonlight Serenade," or Count Basie's "One O'Clock Jump," I'd written the chart that everyone in America other than Benny Goodman, Glenn Miller, or Count Basie used.

Clearly, some of the Pan-Pacific Orchestra's "book" consisted of stock arrangements written by me. I considered it to be my hackwork, but to them, this was like Handel dropping in on the Mormon Tabernacle Choir. I went down the line of the sax, trumpet, and trombone sections like a visiting dignitary greeting the troops.

Like Jack's band, the Pan-Pacific Orchestra traveled with a band boy, who walked behind Fumio Dakuzaku respectfully and helpfully. As a librarian, Fumio was a rather poor choice because he clearly had little musical background, and the band boy had to prompt him as to which sax was a tenor and which was an alto.

Kat took me aside and advised me that the band boy's name was Key Kaisa, pronounced something like Kay Ky-ee-za but without much emphasis on the *ee*. Kat watched warily for my reaction.

I slowly ventured, "Is he aware—"

Kat cut me off. "Yes. He knows about Kay Kyser. He is very upset having the same name as a comedy bandleader."

I was introduced to the boy, who could have been no more than sixteen and seemed very serious about his job. I said his name as accurately as I could, making no reference to Kay Kyser, and asked him about his aspirations.

"I live to be a jazz trumpet player. I am studying with Mr. Oshima, who plays our first trumpet," he said proudly. "In return for that, I am fortunate enough to have obtained this position. The competition was very great." I congratulated him and said I knew I would be hearing great music from his trumpet someday. The boy gave an embarrassed bow and quickly moved away.

Kat looked relieved. "That was very generous of you. It will be the greatest moment of his trip. Now we wonder if we might have the honor of performing one of your arrangements for you. That would be the greatest moment of *our* trip."

In point of fact, I really didn't relish the thought of listening to one of my yeoman-like arrangements when I was anxious to hear Gail's bold work and my own voicing of it. But I could see it meant a lot to the ensemble, and when I nodded my okay, there was an in-stantaneous debate within the band as to which arrangement of mine should be played. At last, Kat opted for my chart of "Down South Camp Meeting."

I was invited to sit with Fumio in one of several white folding chairs that had been set out. The band members all held their in-struments at the ready, whether they played on the downbeat or not. This might be the way a marching band would begin, but certainly not how a swing ensemble would do it. I'd have to slip a word to Kat about this.

As the music began, my first thought was that I should keep in mind what it would sound like if I were asked to perform a Japa-nese folk melody on the *koto,* the *biwa,* or the *shamisen.* Pretty god-awful, I'm sure. Therefore, it was not surprising that the resulting performance by the Pan-Pacific Orchestra was nothing to cause Duke Ellington, or perhaps even Kay Kyser, to lose any sleep. The band was distinguished by its precision, its metronomic tempo, and the absolute internal synchronicity of its ensemble work. Unfortu-nately, while these are outstanding traits for an electric sewing ma-chine, they are among the last things you look for in jazz. The musicians all had rather thin tones and employed a vibrato that seemed far too fast, like a nervous soprano at her first public per-formance.

That said, I was immensely flattered. They did not hit a single clinker, and it was evident that many hours of practice had been put in, both individually and by the entire ensemble. I felt the forced smile on my face gradually turn into a more genuine one.

I felt a hand on my shoulder and saw that it belonged to Gail.

She was dressed in a long black skirt and a dark gray sweater. Her eyes were small and red and had not been bathed in boric acid. She wore no makeup, and her color was pale.

I stood and held her. She let me do so, but it was not romantic, nor should it have been. I wondered how she had allowed Russ to hold her. That too should not have been.

I sat her in my chair and whispered, "I'm so sorry, Gail."

She didn't look at me. "I don't want to talk about it."

"I called you but I couldn't—"

"Ray, shut up. I'm here to do *this*, I don't want to talk about anything but *this*."

The band finished playing my stock arrangement and looked my way. I felt funny reacting in any fashion while Gail was sitting there, clearly in shock and in mourning. But she helped me decide what to do by applauding herself. Fumio and my new pal Key Kaisa joined in. I walked toward them, clapping my hands and calling out, "Bravo! You played it better than Fletcher Henderson himself!" This was, of course, an outrageous lie, but it didn't cost anyone anything. As the band members who understood English translated my compliment for the handful that didn't, I heard an excited buzz sweep across the orchestra.

I introduced Gail to Fumio Dakuzaku, who gave Gail one of his cards and explained to her that, as both the band's librarian and a representative of the imperial government, he was honored to formally accept her work. He added how very sorry he was to hear her sad news.

Gail glared at me as angrily as her mother ever had. "There was no need to tell anyone."

I said gently, "Gail, come let me introduce you to the band."

"There's no need for me to meet the band," she said. "Just have them play my piece so I can leave." I looked at Fumio apologetically and gestured toward Gail as if to say, "It's understandable." He nodded acknowledgment.

I went up to Kat on the bandstand and told him the composer was here. Kat nodded and told the musicians to turn to the *Swing* parts on their stands.

I returned to Gail's side with the score for my original orchestration, from which Jurgen Haffner had extracted the parts that had just been handed out.

There is usually a sense of excitement, anxiety, and (hopefully) elation when an arrangement or composition is performed for the very first time. Until then, the notes have simply been markings on music paper, something imagined in one's head, perhaps with the assistance of a piano. Now, with the downbeat, the orchestration would come into existence. I felt terrible that Gail would always associate this unique moment in her life with the death of her mother.

Gail took the score from me and placed it underneath her original piano score, which she had brought with her. I said, "Good, that's the right thing to do. You should never bury your nose in the score on the first run-through. Just listen to it, the way your audience will."

Whether or not she was paying attention to me, I couldn't say. She turned to her original score's back page, where she had written, *Dedicated to a World of International Understanding*. She took out a fountain pen and inscribed below that *and to the memory of Martha Prentice*. Peeling away the tape on the score's back cover, she handed the page upon which she'd inscribed these additional words to Fumio, who saw what was written and accepted it with solemnity. "I understand," he said quietly. "When the original musicians' parts are placed in our national archives, I will see that this is included as the dedication page."

Kat counted off what we call "two bars for nothing," and the orchestrated *Swing* was heard by human ears for the very first time.

♯

It's how you frame it. Or as an agent at MCA once said to me, "It's all about how you walk in the door."

I've worked vaudeville revues where on opening night a comic owned the audience's bellies and couldn't get them to stop howling. The next morning, the big paper in town says he stank. That night, same comic, same stories, same delivery, the guy can't rent a laugh.

When I'd been reclining on a studio bed in the sunny nest of Gail's bedroom, with an entrancing girl at the keyboard making the notes dance, having the visual of her shoulders, arms, head, and flying mass of hair to delight my eye, *Swing* had struck me as a wild, impulsive, risky, rewarding new direction for those sounds we call music.

And I believe that were we all seated in Carnegie Hall, with the bounce of its reverberant walls adding a sense of drama and intrigue to each lonely line and sharp impact, amidst an audience of intelligentsia who'd been apprised in advance that this award-winning piece had already been pronounced "a breakthrough in modern music" by no less than Deems Taylor, with Benny Goodman and His Orchestra performing the work in confidently supple fashion, *Swing* would have been hailed the next morning as an impudent and innovative composition by a female visionary with whom the Arts would soon be forced to reckon.

However.

In the open air that diluted and dissipated sound to the outer walls of the feudal castle, being sight-read by musicians who played their instruments a bit stiffly and sometimes weakly and whose vibratos sounded a bit like Snow White singing at the wishing well, with a pianist who was having a hard enough time playing his own complex part without also attempting to conduct the piece, *Swing* suddenly sounded like a bunch of noise.

Professor Haffner would have been so pleased.

The Japanese-American girl who had introduced me to Fumio came out into the courtyard, along with Samurai Phil and some other young guides, to see Whatever Was The Matter. A few fled from the a fearful cacophony. The remaining hostesses in kimonos whispered and burst into giggles as if their Japanese sandals had been turned into saddle shoes.

Gail whirled in their direction, and they too quickly withdrew from the garden.

Fumio sat there rigid, his jaw clenched. I'm sure he was wondering what he would say when the piece was performed for the general consul and his wife the next afternoon.

The performance ended. Silence. Finally, Kat got up from the piano, looked our way for a moment, turned back to the band, and hesitantly said something to them in Japanese.

"What did he say?" asked Gail of the band boy.

"He asked if anyone had found any mistakes in their parts," said Key Kaisa.

The first trumpet player raised a hand and spoke a few somber syllables.

"And what did *he* say?" asked Gail.

"He said, 'How would we know?' " answered the boy gravely.

There was a beat of silence and then Shuki, my "beega-fahn," coughed as his attempt to hide a laugh. This set off two other musicians, who were not as successful in covering up.

In another moment, the entire band was laughing in unison and octaves. It was not this one joke that rendered them hysterical but, rather, the cumulative effect of each disbelieving minute they'd spent playing what to their ears was akin to well-organized insanity. That they themselves had been the source of this racket, having had no idea what discordant gaffe might come next out of their own instruments, had left them even more helplessly regaled.

Fumio rose to his feet and moved as fast as he could to the platform without losing his dignity. He barked something that caused them all to stop laughing in an instant. Fumio snapped off some additional sternly-spaced words and called me over.

"They wish to offer their apology," he said.

I told him it was all right, that this was a very new kind of music, and that often it took time to get used to such unusual sounds. I turned to Kat and said, "Would you like me to rehearse it with the band?"

He said, in a voice intended to be heard by the orchestra "No, I will get them to play it with more sensitivity. You are right, of course." He looked at the musicians and said for my benefit, "*Hai?* We are acting like children. It's as if we saw a painting by Mr. Pablo Picasso and said, Look, he has put both her eyes on the same side of her face, and we laughed at that. I have heard many stranger sounds than this in Europe." He added some words in Japanese and they nodded in assent. "As Mr. Dakuzaku has correctly pointed out, this was the selection of the committee in Tokyo. It is not our position to judge their judgment. Our responsibility is to realize the composer's intent."

It was unforgivable that Gail had been forced to endure her first artistic slap in the face on a day when life had already pummelled her into submission. I looked back to see if the composer was hearing any of this.

The composer was not to be seen.

43

A Burning Issue

I excused myself and hurried out of the garden. I described Gail to the kimonoed girl I'd met earlier and she pointed me toward Western Way.

I saw Gail getting on an Elephant Train heading in the direction of the East Bay ferry slip. My best long-distance running speed was somewhat slower than the train's, but I was at least able to keep her in my sight. However, the train didn't stop at the ferry landing as I'd expected. Instead it accelerated and crossed into the parking lot.

A minute later, I could just barely see Gail alighting from the train at the very farthest point of the island's northeastern tip. She went directly to a white convertible that was parked next to a big white trailer truck. From the sports car's trunk, Gail produced a can and walked it over to a large rusted trash receptacle. She tossed something white into the bin, poured the contents of the can over it, and must have tossd in a lit match as well, because by the time I got to her side, flames were pluming up from the bin and I could smell the seductive scent of burning gasoline. I could also see Toby Ackland sitting in the driver's seat of the white Jag convertible, feet propped up on the dashboard.

"Gail," I called, "come back to the rehearsal! They just weren't expecting something so avant-garde, that's all." I was next to her now. I indicated the subsiding flames in the trash bin. "What are you doing?"

"Burning the score to *Swing*," she said, her angry eyes more ablaze than the fire she'd started. "My score for the piano, yours for the orchestra. No one laughs at my music, no one. The hell with them."

I had to remind myself how upset she had every right to be. I looked to see if I could salvage the music she had burned. I had the Photostatic copy of my own orchestration at the hotel, thank God, but it would have been far better to preserve her original piano score. I still believed the piece was remarkable.

There was a man in a slouch cap sleeping in the front seat of the white truck beside us and I thought of waking him to see if he had a fire extinguisher, but it was already too late. The gasoline had served its purpose.

"Gail," I said, "let's go back. They're all very apologetic."

Toby Ackland inquired over his shoulder from the driver's seat of the Jag, "Do you want to stay, Gail? I can pick you up later if you like."

"No, we're leaving," she advised him. He dutifully started the car's engine.

I protested, "Gail, don't go by their first reaction. What you composed is brilliant!"

Gail snapped, "Yes, you're right. For all I know, it's your *arrangement* that loused things up! The piece sounds great on piano, you said so yourself. Today was the first time I heard how you voiced it. It sounded pretty laughable to me, too."

God almighty, so now it was going to be *my* fault? I had to remember that she'd just lost her mother. I was all she had now. And yet I kept thinking of Russ Hewett meeting her in the lobby of the Hotel Oakland.

"Gail. There is nothing wrong with my arrangement," I said as calmly as I could manage.

"Oh, then there *is* something wrong with my composition?"

"No, Gail, it was, it was a combination of things!"

She opened the door to Toby Ackland's Jaguar and stood on its running board. She reached for the purse that was on her seat and took out fifty dollars, which I told her I wouldn't take. She said I'd better take it now, because we wouldn't be seeing each other again.

"What about the concert tomorrow?" I asked. "You're not coming?"

"And be humiliated again? You have yourself the wrong girl."

She tried to push the money on me again, and I told her that since she'd destroyed my work as well as her own, it was as if I'd done it all for nothing, and that's what I wanted to be paid.

She flopped down into the passenger seat and closed the car door as Toby Ackland pulled out of the parking space, almost scraping the rear of the white trailer truck. She turned around in her seat and I saw no anger, only sadness. "Good-bye, Ray. You know I could have loved you if you'd have let me."

"But I *do* love you, Gail," I told her. I just didn't know in what way.

"Go, Toby," she said, and the Jaguar and Gail receded from my life at forty miles per hour, Gail staring at me over the back of the car seat until I could no longer discern her face.

44

Opus None

I got off the ferry to Oakland and walked up to the lead cab on the taxi rank. "You know a cul-de-sac off Fruitvale Avenue called Chancery Lane?" I asked the driver.

"Nope," he said.

"Well, you're going to."

From the street, I could see no lights on in the house. It would have been sensible for Russ to snap off all the switches before heading for the Claremont.

The driveway was, of course, empty.

I walked up the steps to the front door. I hoped Gail was there. I wanted to tell her everything. Under the current circumstances, with her life so suddenly untethered, I wanted her to know she was less alone in the world than she thought.

Forget the above. I couldn't bear to lose her.

I rang the doorbell, but no one answered. I tried the handle of the front door. It was locked.

A slope alongside the house tumbled gently down to Fruitvale Creek. I quickly found myself at the waterbed, staring up at the redwood deck that Russ had built so he could read the Sunday papers while overlooking the stream. I was still limber enough that I could jump, grab the edge of the deck, and hoist myself onto it. The door from the deck into the kitchen was unlocked and I entered the house.

"Gail?" I called out. There was no answer.

A question had gotten itself stuck in my mind and I thought I might find the answer inside Hewett's home. It would run me no additional risk with the law to look around. After all, I was now an intruder whether I examined things or not.

I went to the front door, grabbed its inside knob with my pocket handkerchief, turned it as I gently pulled, leaving the door just slightly ajar. If caught, I could say I'd discovered the door that way and had entered the house out of concern for Gail. I didn't know the law, but perhaps that would make a difference.

Out of sheer curiosity, I first explored the bedrooms of the deceased, hoping to find some insight into their strange relationship. Martha's room was a shrine to the nondescript. Her closet had several brand-new old-looking dresses. Two puce cardigans dominated the top drawer of her dresser, where I also found a rectangular tin originally intended for shortbread cookies. I opened it and leafed through Martha's personal documents: a birth certificate, a list of her important phone numbers, some contracts for two small personal loans back when she and Gail had lived in Cincinnati, an Avondale library card, a red ribbon for second prize in a bake sale.

Russ's room was a continuation of the Russ story. Light pine walls and bed, gray plaid bedspread. Photographs of Russ having caught a fish of modest size. Half his face visible in a shot of Joe E. Brown mugging for the grand opening of something.

Russ had a night table. I opened the drawer. There was a jar of Vaseline petroleum jelly. Rubbers wrapped like shoelaces, with a paper band around the middle. A book called *The Decameron* and a digest-sized edition of *Snap* magazine.

I went to Gail's room, where I believed I'd find the answer to my question, one that Professor Haffner had posed at our lunch together.

This young woman, what else has she written, he'd demanded, *has it all been in this style?* His voice had put mocking quotes around "style."

I stepped over to the orange crates, which were filled to the brim with her compositions. Atop one crate were sheaves of blank score paper, at the ready should she be inspired.

Beneath them was a worn folio entitled *Bach Two-Part Inventions*. Below it, a collection of Clementi sonatinas. Preludes by Liszt and Chopin. Vocal and piano-reduction scores of *Turandot* and *La Bohème*. Beethoven sonatas.

I went to another crate. Gilbert and Sullivan. Gershwin preludes. Tons of sheet music, with an emphasis on Jerome Kern. *The Hits of Fats Waller. A Guide to Stride Piano. Trademark Stylizations of Teddy Powell.*

Yet another crate was filled with Debussy, Ravel, and myriad Russian composers famous and obscure.

I searched through the remainder of the crates, inside the piano bench, under the bed, in the closet.

Nowhere in the room could I find a trace of a single note of music that had come "from the pen of Gail Prentice."

Tucked at the bottom of the last crate that I inspected, in a slim folder secured by a thin red ribbon, I did at least find one handwritten composition: a short piano piece about half the length of Gail's original *Swing*, though it was clearly not in her hand. The notes were clumsily drawn and the pages' many layers of erasures and rewrites made it murderously difficult to read, but no correlation has ever been proven between musical genius and good penmanship.

I took the piece over to the piano. I was very curious to hear how it sounded, because its title was *Self-Portrait* and its composer was Adeline Head.

The one part of the piece that wasn't sloppily written was its opening musical statement, a pleasantly plaintive little fanfare of seven solo notes that were quickly repeated in a sturdy chorale setting. For this part of the song, Adeline's notation seemed assured. It quickly segued, sloppily on the page if not on the keyboard, into a poignant waltz in a minor key. It was not particularly modern and perhaps a little too Romantic for 1940, but as an ètude at a music-composition student's first recital, it would have been nicely received.

While playing a busier passage, one that Adeline probably felt depicted her passionate side, I stopped abruptly and returned to the opening bars. I suddenly realized I already knew the simple theme that began Adeline's *Self-Portrait*.

I had orchestrated it. In Gail's *Swing*.

In fact, I had been so surprised by this unusually consonant theme in the midst of Gail's harmonic pandemonium that I'd voiced it for the entire band in unison. It had been reprised again toward the end of *Swing*, like the last call for reason before madness ruled.

And yet here was the exact same musical statement at the beginning (and end) of Adeline's little tone poem as well.

If Ada had been angered that her faultlessly conventional composition had lost out to Gail's lawless musical mayhem, imagine her rage when she discovered that Gail had stolen a principal theme of hers, placing it not once but twice in her own work. The chance of repetition of the identical theme in both works exceeded the laws of probability.

Why would Gail have committed such needless plagiarism? There was nothing magical or mystical about Adeline's opening melody. It had all the exotic qualities of a door chime.

Unless, of course, it was Adeline who had stolen the theme from Gail. But Gail had said that Ada didn't get to hear *Swing* until after the competition was over. That's when Adeline had given *Self Portrait* to Gail, and asked her if she could study the piano score for *Swing.*

I still felt dazed and numb from losing Gail, though nowhere near numb enough for my liking. I turned to the one arena where I still felt competent, and played through Adeline's *Self-Portrait* on Gail's piano once again.

At this point I was viewing my rumored intellect with such jaundice that my eyes were turning yellow. If there was any part of me I still trusted, it was my ability to comprehend music. So I tried to hear between the notes the way a more astute mind than mine might read between the lines in a stranger's diary.

Listening to Ada Head's bittersweet waltz—taking the composer at her word that this was some sort of "self-portrait"—I tried considering the composition as a kind of musical mug shot. The image it conjured in my mind looked very little like the extremely part-time waitress and Lake Merritt Mata Hari who had leapt from pier to ferry to pier in a pirouette. And I sensed that the answer to much of what was baffling me could be found in the little fanfare that lurked behind the bars of both the reverie I was playing and Gail Prentice's *Swing.*

45

A Major Discovery

SÄTHER GATE, UNIVERSITY OF CALIFORNIA, BERKELEY, CALIF.

I couldn't find a cab to hail on Fruitvale Avenue. I took a bus into Oakland, and from there a trolley direct to Bancroft Way.

Gail was not in at the Berkeley Club. "She hasn't been back since she left early this morning to go to the morgue," said a young woman at the desk rather breathlessly, who was immediately called over by an older woman and informed that the next time she gave out such information about the residents to a gentleman caller, she'd be given notice.

During our hours laboring over *Swing,* I had finally pried from Gail one of Cal Berkeley's most intensely guarded secrets: the location of its music department. It was sequestered in one of the dwindling number of wood buildings on campus, a handsome, boxy barn with banded windows that overlooked the campus's Strawberry Creek. By now it was six on Saturday evening, but practice rooms are as coveted at a music school as phone booths in a maternity ward, and I could hear plenty of wood-shedding in progress as I stepped through the timbered entrance.

A handsome young man, who knew he was, sat at a low desk. He was clearly not only serving as receptionist but in full charge of a clipboard that determined who had rights to what practice rooms and for how long.

"Yes?" he asked.

"Hi there," I said. "I was just trying to track down a composition major named Gail Prentice and I thought I'd pop in and ask if anyone's seen her."

"Pop in and ask who?" he queried, none too politely.

"Well, I guess I could start with you," I said.

"You know Gail well?"

"Yes, I do," I said.

"No, you don't," he said right back. "If you did, you'd know she's not a comp major. She's a piano major. I'm a lyric baritone, and she's accompanied me a number of times."

Nice guy. "So you haven't seen her?"

"Not in days." He looked at the clipboard, flipping pages. "And she hasn't used any of the practice rooms in the last few days either."

This dead end led me off the campus and into an aimless walk along Oxford Street. I wished I'd known other acquaintances of Gail's, but except for Toby Ackland, the only other person I'd met who knew Gail was Adeline Head, and I was just as confused about her as I now was about Gail's composing career.

I wondered if it would cause any harm to try calling Ada at her old number. If that *had* been her at RC Copying, her elopement might have been stymied and she could have gone contritely back to her landlady. I had no idea how close she and Gail had been; perhaps they were nothing more than friendly musical rivals. But Ada might know some other friends of Gail's, or some other phone numbers at which Gail might be reached.

Surely I would learn something. I had nothing to lose but a nickel.

I spotted a Ben Franklin five-and-dime and found a phone booth near the lunch counter. Within the booth there were phone books for Oakland and for San Francisco. I first looked for "Ackland" but could find no listing for a "Toby" or "T" in either volume. He probably lived in a frat house. I then looked up Adeline Head in the San Francisco directory. There she was, on Larkin, a Hemlock exchange. I repeated the number in my head as I put a nickel into the appropriate slot, heard the dial tone, and dialed the number. But I didn't get Adeline.

"Please deposit an additional five cents for the first five minutes," said an operator.

I fumbled in my pocket. Damn. I was out of change. But wait, she had it wrong. "Listen, Operator, I'm quite certain this is a five-cent call."

"I'm sorry, sir, but you are calling from a Berkeley exchange. All calls to the San Francisco zone are ten cents for the first five minutes and an additional five cents for each three minutes after that. Please deposit an additional five cents for the first five minutes."

"Operator, I was with my friend just the other day, and she placed a call to this same number and she only had a nickel, I'm sure of it. There must be some mistake, unless the rates went up."

She said they hadn't. I suddenly realized the operator had it right.

It was Gail who'd done something wrong.

When I'd called Nancy in San Francisco the other day, from the same telephone booth that Gail had used to call Adeline Head, I'd been told to deposit a second nickel. I guess I'd thought Nancy was in a different zone or something. Or more likely I hadn't thought about it at all.

But when Gail had called Adeline, she'd taken my one nickel from me, gotten Adeline's number on Larkin from Information, hung up, gotten her nickel back, put the nickel in again, and called the number. Or, rather, *a* number. I hadn't actually seen what she'd dialed. And then she'd supposedly chatted with Adeline.

Oh, Gail, honey. What have you been up to?

For either Gail had called Adeline at a number in the Berkeley-Oakland area but had wanted me to think Adeline was in San Francisco . . . or Gail had called someone else and pretended that *they* were Adeline.

Or perhaps she'd been talking to no one at all.

46

Swing

Lovers are always "the last to know" about bad things because, of course, they are desperate *not* to know. I had a girl in Chicago named Lois I liked for a short time, just before I met Nancy. Kindhearted as anything, she used to loan her apartment out to a friend named Beryl who lived with her folks. Beryl was quite the man-hungry type. Whenever I blew into town, I'd find some remnant of one of Beryl's trysts at Lois's place: a cigar stub, men's hair cream on a comb, the toilet seat left up. . . . It took us having a fight for Lois to finally scream at me in exasperation, "You blockhead, I don't have any friend named Beryl!"

And parents are often the last to know about their children: that they don't have the job they say they have, that they're in some trouble with the law, that they're just plain no good.

I hailed a taxi outside the Ben Franklin's and asked the driver to take me to the Claremont. In the back of the cab, I tried for the first time to focus steadily, rather than wishfully, on all I'd tried so hard not to consider.

For someone with so much spirit, determination, and pride, Gail had certainly turned out to be a quitter. We had both worked hard on *Swing*. It seemed so unlike her to walk away from a challenge and actually destroy both our scores simply because the first run-through had evoked what I thought was merely nervous laughter. The audience had done far worse to Stravinsky at the premiere of *The Rite of Spring*. They'd whistled and catcalled; fistfights had broken out. He'd been forced to escape the theater by a bathroom window. And yet he hadn't burned his orchestral and piano scores.

Of course, the individual instrumental parts to *Swing* were safe enough under the protection of Fumio Dakuzaku. But trying to evaluate a composition by looking only at each individual part would be like trying to judge the artwork on a jigsaw puzzle by examining one piece at a time.

At least I still had a copy of my arrangement. Gail didn't know that. But there was no Photostat of her original piano score. That had stayed with her when I'd taken my orchestral score to the copyist. Gail's original composition for piano, from which everything had sprung, was gone now . . . except, ironically, for the dedication page she'd handed Fumio moments before *Swing* was first played. So her words still existed, but none of her notes, except, of course, those on the flip side of the page: Gail's abandoned beginning of her Opus 38, the whimsically named "A Bach Ache." I wondered what the gravely serious Mr. Fumio Dakuzaku would make of that.

Jurgen Haffner hadn't been able to make anything of it, and he knew his way around the themes of J. S. Bach as well as anyone on the planet. Had I remembered the theme incorrectly? It had been a simple enough tenor sax part—. "Oh, idiot!" I laughed out loud.

"Excuse me?" asked the hackie.

"Sorry, I was talking to myself. About myself," I added.

Gail had transposed the notes for tenor sax, which is a B-flat instrument. Being a tenor sax player, I hadn't thought beyond that, because that was the right key, from my own instrument's point of view.

But when I wrote the melody out for Haffner, I should have written it in its *concert* key, the key in which it would be played on the piano. That was Haffner's instrument, after all. I'd written out B-C-B-D-C♯-B-D-C♯-F♯, the notes from Gail's tenor sax part. But it was safe to say that Bach never composed a single note in his entire life for tenor sax, since the instrument wasn't invented until a hundred years after he died. If Bach had written the notes for voice, piano, harpsichord, organ, or violin, they would have been notated a whole tone lower: A-B♭-A-C-B♮-A-C-B♮-E. That's what I should have spelled out for Haffner. Maybe he'd have recognized the melody if I'd quoted the notes to him in the correct key.

Of course, Haffner would have wanted me to convey the notes to him in German fashion, substituting an H for the B-naturals and a B for the B-flats. Then it would have been A-B-A-C-H-A-C-H-E-oh God.

A Bach Ache. The melody spelled the title of the piece.

Was that all there was to Gail's inside joke? What else had she notated on that page?

The indication had been that it was a part for a tenor sax. She'd drawn an arrow pointing at the clef sign on the first line. Above the arrow, she'd written a little memorandum to herself—"Clef?"—as if she wasn't sure if that was the correct sign. But the arrow pointed just as much to the key signature. If you knew that she'd written the melody for a B-flat tenor sax, as she'd indicated on the part itself, then you'd also know that you should transpose the notes a whole tone lower to read their correct letter names in the piece's true key. . . .

The word *clef* means "key." Not just in music. In French, it's the word for that which unlocks things.

Was Gail's harmless little sketch, this "Bach Ache," the key to something more than a pun at the top of the page?

The only musical part for "A Bach Ache" had been written in the key of D, and when you transposed it down to its "home" key of C, it spelled its own title because you had unlocked its musical code, so to speak.

Swing was also written in the key of D. What would happen if you transposed it down a whole tone?

The taxi pulled up to the Claremont. I was late; I had less than half an hour before the first set started. Damn Dave Wooster for not being there. There was no way on earth I could beg off.

I ran up to my room, taking the steps three at a time. I reached into my wallet for my key and let myself in, moving quickly to the dresser and opening the drawer where I had put the Photostat of *Swing*. Except for the copy in my room, whose existence was known to no one but Haffner, Gilbert Rice, and myself, the only remaining version of *Swing* (meaning the sixteen individual instrument parts of my arrangement) was now in the hands of a representative of the Japanese government.

I pulled out the score from where I had hidden it, under the white paper that lined the dresser drawer.

Something was adhering by static to its surface. I peeled it back, and it came away easily.

It was an eight-by-ten photograph. It must already have been lying facedown under the white paper lining.

It was a photograph of, from right to left, Gail, myself, and several of the unsavory fellows from the Heritage Picnic, including the fellow in the Bund uniform who had *sieg heil*ed the crowd. I had a look of delirium on my face, owing to Gail's proximity. I hadn't been paying attention to who else was in the shot with me. We all looked like the very best of chums.

Could it be that when my room was broken into, someone had *planted* this photo? But that made no sense. Why turn the place upside down to plant something?

Normally, this little mystery would have occupied my mind for the rest of the evening, but it was the *Swing* score that held all my interest.

I stared at the Photostat's white notes on a black background and found the staff where I'd written the lead tenor sax part of *Swing*. What would they spell if I read those notes a whole tone lower?

The answer, I was both disappointed and yet far more relieved to learn, was nothing. Gail had simply been playing a musical game with "A Bach Ache," and the game had ended there.

I flipped the pages. *Swing* had sounded so credible when Gail had played it for me on the piano in her room. Maybe it *was* my orchestration that had caused all the laughter.

I looked over one section where I'd opted for the keyboard to take a solo cadenza, rather than orchestrate and transpose it for the wind instruments. Perhaps the whole piece should have stayed that way. Still thinking a whole tone lower, I read, in my mind, C#-E-F-A-C-A-D-E . . . I stopped and reread the last six notes.

They spelled *facade.*

Was that just coincidence? I looked around the page and could find nothing. Then I remembered to substitute H for B-natural and B for B-flat, in accordance with Gail's "Bach Ache" code.

Yes, there in the trombones, no more than two bars from the word *facade,* was the word *cache.* I turned the pages. There again. In the bass. *Beach.*

Oh, of course. Trombones, piano, and bass are all instruments written in concert pitch. Their parts don't get transposed. But sax and trumpet parts *are* transposed. If there was a message hidden within the entire chart, you'd need to bring all the notes back to one common key, the way they'd been in Gail's original *Swing* composition for the piano. Undoing—"unexploding," really—what I had done to the piece as its orchestrator. Only *then* would you bring the entire arrangement down a whole tone.

Yes, it would be laborious, but nothing a few copyists couldn't accomplish in a day or two at most, working with what would have been (were it not for my Photostat) the only form of *Swing* now in existence: the individual music parts, the ones the Pan-Pacific Orchestra had played that afternoon. You'd take each part and copy it into a blank score, transposing those instruments that needed to be transposed, until the entire piece was in the same unified key. You'd reduce that down to a piano score and then transpose the entire piano part down a whole tone (as Gail's "Bach Ache" key to the code had indicated) and you'd have all the correct notes.

I looked over just the first two bars of the Photostatic score of *Swing* and found that when I made all the notes that had been distributed around the orchestra into one string of notes in the same unified key, they spelled—surprise—*a Bach ache* . . . which was clearly the Rosetta Stone for *Swing*. Its code breaker.

If this was some kind of cipher, it had actually been quadruple-encoded. The piano score I'd worked from had already been transposed up a whole tone by Gail. Then I'd innocently dealt out the notes across the orchestra to sixteen different instuments, transposing the trumpet and saxophone notes so that they were changed yet again. Then the individual parts were extracted by an equally innocent copyist. Minus the score from which the parts were originally extracted, one couldn't decipher the code without having every single one of the instrumental parts.

I got a blank sheet of music paper from my suitcase and, standing at the dresser, quickly replicated Gail's "A Bach Ache" from memory.

I looked at the clock. Fifteen minutes to get downstairs. A little lower on the same page of music I wrote the first eight letters of the alphabet and below them the corresponding notes in the German scale.

But that was only eight letters. I then wrote the next eight and continued the ascending scale underneath them. That took me about as high as I would write for most instruments.

I tried matching up this two thirds of an alphabet with my "Bach Ache" melody.

It now spelled "A BACH ACHE OP."

O and P . . . perfect. O and P were the last two letters in my scale so far . . . and brilliantly (if diabolically on Gail's part) her subtitle, "OPUS 38," gave a clue to the rest of the cipher. I already knew the notes for the first half of *OPUS*, and I'd bet anything the next two notes of "Bach Ache"'s melody would be the U and S, and would in some way show me where to place the last third of the alphabet.

The two notes that followed O and P in "A Bach Ache" (theoretically the U and S notes) were lower in pitch than any thus far. That told me a great deal.

Maybe, not wanting to ascend any higher, she had started descending from the first available note after the A that we'd started with. I'd try that.

Yes. When I continued the scale downward, I found that its U and S gave me a perfect match for what I'd predicted would be the U and S notes in *OPUS*.

Of course, anything this low would get written in the bass clef so as to be more readable. I hastily rewrote the entire musical alphabet using both clefs so that I could decode the full orchestral score of *Swing*.

No wonder I had noticed Gail's "stylistic" tendency to shun the A in the middle of the piano keyboard, but whenever she did use it, it was always followed by the D below it. "Decoded" down a whole step, these two notes became the letters Q and U.

All you needed now were numbers and you could communicate anything.

"Opus 38," she'd called it. The next two notes would *have* to be how she was going to symbolize 3 and 8.

They were flat notes, E-flat and G-flat. Significantly, there were only four remaining pitches in the chromatic scale that hadn't been taken by a letter: A-flat, D-flat, E-flat, and G-flat. I tried constructing a scale of just those four pitches on the staff above my letter scale, the A-flat representing the number 1 aligned with the first A in my letter scale below it.

Sure enough, the next two notes in the melody line matched the numbers 3 and 8. I'd completed what I hoped was my Rosetta Stone: the key to Gail's *Swing* code, by which virtually any message could be conveyed using little more than three octaves of music. All you needed were the musical parts and the master "key" to the piece (in this case "A Bach Ache," which was on the reverse side of the dedication page that Gail had turned over to Fumio Dakuzaku).

Placing my reconstructed letter-and-number code on the dresser in front of me, I tried applying it to the next two pages of the Photostatic score. I merely took each note in the order it occurred, and where there was more than one note on any given beat or subdivision of a beat, I tried "spelling" out the notes in order from lowest to highest, as is generally the practice among musicians. I added periods where they seemed appropriate.

It all worked.

And dear God, how I wished it hadn't.

For what I'd thought was Gail's jaunty, harmonically audacious intro to *Swing* was now revealed to be the words, "A BACH ACHE OPUS 38 TOP SECRET DECISION HAS BEEN MADE BY US NAVAL—

I felt foolish in more ways than I knew how to count. And yet a single emotion was greater than all my chagrin, embarrassment, and humiliation: fear. For even the very best interpretation I could put on all I'd discovered told me that Gail was lost in a dark place where I might not be able to protect her.

I hurriedly threw on my stage suit and called RC Copying. Gil Rice answered. I asked him how late his office would be open.

"Everybody wants everything for the next morning. I got three guys should be here until midnight at least."

I asked him if I could lease a table, pen, ink, and paper from him and work through the night if need be. I told him I wouldn't be able to be there until one A.M.

He had a muffled conversation with someone in the background and then came back on the line. "Yeah, Twilliger says he'll be here till then, he can let you in. Forty bucks in advance for the use of the place till ten A.M. tomorrow, ink and paper is extra. Don't think about bringing any broads or booze up here. Remember I know where you're staying."

"Thanks, you have a good night, too," I said. I raced down to the ballroom and barely reached the stage in time for the downbeat.

I had three tasks to deal with simultaneously: playing my part, playing Dave Wooster's part, and deciphering the score. Each break couldn't come soon enough for me, and I never left my seat. By the start of the third set I had sorted out this much:

A BACH ACHE OPUS 38. TOP SECRET. DECISION HAS BEEN MADE BY U.S. NAVAL DEFENSE NOT REPEAT NOT TO CONVERT STRUCTURE KNOWN AS TREASURE ISLAND LONG. 122W 22 15 LAT. 37N 49 28 TO SAN FRANCISCO AIRPORT. CONSTRUCTION INSTEAD APPROVED TO CONVERT TO PRIMARY U.S. NAVAL BASE FOR SF BAY AREA. A PRIME TARGET. ALAMEDA DEFENSE ADMINISTRATION HENCEFORTH A.D.A. HEADQUARTERS TO OCCUPY CURRENT ADMINISTRATION BUILDING AT LONG. 122W 22 20 LAT. 37N 49 09 AND WILL HOUSE SENIOR OFFICERS. A PRIME TARGET. AIRPLANE HANGARS WILL SERVICE ALL U.S. NAVAL BLIMPS BOTH RECONAISSANCE AND TARGETING. HANGARS LOCATION ON PUBLIC RECORD AND WILL NOT BE CHANGED. NEW CONSTRUCTION AS FOLLOWS. FIFTEEN PIERS FOR U.S. DESTROYERS AND CARGO SHIPS. TONNAGE OF ABOVE . . .

47

The Last Set

I got that far and then the band had to play "The Music Speaks to Me."

I felt *so* blockheaded as I stepped up to the mike and realized that for months I'd been singing about exactly what Gail had pulled off and still I hadn't caught on: "A trumpet confiding in you alone, a whispered aside from a slide trombone. . . . You hear the moan of reeds who sing in rhythm, and the message they bring with 'em is that soaring speech each poem seeks to be. . . . I tell you, the music it speaks to me."

How, *how* could I have missed it? The title of the song alone had been virtually screaming the truth in my ears. Gail's composition had the power of speech.

I wanted to tap the mike and announce, "Ladies and gentlemen, you are looking at a man who has just spent a week of his life passionately creating a musical arrangement of a *dossier*!"

But it was serious, and I had to keep my notes away from the eyes of Frankie Pompano and Jerry Garden. I was likely the first tenor sax player who'd had top U.S. Naval Department secrets sitting on his music stand alongside "I'm Popeye the Sailor Man."

The only good news was that Carl Brauner, Russ's similarly hale-and-hearty pal, didn't stop by as he'd promised with records for me to autograph on my break. Perhaps he'd been traumatized by the outcome of his Heritage Picnic, or the death of Russ Hewett.

It was easy to guess where the information had come from. Russ would have had all the details Gail was encoding. Because he'd helped oversee the building of the island when it was a civil and not a military project, he was that rare thing, a civilian privy to information that would otherwise have been known only to the navy. Just as he had enlisted the Army Corps of Engineers to help build a world's fair, the government undoubtedly needed his help in transforming what had been intended to become a municipal airport into a U.S. naval base. Once again the go-between, Russ would have had access to facts and figures normally off-limits to a civilian.

The question was, Had Russ knowingly and willingly supplied the information?

Perhaps Gail's letter to him had not been heartfelt at all. It could have been a case of Salome trying to get what she wanted from Herod by feigning an attraction to him. And was it not absolutely horrendous that I was eager to embrace this theory?

I didn't have to decode any more to know that Gail was in a terrible situation, but not much worse than the one I was in. I should be calling the police, the FBI, or the navy at this very moment, but then Gail would be arrested. What was the punishment for revealing government secrets of this nature? I supposed it might even be death.

This was probably not the most propitious evening for Jack to introduce me to a new vocalist he had filling in for the absent Vera. He'd heard the young woman at different clubs along the west coast, had been wowed by (and keeping tabs on) her. Now Vera had given him the perfect excuse to see how she fit in with our sound. The call he'd placed last night had been to her, and she'd taken the train up from Los Angeles this morning. Norma Deloris Egstrom was her name, and yes, she knew it wasn't a great name. She'd tried working under a different moniker in Hollywood, but nothing had panned out, so in the hopes of breaking two years of bad luck, she was giving Norma Deloris a try. She figured the initials N.D. were appropriate for a North Dakota girl.

She was everything Vera wasn't: understated, comfortable, and droll, and she brought a slyness to everything she sang. She sang jazz without making a big deal about it, and the audience liked her a lot. I wouldn't have wanted to be Vera if and when she deigned to return. Jack had more than a bluff card with Norma; I could tell he was just dying to play this ace from up his sleeve. I thought I'd enjoy arranging for Norma's unique voice and manner. But first I had a chart to write that might mean a great deal to me, to Gail, maybe even to the general population. And the grimly hilarious part was, it didn't matter what it sounded like.

I left the bandstand so fast after the last number that I had to weave my way around the applauding couples to get out of the place.

I couldn't let Gail do what she'd done. The trouble was, she'd already done it. My only hope was to create, overnight, a substitute *Swing*—a placebo version of all the music held by Fumio Dakuzaku—and then to somehow switch it with the original.

Had I ever created and copied an entirely new arrangement in one night? Not on your life. But in the taxi on the way to RC Copying, I realized certain things that could make it possible for me to do the seemingly undoable.

First, I didn't have to rewrite the drum part, because none of its notes were in Gail's original score. I'd invented the part from scratch, so it played no part in the code. I could also leave a couple of parts as is, because making gibberish of two thirds of the music would make gibberish of it all. Finally, blissfully, what would speed me along was that, for the first time in my career, I knew *it didn't fucking matter* what notes I wrote! Oh, how I'd labored and agonized over my musical choices when I'd voiced the piece for Gail. But now I was going to lay out each part in a similar range and rhythm to my original, with no regard to the pitches of the notes except that they be different.

But I decided not to change anything until after the words *top secret decision*. Everything prior to that was harmless enough, and this way if anyone tried decoding the music to see if they had the genuine article, the code would pass muster, at first—the equivalent of wrapping a real twenty-dollar bill around a roll of play money.

It would be the most ridiculous arranging job I'd ever done and would have made for a fabulous story to tell the guys, if telling it might not have gotten my possible daughter possibly executed.

48

The Concert Master

It was nine A.M. when I finished. The good news was that I could put the new parts, all sixteen of them, in an envelope identical to the one I'd given Fumio, because that too had originated at RC Copying. The shade of score paper was likewise identical, and I'd done a good job of counterfeiting Haffner's hand in music notation, certainly well enough to pass inspection from the musically illiterate Fumio. These new parts of mine weren't going to be played, after all. I'd created them solely to be decoded—or, rather, to keep those decoding them stymied.

I had a chance to shower, take a nap, and change into my dress suit for *Swing*'s debut on Treasure Island. I called Gail at both her numbers. I got no answer, but I hadn't expected to.

The afternoon concert in the rock garden of the Japanese Pavilion felt very much like the Junior League lawn parties at which I'd occasionally played. The consul general and his charming wife appeared nicely sunned and perfectly suited for an afternoon of canapés and croquet.

When I spotted Fumio, I apologized to him for Gail's sudden departure, as well as my own, the previous afternoon. "She was terribly distraught," I said. "It had been a mistake for her to attempt to come here yesterday."

He asked me what the envelope I had under my arm was. I told him it was a little surprise for the Pan-Pacific's band boy.

Fumio looked about, concerned. "I hope we will not have so much laughter today. It would make things very bad."

You bet it would, I thought to myself. It would look bad if people thought Swing was a strange piece to win such a competition. It might make them suspicious.

I'd had a good chance to dope it all out while I was copying the mindless music contained in the envelope under my arm. The contest had clearly been a ruse to enable the transfer to enemy agents of detailed information about the future conversion of a world's fair into a strategic naval base. How do you get such information—a full year before the public would know of it—out of the country and to Japan, whom F.D.R. and his cabinet already viewed as our future adversary? You could bet that anything heading off to Tokyo, including the luggage of the Pan-Pacific Orchestra, would be thoroughly examined and screened by the government. But how many customs agents or feds would find anything suspicious about Gail's Swing Around the Sun? They could hold it up to the light, search for microfilm in its folds, test it for invisible ink. But the information, reams of it, was all right there, as plain as day, if you knew what you were looking at and how to rearrange it.

Fumio introduced me to the consul general. He apparently spoke English well enough to understand anything that was said to him, but since any statement he made was deemed an official pronouncement of his government, he addressed others only through an interpreter, to be certain he didn't misspeak.

"The consul general says he and Mrs. Sakada are excited to have today's performance ahead of them," stated the interpreter after the consul general had made a comment in my direction. We all nodded enthusiastic agreement as I thought, *And once they've heard it, I'm sure they'll be thrilled they have it behind them.*

I walked over to Kat, who looked gravely concerned. "Listen, Ray, I have done the best I can, but I can make no guarantee it will be sounding much better than yesterday."

"I understand, Kat." I gestured to the envelope I'd been walking around with. "Look, I have a little presentation to make here. Could I leave this within your piano so I have it handy?" There is an area inside an open grand piano, near its crook, where singers can stash Kleenex, glasses of water, flowers, crib sheets. Kat said that would be fine. I added, "And say, why don't you let me introduce the number? Maybe I can frame it in a favorable way."

He nodded gratefully. "Yes, thanks. This performance has my nuts in a vise, I'll tell you."

At three-thirty, all were seated in the rock garden. A pleasant breeze danced around the open space. Fumio introduced various dignitaries and board members from opera and ballet companies, from regional symphonies and music schools, as Gail had once told me would be there. What a shame that she wasn't here. But, of course, I was forgetting for a moment that Gail wasn't a composer. The only true importance of this concert for her was to get *Swing* into a trunk and onto a ship headed for Japan.

Kat was introduced, and he talked about the honor of the Golden Gate International Exposition being included on the orchestra's world tour promoting better international relations. He then led his band in a jazz medley of folk songs from different countries. It proved that in the hands of the Pan-Pacific Orchestra there wasn't all that much difference between an Irish fling and a Russian mazurka, but the number received polite applause.

Then Kat, hoping to hand off all responsibility for what would follow, said he was now proud to introduce the famous American arranger and jazz musician who had helped make possible this world premiere.

I stood before the assembled audience, who looked up at me expectantly. My eyes searched the crowd for Gail, but I was clearly going to have to handle this alone.

I began by explaining, without too many grim details, why the brilliant young woman who'd composed this prize-winning composition could not be here. I said that I carried a message from her: that she was grateful for this honor and hoped that her work would promote better understanding between the United States and the great nation of Japan. This got a small round of applause. When it ended, I stood silently for a moment. Nearly ten years of singing to dance crowds had forever inoculated me against stage fright. If I could perform at the Carpenters and Joiners Union Cotillion Ball of 1938 in Granite City, Illinois, this bunch would be a piece of cake.

"Now is a time," I began, inserting a throb into my voice, "of great international tension. War is raging in Europe. Accusations are made, fingers are pointed, voices are raised in the harsh discord of anxiety, suspicion, and anger. The remarkable woman who composed what you are now about to hear has tried to capture the despair, the hopelessness, the ugly, feeble, insane, laughable, loathsome madness of war. These sounds are not easy to hear. For some among you, they may be almost painful. It matters not. These are the sounds that will torture the world if we do not endure each other, embrace each other, cherish each other. We must swing the pendulum away from the hideous cacophony of conflict and toward the soothing murmur of international peace."

I looked at the audience soberly. "Our composer has asked that, as a prelude to her composition, we listen carefully to thirty seconds of our serene surroundings. And she requests that, when the performance of her composition is over, there be no applause for another thirty seconds, while we hear and savor the silence of tranquillity that denotes an alternative to war. She prays that this work be re-membered for the restfulness that surrounds it rather than the tur-moil within it. And now . . . let us listen to the sound of . . . Peace."

I held up my arms in a stance not unlike Pacifica's. There was a large koi pond just beyond the garden of the samurai house, and we could hear the light and lovely trickling of its gentle fountains. A breeze stirred some wind chimes, and the water of the lagoon lapped sensually against the side of the castle.

Then I gave a sudden, aggressive nod to Kat, who, having bought into my spiel, threw himself into the downbeat.

Oh, the ugliness and foolishness of war! The audience with fur-rowed brow flinched at the jagged shards of sound that sliced the air, the belching and burping leviathan that slithered and crawled and died before us. What unholy intervals and strange, dead whin-ings did the Pan-Pacific Orchestra put forward in all its dribbling vulgarity. Wincing from the brutal candor of the composition, audi-ence members looked to each other with slow nods of respect. We, the assembled, *knew.* Others would not, but *we* could look the re-pugnant kraken in its face and not go mad.

And as suddenly as the inexcusable wailings began, they ceased, and my arms flew high again into the air. Thank God it was over, and we could *hear* God in the slight stirring of the wind chimes, the timid trickling of the koi pond, the light lavings of the lagoon be-yond the castle walls.

I let my arms drop to my sides and bowed my head, signaling that the work was finished.

The audience began to applaud enthusiastically, one person after another rising to their feet. The assistant manager of the San Fran-cisco Opera was particularly demonstrative. I gestured to Kat, he gestured to me, and we put our arms around each other's shoulders.

The crowd applauded further at this display of International Un-derstanding; then people began to chat in excited little groups.

Now the tough stuff.

I watched as Key Kaisa, the band boy with aspirations as a trumpet player, collected the *Swing* parts off the music stands. He quickly carried them over to the side of the stage, where he put them in the RC Copying envelope. Standing over him was Fumio Dakuzaku. As Key closed the envelope, I took the boy by the arm and walked him back to the podium. I called out to the crowd, "Ladies and gentlemen, a brief announcement!"

They turned to look, and I indicated Key. "This young man hopes someday to be a jazz trumpet player and I predict great things for him. As a gift of friendship from the Jack Donovan Orchestra . . ." I walked Key a few steps to the white keyboard, took the envelope with *Swing* in it from him, and set it down in the recess of the piano. I took out the substitute *Swing* envelope and continued, "I present him with the trumpet parts from our recordings of 'Believe You Me' and 'Soup du Jour' "—I withdrew these from the envelope—"and our actual recordings of these same songs, so that he can play along with us when he returns to his homeland! How about that, folks?"

Friendly applause. I went back and pretended to get the envelope with the coded *Swing* parts from the piano but, in point of fact, did a double switch, keeping the envelope with the harmless parts. I said into the mike, "And if I could please have Mr. Fumio Dakuzaku step up to the platform at this time?" I waved him up. He looked vastly out of his element.

I said to the crowd, "Mr. Dakuzaku has been a champion of this composition *Swing*"—I waved above my head the envelope containing the new parts I'd just finished copying that morning—"not only by being on the committee in Japan that selected it, but by supervising its performance here." Much applause for Fumio, led by me. "Mr. Dakuzaku: as thanks for all you have done to promote world harmony, I have been authorized to turn the copyright of *Swing* over to you and your government, with any future royalties on this work to go to the Japanese charitable organization of your

choice, sir. Thank you, Mr. Dakuzaku!" I handed him the envelope
and shook his hand as photographs were snapped.

He opened the envelope to check that all the right-named parts
were there. He counted them and then went through them again, repeating a litany he had clearly memorized, "Alto, alto, tenor, tenor,
baritone sax, trumpet one, two, three, four . . ." Reassured, he again
shook my proffered hand.

"I believe the consul general was signaling to you, sir," I said to
him, pointing to the distinguished gentleman across the garden.
Holding on tightly to the music, Fumio hurried across the courtyard.

I walked casually back to the piano and reached for the envelope
with the "dangerous" version of *Swing*.

It wasn't there.

A few steps away, I saw Kat peering into the envelope. He closed
it and looked at me knowingly. "I saw what you did," he said.

"Really."

Kat nodded. "Yes. You switched parts right now, didn't you?"

I was trying to learn from Lieutenant Culpepper's book. I said
nothing. Let Kat speak again.

"I believe I know why you did it." He smiled and handed me the
envelope with the top secret arrangement. "You took your name off
the parts, didn't you?"

Jurgen Haffner, as a courtesy to me, had put an "Arranged by Ray
Sherwood" credit at the end of each part. Subconsciously, I'd forgotten to do the same.

"I do not blame you one bit," said Kat, lowering the top of the
piano. "That has to be the worst garbage I ever heard. You got away
with it today, and boy, I thank you for that. What a performance!
But you won't be able to introduce this composition everywhere.
You were right to remove your name. You have your reputation to
consider."

I liked him, and it seemed clear he had nothing to do with the intrigue surrounding the arrangement, or he would not have been counseling me with such concern. All the same, I looked inside the envelope. Yes, there was my credit at the end of the parts. I could tell Haffner's hand from my own. I had the version I wanted.

"May I ask why someone with your reputation worked on something that is certainly not worth your valuable time?" he asked. "It's a very forward question, I know, but were you paid handsomely?"

I told him I was losing money on the deal.

He said, "Yesterday, I could only see the girl from the back of the room. She looked very unhappy but capable of being very beautiful. Tell me: did you do it all just for the girl?"

I tightened my grip on the envelope and got ready to leave the castle.

"Yes, Kat. I did it all just for the girl."

49

Meet Me at the Fair

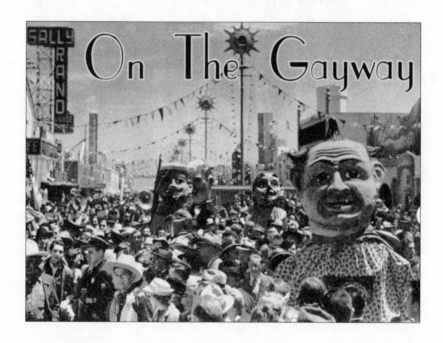

Lying on my bed late that afternoon, wondering what other people did in the situation I was in, and then realizing that there were no other people in the situation I was in, I heard someone outside my door.

I got to my feet and stood by the door's hinges.

There was a sound of something moving at my feet. I looked down and saw a small envelope bearing the Claremont's emblem. I picked it up and opened the door quickly. A uniformed bellboy was stepping down the hall.

"Excuse me, let me give you something for your trouble," I said.

He trotted back to the door and gratefully accepted fifty cents. He had about nine more envelopes in his white-gloved hands. "Do you know if this just came in?" I asked, indicating the envelope I was holding.

"Phone message, sir, probably while you were out. The operator keeps them at her station in case people phone down from their rooms or call in from the outside. Every few hours I make the rounds and deliver copies to make sure our guests got the message." He thanked me again and continued on his mission.

I closed the door and unfolded a little pink page upon which a blue carbon of the operator's handwriting read: *Meet me tonight at eleven-fifteen at the place where I burned my music pages. Take a taxi to the marina. Come the rest of the way by foot. If you tell or bring anyone, or try to contact me before then, it will be very bad for me. Your grateful collaborator, Gail.*

I didn't like it. Anyone could have given the no-doubt wide-eyed hotel operator the message. It could even have been a man, speaking like a woman.

Yet only Gail or Toby Ackland would have known about her burning the composition.

A kidnapper tells a parent, *Don't call the police or your child will die.* Do the parents think the kidnapper will be good to his word? Of course not. Do the parents call the police? Usually not. The police don't have their kid. The kidnapper does.

The night promised to be cool, so I went to the closet for my raincoat. I had no choice but to show up.

I took a cab into downtown Oakland, where Broadway meanders into Chinatown. From there, I visited a pawnshop, a men's haberdashery, and a laundry, hoping that these three stops might save my life.

Then I hailed another cab and had it take me to the marina on Treasure Island's Port of the Trade Winds. At a little bar on the marina, I watched two immense flying boats, the *Yankee Clipper* and the *China Clipper,* bob about in the choppy water like toys in a child's bath while I nursed a beer for an hour.

Nine P.M. I wandered into the fair via Portway Passage, the corridor between the two air hangars. I knew this would almost certainly be the last time I'd see Atlantis before it was torn down. I took the Pacific Promenade past the lagoon, giving a hasty glance to the Japanese castle, now lit by hundreds of lanterns, and turned quickly away from it.

The passing crowd was thinning rapidly. The last remnants of the honest-colored sunset relinquished the job of illuminating the buildings to the island's blue and pink floodlights. I felt like a spirit in an opulent cemetery fighting off an eternal sleep. I wanted away from this polished city, one that seemed to know it had only a few weeks left to live. If there ever actually was an Atlantis, this was how it must have felt a month before its submersion.

I walked quickly to the Gayway. I didn't offer Pacifica more than a passing glance. The Street of the Barkers gave me new life. The crowd was dwindling here, too, but as long as there was a sucker with a few dollars in his pocket, no self-respecting pitchman would ever cease his spiel.

I suppose no one ever simply finds themselves anywhere, not by chance, but I found myself outside Sally Rand's. I turned to a pretty ticket vendor in her kiosk. "I'd like to see Nancy Carmack if she's here."

"She's out on a dinner date," the woman said.

"I had something I wanted to leave for her."

"You can leave it here for her, honey, if you want. I don't know if she's coming back tonight."

I told the woman I'd return in a minute, walked past the tropical drink stand and into a recess that someone was calling a souvenir shop, and purchased a small box of Treasure Island stationery.

At the tropical drink stand I bought a papaya juice and borrowed a pencil stub from the counterman to write: *Dearest Nance, sorry I missed you, leaving town tomorrow, must say a regretful no to Sally's* *offer. I thank you and her so much. I'm always terrified I'll lose the en-* *closed when I'm on the road. Will you keep it safe for me until I'm next* *in town? It was so good to see you after all these years. Always, Ray.*

From my billfold, within a flap right next to Sidney Bechet's broken reed, I extracted and carefully unfolded a little drawing Linney had once made with my fountain pen of a crescent moon and stars. Sometimes, when I said, "Thanks, Linney," I would pat my wallet in my breast pocket, knowing her drawing was there. I hadn't looked at it in over a year. I looked at it now, folded it back up, and put it, along with my note, into the souvenir envelope. I licked the flap and sealed it. I wrote Nancy's name on the front, gave the counterman a tip along with his pencil, and walked back to the pretty girl at the kiosk.

After that, I killed the necessary time strolling about, feeling like the Red Death as the masque approached midnight. Everywhere I went, people were turning away and leaving. I listened to an inverse symphony of music being shut off in midphrase, belly-laughing automatons being unplugged, wood slats rolling as the broad shutters of arcade games were pulled down and padlocked. The brightly colored lights went out like a fireworks display being apologetically retracted. I walked until the fair was so empty that my very presence would cause someone to wonder what I was doing there, then took myself to the East Bay ferry slip, where there were still some people milling about.

I sat on a green wooden bench and watched a man carrying one little girl in his right arm and leading a slightly older one by his left hand. He shouldn't have kept them out so late. I followed them with my eyes as they slowly made their way up the metal ramp onto the ferry.

It would have been nice to know if I'd had one or two daughters in my lifetime, but life was apparently not going to give me that knowledge, and I'd accepted that. I was at least grateful that I'd now been given the chance to *do* something, dangerous as it might be, rather than simply allowing events to buffet me about in their wake. For too many years, I'd done little more than get through each day. This night was going to be mine.

The fog was rolling in. I could actually see it slither along the ground around me. I could make swirls in it with my hand.

"Last ferry, mister," said a man locking the Key Service ticket booth from the outside. "You on it?"

I told him I was being picked up by a friend at the main gate but had thought the park was open later than it was, so I'd had to wait. For his benefit, I got up and started to walk down the Esplanade in the direction of the entrance. I walked slowly until the ferry had carried its passengers and the ticket salesman into the night, then reversed my direction.

I looked at my watch. If I began the trek now across the empty parking area that occupied the northern tip of Treasure Island, I would reach at the appointed time the place where Gail's anger and musical composition had both become inflamed.

I stepped off North Boulevard and onto the vast blacktop that gave way on all three sides, at some merging point my eyes could not see, to the black water of the bay. It took no exertion of my imagination to feel as if I were taking a stroll along the end of the universe. I would not have known which way to walk had it not been for the three stanchions still lighted in the parking lot. They were spaced in a line, each a great distance from the others, like three stars in a constellation.

I wondered how I would locate Gail—or whoever it was my assignation might be with—once I passed the third light. I would have to be careful I didn't walk off the rim of Treasure Island. The last of the stanchion lights was now behind me, making me a fine target, but I doubted I'd been lured here solely to be attacked. Someone, good or evil, needed me here for some function I'd yet to serve. If I was wrong about this, then I'd been a fool to come alone. But Gail had made the choice academic. I didn't feel any particular sense of courage, but I did feel excited, and calm, and purposeful. For one rare evening of my life, I knew I was doing what I was meant to do and had no desire to turn away.

A beam appeared about thirty yards in front of me. Its vague yellow glow was amplified by the fog in the same way that light from a streetlamp becomes brighter during a snowfall.

Now I could see that the light was coming from the dims of an old sedan parked next to the same white trailer truck that had been there the day before.

A woman was walking around the front of the car to face me. She was wearing a gold gabardine trench coat with a belt of gold kid. It was open, and within it she had on a dress of dark crepe.

She looked surprised and extremely unhappy to see me.

"Well, hello, Ray," she said in a low voice. "What the heck are you doing here?"

A second woman stepped around the other side of the car to face me. Her face glowed red in the taillights.

"I sent for him, Gail." She gave me a handsome smile. "Thanks so much for coming, Ray."

Looking completely comfortable with the current situation, and with her striking looks, and with the small black pistol in her hand, was Vera Driscoll.

50

At the End of the Island

I was dazed and dumbfounded. And wrong.

As she came forward to join Gail, I saw it wasn't Vera at all, although it might have been her sister, and if Jack Donovan were offered a trade, I don't know that he would have refused.

It was the late Martha Prentice.

Death had simply done wonders for her appearance. Her hair had been dyed a lustrous blond and was in a pompadour, the sides brushed back into a chignon; her makeup was expertly applied, her lips boldly emblazoned in a pout of Parisian scarlet. She wore a wool coachman's coat with pointed velveteen lapels.

I had a dim notion of why she looked so much like Vera, but at the moment it was far down on the list of things I needed to know.

"Hello, Martha," I said. "Who's that dead person in the Oakland morgue with your teeth?"

"Sorry to bring you out on such a foggy night," she said, ignoring my question. Her eyes flitted up to the sky. "It's supposed to lift pretty soon."

"Let him go," implored Gail.

"Not yet. Soon." She turned back to me. "Now I have a few questions for you, Ray, and I want you to know I'm pretty good at determining when someone's lying, just the way people in your business can tell when someone is playing out of tune. Just be aware that if you lie to me, it will work against Gail's best interests."

"Can't he just leave?" Gail asked. Martha answered by not replying.

In terms of appraising Gail's collusion in whatever unpleasant thing was unfolding here (and I think it was safe to say that nothing really swell was happening), I took it as a bad sign that Gail herself was not flabbergasted that her mother had been resurrected—and with such gorgeous nails at that.

No matter. I'd try to get her out of this mess whether she wanted out or not.

Martha asked me, "Did you arrive alone?"

"Yes. Like Gail told me to in her phone message." I looked over at Gail. "Except I don't think the message at my hotel really *was* from you, was it, Gail?" I turned back to Martha. "I doubt she would have said she burned her *music pages*. She would have called it her *score*."

Martha nodded agreement. "Yes, the biggest handicap I've had in this is that I know next to nothing about music. That's why I've had to rely on you, Ray, to much more of an extent than I've been comfortable with. In fact, that's why I needed to have you on hand here. Just in case there are any last-minute problems."

Gail implored, "But if you sensed it might be a trap, why ever did you come?"

"I had no idea what you were up against. I couldn't risk your welfare just because I was suspicious. So I had to do what the message said." I looked back at Martha. "I suppose I'd do whatever it took to protect Gail. I guess you can figure out why."

Gail said quietly, "Well thanks, Ray, and everything."

"How did you get here?" asked Martha.

"I took a taxi to the marina, as instructed. Two taxis, actually, to muddy my tracks." I had in fact done this, but not for the reason I gave.

"Does anyone else know you're here?"

I thought of Nancy, who would know by at least tomorrow morning that I had been to the fair this evening. I wasn't going to drag her into this. I'd die first, and at the moment the odds of that happening were excellent.

"Not as far as I know. I mean, there's the operator who took the message at the Claremont, but you didn't specify where I was to meet you. There are dozens of marinas around the Bay Area, and only Gail, Toby Ackland, and I would know where Gail burned her music. Now when do I get to ask some questions?"

She smiled cordially. "When you're the one holding the gun. By the way, there was one other person who saw Gail burning her music. The driver of this truck." She nodded toward the trailer, which was marked AMERICAN CONSOLIDATED SHIPPING, LANDSBERG, OHIO. Martha called over her shoulder, "Gunther!"

From behind the truck stepped the man who'd worn the Bund uniform at the German picnic, the one who'd spoken so treasonously and thrown a Nazi salute to the crowd. He was dressed as before, except that as a fashion accessory he'd added a holster and the very nice pistol in his hand, which I recognized as a German Luger.

"Take off your raincoat and throw it onto the ground at my feet," he said.

I did so, tossing the raincoat gently onto the blacktop near where he stood. "I'll be back for it at five," I said. "Make sure you get the stain out of the lapel."

"Ray, don't joke with him," advised Gail. "You'll regret it."

What I regretted was being so completely unrehearsed for this deadly audition. But I did have what might pass for a plan, and I hoped to play it out with enough nerve that Gail would remember me as someone who'd displayed love for her and courage, if not actual intelligence, under fire.

Gunther had been kneeling, searching my raincoat for any signs of a weapon. He found its pockets' few contents and set them aside. "A comb, some loose change, a Chinese laundry ticket, a pack of gum," he reported to Martha.

Martha said, "All right, go frisk him, but give me your gun before you do. I don't want to run the chance of him taking it off you."

"Him?" said Gunther with a smile. He gave Martha his Luger and approached me. "Put your hands above your head," he said, and I more than obliged, locking my fingers together behind my head and stretching my elbows back in a very cooperative manner, which was my intent. He did a thorough job, giving my shoes a careful squeeze, working his way up and around both my legs, having no qualms about squeezing my crotch, then patting up and down my sides. He faced me, checked my jacket pockets, then reached under my jacket and around behind me to check my hip pockets, my waist, and the small of my back.

Gunther walked back to Martha. "He has nothing on him."

Martha gave him back his gun. "It's getting cold," she informed us. "We'll wait inside." She gestured with her pistol toward a lone bungalow that was planted in the very far corner of the parking area. For what we were waiting, I could not imagine, but the others all seemed to know.

"Where's Russ?" I asked Martha, who walked six paces behind me out of deference to the fact that she wanted her pistol aimed at my spine. Gail trailed behind her. Gunther walked alongside me but well to my right, eager to provide cross fire at Martha's slightest command.

"Where's Russ?" Martha echoed. "Russ is dead."

"So are you," I pointed out.

We were about a hundred feet from the rear of the bungalow. One small back window overlooked the parking lot. The building was farther away from the fair itself than anything else on the island.

"All right, turn around," Martha instructed me. "Gunther, go to the front and make sure it's safe for us to enter. I'm not worried about foot patrols, I just want to make sure there's no security guard sleeping on the porch."

Gunther nodded and stepped away, peering about as if he were on safari in Tanganyika.

I observed to Martha, "You know, take away Gunther's gun and you've got yourself Gunther."

"He's an excellent marksman with that Luger."

"Where do you find people like him?" I asked with immense curiosity. "I mean, is he salaried? Is this his *job*?"

"There is a network of people, Americans and émigrés. The Bund and other organizations are a helpful nursery. You might be surprised to see the list of people across the country—travel agents, financiers, photographers, doctors, all walks of life, really—who can be helpful to know."

"And you're at the top of that list?"

Gail warned me, "You're asking too many questions, Ray."

Martha assured Gail with a small laugh, "It's all right, Gail. The more Ray knows, the better he can assist us. He's not going to let you down." She replied to my question, "No, Ray, I'm not on that list at all. I'm here in a professional, military capacity. This is my *work*, my life's work. Not, as it is for Gunther, an avocation."

"You're a spy," I said. I'd never met one before.

"Oh, please, such a ridiculous term. Think of me as the advance guard of a new ruling class."

"Aw, I liked you much better as a spy."

Gail gave me a warning glance and beseeched Martha, "Ray doesn't know anything. Let him go."

"Not until I know we don't need him," her mother responded firmly.

Gail looked straight into my eyes. "Ray, you like me, don't you? In the beginning, I thought you liked me an awful lot. I thought, well . . . I thought lots of things. But once we started work, you seemed to like me less, and that hurt, but listen: you still like me enough that you wouldn't tell anyone anything that would destroy my life, would you? Right?"

There seemed no point in lying. "Right."

"Well, Ray, if anything bad were to happen to"—she looked at Martha—"were to happen to my mother, I assure you, my life would be ruined." She pleaded my case to Martha. "You said it yourself. He won't tell anyone anything if he thinks it might harm me. You can let him go."

She was making the best argument for not killing me. I doubted it was good enough to save me, but I appreciated the effort.

Martha made a few impatient circles in the air with the barrel of her pistol. "Enough. We're going inside."

Gail went to pick up my raincoat from where Gunther had left it. "What are you doing?" Martha asked.

"I'm . . . getting his coat. He'll be needing it later, won't he?"

Martha didn't immediately reply.

"Won't he?" Gail repeated.

"Yes, sure," said Martha. "Come on."

We walked to the bungalow, where I expected to learn a great deal. Including whether or not there's life after death.

51

A Bungalow on the Bay

The bungalow turned out to be Russ Hewett's office on Treasure Island. There was a desk and a chair, a drafting table and a display easel, some functional shelves, and a leather armchair fronted by a coffee table and flanked by two straight-backed chairs. To the immediate left of the entrance was a door marked WASHROOM with a key in its lock.

For nights like these, the space heater in the corner would have made the room comfortable. We did not turn it on, though. Comfort was apparently not high on the agenda.

It's eerie to enter the office of a person who had not expected to die. Paperwork that assumed it would be finished was waiting in a patient litter on the desk. Photographs of the Heritage Picnic lay about. A mystery novel, open midway with its spine facing up, rested on the right arm of the leather chair. It was, for Russ, the first case that Perry Mason would never solve. A small bottle of violet ink on the desk lay open and on its side, but rather than having been blotted up, the ink had simply dried where it was, forming a thin violet cake that went right up to the desk's edge. It had miraculously stopped short of spilling onto the carpet. A table radio was staying tuned with admirable loyalty to a radio station that had gone off the air for the night; the dull static created the aural illusion of soft rain outside.

Gunther went to turn off the radio, but Martha stopped him and did it herself. "You can't touch anything in this room with your bare hands," she cautioned him. "Gail and I have both been here during the last year, but you haven't. If the police ever decide to give the place the once-over, I want everything as Russ left it."

Gunther nodded and, lowering the gun in his right hand, unbuttoned his shirt pocket with his left and took out a pack of cigarettes. He held the pack to his mouth and plucked out a cigarette with his lips. He'd likely seen someone do this in a movie, and so far he was okay. But then he produced a box of matches from the same pocket and stared at it as he tried to figure out how to light a match with only one hand. He finally abandoned the project, dropping the matchbox back into his shirt pocket, which he quickly rebuttoned. He glared briefly at me, embarrassed that I'd witnessed his clumsiness.

"Make yourselves comfortable," Martha said. "We'll be here for a little while."

Gail hung her coat and mine on a rack as I peered around the room. "So . . . no surprise visit from Russ?" I asked her.

"That's it for him," she said, with the same amount of anguish as a soda jerk saying he was out of butterscotch.

"And where was he on the totem pole, Martha?"

"On top of me, the hog," she said, displaying an expression of such loathing that I knew she'd had some part in his death. "Or when I was lucky, beneath me. Then I could just stare straight ahead."

"Sex is a part of what you do?" I asked. My chance to act was approaching and I wanted to keep her talking.

"We enter into this work knowing what is expected of us. Hewett had unique information we wanted." She shrugged. "He was drawn in first by the sex. That was the easy part for all concerned—except me, of course. Then I began to paint a picture on his pillow of the exalted role a man like himself could take in a new global structure, and how I happened to know a number of well-placed citizens who'd be involved in this transition. He found himself being treated with respect by those who normally wouldn't have given him the time of day. That's what he cared about—that and the things I let him do to me." Her lips formed into the definition of a smirk. "Russ Hewett was no more a Nazi than I'm a Roosevelt Republican."

So the litany Russ had spouted at the Heritage Picnic, his envisioning of how the United States might someday be dominated by Germany, was in fact what he had actually hoped for, and what Martha had made him feel he would be a part of.

It was time. I asked, "Can we turn on the space heater just for a while? It's cold in here."

"We aren't turning on anything," said Martha.

I asked Gail, in a concerned voice, "How are you, honey? Are you feeling cold?"

Gail shrugged. "A little, but I'm okay." She sat down in a chair by the coffee table.

"Here, you can keep this around your shoulders." I took off my suit jacket as if to offer it to her.

"She doesn't need it," said her mother.

"I'm not up to something, if that's what you think. I just don't want her getting a chill," I said, ever solicitous of Gail's welfare. I stood there, holding my jacket by its collar. Martha was immediately to my left, only two feet away, while over by the desk, Gunther continued to eye me warily. "Look, Martha," I reasoned, "your deputy here already searched my pockets. If you want him to do it again, that's fine with me. Here you go, pal."

I gently tossed the jacket over to Gunther, who was surprised to see it land on his right hand, momentarily draping his gun. But he was not as surprised as Martha, whose eyes had been reflexively following the arc of my jacket, and who now discovered that I suddenly had a gun of my own and was pressing its barrel hard against her right temple.

"Nice trick," said Martha.

"I would have so little problem killing you," I advised her. "You're already dead, remember?"

Still holding my gun against her head, I stepped behind her and wrapped my left arm around her waist, clamping my hand around her right wrist, but she was not even trying to struggle.

"Ray!" Gail cried, distraught. "You don't know what you're doing."

Gunther had pulled my suit jacket away from his arm and was pointing his Luger at both of us. Marksman or not, there was no way at this angle he could shoot me without hitting her. "What do I do?" he implored of the woman who gave him his orders.

I counseled Martha, "Tell him to put his gun in the bottom desk drawer or your brains will be wallpaper." I sounded like I meant it, and maybe I did. "I could shoot you right now in cold blood, call the police, tell them what I know, and I'd be getting my picture taken with the mayor at noon tomorrow. The only hope you have right now is my concern for Gail. Let go of your gun."

Martha did so. As it clattered to the floor, she advised Gunther to do as I'd said. Advantage, Mr. Sherwood. I had Martha kick her pistol across the room toward Gunther, who followed my instructions and placed first her pistol and then his holstered Luger deep into the well of the desk's left bottom drawer.

Gail was close to despair. "You're going to ruin everything, Ray."

I told Martha to sit, and she did so without a peep. I moved quickly to the washroom door, always keeping her in view. A quick glance inside showed me there was no window and no vent large enough for a person to escape. "Get in here," I told him. He stared at me like a rabid dog whose jaws had been tied shut. I had him sit down on the toilet seat and locked him in the washroom from the outside, pocketing the key.

I walked back over to the two women. Gail was silently mournful, and although I was the one with the gun, she stared at Martha as if her mother had all the answers.

"Gunther usually knows how to frisk people," commented the strangely assured Martha, who asked, with what seemed like professional curiosity, "How'd you get the gun?"

It gave me immense pleasure not to tell her. En route to Treasure Island that evening, I'd stopped off in Oakland's Chinatown and visited a pawnshop that had nearly a dozen musical instruments in its front window and some two hundred unregistered pistols under its rear counter. The proprietor advised me that the petite .38 that most interested me was considered a lady's gun, and I reassured him that this was fine, as I intended it for a lady. I then walked two doors down the street to a haberdashery, where I asked if they might have a suit one size larger than mine that fitted tight in the shoulders, causing the back of the collar to puff away from the neck. The suit they sold me might have been a bit snug on Quasimodo, but it suited my needs admirably. I then visited the nearest Chinese laundry and paid a seamstress seated at a table in the window to sew a pouch for me in the lining of the jacket near its collar, one that would be just big enough to hold the trim .38 invisibly between my shoulder blades.

I'd worn this less-than-fashionable suit to my appointment on Treasure Island, the gun's weight settled reassuringly between my shoulders. When Gunther had frisked me, I'd placed my hands behind my head and moved my elbows outward in what seemed like a maximum effort to cooperate. But this had actually elevated the pistol even farther from his searching hands, in a location Gunther would never have thought to frisk: the momentarily cloaked nape of my neck. When I'd whisked off my jacket, supposedly to drape it around Gail's shoulders, I'd kept the lining side toward me. It had been a breeze to extract the gun, the jacket effectively hiding the pistol in my hand until the moment I'd tossed the jacket toward Gunther and held the gun against Martha's head.

My plan now was to hit them with all I'd pieced together in the last forty-eight hours so as to jar Gail, and possibly even Martha, into telling me everything I didn't already know. Not that I was trying to be some kind of detective; I was just compelled to see if there was some way, any way, that I could extricate Gail from the corner she'd backed both of us into and buy her a future, even if it was at the expense of my own.

"Gail."

She looked up at me.

I said calmly, evenly, like a knowing but forgiving parent, "Gail, I know that *Swing* is actually a coded message giving detailed information about the naval base that's going to be built on Treasure Island."

The wind went out of her, while her face displayed the opposite of a blush, turning a deathly white. Her mother was stunned as well. To see fear register on Martha Prentice's face was akin to bliss for me. But she didn't hem and haw about it. "When did you catch on?" Martha asked in a controlled but concerned voice.

I had no obligation to tell her the truth. I wanted the people who'd be attempting to decipher *Swing* to slave hopelessly over the meaningless parts for months.

I gave Martha the most credible expression of regret I could muster. "I'm afraid I didn't catch on until just before I came here this evening," I said in what I hoped was a bitter, rueful tone.

She looked relieved, which displeased me, so I decided to shake her up further, starting my riff as confidently as when Jack Donovan would signal to the band that he was having me solo for an extra chorus.

"As it happens," I began, "I'm not the only one who broke the *Swing* code. Adeline Head did as well. That's why she had to die." I looked from Martha to Gail. "She's the one whose nearly faceless body fell from the Tower of the Sun, not Marie Prasquier . . . which in turn allowed Marie to assume the vacated role of Adeline Head, becoming a citizen of the United States and a waitress without portfolio."

I hadn't figured out absolutely everything yet, but Gail and Martha sure as hell must have thought I had. God, I felt alive. I was so damn proud of myself and would remain so for at least another few minutes.

Gail could barely manage to speak. "What . . . why would you think such things, Ray?"

"I thought it strange that Adeline Head's *Self-Portrait* began and ended with a musical theme identical to one in your *Swing Around the Sun*. At first I thought you might have stolen the melody from her, but I ruled that out when I realized you hadn't really chosen the notes of your composition at all . . . they were, in fact, just part of a code. And certainly Ada would have had no reason to steal from you. Her work was in a very traditional romantic style, completely unlike your own.

"And then it dawned on me: Adeline's musical portrait of herself began with her own name. A-D-A-H-E-A-D. Being a music student, she had probably been told more than once that her name could be spelled out with musical notes. Unfortunately for you, Gail, that name also occurred in the *Swing* code, when it referred to the 'Alameda Defense Administration, henceforth ADA headquarters.'" I hummed the musical phrase that had begun and ended Ada's *Self-Portrait*. "She'd been hearing that little sequence of notes for years. It was 'hers.' Yet when she got to play your winning composition, Gail, she heard her musical name in *Swing* several times, and recognized the melody even though it was in a different key. Having accidentally broken the code by transposing the original piano music so that it correctly spelled her name, she spotted other words that needed no further deciphering, just as I did: *beachhead, cache, facade.* I looked down at Gail. "Ada confronted you with this, didn't she? So you told Martha and Russ she was on to you, and they said they'd take care of her."

Gail's hands were agitated. "No, Ray, no, listen, I had no idea anyone was going to die. I made a deal with Ada, I told her I'd pull my work out of the competition if she'd just let the band play *Swing* one time in rehearsal, so that they'd get possession of the music. I told her the coded information was for a Japanese construction company that wanted to underbid the competition. She may not have believed me, but I don't think she really cared about anything as long as she won. I admit, okay, I *did* have to tell Russ and my mother what I'd agreed to, because it would change our plans—"

"Oh, Gail, did you really think they'd ever let Ada walk around knowing what she knew?" I raised my eyes to the heavens, or at least to the cracked plaster ceiling of the bungalow, hoping that her naïveté was genuine. "They *had* to silence her before she could talk to anyone about what she'd learned."

Gail pleaded with me. "I swear I didn't know what they were going to do. I wasn't a part of that in any way!"

I remembered the afternoon she'd supposedly spoken with Adeline Head. "Really? Then why did you have a telephone conversation with a dead girl?"

Gail looked stunned yet again. She turned hurriedly, maybe even fearfully, to Martha. "I never told him a *thing* you didn't want me to tell him, you have to believe me. I don't know how he knows so much, but I promise you, he didn't hear it from me."

Martha seemed inexplicably calm, considering her current circumstances. "It's all right, Gail. Let him have his moment, since he's been good enough not to tell any of this to the authorities. You haven't, have you, Ray?" Martha knew damn well I hadn't, and only she and I understood why.

Gail turned back to me, seemingly as desperate to prove her innocence to me as she was to prove her loyalty to her mother. "The afternoon you met me at the Campanile, I called Russ's house from the Rexall drugstore while you were waiting for me outside. I was always supposed to report anything unexpected, and I had to let them know you'd agreed to work with me on Swing. That's when I learned that it was Adeline who had died. I was horrified, but Russ told me tears weren't going to bring her back, and that I had to pretend to talk to Ada in front of you and other people that day, to make it seem like she was alive, and to explain why no one would be seeing her again.

"Just the day before, Adeline had confronted me about the Swing code and I'd told Russ and my mother about the deal I'd made with her. I found out later that Russ immediately contacted Marie Prasquier—who'd already proposed to him and half the male population of Treasure Island—and told her he had a way she could get a new identity for herself. Marie said she would do absolutely anything. Russ fed her some story about an accident at the fair: a young woman had been killed, he didn't want Treasure Island to get bad publicity. If things could be staged so that it looked like it was Marie who had died, as a suicide, she could have a new life as an American citizen named Adeline Head."

"Did Marie really buy his story?" I asked.

I was speaking to Gail but it was Martha who replied, in a disturbingly casual voice. "People will believe whatever they need to believe," she said with a half smile, "if they're desperate enough. Marie *had* to have guessed, and yet she never questioned me once, not when we went shopping that same afternoon for two identical outfits, one for her and one for the victim of the terrible accident—"

"Which hadn't happened yet," I added.

"Nor was she surprised when I bought all those barrettes and fixed her hair in a very distinctive way. She did just as she was told."

I pictured Marie at the Café Lafayette my first morning on Treasure Island. "Such as making certain that several witnesses took note of her appearance and her distress just before her supposed death."

Martha nodded amused assent. Her lack of concern was causing me to have plenty of my own. You'd never know by her demeanor that I was armed and she was in a sea of trouble. But as long as I had her talking, I wanted to get the facts firsthand. "The only big question I have is when Ada was actually murdered. Do you mind filling me in?"

Martha sat back comfortably in her chair. "I don't have a problem telling you anything. We both know that if you turn me in, Gail will suffer as well. I don't think you'll let that happen." She looked over at her daughter. "You notice he hasn't called the police. The only effective option he has would be to kill Gunther and me. Then there'd be no one who knew of your involvement in all this."

Gail looked at me, terrified. "Ray, don't even think about hurting her—"

"Don't worry, Gail," Martha reassured her. "Murder's not in Ray's repertoire."

I countered, "I have no qualms about shooting you where you're sitting if you try anything."

"Understood," she nodded. "Permission to stretch my shoulders?"

"Slowly."

She stretched them as directed and gave a short sigh. "Well. Since you clearly have the upper hand here, Ray, why don't I tell you what you're dying to know."

She proceeded to share a horror story with me as if it were a weather forecast.

That Monday night, she and Russ had entered the Tower of the

Sun just as Adeline was finishing the carillon piece that signified the closing of the fair. There was no guard there, and besides, Russ was known to most of the staff; his presence would never have been questioned anywhere in the park. They took the service elevator up to the carillon's keyboard, where Martha pointed her gun at Ada as she finished playing and told her she'd be staying there with them until the next morning.

To pacify her, they explained that they needed to keep her out of circulation until Gail could fly to Mexico, in case Ada changed her mind about the deal she'd made and decided to report Gail to the police. They said that if she promised not to make any noise, they wouldn't have to gag her. Adeline agreed, as long as they swore she could leave her perch in the morning. They assured her that she would.

There were sandwiches for her and a thermos of warm milk, a blanket and pillow. They gave her the barrettes as a gift, and in the morning, to pass the time, Martha plaited Ada's hair to see if she liked the way they looked. Then they told her to change into a new outfit they'd brought with them, so that anyone who'd seen Ada the night before wouldn't wonder why she was still wearing the same clothes. Ada thought this unnecessary, but she liked the plaid frock very much. Russ turned his back like a gentleman as she changed. And when she was all ready, he clubbed the back of her head with a deadblow hammer he'd brought specifically for this purpose.

"He was also supposed to smash in her face after she was dead, so that no one would recognize her," Martha concluded dispassionately. "He couldn't stomach that, so I had to. I put a small tarpaulin under her to catch the blood and left her body there for Marie to push off the tower at a little before ten. I also left a disguise for Marie to put on over her own frock before she left the Tower. A nun's habit. It's the best way for a woman to make herself invisible. No one ever questions a nun, or can describe what she looks like. In the commotion, Marie had plenty of time to take the elevator down, slip out one side of the tower, and swing back around to give Adeline a last blessing."

I remembered the nun, and now realized she'd touched Ada's corpse in order to hide the fact that blood was already on her own hands. She'd pretended to be sickened by this and had run to the restrooms, where she'd later have been able to simply stroll away, the folded tarpaulin and its dried bloodstains tucked under the cinched waist of her habit, and take the next ferry home.

It had all gone perfectly. By the time Adeline's body struck the Court of the Moon, Martha was already back in Oakland working in Dr. Corwin's office, and Russ had brought Bob Culpepper to the very site where Ada's body would land in order to establish his alibi, not that anyone would ever have suspected Russ of murder. He'd told Gail to meet him there just before her concert, without telling her why, not only to keep her in the clear until she'd served her purpose with *Swing*, but also to graphically demonstrate how he and Martha dealt with anyone who crossed them. By making her appointment with me that same morning, Gail had unwittingly drawn me deeper into the conspiracy than anyone had intended.

The rest I'd already figured out. Marie had taken on Adeline's identity, but she had to find a way to earn a living, preferably far from the Bay Area. She'd heard Sally Rand's tour was having trouble finding dancers, and Marie had hoped she could wangle herself the chance for an audition with Nancy. But when Marie saw Nancy sitting with me, one of the last people to have seen her alive, she'd had no choice but to walk out the door and never come back. What if I'd recognized her and returned with the police?

I looked at Gail, and although I said nothing, something in my expression must have prompted her to say, "I know I must seem like a monster to be involved in all this, Ray, but everything I've done has been for a very good reason."

I wanted to embrace her, tell her I understood, that what she'd done was human, but I couldn't, I didn't, and it wasn't. "Gail, what about the bodies on Grizzly Peak?"

The words tumbled out of her. "I don't know anything about them. I got a call yesterday morning from the police, saying they believed my mother and Russ had been killed and would I come to the morgue to view their remains—"

"Immediately after which," I interrupted, "you got another call from your mother, letting you know she was all right?"

Gail said nothing.

I looked at Martha. "I imagine you have a second residence in Oakland?"

Martha said, "Nothing to brag about. A one-room flat with a Murphy bed, near Lake Merritt."

"I bet it's been a busy place, with you lying low there since you died, and Gail staying with you last night and today. And the woman who became your corpse." I turned to Gail. "Do you know who that was?"

Gail shook her head. "At the morgue . . . sickening . . ."

"It was Marie Prasquier," I said. "You can't change the teeth in someone's mouth, not without surgery that would be easily detected. But it doesn't take surgery to change someone's dental records. Especially not if you're a trusted office worker who handles the filing for doctors and dentists around the area." I said to Martha, who looked very different now than she had in her severe white medical uniform, "It only took changing the name on Marie Prasquier's dental records to your own, and placing them in the files of a dentist whose practice had been taken over by someone else. Culpepper told me there'd been a list in your metal clutch bag—metal because you didn't want the list to burn—of your important phone numbers, including the dentist who had your falsified records. The police went straight to where you wanted them to go.

"Poor Marie gave you her dental records thinking you were going to put them in a file marked 'Adeline Head,' so she could start building a new identity for herself. You put Marie up in your apartment, and to further build her trust, you made the call to Nancy for her, putting on a Georgia accent. You had her spy on Gail and me at the lake while you were changing into your flapper outfit. Gail must have called and told you where we were when she left me to get us sandwiches that morning.

"But the moment Marie gave you her dental records, you knew she could die in your place, once the *Swing* charts were completed and you were ready to clear the books on Martha Prentice of Oakland."

I asked her with genuine curiosity, "Only why'd you kill Russ? Didn't he still have some value to you?"

She shook her head. "The *Swing* chart has in it everything he knew or was going to know. The navy had decided to do the construction without him. You heard him at the Heritage Picnic. He'd learned too much about my contacts and not enough about discretion." Her eyes turned to onyx. "And I couldn't bear to screw him anymore."

"But what did he think was going to happen on Grizzly Peak?"

She laughed. "Not that he was going to die, that's for certain. He'd pretended to get drunk at the hotel to establish that he wasn't fit to drive. He actually was pouring his pink gins into a sponge within his handkerchief. He reeked of gin because he was mopping his face with it. After you left him in the men's room, he tossed the sponge into a fish tank."

I recalled the tank full of dead tropical fish, and the sponge that lay within it.

"He purposely pawed Gail to get her to leave and be out of our way. We drove back to Oakland and picked up Marie at my apartment. Once we were up on Grizzly Peak, Russ pretended there was a problem with the car, then he knocked Marie out, put her in the passenger seat, and poured gasoline over her body. He thought the story was going to be that while he was changing a tire, the emergency brake had slipped and I'd gone over the cliff. I was supposedly going to move to another town and he was to join me a few months later, after I'd established a new identity. But while he was pouring the gasoline on Marie, I hit him over the head with the same lead pipe he'd used on her." Her eyes narrowed. "He didn't quite pass out, and that was a little frightening. Luckily, he was stunned enough that I could hit him several more times until his skull caved in. I pushed him into the driver's seat and let the car go over the edge. After it started burning, I tossed my silver mesh bag down into the ravine where it would be found by the police, then walked about a quarter mile to a van that Russ had parked up a dirt road earlier that day, and drove back to my flat in Lake Merritt. End of me, end of Russ."

She was almost too forthcoming. Was it simply because she believed I'd never blow the whistle on anything that might hurt Gail, or was there something she knew that I didn't? "Who do you work for, Martha?"

She brushed the skirt on her lap. "It will be announced very shortly that Japan has formed an alliance with the Third Reich. Any conflict with either Axis country will cause the United States to face us on both your European and Asian flanks. So you can understand why a new naval base vital to the defense of your West Coast is of great interest to Germany as well as to Japan. But officials of the German government can't enter or leave the United States at will; we had to act quickly while our Japanese counterparts still have that right." She laughed. "You let Japan, who as everyone knows you plan to go to war with, have a pavilion on the very island you'd use for your destroyers and aircraft carriers." Her giggle was an unimaginable sound. "I love the way America prepares for battle."

I moved over to Gail, who'd sat frozen since Martha's account of Hewett's murder. "Honey, what I don't get about your involvement in all this is . . . *why*?"

She replied numbly, "People will do things for a parent they wouldn't do for anyone else."

How I could possibly get her out of this? "You knew nothing about Russ Hewett's death?"

She shook her head emphatically. "Nothing. Not that I liked him."

I grabbed her arm. "You swear to me you had nothing to do with what happened to Marie Prasquier on Grizzly Peak?"

She looked at me good and true. "Yes. Nothing."

"Then listen," I said, energized, "I think we can get you off the hook. No one has to know about *Swing*. There's no proof you did anything wrong." I figured I'd tell her later, in private, that what the Pan-Pacific Orchestra had taken with them was worthless, that despite her best efforts, she hadn't been a traitor. If anyone ever learned what Gail had tried to do, I could always say she'd changed her mind and ordered me to make the chart meaningless. "Let's think. Outside of writing *Swing*, what did you do wrong? You helped cover up a murder, but you weren't an accomplice to one. Besides, you were protecting your own mother. If you turn state's evidence, I'm sure we could make a deal on that. Is there anything else, honey? I have to know before I call the police."

"Nothing else, Ray, I swear," Gail vowed.

I thought, Damn, I just may have saved her.

For the first time, Martha looked like something other than her calmly confident self. "Gail, you'd condemn your parent to a certain death . . . ?"

Gail stood. "I'm doing the right thing, you'll see." Her face lit up. "You know, Ray, I think Russ had a list of my mother's contacts locked up in his desk. Turning that over to the police might help my case, don't you think?"

I told her I agreed. Keeping the gun trained on Martha, I went to call Bob Culpepper. For this arrest, I thought he wouldn't mind being wakened.

"I think Russ kept the list here," said Gail, crouching down to rummage through the lower left-hand drawer of the desk.

I picked up the phone, dialed Information and said, "Hello, I'd like to—Don't do that, Gail."

Her hand had been reaching for Gunther's Luger. I couldn't call the police. She was clearly not as innocent about this as I'd hoped. I replaced the receiver in its cradle and pointed my gun at her.

"I'm sorry, Ray," she said, almost tenderly. Still kneeling at my side, she continued to move her hand slowly toward the pistol. I was lucky it was on top of Martha's gun and strapped in its holster. It was not something she could pull from the drawer in one swift motion.

"Gail, move your hand away," I said.

"I'm sorry. I have to get the gun," she said, but her hand stayed where it was. She eyed me carefully.

"So you're as bad as they are," I said. If my heart hadn't been broken so many ways a long time ago, it would have been broken now. Gail.

"No, Ray, you got me wrong. I'm really quite the good person. Now let me take the gun and I'll send you back out into the night, I swear to you. You tried to come to my rescue, and you were brave and my hero. But you're fooling around with my whole world and you think you know what you're doing and you don't."

She started to reach again for the Luger. I placed the barrel of my revolver against her hand.

She said, "You won't shoot my hand. I play piano with this hand. You won't shoot me at all." Her ample eyes looked up at me for reassurance. "Now I'm going to take the gun and then I'll let you leave, I promise."

Could I shoot her? I could shoot her in the calf, that would stop her without permanently crippling her. I wouldn't want to shatter the bone. I looked at her leg to find the safest location to—

"That's enough," said Martha, as I felt the barrel of a gun against my head.

52

The Final Notes

"Oh Gail," I said quietly. "What have you done?"

Martha spoke so close to my ear that I could smell her breath. It was poison to me. "When you take a gun away from someone who does this kind of work on a regular basis, you don't simply assume that's the only gun she has on her person. You should have checked my inside left thigh. Now it's your turn to drop the gun. Don't worry, Ray. I'll let you go when I'm sure I don't need you any longer."

I didn't believe her for a second, but I didn't seem to have a choice. Her gun was at my head; mine was, brilliantly, pointed at Gail's leg. I dropped the gun, and damned if Gail didn't scoop it up and hand it to her mother, saying, "I told you you'd see I was doing the right thing, remember? You wouldn't have had the chance to sneak up on him if I hadn't distracted him. We're still on, right?"

I was beyond anger and rage. "Gail," I lamented, "don't you understand she's going to murder me?"

Gail pleaded, "Forgive me, Ray, I don't have a choice! If you would have just let me take the gun, I'd have let you leave—" She looked at Martha, desperately afraid of the words she'd just spoken. "Oh God, I shouldn't have said even *that*."

I was no longer going to keep the secret of who I might be from her, not if I was going to die because of it. "Gail, you don't understand."

"No, *you* don't understand!"

"Gail, you could be killing your own father!"

"I know!" she cried in despair.

What on earth did *that* mean?

The telephone rang a shrill alarm. "Don't answer it!" Martha snapped at Gail. The phone rang a second time and went silent. Martha stared at it, willing it to ring again. It did, and Martha picked it up, saying nothing. A male voice crackled from the receiver. She said, "*Bestätigt*," then hung up.

She turned to Gail. "The plane should be here in a matter of minutes."

"What plane?" I asked.

"A seaplane," said Martha.

"I'm still going?" said Gail hopefully.

Martha nodded. "You've truly earned it." She turned to me. "And I'm going to let you go, as I promised. I honestly believe you won't tell anyone anything, because it would be very bad for Gail if you did. Gunther will be guarding you until after we're on our way. Gail, let Gunther out of the bathroom."

As Gail stepped over to the washroom, Martha gave me the same look of contempt she'd shown me at the Claremont. She said quietly, "Before we go, I've prepared a little surprise for Gail to give you."

I could hardly wait.

Gail was back with Gunther, who angrily strapped on his holstered Luger.

Martha said, "Gail, I want you to share your good news with Ray."

Gail's face brightened. "It's okay? You're sure?"

Martha nodded.

There was nothing mean-spirited in Gail's tone. "I'm glad I can tell you, Ray, because maybe this will better help you understand the things I've done. We're flying from here to Mexico City. Then to Buenos Aires, Morocco, Lisbon, and from there to Berlin. After that, I'm not sure where I'll be going. Lisbon, most likely. But I won't be alone."

"Tell him what you're picking up in Berlin," Martha prodded.

Gail's eyes grew wide. "Ray, I'm going there to get my father."

Her father.

Oh.

I looked at Martha. "You know who her father is?" I asked.

"Yes," said Martha. "I've known all along. I'm told he's a wonderful man, warm and gentle and creative."

It was good that Martha was holding a gun on me, because I would otherwise have slain her with my hands. "You let me think—" Oh, the delighted smile on Martha's face.

Gail perceived none of this. She was too full of her own happiness. "Do you remember when I was talking about my uncle Joe, the composer, who taught me what I know about music? Ray, I was really telling you about my *father*. I so wanted to let you know about him but"—she cast a glance toward Martha—"I'm not allowed to, so I pretended I was talking about my uncle."

Numbly, I asked, "What do you mean, you're not allowed?"

Gail again looked to Martha for permission. It was not an optimistic indication of how long I was going to live that Martha informed Gail she could tell me everything.

"My father is under arrest in Berlin for his political and artistic beliefs. I'm allowed to write to him and I've gotten a few short letters back, but there have been so many rules imposed upon my life this last year. I've done whatever I've been told to do, in order to get the authorities to permit me to bring him back home. That's why I wrote *Swing*. I'm not really an aspiring composer, you know. I'm simply a pianist."

I croaked, "Gail, are you aware that I was led to believe I might be your father?"

Gail gave a nervous laugh. "What?"

"Did you know that I was led to believe that?" I said, raising my voice.

"But how could you think that?" She looked at me as if I were mad.

I nodded at Martha. "We—" I didn't want to be coarse in front of my daughter, except she wasn't. "Martha and I slept together years ago. Nine months before you were born."

"But—" Gail looked at Martha with a strange expression. "Can I tell him? You've let me tell him everything else."

Martha nodded. "Yes, it's all right now. We'll be leaving in a few minutes."

Gail said, "Martha isn't my mother. That's one of the rules: I have to say she is. I've even been referring to her as my mother this evening. I *can't* break the rules. Being my mother has allowed her to monitor me, check up on me at school, meet my friends, and keep me tethered to her on the weekends without arousing the curiosity of others. It also has given her an identity. You know, a birth certificate, a driver's license. If I can prove I'm Gail Prentice and I say she's my mother, then she must be Martha Prentice, right?" Her eyes lowered. "My real mother died many years ago. In Cincinnati."

"And yet in many ways I became Gail's mother," said Martha. "Because, in a manner of speaking, I adopted her." I thought of the tin in Chancery Lane that contained all of Martha's important documents, which had, of course, belonged to the real Martha Prentice. "I'd gotten very specific information from Russ Hewett regarding a new naval base that was to be built on the island he'd helped to construct. I had to get this information across the water. But, of course, all communications with Japan and Germany are carefully screened by your government. On the other hand, a Japanese orchestra was going to be performing here very soon. No one in the government or from customs would question the most universal code of all: music notation. Could we find someone free from suspicion in the Bay Area to create what we needed?

"When we impound certain prisoners who have family in other countries, we encourage them to write home, so that we can learn where their relatives live. Here we have a composer imprisoned in Germany, writing to his equally musical daughter in Berkeley, California. *Vollkommen.* I hand-delivered her father's letter to Gail myself."

Gail said to me, impassioned, "Now do you see, Ray? They said they'd kill my father if I didn't do what they wanted. The letter was clearly from him—I know his handwriting and his way of speaking. I *had* to do what they told me. After all, it isn't like we're actually at war with Japan or Germany. So I invented the *Swing* code and encrypted all of Russ Hewett's information into my composition, knowing in advance that the judges in Japan had been told whose entry should win. I just had to have the code orchestrated and split into many parts, then destroy the original score myself, so that only someone with all the music for all the instruments could reassemble the message. That's why I needed you."

Martha took some fruity pleasure in outlining my pitiful gullibility for me. "You see, Gail had to report all your conversations back to me, not realizing how helpful some of what you told me was. Even before Russ learned about the daughter you lost, I'd heard that you'd been at the Claremont at just the right age, in just the right time frame, that you drank heavily back then and now had very lit-

tle memory of your trysts, I realized I'd been given the chance to
have a powerful hold over you and your loyalty."

"So you stabbed me."

I could see she enjoyed the memory. "Well, that was to lend cre-
dence to my story, as well as to help me align my fabricated tale with
your real blood type. When Russ phoned and told me about your
daughter's death, that clinched the deal."

"How did you know about the clarinet reed in my wallet?"

"Russ found your wallet after a fight you'd had. He went through
it thoroughly before he returned it to you. That's how I knew your
middle name. And if a musician carries a reed in his wallet, autographed by a jazz legend, it must mean a lot to him."

I looked at Martha in amazement. "You're the devil," I said. "You
knew that even if I had not lost my own child, if I believed Gail might
be my daughter, I'd do anything for her. And if at any point I realized
the significance of *Swing,* you knew I'd keep silent. If it were anyone
else, I'd be headed straight to the FBI. But for a daughter, I'd make
any sacrifice. Why, you even covered yourself if you or Gail got
caught. I had written the orchestration, it was in my handwriting,
the original had been destroyed . . . the *Swing* code could have all
been *my* doing." I realized just how smart Martha had been. "That's
why you had the photos taken with me and those Nazi sympathizers
at the picnic, to show that I was in league with them! And if I was
blamed for revealing the coded information in *Swing,* you knew
there was every likelihood I'd take the fall for Gail. You could have
framed me and, for her sake, I would have kept quiet."

I turned on Gail, wounded, and asked again, "Did you know I'd
been told you might be my daughter?"

Her face seemed genuinely anguished. "Oh, Ray, no, of course
not! It really happened the way I said—I *am* a fan of your work.
When it turned out you were in town, well, it was perfect! I'd figured a regular jazz arranger, he'd hear what I'd written and just
laugh me out of the room, like the Japanese band did. But someone

like yourself, knowledgeable about very modern music, would hear my piece as something daring and adventurous." Despite our grim circumstances, a pleasurable realization flitted across her face. "Oh my gosh, no wonder you never made a real pass at me! I was so insulted that you didn't even once try to kiss me! Oh, Ray . . ." She moved to embrace me, but I reflexively pushed her away.

"Don't! It's not that simple! I'm all mixed up. You don't know what you've—" She was just a college girl who'd taken advantage of me and now she wanted to kiss me? "I'm not Russ Hewett, you know!"

She looked baffled. "What do you mean by that?"

"I saw the love letter you wrote to him, Gail! It was in his cigar case when he died."

"Are you crazy?" she asked. "Me, write a love letter to *him*?"

"Gail, you forget I orchestrated your score, I know your handwriting by heart. Culpepper showed me the letter. It had a violet ink stain . . ."

A violet ink stain.

"Enough now," said Martha. She turned to Gunther and gave him a pointed look. "The plane should be landing any minute now. Go take care of things. You understand?"

Gunther nodded and left the bungalow.

I said to Martha, "Before you go, there's something that might be very important for both of you to know. You see this dried-up stain on the right side of the desk? That's from this bottle of violet ink that spilled. The ink ran all the way to the edge, but if you look down, strangely enough, not one drop spilled onto the carpet."

Martha said, "I'm not looking down at anything." She kept her gun trained on me.

"Well, Gail, *you* can look. Like I said, there were violet ink stains on the letter I thought you wrote to Russ." I'd figured something out. Something dreadful. And the only reason Martha was letting me talk about it was because she didn't have a clue what it was. I tried to sound chatty. "I'm betting the reason the violet ink didn't spill onto the carpet was because it spilled into something else first. Like this lower right-hand drawer. I think that when the bottle spilled, the drawer was open."

Gail blinked at me. "This doesn't seem very important, Ray."

I told her, "At the Claremont, the last night of his life, Russ apologized for being late. He told me he'd had to stop off at his office." I pointed to the pictures on his desk of me, Russ, and Gail flanked by the Nazi sympathizers. "I think he came by to pick up some of these photos. While I was on the bandstand, he was supposed to plant one of these pictures in my room, in case you needed to frame me somewhere down the line. Gail was in the picture, too. You could have framed her as well."

Martha said, "Only if she didn't cooperate, and she did. Gail, I think I hear the plane's engines."

I continued: "Here in his office, Russ had a brainstorm, one he couldn't tell you about, Martha, because Gail and Toby Ackland were already with you. He decided he'd also plant a page from a letter he kept locked in this lower right-hand drawer. When found in my room, it would make it seem like Gail and I were co-conspirators because we were lovers, or vice versa."

I quoted words that had upset me so much when I'd first read them that they were now branded on my brain. " 'I lie in my bed here and in Chancery Lane praying that love can travel through walls and reach you, and that you can feel my embrace.' "

Gail looked stunned. "How do you know those words?"

"Yes, how *would* I know them? They're not from a letter you wrote to Russ. They're from a letter you wrote to your *father*. One that Martha said she sent to him in Berlin. Am I right?"

"Yes, weeks ago . . ." said Gail. I saw a terrible fear rising in her face.

"And yet I read it, Gail, I held it in my hands just yesterday. The original. In your handwriting. With an ink stain on it from this bottle that spilled only two nights ago, when Russ was getting your letter from this desk." I had to say it to her, even knowing what it meant. "Why was that letter still in this country, Gail?"

Gail looked from me to Martha and to the lower right-hand desk drawer.

Martha started to speak, but Gail had already opened the drawer and was going through its contents.

In the background, I could hear the powerful engines of a seaplane revving.

"Oh no." Gail spoke in a frightened little voice. Trembling, she held up several sheaves of notepaper, all of which bore her handwriting. "These were the letters I wrote to him." She flipped through the pages. "August, July . . ."

Martha made no effort to explain, as if there was no longer any reason to lie.

"I guess you know why they were never mailed," I said sadly.

"Oh no, and *these!*" moaned Gail, flipping through other, smaller notes, on cheaper paper. "Letters from him. Letters I never received."

I said, "Gail, I'm sure they let him write to you every day but told him not to mention time or events. They're all real expressions of his feelings, I'm sure. But I think they kept the letters here, and delivered one of them to you every month or so. Who knows how long ago he wrote them." In despair, Gail turned to Martha, who was making no pretense of kindness or concern now. Gail fell upon the room's carpet, holding her arms around herself, sobbing without sound. I held her, trying to comfort her. She shook me away.

The front door opened, and Gunther stepped in.

"Things are ready," he said. His gun was drawn.

Martha went over to Gail, took her arm, and pulled her up with a strong tug. "Come on," said Martha. "We have a plane to catch."

53

The Seaplane

Gail and I were being marched from the bungalow toward the water near the parking lot's edge. Martha and Gunther walked behind us, their guns aimed at our backs. Martha had advised us we would be shot without hesitation if we stopped. We would be shot if we ran. This much I knew: we were going to be shot.

"If my father is dead, why am I flying anywhere?" Gail asked aloud.

"We're taking you to pick up his body, so that you can bury him where you wish. We're very sorry he died. He became ill in prison."

I had the choice of soothing Gail until a bullet entered her back or letting her know what we faced, so that we might try to do something to save ourselves. Although what that might be, I had absolutely no idea.

I said to Gail, not even trying to whisper, "You see how she works? She holds out hope, tells you the good thing that's going to happen if you just cooperate. You'll see your father, she'll let me go. It's to make prisoners as manageable as possible until it's too late. They're not going to fly you to Germany. *She's* going back, I bet, probably by the route you thought you both were going to take."

"Shut up," said Gunther.

"Gail, both of us were always going to die. Martha's only been allowing us to live in case any problem arose on the musical front. My guess is that the phone call she just got told her the charts are now out of the country, or that they've checked some of the music and decoded it successfully." I was so glad I had left the first few harmless bars intact.

"The phone call confirmed both those things," said Martha. "Also that the seaplane was arriving. I'm willing to let both of you live if you work for us."

"Really?" I asked. I peered around. "Where's this seaplane?"

"You heard its motors when you were inside the bungalow. The pilot has cut his lights and engines now. We don't want to be spotted."

We were almost by the white truck in the parking lot. It was about eighteen feet long and seven or eight feet wide. I remembered the lettering on the side of the truck had said it was from Landsberg, Ohio. Where was that? I wondered.

"Take off your clothes," said Martha.

"What?" I demanded.

"After Gunther failed to frisk you properly, I'm playing it safe. Strip quickly and you can keep your underpants. Gunther, is that all right?"

Gunther said it wouldn't make a difference. Why he suddenly had jurisdiction over this was puzzling. He purposely shaded himself to Gail's side to better enjoy the view as she undressed.

We stood there, nearly naked, in the chill wind that came off the water.

"Okay, Martha, see? No weapons," said Gail. "Can we get dressed now?" The cold and indignity seemed to have revived Gail momentarily.

Martha ignored her. "Oh, by the way, the seaplane isn't here after all. We're going to drive to it. You'll ride in the back of the truck."

54

The Truck

Gunther pulled up on a jointed latch, opened the truck's cargo door, and turned on a battery-powered electric lantern that stood on the truck bed's floor. It was surprisingly powerful and revealed the truck to be completely empty. "Sit down in the front there," he said. "It's a good night for a little drive."

To where? I wondered. What canyon or cliff? Or would they simply drive the truck off the edge of Treasure Island?

Gail and I stepped up into the truck and Gunther followed, walking us to the front of the trailer. I knew this would be my only chance. If I could overpower him and get his gun, I could shoot it out with Martha, using Gunther as a shield. Not that I thought Martha would have any hesitation about shooting him. I simply thought that he might be able to catch a bullet for me. I felt fine with that.

I appraised Gunther. In a fair fight, I could easily take him. My additional advantage was that I'd be fighting for Gail's life and mine. That was a terrific edge for me. He had a gun. That was a far more terrific edge for him.

I figured, in the half second that it took me to reason all this, what any private detective would have known off the bat. The gun was the target, not Gunther. I'd always been pretty good at pool, and I tried quickly to calculate the angles. Gunther was directly behind me. The Luger was in his right hand. Gail was on my right. If I swung counterclockwise and pushed his arm aside, he might fire and hit Gail. I'd have to swing around to my right and push his right arm across his own body so that the gun pointed toward his left.

"Listen, Gail, honey," I said caringly, "always remember *ottava bassa*." It was musical nomenclature for dropping a note down an octave.

"What's that?" Gunther demanded.

Gail understood what I meant and threw herself to the floor. I whirled clockwise but had not anticipated that, seeing Gail move, Gunther would whirl to his right. My body didn't connect with his arm at all and almost spun in a complete circle. I was off balance and facing the wrong way, but I had to do something, so I barreled my entire body into him, leading with my left shoulder. As we both went down, the gun fired and the bullet caromed off the walls as fast as a drummer's paradiddle. I groped with him on the floor, trying to get his right arm under control with both my arms, an objective that, regretfully, caused the right side of my neck to be stretched and exposed. He bit into it lustily, like a timber wolf. It hurt like I couldn't believe. Luckily, his teeth had dug in low and caught more of my collarbone than my neck. Rather than pull away, I rammed my right shoulder down into his mouth, making his head bounce off the metal floor. "Kill! Kill! Kill!" I screamed in order to bear the pain. I wanted to split his head open. I wanted his face to be a bigger mess than Adeline's face had been.

Realizing his strategy had been a poor choice, he unclenched his teeth and tried to find a new line of attack. As we nastily grappled, both my hands still locked around his right forearm, he started to make bleating noises of pain. I turned to see Gail stomping with her right heel on Gunther's hand and wrist. Stupidly, I'd forgotten that I had a weapon Gunther didn't have: a twenty-one-year-old woman who could ply the levers of a carillon so that its bells could be heard for miles. She wasn't using her hands right now, though. She knew we needed the gun, and she was slamming her heel down as if Gunther's hand was a brush fire she could put out with her feet. The gun fired again, its bullet repeatedly stinging the sides of the truck.

It would have been disastrous to let go of Gunther's arm, which left my choices for further assault sorely limited. So I kneed him repeatedly in his groin, wincing to myself as I considered what it must feel like to be him. I tried kneeing him in his stomach a few times but I couldn't get quite the right angle, so I went back to his balls, where I seemed to be getting the best return of pain for the investment of my energy. This and Gail's constant stampede at almost one hundred and fifty-two beats per minute finally caused Gunther to drop the gun.

We had been assaulting him so mindlessly that my brain had been free to wonder why Martha, who was outside the truck and had her own gun, was doing nothing to stop us. I received my answer the next instant, as I heard the door to the rear of the truck slam closed. There was a deep rasping sound like the tumblers of a vault sliding into position. Instantly, Gunther stopped struggling, even as his entire body tensed beneath me.

"Oh no," he gasped, softly, with such a look of fear on his face that I was newly frightened without knowing why. The adrenaline was no longer working for me. I pinned him down, but he wasn't struggling. Gail found the gun on the floor of the truck and quickly picked it up.

The truck was so black now that the battery-powered lantern seemed even more brilliant. We could hear and feel the truck's powerful engine roll over and rev like a horde of synchronized motorcy-cles, then settle into a low, steady drone. What I'd earlier thought had been the sound of a seaplane's engines had clearly been the truck's powerful motor being tested under Gunther's supervision.

"Where is she taking us?" I snapped at the horrified Gunther.

His eyes darted about the inside of the truck as if he were esti-mating how much of a load it could hold.

I said, "Gail, give me the gun."

She did so, and I held the barrel of the Luger against his head. "I said, tell me where she's taking us."

"To hell," he whispered in terror. "We're already on our way."

At the End of the World

Gail felt the side of the truck. "It's just vibrations," she said. "I don't think we're moving."

Gunther shook his head, "We won't move. All the same, we're being taken somewhere. And I am the mechanic of my own destruction."

"What are you saying?" Gail asked.

His eyes were wide and bright with horror.

"This is a death truck. I did the modifications myself. It's a simple matter to switch the truck's venting system, which I did just a little while ago. The exhaust from the two pipes that vent above the rear of the cab is simply diverted into this trailer above the false ceiling, there." He pointed, and I could see that on one side of the shiny metal ceiling there was a two-inch-wide vent that ran the length of the trailer. A specter of thin smoke was fingering its way down into our long metal chamber from the front end of the vent.

As we spoke, the smoke extended ever farther along the vent, moving toward the back of the truck.

Gunther said, "What you see and what you'll smell are the chemical by-products of burning gasoline. It would suffocate us eventually, but it would take hours. The gas that will kill us long before that is invisible and has no odor or taste. I've tuned the engine to maximum efficiency for the manufacture of carbon monoxide. I've used this before. It works. You'll see."

"Listen, you idiot," I demanded, shaking him. "Don't you want to live?"

He straightened himself up and sat against the side of the trailer. "Of course. If I knew a way to save myself, I would. But I built this," he said with a tinge of pride in his voice, "and I know how well I built it. Did you see on the truck, how it says 'Landsberg, Ohio'? I painted that. I am from Ohio, but Landsberg is the prison where the Führer wrote *Mein Kampf*. We should," he added, trying to convince himself, "we should be honored to end our lives in a place with such a name." He looked about fearfully. "There is a way that great men die. So I must collect myself. And since I'm taking both of you with me, I may yet be granted a warrior's fate in Valhalla." He added quietly, "If there is a Valhalla."

I rushed to the door of the truck, which Gail was already shaking and banging uselessly. "Maybe I can shoot the lock off," I said.

From his seated position, Gunther informed me, "Ten strong men couldn't force it open. And your bullets won't penetrate the metal. Or didn't you notice that the bullets I fired all ricocheted? You shouldn't waste the ammunition. You may want to save the bullets for yourselves."

I asked him how many bullets were in the Luger's magazine. He said sixteen, of which we'd spent two.

Gail yelled, "Martha!"

Gunther laughed. "She is long gone. She doesn't know how to drive a truck like this, and there's no point in her staying around.

She has much greater work to do in Berlin, and reaching there is a long and complicated route." He groaned to himself. "The plan, if I'd not been so incompetent, was to kill the two of you in the truck, then put you together naked in the bungalow and blow out the pilot light on the space heater. We were going to scatter your clothes on the floor. It would look like you'd been having sex and been gassed in your sleep. That was the plan." A look of concern came over his face. "Or do you think she always meant for me to die with you? We may not be found until the fair is torn down and someone wonders who belongs to this truck."

Gail and I shouted for help. Gunther told us not to bother, that even if someone was close enough to hear, the truck's engines would blot out our cries. Even gunshots would be muffled.

He moved to the rear of the truck and squatted down against its wall. "There is one car that patrols the roadways of the entire island and the approach from Yerba Buena. It passed here at 11:50. It won't be back again until two A.M. We'll be dead long before that."

I looked at the mechanism that sealed the door shut to see if it had any vulnerable spots, but there was simply nothing to shoot at. Everything was on the outside. Still, I had to try. I pointed the gun at a big metal hinge, angling my body so that, with luck, the shot wouldn't ricochet into me, and fired. The result was negligible. The hinge ended up slightly chipped, and there was some scorching around it. I shot again. I could have fired until the gun was empty and we'd be just as dead.

I'd heard that it could take less than ten minutes for even a moderate amount of carbon monoxide to make someone unconscious in a closed garage. Already I could feel the effects of the gas. I felt far more fatigued than I'd been a minute earlier, and dizzy. My head was beginning to ache, sending a very sharp and throbbing pain into both sides of my skull. My feet were getting weighty.

Gail said, "We have to block the vent. Make Gunther give us his clothes."

Gunther scoffed. "Do you think I would have designed it so that half a laundry basket of clothing could obstruct the gas? This truck can kill up to sixty people without taxing itself. Look for yourself—the vent is the length of the trailer."

He slumped forward over his raised knees. "Exertion only speeds death. Carbon monoxide combines with the blood more quickly than oxygen and is reluctant to leave. The best hope you have is to do nothing."

I turned to face Gail. It greatly saddened me that she looked so lovely. "I can't just stand here waiting to die!" Gail cried, which was a mistake because her ensuing sharp intake of breath caused her to double up in wracking spasms. I was able to grab her before she hit the floor, and I helped her to the back of the truck. I set her down against the wall next to Gunther, who, despite his lack of movement, was beginning to cough as if from the croup.

My years of playing tenor sax were, for the moment, helping me fare better than the others. My lung capacity was surely greater, and I could go much longer between breaths.

I shook Gunther. "There must be some opening, hole, seam, where we could breathe fresh air, even if we had to take turns," I said. My legs felt as if they were cast from iron, my arms from lead.

He said nothing, which gave me hope, because each prior time I'd suggested something, he'd scoffed.

I said, "Listen, you can stay alive underwater if you just have a straw. All I'm asking for is a straw."

He said, "It's not like being underwater. The carbon monoxide invades, it's a poison."

I begged him. "A crack! I'll take anything." I put my mouth by his ear and whispered, "I don't want her to die without hope." At this point, I was no longer looking for the way out. I was looking for whatever might make Gail *think* there was a way out.

"It won't save us," said Gunther. He crawled on his hands and knees, as I followed him, to the left front corner of the trailer. He pointed to a tiny seam in the metal. "Here. This little join. It was soldered to be airtight, but the solder must have been cheap—it came off. I put five layers of medical tape over it, on the outside."

I probed the corner with the nail of my pinkie finger, which clicked against an edge of metal. "Do you have a knife?" I asked him. "A fountain pen? Anything small or sharp? I just want to make a breathing hole."

I knew the answer was that he had nothing.

"Bring Gail over here," I ordered. He didn't move. I grabbed his throat. "Bring her over or you'll go to Valhalla with your balls shot off."

He crawled back toward Gail.

While he did, I held the barrel of the gun down against the corner of the truck. The seam in the corner was no bigger than a dime. All I could hope to do was pierce the medical tape that covered the tiny crevice on the outside of the truck. I took a breath and held the gun down hard, clamping my left hand on my right, vowing not to let the gun recoil.

I screamed my daughter's name for willpower as I pulled the trigger. The gun exploded, and I felt a kind of pain I'd never known before. I couldn't tell if I'd sprained, broken, or shattered my right wrist. But there was such pain.

I bent down to feel the scorched metal with my left pinkie finger. The shot had opened up the corner join just a little.

I would have to fire again. The question was, Should I use my left hand and thereby possibly break both wrists, or stay with my right, since the damage was already done? I decided to stay with my right. A little less pain was not as valuable as having the ability to do something with my left hand.

I fired the gun again. Pain to the third power. My eyes dispensed a flood of tears that were unconnected to emotion. I tried to remind myself that there was actually a time in my life when I hadn't known such agony.

But the gunshots had made a slight difference. I'd seemingly shot off some of the tape. I was now able to force my left pinkie finger through the hole, though in withdrawing it, I cut myself badly. I tried to force the barrel of the gun through the aperture. It was the only tool I had.

Gunther had brought over Gail, who was dazed. "Gail," I gasped. "Put your mouth down against the floor and see if you can breathe in some air." I guided her head down, trying to position her mouth where the aperture might be. After half a minute, she pulled away. "Now you," she gasped.

I lay on my belly and tried to get my mouth close to the tiny space. I didn't get much air, but it was something. Then I signaled her to go again. I let her go twice because I had the gun. After that, I gave Gunther his turn.

We went on like this for minutes, but it was a losing battle. Each thin sip of air we were able to suck in was no match for the glacier of lethal gas that was burying us, although we couldn't identify it with any of our senses, but only by our growing delirium and utter debilitation.

Finally, while Gunther was at the airhole and I realized that in another ten minutes we would be unable to move and therefore would die, I said to Gail, "So . . . I have a plan."

"Well, yes, dammit, Ray," rasped Gail. "I've been waiting."

I said, "One or two more shots from this gun and maybe I can force a hole big enough to put its barrel through."

Gail had to take another ration of thin air. When she was done, I took my turn, then let Gunther go again, as I told her, wheezing, "You two will get to the back of the truck. Then I'll try to . . . angle the gun to shoot the gas tanks at the back of the cab. If I'm lucky . . . they might explode . . . and open a way for us to get out."

Gail's breathing was that of an aged man on his deathbed. It was a horrible sound to come from someone so young. "Is there more to the plan?" she asked me.

I shook my head. "No. Did you hear that, Gunther?"

Gunther took his mouth away from the hole and nodded yes.

I coughed again. "All right, so that's my plan."

Gail said, "And you, Ray, what'll happen to you?"

I coughed and smiled. "That's part of God's plan."

Gail made what little protesting noise she could make, but I ignored her. "Both of you, take your last air and go to the back of the truck, in case I explode the tanks. Gunther, you first."

I was feeling dizzy, and I was afraid I might pass out before I could try my pathetic ruse. I would try to make it work, but the best I could likely hope for was that Gail would drift off into a sleep of death at the back of the truck, with the belief in her brain, as it shut down, that any minute I would save her. It would be much like Linney's death, but at least Gail was not as alone, and would slip under with a little more hope. That was probably the best I could do for her now.

In a way, life had been kind to me at the end after all. Yes, I was going to die now, one way or another, but having learned that Gail was no more my daughter than any other girl on earth, I knew it was all right for me to kiss her good-bye the way I'd wanted to kiss her when we'd first met.

We kissed, trying to put into it everyone we'd ever loved, ever wanted to love, ever loved who hadn't loved us. This kiss would have to cover all of that. It wouldn't be enough, not nearly, but it was all we were going to have.

Then we were done.

I pulled Gunther away from the airhole with my left hand and told Gail to take a last ration of oxygen.

Finally, I said, "Now get back there."

She looked at me.

I choked out, "Get back or you'll ruin my plan!" I told Gunther to take her, and he remembered my earlier threat. Together, they crawled to the rear of the truck.

I shot at the hole once, from a foot away, holding the gun with both hands. The recoil hurt my right wrist indescribably. I fired again . . . and found I was now able to force the barrel through the widened hole and twist it straight and forward.

I looked back at Gail. Her knees were up against her chin.

The damage to my wrist had made it impossible for me to pull the trigger with my right hand any longer, but this worked out all right, because I actually had a better angle using my left. "Thank you, Linney," I murmured.

This would probably be it for me. I framed my thoughts around my daughter, particularly a mental image I had of Linney with her mother, strolling toward me after they had gone for a morning walk around our neighborhood. I wanted to take it with me . . .

. . . as I pulled the trigger with my left hand.

I heard a *clank*, but there was no explosion. I fired over and over again. Nothing.

I had only one bullet left. Sucking a thread of air up through the hole and into my abraded lungs, I struggled back to Gunther and somehow said, "I don't know if I hit the gas tank, I can't see. I need a fuse. All we have is your clothing."

"My uniform," he said.

I pointed the gun at his crotch. "Your tie and shirt."

I carried them back across the truck as if they weighed three hundred pounds and I weighed more.

Could you set fire to a tie by shooting it with a gun? I didn't know. I had only one bullet to help me find out. I prayed that gasoline was trickling underneath us. If that was the case, one good spark—

I suddenly pictured Gunther trying unsuccessfully to light a cigarette by the desk in the bungalow. I fumbled for his shirt pocket.

The box had six wooden matches. I struck one and tried to set fire to the tie. It didn't want to burn. I struck two at the same time and got the tip ignited. I eased it down through the airhole, waiting until the flame became a plume before I let it drop.

I tore a strip of cloth from the silver shirt, but it wouldn't light. The carbon monoxide snuffed out the flame even as it ignited. I tried again. This time the match itself didn't want to ignite. I moved closer to the airhole so that the match would have the benefit of a little more oxygen, and it lit. I lowered the shirt strip through the hole until I was holding only the tip, and touched the flame to it. The shirt began to burn and I dropped it, hoping that the fresh air would help the flame rather than blow it out.

I still had one bullet left. I'd try to fire straight down. Hopefully there was some gasoline directly below me.

I smiled as I remembered that if luck was with me, I'd be dead in another few seconds. I looked back at Gail, said Linney's name, and shot the gun.

Nothing happened, except for all hope leaving my heart.

I crawled back to Gail, leaned against the wall, and took her in my arms.

There was a ringing, a singing in my ears. Not of any voice I knew. High-pitched, like violins that could speak. They were singing what I used to sing to Linney, when I'd push her so high . . .

How do you like to go up in a swing,
Up in the air so blue?
Oh, I do think it the pleasantest thing
Ever a child can do . . .

"What do we do now?" Gail croaked.

"Don't worry," I said. "I have another plan."

"What is it?" she mumbled, her speech slurred.

"Very good plan, honey."

"It'll work?"

"It's working already."

She coughed. "I'm cold," she said slowly. The battery-powered lantern was beginning to dim, or perhaps it was my eyes. She said, "Hold me so no one can take me away."

I cradled her. She must have been hearing her own hallucinatory singsong as well, because her lips whispered, almost airlessly, "Where's the music coming from?"

"Don't worry," I reassured her.

"I'm scared."

"No, no, it's just little notes on paper," I soothed. "Dots on paper."

"Dad."

"I won't leave, you, Linney." I held her tighter. "I won't leave you."

She went limp in my arms.

And then there was simply no air in the truck. Not that our lungs were straining to find it, but rather it simply wasn't there. I felt the vacuum reach down my throat and grab my heart and hold it still.

I tried to tell Linney I loved her, but I couldn't make a sound. If I'd had an epitaph ready to pronounce, I wouldn't have been able to speak it as I died.

56

Allegro con Fuoco

The explosion momentarily lifted the front of the trailer off the ground.

The good thing that happened was that instantly there was a hole gouged in the front of the truck. This let in a wave of air and was a big enough aperture for us to fit through.

The bad thing was that a wall of intense fire covered the entire aperture. And just as I felt the oxygen touch my lungs, the fire started sucking it all back.

Gunther was revived enough to start crawling to the hole. "Wait!" I cried.

He didn't waste his time talking to me. He clearly thought he stood a chance of jumping through the flames. Perhaps he did. I didn't blame him for wanting to escape, but he'd forgotten that many trucks have two fuel tanks, and if one goes, the second usually blows shortly thereafter.

As he reached the waterfall of black and crimson fire that poured past the newly made mouth of our metal prison, there was a second explosion, much bigger than the first, and Gunther found himself in Valhalla on the day that it was immolated. He turned toward me, his body now a seven-foot-high torch. He was tall at last. Every part of him was burning except his brain, and I believed he could see us. Was he trying to salute? He began to twist and curl into himself the way a sheet of paper does when thrown upon a hearth.

I shook Gail awake. The second explosion had caused another flaming tear in the truck, this one somewhat larger but just as filled with fire. Again, more oxygen was available, but the flames were drawing it in with lungs more powerful than our own. And now it was becoming academic who would win the battle for the air, because the air was becoming too hot to breathe. We were lucky (within a very broad interpretation of the term) in that there was nothing in the truck to catch fire, with the exception of us. But the metal hull would soon be too hot to stand or sit on.

We were part of a very cruel scientific equation. We desperately needed oxygen. But more oxygen for us meant more for the fire, making its flames and killing heat ever stronger. At the same time, the carbon monoxide that still filled the truck had the power to retard and smother the deadly flame, but not before it would poison us. Between the oxygen, the carbon monoxide, and the fire, it was hard to choose whom to root for.

"Do you want to try going through the flames?" I asked Gail. She shook her head no. Gunther had served us some good, after all, because we'd seen how he'd met his end, and we knew we didn't want that for ourselves.

"There's a chance," I shouted in her ear over the din of the bellowing inferno, "that all the carbon monoxide will put out the fire, or bring it down enough that we can get out."

At that moment, there was a further eruption of gasoline, and the flames increased.

"But what I'm really banking on," I added, "are April showers." The temperature of the metal would soon reach a point where we would end up scorched to death like steak slapped down on a pre-heated skillet. I was suddenly nostalgic for the good old days of carbon monoxide poisoning.

The door to the back of the truck swung open. We felt the best breeze in the history of the world—cold, laced with gasoline smoke, but sweeter to us than a field of wet clover on the first sunny morning of spring.

It wouldn't have mattered if the doors had been opened by Martha and Gunther the Second—we would have gratefully embraced them, and so we did as they helped us down from the truck and carried us in their arms away from the flames.

Seeing as I was only in my undershorts, I think Bob Culpepper was anxious to get me out of his arms and onto the ground as quickly as possible. As he set me down on the grass by the perimeter of the parking lot—had we never left Treasure Island? I could have sworn we really had traveled, as Gunther had promised, to hell—I saw Gail being wrapped in a blanket by Nancy, who did this as caringly as would the mother of a nearly drowned child.

57

Breathing Space

Officer Ciancimino was trying to determine where the little fire extinguisher he'd removed from the trunk of the squad car might be most effectively employed against the inferno at the front of the truck, which was somewhat like determining where to apply Mercurochrome to Marie Antoinette's neck, post-guillotine.

Culpepper said to Nancy, "There ought to be a small tank of oxygen in the trunk of the squad car as well," then stepped away quickly to get it.

I coughed out my words to Nancy. "Her clothes should be behind the truck. Mine, too. Don't you get too close, though."

Nancy said she'd be right back and went toward Ciancimino.

I crawled over to Gail and put my face close to hers.

"Can you hear me?" I asked.

She nodded yes.

"Okay, listen. The *Swing* chart . . . I changed it before it left the country. Whoever has it now has nothing." Despite our ordeal, Gail's face immediately became twice as alive. "If they get Martha and she talks—listen carefully—say you only made the first few bars in code; the rest was gibberish. If the music ever turns up, it'll bear this out."

She looked up at me like a child, showing more gratitude than I'd ever been offered. My head shook the offering away. "No, don't think I'm your hero. The *Swing* chart, that's my gift to you, but the rest of it . . . I'm telling the police what I know. You'll have to answer to them."

She spoke through grime-crusted lips. "Ray. So you know . . . All I did was make that phone call to Adeline after she was dead."

I frowned. She didn't understand yet, but she would. "Gail, you knew about a murder and you didn't tell anyone."

"But . . . my father would have died."

"I know. And we have his letters, and yours, and my testimony to everything that Martha admitted. You'll tell this to the police—" I gasped for air "—and if you must, to a judge and jury, and they'll decide what should be done. That's not up to me."

I was no longer her big hero. That was okay. I was no longer her father either.

I told her, "You got me caught up in this. That was wrong."

"Forgive me."

"I can do that. A lot of what happened was my own fault. I was so taken with you, and so needy." I brushed some of her wild mane away from her eyes. "Whatever happens from here on will be a lot better than whatever was going to happen in there." I nodded at the truck, which was now engulfed in dense black smoke. "And if you want, I'll stand by you as long as you need me to."

Culpepper came back with a small tank of oxygen and clamped its small mask over Gail's mouth. She coughed violently as the pure air hit her lungs.

Nancy returned with our clothes and helped Gail into hers.

"How did you know we were here?" I asked Culpepper.

"I didn't know anything," he said, and indicated Nancy, who was slipping a dress onto Gail as if readying her for her first day of school. She said, "I'd had dinner with Bob in the Chinese Village by the Gayway, then came back to Sally's on my own and found that little drawing of Linney's you'd left with me for safekeeping. Despite your casual note, I knew you'd never part with that unless you thought something might happen to you. I was so alarmed, I went to the Claremont, and when you weren't there by eleven-thirty, I asked the front desk if you'd had any messages in the last twenty-four hours. They said you had, but they wouldn't tell me what it was. I told them I'd been your wife, and that made them clam up even more. So I called Bob and, thank God, he came over, flashed his badge, and we learned you were meeting someone near a marina."

Culpepper said, "That could have been anywhere. But everything you've been doing these last two weeks has seemed to center on Treasure Island. Trouble is, by the time we got here, there was nobody left to question. So we just poked all over the place, wondering where Gail might have burned her music, like she said in the note."

"The note wasn't from Gail," I said. At least I could exonerate her on that count.

Nancy wrapped her own cloth coat around Gail and then wrapped her in the blanket again. "We'd given up and then we heard the truck explode."

Culpepper took the oxygen tank from Gail and, over my protests, made me breathe from it for a minute. As I wheezed louder than a concertina, he said, "Listen, I wish I didn't have to bother you with this now, but we can't let whoever did this to you get out of the area. I'll take the full story from you a little later. Right now what I need is a description and the name of who we're looking for."

I gave him a very accurate description. It was even a bit poetic. The name I offered him, in all good faith, was a name he'd never heard before.

58

Dal Segno al Fine

"The name is Vernon, Edna Vernon," said the absurdly attractive woman as a redcap deposited her lone suitcase at the sales counter. "I called early this morning. You're holding a reservation for me on the *Flying Cloud* to Mexico City, unless a seat has become available on your Buenos Aires flight."

The Pan Am clerk consulted a clipboard and smiled. "I think I may have some good news for you, Miss Verne."

"Vernon."

"Beg your pardon. Well, I'm pleased to say we've had a cancellation on the flight to Buenos Aires. So it's really your choice. Which would you prefer?" He waited as she considered. "Please don't let me rush you."

After a moment, she decided. "Yes, good. Buenos Aires."

"Buenos Aires, then. That will be, um, nine hundred and thirty-two dollars, I believe." His tone was apologetic, because it really was so much money. "Would you prefer to pay by cash or with a check?"

She opened her pocketbook. "Cash."

"Excellent. And because this is an international flight, I'll be needing to see your passport."

She gave it to him. He compared the photograph to the woman. *Edna Drisch Vernon,* it said. The picture was clearly a few years old, but she was even more stunning now, her angled pompadour sweeping back into a chignon.

He handed the passport back to her. "Thank you so much. Now if you'd like, you may wait for your flight in what we call the Pawala Lounge. I know it sounds like a Hawaiian village, but it actually stands for Pan American World Airways Los Angeles Lounge, exclusive to our customers." He winked at her. "It's an awful lot better than the hamburger sandwich counter by Gate 3, I promise."

He indicated a door, and the redcap followed her through it.

She walked into a small room with a number of occupied chairs and not much else. She was dismayed to see that there was no bar, no table with hors d'oeuvres. She gave the redcap a quarter and sat by a table with some magazines on it. It surprised her that the magazines were so old.

There were six or seven men seated about the room. A burly-looking lady in the corner was the only other woman. The men, all dressed in commonplace suits, seemed uniformly engrossed in the morning's *Los Angeles Times.*

A Pan Am steward in a peaked cap and epauletted jacket stepped over to her. He had some cheeses under glass on a tray and a sharp-tipped knife in his hand for cutting slices of same. "Cheese board, Miss?" he asked. Well, this was a little better. "We have some Stilton, Cheshire, American, and Limburger."

She looked over the selection. "What I really would like is a drink, if I can get one."

"Certainly. I can offer you a carbonated beverage, or perhaps a pink gin? But are you sure you won't have some cheese?" She looked up and wondered why he was wearing sunglasses indoors. He proffered the board once again and, in moving it toward her, accidentally jabbed her arm just a bit with the tip of the sharp knife that he held in his hand, which was wrapped, she noticed, in a cast that extended into his sleeve.

As she reacted, the most surreal thing occurred. All the men put down their newspapers and rose at the same moment as if there'd been an announcement for their flight's departure. But instead of heading toward the door, they all slowly moved toward her. She quickly got to her feet.

The burliest of the men wore glasses, a fake mustache, and a panama hat. He said to the steward in sunglasses, "Is this her?"

I replied, "Yes, Bob, this is her."

I took off my cap and sunglasses and smiled at Martha Prentice, or whatever her name was.

Martha's eyes darted in every direction, but she was surrounded.

I reassured her: "I know. You're surprised to see me. It's such a shock when you think someone is dead and then they come back to life. It's happened to me twice. Marie Prasquier and, of course, yourself. And looking at you now, one would almost think Vera had come back to life as well."

I gestured toward Martha's lustrous hair, which now duplicated Vera Driscoll's trademark coif. "You know, when I mistook your resurrected self for Vera on Treasure Island, I tried to imagine why someone who would want to slip out of the country as quietly as possible would dress and style herself to look exactly like the stunning Vera Driscoll, who is, after all, something of a public figure. The only reason I could come up with was that you'd gotten possession of something so helpful to your departure from the United States that it made it worth your while to look like the former Edna Drisch Vernon—something like, say, Vera's passport. Vera had shown it to me one night when she'd sneaked into my hotel room.

Funnily enough, Russ Hewett had also broken into my room at the Claremont, on the last night of his life. Which was also the last time anyone saw Vera. I'd thought it odd that although Russ was planting something in my room rather than searching it, I found it in a shambles. And then, of course, I knew everything."

Vera. She fooled us so skillfully that, when she was murdered, we almost didn't know it. She'd had me genuinely believing she was running off to see Dave Wooster in San Diego. And she knew full well that if I was the one who had to explain this to Jack, I'd do such a well-intended but inept job that he would realize the supposed truth, consider me to be a loyal friend, and not expect to see Vera until Seattle. Meanwhile, Vera had bribed her way into my hotel room once again and was lying in wait for me, certain that this time I'd have to succumb and spend the night with her. After all, it would have been very difficult for me to call Jack and explain that, although I'd told him an immense lie about Vera going to southern California, and although she was now in my bed, I was blameless in the entire affair.

She'd heard me enter my hotel room, but when she turned on the bedside lamp, she didn't see me. Instead she saw Russ Hewett, to whom she'd just been introduced in the ballroom, who was planting an incriminating photograph in my dresser drawer. She knew who he was, and he knew she knew. He *had* to silence her. They struggled, sending furniture flying in every direction, until he finally suffocated poor Vera, lowered her over my windowsill, walked her corpse as if she were drunk around the far side of the hotel up to the parking lot, and stashed her in his car.

No wonder the letter Gail had written to her father was still in Russ's cigar case when he was found dead. He'd never had the chance to plant it.

And no wonder he had looked so pale and sober and was in need of a stiff bourbon when he came back to the ballroom that evening. He'd just committed an unpremeditated murder.

At least he'd taken away Vera's pocketbook and her passport within it. Martha had instantly realized how that could serve her.

"Where'd you dispose of Vera's body?" I asked Martha.

"Mount Diablo," she replied, without a hint of surprise at my deduction. "Russ and I ditched her in a ravine before we picked up Marie Prasquier. You'll find Vera there one of these days."

She looked around, trying to find a way out. She was a professional and as Culpepper took her pocketbook from her, immediately identified her one avenue of escape.

I said, "Don't feel bad, Martha. If we hadn't nabbed you, they'd have gotten you at customs. Your new name and description is at every international terminal in the country. It was a good idea to travel with the passport of a swing band singer who no one knew was dead. It would have been an even better idea if you'd made sure I was dead as well. All the airlines and shipping agents were on the watch for anyone trying to leave the country under the name on Vera's passport. Pan American took your reservation, called the Oakland police, and Bob and I flew down to greet you."

Bob removed a black pistol from Martha's pocketbook with his handkerchief. "You're under arrest. We're taking you back to Oakland for arraignment, where the FBI is interested in speaking with you as well."

She said, "I know this sounds ridiculous, but if we have a long trip, might I use the bathroom quickly? I have to. It's because I'm afraid."

Culpepper walked over to a door marked EMPLOYEES ONLY and looked in. There was a toilet and a sink but no windows.

"I'm standing outside the door, and in five minutes I open it, no matter what," he told her.

Gratefully, she replied, "Thanks so much. I won't need anywhere near that long."

She gave me a look I'll never forget, entered the bathroom,

Culpepper shut the door, and within fifteen seconds the gunshot I expected to hear rang out.

Culpepper, being a professional, should have realized that when you take a gun away from someone who does this kind of work on a regular basis, you don't simply assume that it's the only gun she has on her person.

I could have told Bob this before she stepped into the bathroom, but it was something he needed to learn, and people learn best by experience.

Besides, it was better for all concerned that it ended this way.

Every Good Boy Does Fine

Bob asked me what I was doing.

I told him I was finishing up something I'd been writing. I placed my current yellow legal tablet, now full, in the nearest of the four orange crates that contained nothing but other such yellow tablets in my workroom. I set my Eberhard Faber No. 2 pencil atop it.

Bob didn't have much interest in the contents of the crates. As usual, he was more taken with my odd drafting table. I'd had it mounted to a beat-up baby grand that had nothing to lose in the looks department. It allowed me to create an arrangement at the piano without having to constantly twist to my right each time I wanted to write a note. I was in pretty good shape for a man who was bidding good-bye to his forties, but it saved me a lot of wear and tear.

"What's all this?" he asked, pointing to the big orchestral chart upon which was mapped out my latest arrangement for big band and strings.

"It's music for your aunt Peggy to sing," I said.

"She's not really my aunt, right?" asked Bob for about the tenth time that year.

"No, you know that. She's just our friend, but she likes you like an aunt."

"Yeah, she's okay," he said, staring at the piano keys, dying to bang on them. "How come you always call her Norma?"

"Because when I met her, that was her name. And her last name was Egstrom. That was before she went back to using the name Lee."

"And she's your boss?"

"No, I work for lots of people, but a lot of the time it's for her." I indicated the arrangement. "She's going to sing this on the television. On a show called *Cavalcade of Bands*. Your uncle Jack's group is going to be the band of the week."

Bob frowned. "Yeah, well we won't be able to see it. Unless we go to Nick Michael's house. He has a TV machine."

I said, casually, "Well, I thought it was time we got one, too."

His eyes nearly burst out of his head. "We're gonna have a TV?" he asked. I nodded in the affirmative. "Holy cow. Wait till I tell everybody."

"You going outside?" I asked.

"Yeah, maybe later."

"Where?" I asked.

"I don't know. Why do you always want to know?"

"Because I like to know lots of things. What are you going to do?"

356 · Rupert Holmes

I had to remember that he must be allowed to do the things other kids did, even if it meant he might skin his knee or get hit in the head with a football or step on a nail. As his namesake had once told me, "It's a miracle any kid gets through life, but most of them do." With luck, this lifetime the odds would be in my Bob's favor.

I told him a list of twenty things not to do while I was out of the room, took the very first of the yellow pads from orange crate number 1 and went downstairs to show it to his mother. As I left, I looked at the photo of Linney that always sat on the table where I'd been writing. Bob reminded me in absolutely not one way of her . . . except that he, too, was my child, and I would think about him and love him every day I was alive.

Maybe even after that, but that was not up to me.

I went through the kitchen door and saw Gail at the table, sipping a cup of coffee.

"Have you finished the chart yet?" she asked. "I'd love to see it when it's done."

I told her I hadn't, that I was just finishing something else first. She looked at me imploringly. "Well, please, as soon as you can. I love Peggy and she's wonderful to me, but when I back her up, she has no idea how much prep time I've put in. I'd hate to spoil the illusion she has that I'm brilliant."

I laughed. "It's no illusion."

She took another sip of her coffee. "Where's Boberino?"

As an answer, there came a very unmusical noise from my piano upstairs, the sound of a kid hitting a bunch of low piano keys in clusters, with the right damper pedal pressed down so that the notes reverberated. It resembled discordant thunder. Kids love to do this. Leave a kid who's never seen a piano before alone with one in a room for no less than fifteen minutes and he or she will discover, all on their own, that this can be done. It makes them feel powerful.

To anyone else, it would sound like noise. To this father, it was a symphony.

"Enough," said Gail, standing forthrightly. "You've put me off too long. I'm going up there to give him his first piano lesson."

"Oh, thank God, please do," said Nancy, joining us at the kitchen table. "His father thinks it sounds wonderful when he does that, but I can't take much more. My nerves aren't what they used to be."

I mock-protested, "No son of mine is going to be a musician. They're a bunch of scoundrels and rogues. He's going to be a marine biologist, or an astronomer, or an encyclopedia salesman—anything but a musician."

"You can't help it, if it's going to happen," said Nancy. "That's pretty much out of your control."

"Is he as much of a handful as ever?" asked Gail.

"Do you mean Ray or Bob?" Nancy asked back. The two of them laughed, sharing their resigned tolerance of me. "I suppose Bob's the one who runs me the most ragged. I thought the hard part was having a baby at thirty-eight. That was a milk run, figuratively and literally, compared to having a ten-year-old."

"Scott and I can't wait to have those problems," said Gail. She downed the last of her coffee, and sighed. "Well, let's see how much Bob loves me when we're playing scales instead of catch." Smiling, she left the room and went up the stairs.

I took Gail's coffee cup over to the sink, where Nancy was rinsing off some tomatoes she'd miraculously managed to grow in an unpromising patch of our backyard. She examined them with the same thoughtful, hopeful eyes she and Linney had always had in common.

She'd given life to Linney, and it was from half of her that Linney had been created, the other half stemming from what must surely have been the very best part of me.

When Nancy and I are together, our shared love is as close as we can come to having Linney alive again, at least on earth.

She caught me looking at her and was somewhat flustered by it. She turned and saw the yellow writing tablet on the kitchen table. "What's that?" she asked.

"Nothing urgent," I said. "You can look at it later." I took hold of her hand. "I treasure you, Nance."

She laughed shyly.

"Treasure you," I said again, and not letting go of each other's hands, we walked up the stairs to watch Gail teach our child the letters of the notes on a piano.

Acknowledgments

I am hopelessly indebted to Jon Karp, editor in chief of Random House, for the existence and nature of this book. He has inspired and guided me, helping me to shape and sculpt this story in every way imaginable. What I owe Jon continues to compound itself daily at a rate any loan shark would envy.

I'm profoundly grateful to Random House president and publisher Gina Centrello for giving my work the most admired home on the block in which to live.

Random House has also provided Ray Sherwood and company with an accomplished, supportive family. It has been a pleasure to work again with savvy copy editor Bonnie Thompson and to be adroitly, patiently, and wittily overseen by production editor Evan Camfield. In matters both practical and creative, associate editor Jonathan Jao has been a tremendous help since the novel's earliest inception. I'm very grateful to clever and insightful senior editor Caroline Sutton and to managing editorial associate Jennifer Rodriguez for their creative input, and to Amit Kumar for his encouraging comments. Production manager Molly Lyons and designer Mercedes Everett have done their usual splendid job of giving my words a clean and handsome look.

Managing editor Benjamin Dreyer has been a joy to confer with since he oversaw my first novel. He has generously continued to lend me creative insight as well as free access to his astute mind in the creation of this book. I would express my gratitude much more eloquently if he were helping me write this paragraph.

Heather Schroder, my literary agent at ICM, continues to be an insightful voice of reason, and a lilting voice it is, at that. For her valuable advice, insight, candor, and friendship, a plethora of thanks.

Although I've inscribed every word (and note) of this novel myself, my author's credit might just as well bear the subtitle "as told to Teressa Esposito," because, in fact, each sentence was first recounted to (and frequently rejected by) my above-named gifted and trusted associate, as has been the case with all my words and music for almost a decade. It is a wondrous thing to have in my life a friend whose counsel I can heed and whose criticism I can accept without question or the reflexive need to defend myself. Teressa is all that and much more. She also proofed and prepared my penciled orchestrations for the *Swing* CD more skillfully than Gail Prentice did for Ray Sherwood, and infused my compositions with her own significant musical talent. She is always at the heart of my work, whether singing on Broadway eight times a week or steering me away (hopefully with occasional success) from my most dangerous shallows. To her, my lifelong gratitude and admiration.

For this book, I had to recreate a world I never knew, in a time before my time. In addition to Teressa Esposito, two people were astoundingly helpful in aiding my attempt to replicate the Treasure Island, Oakland, and Berkeley of 1940.

The first was my dear friend Deborah Corwin, who had skillfully assisted me with the orchestrations for *The Mystery of Edwin Drood* on Broadway and was an associate producer of its original cast recording. (I will also add here that when my ten-year-old daughter, Wendy, died in 1986, Deb shouldered me and my inconsolable grief through the next several years of my existence, smoothing my path wherever she could and dealing with a world I was not yet capable of rejoining.) Deb later married a sterling fellow named Dr. Jan Corwin and the two have lived for many years in the lovely East Bay town of Orinda. When I told Deb that part of my story was to be set on Treasure Island, it was she who first mentioned the Claremont (where I stayed while researching the novel) and walked with me across the causeway from Yerba Buena and into one of the few buildings that remain from the Golden Gate Exhibition. As with my Broadway plays of the eighties and nineties, I am once again deeply grateful to Deborah for her assistance, valuable feedback, and priceless friendship.

The other contributor who was immeasurably helpful to my research is also a resident of the Bay Area. I first met Linda Arce Hodges when I was performing at the highly esteemed Tomorowland Terrace in Disneyland twenty-something years ago. She was a particularly vociferous voice in the crowd, but as the years went by, she evolved from fan to friend and pen pal, especially regarding our shared interests in theology. Last year, when I asked Linda a minor question about the layout of the approach to the Bay Bridge, her interest became sparked by Ray's story and the lost world of Treasure Island. Soon, she was playing Paul Drake to my Perry Mason, sending dispatches from the Oakland front as if we were on a transcoastal scavenger hunt for obscure information important only to us: the names of every telephone exchange in San Francisco in 1940, the history of dirigible bases in California, the cost of parking on the Magic Isle. It was Linda who tracked down the lethal ledge on Grizzly Peak and convinced the Alameda Museum (many thanks, Diane Coler-Dark) to let me view a remarkable color home movie taken in 1940 by the Pagano family at Treasure Island, allowing me to see scenes of the Gayway that could not be found anywhere else. I have found my own way of acknowledging Linda, her husband, and her family within this book. It is small recompense for the privilege of having such a fabulous partner in crime.

For their input, I must also thank gifted mystery and romance novelist Laura Hayden, who has always been a generous sounding board for my own work; the deep-feeling Susan Little, educator par excellence, who created a veritable annotated guide to *Swing* in real time as she read the first draft; and the sensitive and artful writer Lisa Filadelfia, who made a very strong case for a number of important adjustments in the first part of this novel. And I gratefully thank the delightful Emma Esposito, who has been one of my best reference sources on all matters under the sun.

I'm privileged to be the husband of Liza Holmes. If anywhere in this story you find a smattering of goodness, strength, courage, or kindness, then you've found Liza, who has given me all of this, and her sustenance, care, guidance, and laughter, for several lifetimes. We have also had occassion to cry together. I treasure you, Liza.

I thank my beloved sons, Nick and Tim, for all the joy, purpose and hope they have given me. Tim is autistic and can't decipher these words at the present, so I'll tell him more when I can next embrace him. Nick has done great things with his life while I have been writing this book, and he can take all the credit for that. Each day I feel lucky and proud to be his father.

As you may also have surmised from this volume's dedication, this book has been, like me, graced by the lovely spirit of my late daughter, Wendy, and haunted by her tragedy. She was the loveliest of God's creatures. It is my honor and heartbreak to be her father.

I remember you every moment, Wen.

My best male friend is Rob Sisco. That doesn't mean we go pike fishing very often. We haven't played a round of racquetball in, oh gosh, ever. He signed on for the job in 1980 and has been there for me ever since. He is the first fellow to whom I show my work, and he has assisted and supported it just as he has my life.

Like Ray Sherwood, my father attended the Juilliard School of Music. By age nineteen, he was playing a remarkably suave lead alto sax for xylophonist Red Norvo and his Orchestra, which also featured the vocalizations of Red's wife, Mildred Bailey. Although Ray Sherwood, Jack Donovan, and Vera Driscoll bear no resemblance whatsoever to my father, Red, or Mildred, the tales my father spun for me about touring with a big band in 1940, and his jazz recordings, which I first spun on our record player at the age of five, greatly motivated this novel. An image of him playing with the Bobby Parks Orchestra at the Hotel Syracuse in the same year in which this story is set can be seen below. That's Lenny there, third sax from the left. A witty, spry eighty-five as of this writing, he has always known what "swing" should sound like. Every day to this day, Jazz inspires Lenny's life. I love you, Dad, for inspiring mine.

About the SWING CD

The enclosed CD has seven tracks containing nine pieces of music referenced in the novel *Swing*: three instrumental numbers, four songs with vocals, Adeline Head's composition for piano entitled *Self-Portrait,* and Gail Prentice's *Swing Around the Sun,* as orchestrated by Ray Sherwood and performed by the Pan-Pacific Orchestra.

All the cuts, with the exception of the solo piano on *Self-Portrait,* are performed by four trumpets, four trombones, five saxes, and rhythm. No synthesized instruments are used. The only thing electrical on this CD is the pickup on the rhythm guitar. The odd sounds you may occasionally hear in *Swing Around the Sun* are generated solely by the above-described instrumentation. Also be assured that this recording of Gail's composition is an exact replication of that which is described in the novel. I wrote and arranged it exactly as Gail and Ray did, every step of the way, based on the same source material.

This accompanying CD is intended, first and foremost, to enhance your reading experience, hopefully putting you in the mood to spend a long weekend in the Big Band era with Ray Sherwood and his cronies, friends, enemies, and loves.

The novel *Swing* was written long before this bonus CD was ever contemplated. You don't need the CD to solve the book's mysteries, although Random House hopes that, with or without this recording, the story will keep you guessing to the very end. However, among the nine musical selections on the CD can be found a few clues that, when coupled with information contained within the novel itself, may enhance your chance of solving the puzzles of *Swing*.

If you're reading these words prior to reading the novel itself, allow me to spare you from too many chasings of wild geese: Please don't go looking for clues by poring over the lyrics, or playing the CD backwards, or listening for embedded subliminal messages. The clues can be found simply within the gist of a lyric and within the musical themes of more than one composition. Detecting this requires no more formal musical training than the ability to recognize a familiar tune. The CD's lyrics are included here more for your reading pleasure than to assist you in locating buried treasure, and there are many red herrings among the blue notes in these songs.

If, after reading *Swing* and listening to the CD, you still have any questions regarding where the clues lie within the music, you are encouraged to write to SWING@RupertHolmes.com, where no reasonable inquiry will go without reply.

To learn more about the very real but forever lost world of Treasure Island, visit www.RupertHolmes.com.

SWING

CD Songs & Lyrics

1. The Music Speaks to Me (*instrumental version*)   4:29

2. Believe You Me   4:16
   vocal by Chrissy Faith

3. Beef Lo Mein   3:38
   vocal by Rupert Holmes

4. A Night at the Claremont   5:26
   Soup du Jour (*instrumental*)
   A Temptress in Taupe (*instrumental*)
   Too Bad for You
   vocal by Rupert Holmes

5. The Music Speaks to Me (*vocal version*)   3:43
   vocal by Rupert Holmes

6. Self-Portrait (*a composition for piano*   2:58
   "by Adeline Head")
   performed by John Baxindine

7. Swing Around the Sun   5:02
   (*Opus 37 "by Gail Prentice,"*
   orchestrated "by Ray Sherwood")

All words and music by Rupert Holmes
© 2005 Wendy Isobel Music. (ASCAP)

Arranged and conducted by Rupert Holmes except band 5:
The Music Speaks to Me (*vocal version*)
Arranged by Lanny Meyers

Produced by Jeffrey Lesser
Engineered and mixed by Jeffrey Lesser
Musical contractor (and killer drums): Jimmy Musto
Musical supervision: Teressa Esposito
Postproduction supervised by Jeffrey Lesser

1. The Music Speaks to Me
(Instrumental Version)

Composed and arranged by Rupert Holmes

2. Believe You Me

Words and music by Rupert Holmes

Doubt me if I've sworn that morning rises in the east.
Doubt me if I've said that bread won't rise without the yeast.
Doubt me 'til each word you've heard is tested, tried, and true.
Doubt me forever,
But doubt me never
If once I say to you:

Believe you me,
Adore you I.
Conceive you how
You now reply?

You need but choose the words and say you'll keep me warm.
Just break the news in any way, or shape, or form.

Perceive do we
What have we here?
Believe you me,
I'll make it clear.
I'll turn each line around
'Cause mine you're bound to be.

And know you this—
When once we kiss,
All this you'll see.
Believe you me.

3. Beef Lo Mein

Words and music by Rupert Holmes

There was a guy on a second date
And he had reckoned that this girl would be his own first mate
But she said, "I'm starvin' so's I'm half insane!"
He said, "I know this place in Chinatown with Beef Lo Mein."

They hopped a train down to Doyers Street
Where all the Moo Goo Gai Pan, Wor Shu Opp enjoyers eat.
"Hey waiter! My girl has food upon the brain,
Go do your part, she's got her heart set up for Beef Lo Mein."

They ordered ribs and some Won Ton soup,
But come the day for the entrée the waiter's head did droop.
He told them, "So sorry, I am racked with pain—
Chef says he's run fresh out of noodles for your Beef Lo Mein."

And oh, the lady looked fit to be hung.
My buddy felt like Egg Foo Yung was on his face.
And so he knew he'd lost the whole caboodle
For the lack of any noodle in the place.

There went the date, and the whole shebang.
The diamond ring he planned to spring on her, it never sprang.
There went the three-bedroom on a shaded lane.
He'd lost his pride and blushing bride for lack of Beef Lo Mein.

There went the son who would run the bank,
And marry into money with some honey born with swank . . .
There went the new gov'nor of the state of Maine,
And his ascent to President because of Beef Lo Mein!

Each day, life is a chain of main events
Without the slightest grain of sense that can be found.
And way back down the line the weakest link
Determines if you swim or sink into the ground.

So take a tip from this hip refrain,
The best-laid plan of any man can tumble down the drain,
I tell you, each picnic holds the threat of rain:
In disbelief, some call it grief . . .
I call it Beef Lo Mein.

4. A Night at the Claremont

Jack Donovan and His Orchestra of Note
Live from the Garden Room
Berkeley, 1940

Soup du Jour

(instrumental)
Composed and arranged by Rupert Holmes

A Temptress in Taupe

(instrumental)
Composed and arranged by Rupert Holmes

Too Bad for You

Words and music by Rupert Holmes

You lost your poise by nine o'clock.
By ten, you'd lost your shoes.
You've not much left to lose,
Too Bad For You!

You say champagne goes to your head
When you paint Old New York . . .
Well, I just popped my cork,
Too Bad For You!

Too bad for you!
(*Too bad for you!*)
Too sad but true!
(*Too sad, too true!*)
Too bad your destiny must rest in me
'Cause I've got plans for you.

You're *hoi polloi* but here's the boy
With whom you will debut.
You're much too good for me,
Too bad for you!

Too bad for you
(*Too bad for you!*)
That I'm mad for you!
(*Too sad, too true!*)
I gladly promise that you'll hit the mat
'Cause we've got fat to chew!

Your fate tonight would be a shock
No gypsy could foresee.
Though you're too good for me,
I'm in the mood to woo,
And claim and tame the shrew,
Too bad for you!

5. The Music Speaks to Me

Words and music by Rupert Holmes

A trumpet confiding in you alone,
A whispered aside from a slide trombone,
You hear the moan
Of reeds who sing in rhythm
And the message they bring with 'em
Is that soaring speech each poem seeks to be.
I tell you, the music it speaks to me.

The brass comes to blows in a thousand sighs,
And cries what, in prose, heaven knows ain't wise to vocalize.
My spirit cheers in sheer bliss
Yes and I'm all ears to hear this
As it talks and squawks and shouts and shrieks, *Oo-wee!*
I love that this symphony speaks to me.

Speak out,
Speak low,
A horn part is the part of speech I know, so

Let's jump on the bandwagon with the band
The tale in the wail of a baby grand, I understand.
To some it might be garble
But to me it's carved in marble.
What is Greek to some is not to Greeks, you see.
Doo-wot, doo-wot, do what you wanna,
I got to speak Americana,
And lover, the music speaks to me.

So don't bother to ask of me, "What's the word?"
The news of a blues with a minor third is all I've heard.
So jitterbug or bounce it,

Cut a rug as you pronounce it,
Treasure all the bloops and cracks and squeaks do we!
A hist'ry far greater than fiction
A myst'ry with musical diction
The music it speaks and it speaks to me!

6. Self Portrait

A Composition for Piano
"by Adeline Head"*

7. Swing Around the Sun

Opus 37
Composed "by Gail Prentice"*
Orchestrated "by Ray Sherwood"*

*In actuality, composed and orchestrated by Rupert Holmes.

ABOUT THE AUTHOR

Twice a recipient of the Mystery Writers of America's coveted Edgar Award, RUPERT HOLMES is no stranger to the worlds of mystery or music. His first novel, *Where the Truth Lies,* has been made into a major motion picture by director Atom Egoyan starring Kevin Bacon, Colin Firth, and Alison Lohman. For his Broadway musical *The Mystery of Edwin Drood,* Holmes became the first person in theatrical history to solely win Tony Awards for Best Book and Best Music and Lyrics, while *Drood* itself won the Tony for Best Musical. His comedy-thrillers for the stage include Broadway's *Accomplice* and *Solitary Confinement.* His most recent work for Broadway, *Say Goodnight, Gracie,* earned Holmes the 2004 National Broadway Theatre Award and a Tony nomination for Best Play. He also created and wrote all four seasons of the critically acclaimed, Emmy Award–winning television series *Remember WENN,* set in 1940. Serving as background to the writing of *Swing,* Holmes received a Drama Desk Award for Best Orchestration and arranged and conducted Barbra Streisand's classic album *Lazy Afternoon.* The *Los Angeles Times* has called Rupert Holmes "an American treasure."

To learn more about *Swing* and other works by Rupert Holmes, visit www.RupertHolmes.com.

ABOUT THE TYPE

Berkeley Oldstyle, designed in 1983 by Tony Stan, is a variation of the University of California Old Style, which was created by Frederick Goudy. While capturing the feel and traits of its predecessor, Berkeley Old Style shows influences from Kennerly, Goudy Old Style, Deepdene, and Booklet Oldstyle, all of which were also designed by Goudy. It is characterized by its calligraphic weight stress, and its x-height, now described as classic, is smaller than that of most other designs of the day. The generous ascenders and descenders provide variations in text color, easy legibility, and an overall inviting appearance.